GRANTA

Best of Young British Novelists

7

EDITOR: Bill Buford
ASSISTANT EDITOR: Diane Speakman
GERMAN EDITOR: Michael Hofmann
EXECUTIVE EDITOR: Pete de Bolla
DESIGN: Chris Hyde
ADMINISTRATION AND PRODUCTION: Jane Nellist
EDITORIAL ASSISTANTS: Graham Coster, Francis Spufford
EDITORIAL BOARD: Malcolm Bradbury, Elaine Feinstein, Ian Hamilton,
Leonard Michaels
U.S. EDITOR: Jonathan Levi, 6WR, West 104th St, New York,
New York 10025

EDITORIAL CORRESPONDENCE: GRANTA, The Hobson Gallery,
44a Hobson Street, Cambridge CB1 1NL. (0223) 315290.
All manuscripts are welcome but must be accompanied by a stamped,
self-addressed envelope or they cannot be returned.

SUBSCRIPTIONS: £10.00 for four issues. Back issues are available for
£2.50 including postage (issues 1 to 4) and £2.95 including postage
(issue 5 onwards).

GRANTA is photoset by Lindonprint Typesetters, Cambridge, and is
reprinted in 2010 by CPI Antony Rowe, Chippenham, Wiltshire

GRANTA is published by Granta Publications Ltd. and distributed by
Penguin Books Ltd., Harmondsworth, Middlesex, England; Penguin
Books Australia Ltd., Ringwood, Victoria, Australia; Penguin Books
Canada Ltd., 2801 John Street, Markham, Ontario, Canada L3R 1B4;
Penguin Books (N.Z.) Ltd., 182-190 Wairau Road, Auckland 10, New
Zealand. Copyright © 1983 by Granta Publications Ltd. Each work
published in GRANTA is copyright of the author.

GRANTA acknowledges the assistance of the Eastern Arts Association.
Cover design by Chris Hyde
ISSN 0017 - 3231
ISBN 978 0 14 01 4082 8

CONTENTS

GRANTA

MARTIN AMIS
MONEY

Martin Amis was born in Oxford in 1949, and was educated in Britain, Spain, and the United States, attending over thirteen schools and a number of crammers in London and Brighton. He was an editorial assistant on the *Times Literary Supplement* and the Literary Editor of the *New Statesman* from 1977 until 1979. He is now a Special Writer on the *Observer*. He is the author of four novels, the most recent of which is *Other People: A Mystery Story*. 'Money' is the first chapter of the new novel that Martin Amis is currently completing.

As the cab pulled off FDR Drive, somewhere in the early Hundreds, a low-slung Tomahawk full of black guys came sharking out of lane, sliding off to the right across our bows. The cab swerved and hit a deep crater in the road: to the sound of a rifle-shot the roof dropped down and smacked me on the core of my head. I really didn't need that, with my head and face hurting a lot all the time anyway, and still drunk and crazy from the plane.

'Oh, man,' I said.

'Yeah,' said the cabbie from behind his screen. He was fortyish—balding, but what a rug he had falling straight and damp over his shoulders. I couldn't see that much of his face. The back of his neck was mottled and pocked, with traces of adolescent virulence—'of fire, of flame'—in the crimson underhang of the ears.

'Need only about hundred guys like me,' he said loudly, 'take out all the fuckin' niggers and PRs in this fucking town.'

I listened from the back. My ears have started hearing things recently. I mean, they've started hearing things that aren't really audible. It happens mostly in the mornings, but at other times too. It happened in the plane, for instance, or at least I think it did.

'What?' I shouted. 'A hundred guys? That's not many guys.'

'We could do it. With the right gunge, we could do it.'

'Gunge?'

'Gunge, yeah. 48s. Automatics.'

I sat back with a grunt and rubbed my head. I'd spent *two hours* in immigration, half an hour in customs, and another twenty minutes before I secured this cab—yeah, and the usual maniac fizzing at its wheel.... I've driven in New York. Five blocks, and you're reduced to tears of blood-lust and self-pity. So what happens to the guys who do it all day? You try it. I said, 'Why would you want to do that?'

'Uh?'

'Kill all the niggers and PRs.'

He lifted one hand limply from the wheel. 'They think, you know, you drive a yellow cab, you must be some kind of a scumbag.'

I sighed and leaned forwad. 'You know something?' I asked him. 'You really *are* a scumbag. You're the first one I've met.'

We pulled over. Rising in his seat, he turned towards me. His face was much nastier than I'd banked on it being—old and girlish with bright eyes and shapely lips, as if there were another face, the second face, beneath his mask of skin.

'Okay. Out the car.... I said out the fuckin' car!'

'I heard you,' I said, and pushed my suit-case along the seat.

'Twenty-two dollars,' he said. 'There onna clock.'

'I'm not giving you anything, scumbag.'

Without turning he reached below the dash-board and pulled something. All four door locks clunked shut with an oily, chockful sound.

'Listen, you fat fuck,' he began. 'This is Ninety-ninth and second. The money. Give me the money.' He said that he would drive me uptown twenty blocks and kick me out on the street right there. He said there'd be nothing left of me but hair and teeth.

I had some notes in my back pocket, from my last trip. I gave him a twenty. He flicked the locks and I climbed out. There was nothing more to say.

So now I stand with my case, in industrial light and island rain. It must be pushing eight o'clock, but it isn't darkening yet. The weepy breath of the day is still holding its glow. Across the dirty street some black kids sit hunched in the doorway of a dead liquor store. They look too depressed to come and check me out. It's past midnight, my time. God, I hate this movie. And it's only just beginning.

I looked for cabs, and none came. I was on First, not Second, and First is uptown. All the cabs would be heading the other way, getting the hell out on Second and Lex. So now I get to take a stroll down Ninety-ninth Street.

I wouldn't have done this a month ago. No, I wouldn't have done it then. Then I was avoiding the awful thing. Now I'm just waiting for it.... Inflation, they say, is cleaning up the city; money is cleaning it up. But things still happen here. You climb out of the cab, look around, take a deep breath—and come to in your underpants, somewhere south of SoHo, or on a midtown traction table with a silver tray and a tasselled tab on your chest, and a guy in white saying, 'Good morning, sir. That'll be fifteen thousand dollars....' Yes, things still happen here. Something is waiting to happen to me. Damage is. Damage is waiting. I am waiting. Soon, damage is going to stop waiting—any day now. Awful things can happen any time.

That is the awful thing.

Fear walks tall on this planet. Fear has really got the whammy on all of us down here. Fear takes no shit from anyone. Oh, it's true, man. Sister, don't kid yourself.... One of these days I'm going to walk right up to fear. I'm going to walk right up. Someone's got to do it. Courage! I'm going to walk right up and say, 'Okay, pal. It's over. You think you're such a hard-on. You've pushed us around for long enough. Here is someone who *would not take it*. It's over. Outside.' Bullies, apparently, are all cowards deep down. Fear is a bully, but something tells me that fear's no coward. Fear, I suspect, is really incredibly brave. Fear will take me straight through the door, prop me up in the alley among the crates and empties, and show me who's the boss. I might lose a tooth or two, or he could break my arm—or fuck up my eye! Fear might get really carried away, like I've seen them do. Maybe I'd need a crew or a tool or a gun. Maybe I'd better let fear be. He's too good at fighting, and I'm too frightened anyway.

I walked west for a block, then south. On Ninety-sixth street I jumped into a cab at the lights. The cabbie turned, and our eyes met horribly. 'The Ashbery,' I said without expression, and told him the address for the second time. He took me. I gave him the two dollars I owed him as a tip, plus a couple more. They money changed hands very eloquently.

'Thank you, friend,' he said.

'You're welcome,' I told him. 'Thank *you*.'

I'm sitting on the bed in my hotel room. The room is fine, fine. No complaints: it's terrific value.

The pain in my face has split in two, but hurts about the same. There's a definite swelling in my jaw now, on the upper east side. It's a fucking abscess or something, maybe a nerve or a gum gimmick. Oh Christ, I suppose I'll have to get it fixed. It will cost me. You have to spend big for everything like that out here, as you know, as I've said. All these people in the street, these extras, they all cost money to keep on the road. There are taxi-meters on the ambulances in this city: that's the sort of place I'm dealing with. I can feel another pain operating in the slopes of my eyes. Hello there.

I'm drinking tax-exempt whisky from a tooth mug, and listening to see if I'm still hearing things. The mornings are the worst, and this morning was the worst yet. I heard jet take-offs, computer fugues, didgeridoos. What is my head up to? I wish I had some idea what it's got in mind for me. I want to telephone Serena and give her a piece of it, a piece of my mind. It's two in the morning over there. But it's two in the morning over here too, in my head anyway. And Serena would be more than a match for me, with my head in the shape it's in.... Now I've got another evening to deal with. I don't want another evening. I've already had one, in England and on the plane. I don't need another evening. Alec Llewellyn owes me money. Barry Sleep owes me money. Serena Fox owes me money. Outside, night has fallen quickly, and the banked lights aren't really steady in the tall sky.

The mirror looked on quite unimpressed as I went through a series of rethinks in the windowless bathroom next door. I cleaned my teeth, combed my rug, clipped my nails, bathed my eyes, gargled, shaved, showered, and still looked like shit. I'm so fucking fat these days. I tell you, I disgust myself in the tub and on the can. I sit slumped on the ox-collar seat like a sack of plumbing, the winded boiler of a thrashed old tug. How did I get like this? It can't just be the booze and all the junk food I put away. I must have been booked in for this a long time ago. Can money fix it? I need my whole body drilled down and repaired, replaced. I need my body capped, is what I need.

That Serena.... Today someone told me one of her terrible secrets. I don't want to talk about it yet. I'll tell you later. I want to go out and drink some more and get a bit tireder first.

The steel doors parted, and I stepped out into the hall. Uniformed men stood by impassively like soldiers in their trench. I flicked my key on to the desk and nodded. I was too drunk to be able to tell whether they could tell I was drunk. I turned and headed for the door.

'Mr Sleep.'

'That's me,' I said.

'Oh, sir. There was a call for you. Miss Caduta Massi.... Is that *the* Caduta Massi?'

'That's her. Any message?'

'No, sir. No message.'

'Thanks.'

'Mm-hm.'

So now I strode south down bending Broadway. I walked through urban genies of subway gas. I heard the distant chirrup of sirens, the whistles of cyclists and skateboarders. I saw the lurching cars and cabs, shouldered on by the power of their horns. I felt all the contention, all the democracy, in the air. These are people determined to be themselves: try telling them any different. A big pale screamer shadow-boxed in the entrance of a space-game arcade. He babbled of betrayal and fraud, grievance and eviction. The city is full of them, people who bawl and shout and weep about nothing all the hours there are. I'm told they're chronics from the city madhouses. They all got let out when money went wrong ten years ago. Now there's a good joke, a global one, cracked by money. An Arab pulls up his zip in the sheep-pen, gazes across the stall, and says, 'Hey, Ahmed. Let's hike oil.' Ten years later a big whiteman flails on Broadway, for all to see.

I hit a topless bar on Forty-fourth. Ever checked out one of these joints? I always expected a shadowy dirtbox patrolled by half-clad waitresses. It isn't like that. They just have a couple of chicks in pants dancing on a ramp behind the bar: you sit and drink while they slink their stuff. I kept the whiskies coming, at $5.30 a time, and sloshed the liquor round my upper east side. I also pressed the cold glass against my buzzing cheek. This helps, or seems to. It soothes.

There were three girls working the ramp, spaced out evenly along its mirrored length. The girl dancing for my benefit—and for that of the gingery, hermaphroditic figure seated two stools to my right—was short, shy, and puppyishly built. Well, she was my girl, for the next half-hour anyway. Her skin shone pale in the light, and had a sore look, as if she were given to rashes, allergies even. She had large woeful breasts, concave at the heart, and an eave of loose flesh climbed over the rim of her pants, which were navy-blue and fluff-flossed, like gym knickers. The upper grip of her breasts bore soft crenellations, greyer than the rest of her. Stretch-marks at twenty, at nineteen: something wrong there, the form showing fatigue, showing error, at a very early stage. She knew all this, my girl. Her ordinary tomboy face attempted the standard sneer of horny defiance and yet was full of shame—shame of the body, not the other shame. The other two chicks along the ramp looked a lot more useful. But my

11

face hurt when I turned their way. And I had my girl to consider, her own feelings in the matter. She smiled my way every now and then; the smile was so uncertain, so ashamed.

'You want another Scotch?' said the matron beind the bar—the old dame with her waxed hair and scrapey voice. The body-stocking or tutu she wore was an anomalous dull brown. It spoke of spinal supports, hernias.

'Yeah,' I said, and lit another cigarette. Unless I tell you otherwise, I'm always smoking another cigarette.

By the time I looked up again my girl was gone. In her stead there writhed a six-foot Mex with wraparound mouth, hot greasy breasts, and a furrow of black hair on her belly which disappeared like a trail of gunpowder into the sharp white holster of her pants. Now this is a bit more fucking like it, I thought. She danced like a wet dream of vicious inanity. Her forty-tooth smile went everywhere and nowhere. The face, the body, the movement, all quite secure in their pornography.

'You want to buy Dawn a drink?'

I straightened my head. The old boot behind the bar gestured perfunctorily towards the stool beside me, where Dawn now perched—Dawn, my girl, swaddled in a heavy dressing-gown.

'Well—what's Dawn drinking?' I asked.

'Champagne!' A squat glass of what looked like glucose on the rocks was cracked down in front of me. 'Six dollars!'

'Six *dollars*?' I said, and flattened another twenty on the damp wood.

'Sorry,' said Dawn with a wince. She used the long Borough's vowel. 'I don't like to do this part. It's not nice to a girl. What's your name?'

'John,' I said.

'Oh. What do you do, John?'

'I'm in pornography,' I said. 'Right up to here.'

'That's interesting.'

The stripper loomed over us with my change. 'You want another Scotch?'

'Christ! Yeah, okay—do it.'

'...Are you English, John?' asked my girl, with great understanding, as if this would answer a lot of questions.

'Tell you the truth, Dawn, I'm half American and half asleep. I just climbed off the plane, you know?'

'Me too. I mean the bus. I just got off the bus.'

'Where from?'

'New Jersey.'

'No kidding. Where in New Jersey? You know, I—'

'You want to buy Dawn another drink?'

I felt my shoulders give. I turned. I said, 'What does it cost to keep you away from me? Will you fucking get out of here? Tell me something.' But I said a whole lot more. She stood her ground, this old dame. She was experienced. I gave her all my face, and this is a face that can usually face them down, big and grey, full of adolescent archaeology and cheap food and junk money, bearing all the signs of its abuse. For several seconds she just gave me her face too, full on, a good look at the eyes, which were harder than mine, oh much harder. With her fists on the bar she leaned towards me and said:

'*Leroy!*'

Instantly the music gulped out. Various speckled profiles turned my way. I looked up at the ramp. My Aztec body-artist, hands on hips, stared down at me with an expression of nauseated boredom. She just wanted to dance. I just wanted to watch her doing it. And why should I pay good money to look elsewhere?

'I'm looking for things.' This was Dawn. 'I'm really interested in pornography.'

'No you're not,' I said. 'And pornography isn't interested either. It's okay, Leroy! Relax, there's no problem, Leroy. I'm going. The money's here. Dawn, you take care now.'

I slid down the stool. I stumbled. The stool wobbled on its base, like a coin. I waved to the watching women—get your staring done with—and lit out for the door.

I walked back to the hotel. Nothing happened. It never does, but it will. The revolving door shoved me into the foyer and the desk clerk started bobbing about in his stockade.

'Sir, while you were out tonight,' he said, 'Mr Lorne Guyland called.'

He offered me my key, which I accepted.

'Would that be the real Lorne Guyland, sir?'

'Oh, I wouldn't go that far,' I said, or maybe I just thought it. I rode the lift. My face was still hurting a lot all the time. In my room I picked up the bottle and sank back on the bed, waiting for the noises to come. I thought about travel through air and time, and about Serena.... Yes, I think I can fill you in on that now. Perhaps I'll even feel a little better, when I've told you, when it's out.

Earlier today—it seems like childhood—Alec Llewellyn drove me to Heathrow at the wheel of my powerful Fiasco. (Alec is down on his luck at the moment. All he's got is a clapped-out little Culprit, a 990. He's borrowing the Fiasco while I'm away.) I was fuddled with drink and tranquillizers, for the plane. We didn't talk much. I was on standby; something in me hoped that the flight would be full. It wasn't. After some last-minute confusion, they gimmicked me a seat. 'But you'd better hurry,' said the girl. Alec jogged at my side to passport control. He slapped me on the back and I went through.

'Hey, John!' he called from the other side of the barrier. Beside him an old man stood waving at no one that I could see.

'What?'

'Come here.'

He beckoned. I came panting up to him.

'What?'

'Serena. She's fucking someone else—a lot, all the time.'

'Oh, you son of a bitch.' And I think I even took a weary swipe at his face. Alec is always doing things like this. You can never tell whether they're true. And something bad always comes out of them in the end.

'I thought you ought to know,' he said woundedly. He smiled.

'Oh yeah. Who? Come on. Christ! Why are you doing this to me? Who, who, who?'

But he wouldn't tell me. He just said it had been going on for a long time, and that it was someone I knew pretty well.

'*You*...,' I said, and turned, and ran.

There. I don't feel better. I don't feel better at all. I'm rolling over now, to try and get some sleep. London is waking up. The distant fizz or whistle or hiss in the back of my head is starting again, modulating slowly, searching for its scale.

14

Oh man, sometimes I wake up, feel like a cat run-over. What have you gone and done, boy, What are you going to do now? Are you familiar with the stoical aspects of hard drinking, of heavy drinking? Oh it's heavy. Oh, it's hard. It isn't easy.

The disease I have, called tinnitus—more reliable and above all cheaper than any alarm call—woke me promptly at eight. Tinnitus woke me on a note of exasperation, as if it had been trying, ringing, whining to wake me up for hours. I let my dry tongue creak up to check out the swelling on my upper east side. About the same. My throat apprised me that I had a snout hangover on, too. The first cigarette would light a trail of gunpowder to the arsenal, the magazine, the dancer's holster inside my chest. I lit it anyway.

As I emerged from some X-certificate work in the equatorial bathroom the telephone fixture by the bed did its chirrup, causing me to moan with fear. I lit another cigarette.

'Hello?'

'John? Lorne Guyland.'

'Lorne! Hi! How are you?'

'Good,' he said. 'I'm good, John. How are you?'

'I'm fine, fine.'

'That's good, John. John?'

'Yes, Lorne.'

'There are things that worry me, John.'

'...Are there?'

'I don't happen to be an old man, John.'

'I know that, Lorne.'

'I'm in great shape. Never better.'

'I'm glad, Lorne.'

'That's why I don't like it that you say I'm an old man, John.'

'I don't say that, Lorne.'

'Well okay. You *imply* it, John, and that's, it's, that's about the same thing. In my book, anyway. You also imply that I'm not very sexually active and can't satisfy my women. That's just not true, John.'

'I'm sure it's not true, Lorne.'

'Well, don't you think we should meet and talk about these things?'

'Absolutely. When?'

'I'm a very busy man, John.'

'I respect that, Lorne.'

'I mean, you can't expect me to just drop everything, just to, you know, meet with you, John.'

'I realize that, Lorne.'

It went on like this, I swear to God, for an hour and a half. After a while I fell silent. This had no effect on anything. So in the end I just sat through it, smoking cigarettes and having a really bad time.

When it was over, I took a pull of Scotch, wiped away my tears, and rang down to room service. I asked for coffee.

'Coffee how?' came the suspicious reply.

'With milk and sugar. How big are the pots?'

'Serve two.'

'Four pots.'

'Check.'

I lay back on the cot with my address book. Using the complimentary pad, I made a list of all the places where the nomadic Serena might be hanging out. I made a list of all the people who might know her movements. I wondered how much money all these calls were going to cost me.

Then the impeccable black bellhop arrived with my coffee. I came over, signed the check, and gave him a buck. He was in good shape: he had a pleasant agitation in his step, and a piercing smile. He sniffed the air.

He could take one look at me—at the ashtray, the whisky bottle, the four pots of coffee, my face, and my gut set like a stone on the white band of the towel—he could take one look at me and be pretty sure I ran on heavy fuel.

I'd better give you the lowdown on Serena, and quick. It was inevitable, I suppose, that someone like me would end up with someone like her. Spectral sexologists must have been nodding their heads complacently when they saw us moving in the same direction. Put her this way....

Like many girls (I think)—and especially small, delicate, swervy, gymnastic bed-wise ones—Serena lives in hardened fear of assault, molestation and rape. Lying in between the sheets, or propped at my side during long and anxious journeys in the Fiasco, or across the table deep in the lees of high-tab dinners, Serena has often refreshed me with tales of ravishment and violation from her childhood and teenage years—a musk-breathing, toffee-offering sicko on the common; the tool shed interrogations of sweat-soaked parkies; some lumbering retard in the alley or the lane; right up to the narcissist photographers and priapic prop-boys who used to bother her at work. And now the scowling vandals, bus-stop boogies, and soccer trogs malevolently lining the streets and more or less constantly smacking their lips and squeezing her ass or flicking her tits and generally making no bones about what they need to do.... It must be tiring knowledge, the realization that half the members of the planet, one on one, can do what the hell they like with you. Yeah, we've got the whammy on you chicks all right. We caught on to this in the cave and never look like looking back.

It must be extra hard on a girl like Serena, whose appearance, after many hours at the mirror, is a fifty-fifty compromise between the girlish and the grossly provocative. I've followed Serena down the street, when we're shopping, say, and she walks on ahead, wearing sawed-off jeans and a wash-shrunk T-shirt, or a frilly frock twirling on her golden thighs, or a see-through coating of gossamer like a condom, or a *school uniform*.... The men wince and watch, wince and watch. They buckle and half turn away. They look appalled, winded, mock crazy. And sometimes, when they see me cruise up behind my babe and slip an arm round her slender but cable-muscled waist, they look at me as if to say: Do something about it, will you pal? Don't let her go around the place looking like that. Come on, it's your *responsibility*.

I have talked to Serena about the way she looks. I have brought to her notice the intimate connections between rape and her summer wardrobe. She laughs about it. She looks flushed, pleased. Funny, isn't it? The oddest people nurse a sneaky interest in power. Serena would stand stock still in the path of an advancing juggernaut, so long as the driver never once took his eyes off her tits.

In addition to rape, Serena is frightened of mice, spiders, dogs, toadstools, cancer, mastectomy, chipped mugs, ghost stories, visions, portents, fortune tellers, deep water, fires, floods, thrush, poverty, entopic pregnancy, lightning, swimming, flying, and ageing. Like her fat pale lover, she never reads a book. She has no job, no money. She is either twenty-nine or thirty-one, or just possibly thirty-three. She is leaving it all very late, and she knows it. She will have to make her move, and she will have to make it soon.

I don't believe Alec, necessarily, but I won't believe Serena either. The thing about girls is—you never know. No, you never do. Even if you actually bust her, catch her red-handed—bent triple, upside down in mid-air over the head-board, say, and flossing her teeth with your best friend's dick—you never know. She'll deny it. Even if she has to cough the dick out of her mouth to facilitate speech, she'll deny it. She'll look you in the eye and tell you it isn't so. She'll *believe* it, too. That's their strength—that's why you're never sure.

Ah, Serena, tell me it isn't so.

I worked up a big sweat over the console that morning—yeah, and a big tab too. I was just a hot robot, a jangling grid of jet-lag, time-jump, and hang-over. The telephone was an antique: a dialler. My fingers were so chewed and sore I could hardly do up my shirt buttons. Halfway through the session I was dialling with my left pinkie. And every time, every time, the soft intrusion of the telephonist as she purred on to the line with her unvarying, asphyxiating voice. 'Me again,' I kept saying. 'Me again, me again.'

I tried my own number first and repeatedly thereafter. Serena is always in and out. She has her keys. No luck. I spoke to Flora and Debbie, Serena's flat-mates. I rang her old office. I rang her gym. I rang her hairdresser. I even rang her gynaecologist. No one knew where she was. On a parallel track, I searched the air waves for Alec Llewellyn. I talked to his wife. I talked to three of his girl friends. I talked to his probation officer. I talked to his mother. Ditto.... Oh, these are pretty thoughts for me to entertain, three thousand miles from home.

My right ear felt red and fat. For a while I slumped back and stared at the telephone. It held out for several minutes. Then it rang.

'—Hello?'

'John Sleep? It's Caduta, Caduta Massi.'

'At last!'

'John, it's good to talk to you. But before we meet, I think we should sort some things out.'

'Like what, Caduta?'

'For instance, how many children do you think I should have.'
'Well I thought just the one.'
'No, John.'
'More?'
'Many more.'
I said, 'About how many?'
'I think I should have many children, John.'
'Well, okay. Sure. Why not? Say, what, two or three more?'
'We'll see,' said Caduta Massi. 'I'm glad you're amenable to that, John. Thank you.'
'Forget it.'
'And another thing. I think I should have a mother, a white-haired lady in a black dress. But that's not so important.'
'Whatever you say. Caduta—let's meet.'
Later, I had them send me up a rack of cocktails and canapés. The same bellhop walked skilfully into the room with the silver trays on his tense fingertips. I had nothing smaller, so I flicked him a five. He looked at the note and he looked at me.
'Have one,' I said, and picked up a drink.
He shook his head, resisting a smile, averting his mobile face. But the smile wriggled out.
'What's up?' I said coolly, and drank.
'You party last night?' he asked. He couldn't straighten his face for more than a couple of seconds at a stretch.
'What's your name?'
'Mike.'
'No, Mike,' I said, 'I did it all by myself.'
'...You gonna party now?'
'Yes. But all by myself again.'
He lifted his round chin, nodding his head tightly. He looked very serious. 'I take one look at you, man,' he said, 'and I know you ain't *never* gonna stop.'

I didn't attempt anything else that day. I drank the drink and ate the grub. I had a bath. I had a shave. I had a hand job. Or I tried. Then me and my sore tooth throbbed our way through a few hours of television—I sat flummoxed like a weary ghost, all shagged out from its hauntings.... There was some kind of variety show, hosted by an old entertainer, someone who was pretty well over the hill when I was a kid. Amazing to think that these guys are still around, still alive, let alone still earning and doing their shit. They don't make them like that any more. Or, let's be accurate: only now, in 1981, do they make them like that. They couldn't before—they didn't have the technology. Jesus Christ, this old prong has been sutured and stitched together in a state-of-the-art cosmetics lab. The scalloped blaze of his bridgework matches the macabre brilliance of his flounced dicky. Check out the tan on the guy—it's like a paint-job. He looks terrific, positively rosy. His Latin rug sweats with vitamins. His ears are sharp and succulent.... Then this old android starts bringing on a string of even older guys, also spruce and metallic, a chorus line of tuxed fucks called things like 'Mr Music' and 'Entertainment Himself'. Wait a minute. Now I *know* that one has been dead for years. Come to think of it, the whole show has the suspended air and sickly colour of treated film, that funeral-parlour glow, numb and shiny, like a corpse. I've been warped out of time here, into a necropolis of the old American gods.

Time passed until it was time to go. I climbed into my big suit and brushed my hair. I got one more call that afternoon. It was a curious call, a strange call. I'll tell you about it later. Some whacko. No big deal.

Where is Serena Fox? Where is she? She knows where *I* am, that hot bitch. My number is up there on the kitchen wall. This is punishment. Punishment is what I'm taking here.

I ask only one thing. I want to get back to England, and track her down, and be alone with her—or not even alone, just close to her, close enough to smell her skin, see the flecked webbing of her green eyes, the supple line of her lips—and put in one good, clean punch. That's all I ask.

So now I must go uptown to meet with Fielding Goodney at the Carraway Hotel—Fielding, my money-man, my contact, and my pal. He's the reason I'm here. I'm the reason he's here too. We're going to make lots of money together. If we don't, then I'm going to fucking kill myself, is all I'm going to do. It's as simple as that.

I came down the steps and into the street. Above, all was ocean brightness. Against the open sky the clouds had been sketched by a wonderfully swift and confident hand. Ah, where would I be without the sky? I know: I'd be in England, where we don't have one. Through some physiological fluke—poison and chemistry doing a deal in their smoke-filled room—I felt fine, I felt good. Manhattan twanged in its spring ozone, girding itself for the fires of July and the cellar heat of August. Let's walk it, I thought, and started across town.

On masculine Madison Avenue, as trimly buttoned as a snooker waistcoat, I took my left and headed north into the long vista. The angry cars swore loudly at each other, looking for trouble, eager to fight. At the corner of Fifty-fourth, a big black guy writhed within the glass and steel of a telephone kiosk. He was having a terrible time, that much was clear. Often as I approached he slapped the hot outer metal of the booth with his wide palm. The powerful back leaned into the sentry box, giving it all his shoulder and buttock. He was shouting—I couldn't really hear him. I bet money was involved. Money is always involved. Maybe women too. In the cabled tunnels beneath the street and in the abstract air paths of the sky, how much obscenity, imprecation, and threat were crackling through New York? How would it balance out? Poorly, probably. Every line that linked two talkative lovers would be flexed and snarled between a hundred more that promised violence in its intense and sexual, its special language.... I've hit women. Yeah, I know, I know. It's hard to do, in a sense. Have *you* ever? Girls, ladies, have you ever copped one? It's quite a step, particularly the first time. After that, though, it gets easier and easier. Afte a while, hitting women is like rolling off a log. But I'm going to stop. I'm going to kick it. Just you see if I don't.... As I passed, the black cracked the telephone back into its frame and lurched off-balance out towards me. Then his head dropped, and he slapped the metal one more time, but feebly now. Time and temperature flashed above.

Fielding Goodney was already in attendance at the Carraway's Stahrlight Bar when I strolled into the cinematic gloom, a little after six. He stood with his back to me in the depths of this grotto of glass, leaning among the stools with a forefinger extended towards the bottles. An amused barman bobbed about to his instructions.

'Just wash the ice with it,' I heard him say. 'None in the glass, okay? Just wash it.'

He turned. 'Hey there, Slick.' We shook hands. 'When did you get in?'

'Can't remember. Yesterday.'

He looked at me critically. 'You fly Coach?'

'Yeah. Standby.'

'Pay the extra, Slick. Fly in the sharp end. Coach kills. Hell, it's all on the house. Bob: give my friend here a Rain King. And just wash that ice. Relax, Slick, you look fine. Bob, am I wrong?'

'That's right, Mr Goodney.'

Fielding leaned back against the dark wood, his weight satisfyingly disposed on two elbows and one long Yankee leg. He regarded me with his embarrassing eyes, super-candid cornflower blue—the kind made fashionable by the first wave of technicolour American filmstars. His thick unlayered hair was swept back from the high droll forehead. He smiled.

'Just how old are you, Fielding?' I asked.

'I'm twenty-five.'

'Jesus Christ.'

'Don't let that spook you, John. Here. Here's your drink.'

Barman Bob expectantly slid the frosted glass towards me. The liquid looked heavy and viscid, like colourless mercury.

'What's in this?'

'Nothing but summer skies, Slick. You're still a little lagged, no?' He placed a bronzed hand on my shoulder. 'Let's sit down and talk. Bob: keep them coming.'

I followed him to the table, thankful for that human touch.

Fielding straightened his cuffs and said, 'Any thoughts on the wife?'

'Well I just spoke to Caduta Massi.'

'No kidding? She called you?'

'Yup.'

'So she's hungry. What did she say?'

'She said she wanted lots of kids.'

'Huh?'

'In the film. She said she wanted at least three more kids.'

'That figures,' said Fielding. 'Word is she had herself snipped. Sometime in her late twenties. You know, no more abortions. Didn't want kids in case it fucked her body. So now she wants kids.'

'She's a bit old for us, isn't she?'

'Have you seen *The Succubus?*'

'Yes. It was terrible.'

'Sure, the film shat, but she looked great.'

'True. Who else is there? Happy Elexa?'

'No good. She's in the Hermitage.'

'Really? What's up?'

'Depression, deep, practically catatonic. That girl is real pissed off, I tell you.'

'Really? What about Norma Wand?'

'Ditto. Fat farm. Two hundred and twenty pounds.'

'Wow.'

'I say Caduta, Slick. She's perfect for us. Think about it. Have you spoken with Lorne?'

'Yeah.'

'This is a very difficult time for Lorne.'

'You're not fucking kidding.'

'He's low right now. He just had eighty grand's worth of dental work.'

'But look, man, he's going to roast me. I won't be able to handle him.'

'Stay icy calm, Slick. The truth is, Guyland will do anything to be in this picture. Have you seen *The Prairie Oyster?*'

'No.'

'*Pookie Hits the Trail? Big Bad Bill?*'

'Of course not.'

'He's doing anything now. Road movies, good-ole-boy stuff, TV specials. His agent straps him on the horse and out he rides. This is the first real part that's come his way for four-five years. He's crazy for it.'

'Then why do we want him?'

'Trust me, Slick. With Guyland in the package it respectabilizes the whole deal. It ups the TV and cable sale by 50 per cent, means we clean up in Taiwan and Guadeloupe, reassures certain backers.... I have a dozen old farts with fifty grand under the cot. They won't haul it out for Drew Tatler or Butch Beausoleil or Spunk Davis. Never heard of them. Lorne's our man, Slick. Face it.'

'But he's a maniac. How do I deal with him?'

'As follows. Say you'll do everything he wants and then when the time comes don't do any of it. If he goes bananas, you shoot the scene then lose the film. You'll have final cut, Slick. That I swear.'

Well, this made pretty good sense to me. I said, 'How's the money?'

'The money,' said Fielding, 'the money is beautiful. Ever take any exercise, Slick?'

'Why? I mean yes.'

'What kind of stuff?'

'I swim sometimes, and I play tennis.'

'No kidding.' He called for two more and the check. I reached for the squashed notes I kept in my trouser pocket. With a strong left hand Fielding seized my wrist. As I drank I saw him take a fifty, one of many, from his shining clip.

Fielding had the car waiting outside—an Autocrat, half a block long, with chauffeur, and with black bodyguard riding shotgun. He took me to an old gangster steak house in the Heights. It was brilliant. We talked money. Everything looked cool. Fuck it, I thought: worst case, his dad will end up tabbing the whole deal. Fielding's father is called Beryl Goodney, and owns half of Virginia. Maybe his mum is called Beryl, too, and owns the other half. You never can tell with American names. I once had a cabbie called Supersac Morgan. (Supersad's eyes were brown and melancholy. His eyes were supersad.) New Yorkers will tell you that the surname comes first on the cabbie's ID. But who says? Even with Smith John and Brown David, how can you be really sure over here? And another thing: is Alec Llewellyn fucking Serena Fox? Well, what do you think? Could be, no? What's your personal opinion? Has he seen the single dead flower in the jam jar beside her bed? Has he heard her peeing and humming in the bathroom, the black pants like a wire connecting her slender calves? Girls always fancy your best friends. I always fancy their best friends too. Girls and their best friends are very alike, except in one important respect. You don't see and fuck the best friend all the time. They give you the one thing your girl can't give you: a change from your girl. I don't think she is. I don't think Serena Fox *is* fucking Alec Llewellyn. How come? Because he hasn't got any money. I have. Come on, why has Serena stuck it out with me? For my pot belly, my gumline filings, my basement rug? She's not in this for her health, now is she?

Fielding signed the check. I signed some contracts, directing more and more money my way.

He dropped me off on Broadway. Eleven o'clock. What can a grown male do alone at night in Manhattan, except go in search of pornography?

Me, I spent an improving four hours on Forty-second Street, dividing my time between a space-game arcade and the go-go bar next door. In the arcade the proletarian triffids of the New York night, these darkness-worshippers, their terrified faces reflected in the screens, stand hunched over the consoles. They are human forms of mutant moles and bats, hooked on the radar, rumble, and wow of these stocky new robots who play with you if you give them money. They'll talk too, for a price. Launch Mission, Circuit Completed, Firestorm, Flashpoint, Timewarp, Crackdown, Blackout! The kids, tramps, and loners in here are the displaced mineshaft spirits of the new age. Their grandparents must have worked underground. I know mine did. In the go-go bar men and women are ranged against each other, kept apart by a wall of drink, a moat of poison, along which conciliatory matrons and bad bouncers stroll.

At eleven-thirty or thereabouts the old barmaid said to me, 'See? She's talking to you. Cheryl's talking to you. You want to buy Cheryl a drink?'

I looked up. The barmaid might have been last night's sister. I paid the ten, and said nothing.

An hour later the barmaid said to me, 'You English? We got an English girl here. Hey, English! *Cmere.* This is English. He's English. You want to buy English a drink?'

I said, 'I do want to, but I haven't got any money.'

An hour later the barmaid said to me, 'Okay. Beth's talking to you. You want to buy Beth a drink?'

I said, 'I haven't got any money, and anyway I don't even want to.'

She didn't ask me again after that, which was shrewd and experienced of her. She could tell by the way I sat coiled over my Scotch that it would be better to let me be. I had a few more, then

25

made a break for the streets.

I wheeled round Times Square, looking for damage. I found some too. A very young prostitute approached me. We got a cab and rode thirty blocks, downtown, west, Chelsea way. I glanced at her only once in the bucking car. She was dark, with lips the colour of blood and black hair too tangled to shine. I consoled myself with the thought that, along with a bottle of *Je Rêve*, a carton of Executive Lights, and a punch in the tits, I'd be taking back a real lulu of a VD for Serena—Herpes I, Herpes II, Herpes: The Motion Picture. I can recall the rudimentary foyer of some thriving flophouse. I paid for the room, up front. She led me there. The figure of fifty dollars was mentioned by her and okayed by me. She started getting undressed and so did I. Then I stopped.

'...But you're pregnant,' I remember saying in childish, open-ended surprise.

'It's all right,' she said. I stared at the strong gleaming belly; you expect it to be soft but it looks so strong.

'It's not all right,' I said. I made her get dressed and sit on the bed. I held her hand and listened to myself talking crap for an hour and a half. She nodded. I had paid her the money. She probably listened to some of it; this was easy work, really. Towards the end I thought I might try and wangle a hand job out of her. She would have obliged readily enough, no doubt. She was like me, myself. She knew she shouldn't do it; she knew she shouldn't go on doing it. But she went on doing it anyway. What is corruption, if it isn't seeing the difference between good and bad and choosing bad—or consenting to bad, okaying bad?

Nothing happened. I gave her a further ten for car fare. She went off to look for more men and money. I went back to the hotel, lay down fully clothed, and backed off into sleep for the second night running in this town where the locks and light-switches all turn the wrong way and where the sirens go 'you' and 'whoop!' and '*ow, ow, ow.*'

My head is a city, and various pains have now taken up residence in various parts of my face. A gum-and-bone ache has launched a co-operative on my upper east side. Across the park, neuralgia has rented a duplex in my west Seventies. Downtown, my chin throbs with lofts of jaw-loss. As for my brain, it's Harlem up there, expanding in the summer fires. It boils and swells. One day soon it will have to burst.

Memory's a funny thing, isn't it?

You don't agree?

Funnily enough, I don't agree either. Memory has never amused me much, and I find the whole gimmick progressively unfunny as I get older. It's funny: perhaps memory just stays the same but just has less to remember as the days and days lengthen, and life gets less memorable. Lying in the bath some slow afternoon, can you remember if you've washed your toes? (Peeing is boring, isn't it? Whew! Isn't *that* a drag?) I can't remember half the stuff I do any more. But then I don't want to much. Whichever way you look at it, memory's a funny thing, isn't it?

Waking now at noon, for instance, I have a strong sense that I spoke to Serena in the night. It would be just like her to haunt me in the black hours, when I am weak and mad. What did she say, if indeed she said anything, if the talk weren't just dawn fears and dream babble? Serena knows something that everyone ought to know by now. She knows that people are easy to frighten and haunt. People are terribly easy to terrify. It seems that we are all pretty weak down here. We are all aching for reassurance and praise. No one gets enough of it.

I could certainly use some...I didn't get any yesterday. I haven't told you about my mystery caller yet, have I? I think you'd better check it out.

I was sitting in front of the television, as you know, and torpidly splashing my way through the drink. The telephone rang: I snatched at it, and juggled with the grey doll's arm.

'Yeah?'

There was silence—no, not silence, but a distant parched whistle, dreary and remote, like the sound that lives inside my ear. Perhaps this was the sound the Atlantic made with its volume and its space.

'Hello? Serena? Say something, for Christ's sake. Who's paying for this call?'

'Money,' said a man's voice. 'Always money, the money.'

'Alec? Who is this?'

'It isn't Serena, man. I'm not Serena.'

I waited.

'Oh, I'm not anybody very special at all. I'm just the guy whose life you fucked up. That's all I am.'

'Who are you? I don't know you.'

'The man says he doesn't know me. How many guys' lives have you fucked up recently? Maybe you ought to keep score.'

Where was this call coming from? Would the hotel telephonist know? *Had* I fucked up anyone life's recently? Not that I could recall....

'Come on,' I said, 'what is this? I'm hanging up.'

'*Wait!*' he said—and I thought, at once, with relief: Oh, he's *mad.* So there's no real problem. Everything's fine, fine.

'Okay. Say your bit.'

'Welcome to New York,' he began. 'Flight 101. Thank you for flying Trans-American. Don't fight with cabbies. Don't go to topless bars. You want to buy Dawn a drink? Keep away from those porno stores you've been eyeing. They'll wreck your head. Take it easy. You're a very sick man, John.'

'...Wait. What's your name?'

The line died. I put down the receiver and picked it up again.

'It was a local call, sir,' the girl told me. 'Everything all right, sir?'

'Yes,' I said. 'Thank you. Everything's fine, fine.'

Wow, I thought—this is a new wrinkle. It was a local call all right. It was very local indeed.

Half past two, and I was out on Broadway, heading north. Now, how bad do you assume I'm feeling?.... Well, you're wrong. I'm touched by your sympathy (and want much, much more of it: oh brother, sister, could I use some more of that), but you're wrong. I didn't feel too great this morning, true. A two-hour visit to Pepper's Burger World, on the other hand, soon sorted that lot out. I had four Wallies, three Blastfurters, an American Way, plus a six-pack of beer. I'm a bit full and sleepy, but apart from that I'm ready for anything.

I wondered, as I burped up Broadway, I wondered how this town ever got put together. Someone was dreaming big all right. Starting down in Wall Street and nosing ever upwards into the ruins of the old West Side, Broadway snakes through the island, the only curve in this world of grids. Somehow Broadway always contrives to be just that little bit shittier than the zones through which it bends. Look at the East Village: Broadway's shittier than that. Look uptown, look at Columbus: Broadway's shittier. Broadway is the moulting, scuffed-up python of New York. I sometimes feel like that myself. Here the fools sway to Manhattan time.

'I ain't got to hear that shit,' one of them said to the other as he passed me by.

Now what's all this about me playing tennis with Fielding Goodney? Do *you* remember him making this ridiculous arrangement? Remind me.

As I sat sobbing over my snout and coffee this morning, Fielding rang and said, 'Okay, Slick. I fixed the court. Let's do it.'

Well, of course I played along, and obediently wrote down the address he gave me. As it happens I've got an old pair of sneakers with me, and a T-shirt of sorts. Fielding said he'd lend me some trunks. As for tennis, I thought to myself—yeah, I can play that shit....

Carrying my stuff in a plastic duty-free bag, I followed leaning Broadway up past the loops and circuses at the corner of the Park and into the West Side with its vacant lots and car chutes. The numbered street plodded slowly past. I kept expecting to see a sports centre or a gymnasium, or one of those shady squares of green that sneak up on you in the streets of London. You've fucked up again, I thought when I came to the building that corresponded to the address on my slip. It was a skyscraper, whose glassy lines climbed without any nonsense into the open blue. I went in anyway and asked the man.

'A fifteenth,' he said.

What was Fielding playing at? I rode the lift, which barrelled me up through the dead floors marked with an X. In the corridor I passed a familiar face—that of Chip Fournaki, the swarthy pro who usually flopped bad-temperedly in the semi-finals of the major competitors. A second later I passed Bob Karebenkian, Chip's doubles partner.

The door buzzed and I stepped into the loud green of a tropical ante-room. On the Astroturf carpet stood Fielding Goodney, drinking real orange juice from a tall glass. His skin was deeply tanned, setting off the milky down of his limbs and the clean lines of his pristine shorts and shirt, the chunky white of his footwear.

'Hi, Slick,' he said, and turned towards the glass wall when I joined him. As if from the bridge of a ship, we looked down on to the empty court. At the far end of the deck was another window, behind whose gloom sat fifteen or twenty people. The court must have been three floors deep. A hundred dollars an hour? Two hundred?

'Who are they over there?' I asked.

'They just come in and watch. As I say, don't be spooked by the occasion, Slick. These are your trunks.'

He pointed to the door.

'Oh, Mr Goodney,' I heard the white-smocked lady sing. 'You'll finish prompt, won't you? Sissy Skolimowsky is on at four, and you know what *she's* like.'

I knew what Sissy Skolimowsky was like too. She was the current world champion.

So I slipped into my gear next door. Hippie-red, tank-top drummer's T-shirt; Fielding's horrible trunks (they weren't tennis shorts at all: they were skirt-tight Bermudas, with golfing check); black socks; my cracked and parched gym-shoes. Then I tiptoed to the can. The shoes pinched like crazy; my feet must still have jet-lag, jet-swell. I unzipped the trunks and did my thing. The pee looked awful pale against the Vitamin-B steeped mothballs of the curved jug. I turned. There was a mirror. Oh forget it. They won't let you play anyway.

But they did. The lady gave me a startled glance—at the tureen of my gut, no doubt, and at the crushed bullybag in the wide-checked Bermudas—but she gave me my racket and opened the door. I came down the steps and on to the deck. Fielding had already loped hungrily to the far end, holding his barndoor-sized steel racket in one hand and a dozen yellow tennis balls in the other.

'Want to hit for a while?' he shouted, and the first of the balls was burning through the air towards me.

I should have realized that when English people say they can play tennis they don't mean what Americans mean when they say they can play tennis. Americans mean that they can play tennis. Now I am nothing more than an all-weather park-player. A certain wrong-footing slyness has sometimes enabled me to dink and poke my way to victory over more talented players; but basically I'm a dog on the court. Fielding was good. Oh, he was *good.* And there were differences of health, muscle-tone, and co-ordination to be accounted for too. Fielding, tanned, tuned, a king's ransom of orthodonture having passed through his mouth, reared on steaks and milk sweetened with iron and zinc, twenty-five, leaning into his strokes, and imparting top-spin with a roll of the wrist. Me, I lolloped and leapt for my life at the other end; fourteen stone of yob genes, booze, snout, and fast food; ten years older; choked on heavy fuel; with no more to offer than my block drive and backhand chip. I looked up at the glass window above Fielding's head. The middle-management of Manhattan stared on, their faces as thin as credit cards.

'Okay,' said Fielding. 'You want to serve?'

'You do it.'

I watched Fielding bend forward, pat the ball, then straighten up to aim his gun. *My* serve is no more than a convulsion which occasionally produces a baseline overhead. But Fielding was precise in his stance, fluid in his action, with a touch of the severity that all natural ball players have. What is it with ball players? What is it about roundness that they understand better than we do?

His opening serve I didn't see at all. It fizzed past me, losing its definition for a moment on the centre line, before thwacking first bounce into the green canvas behind my back. The passage of the ball seemed to leave a comet's trail of yellow against the artificial green of the court.

'Nice one,' I called, and trudged across in my black socks and checked Bermudas. This time I managed to get a line on Fielding's first serve: it smacked into the tape with a volume that made me whimper—the sound of a strong hand slapping a fat belly. I edged up a few feet as Fielding daintily removed the second ball from the pocket of his tailored shorts. I twirled my racket and swayed around a bit.... But his second serve was a real dilly too. Hit late and low with what I guessed was a back-hand grip, the ball came looping over the net, landed deep, and kicked like a bastard. It jumped so high that I could return it only with a startled half-smash. Fielding had come thundering up to the net, of course, and angled the ball away with acute dispatch. He aced me again at thirty-love, but on the last point of the game I got another crack at his second serve. I stood my ground and lobbed the brute, quite accurately, and Fielding had to stroll back from the service line to retrieve it. That lob was my last shot, really; I was never a contender after that. We had a rally of sorts: i.e. Fielding stood at the centre of his base line while I hurled myself round the court. *Put it away*, I kept telling him, but there were a good few strokes exchanged before he elected to place the ball beyond my reach.

We changed ends. I didn't meet his eye. I hoped he couldn't hear my hoarse gasps for air. I hoped he couldn't smell—I hoped he couldn't see—the junk-fumes swathing my face like heat-ripple. As I took position I glanced up at our audience in their aquarium. They were smiling down.

My opening serve flopped into the net, six inches from the ground. My second serve is a dolly and Fielding murdered it in his own sweet time, standing back before putting all his weight into the stroke; I didn't even chase his return. The same thing happened on the next point. At love-thirty, I served so blind and wild that Fielding simply reached out and caught the ball on the volley. He pocketed it and strolled forward a few paces—several paces. I moved wide and, in petulant despair, hit my second serve as if it were my first. And it went in! Fielding was less surprised than I was, but he only just got his racket to the ball; and he was so insultingly far advanced that his return was nothing more than a skied half-volley. The yellow ball plopped down invitingly in the centre of my court. I hit it pretty low, hard, and deep to Fielding's backhand and lumbered cautiously up to the net. A big mistake. Fielding chose this moment to untether a two-fisted topspin drive. The ball came screaming over the tape, skipped a beat, regathered its tilt and momentum—and punched me in the face. I toppled over backwards, and my racket fell with a clatter. For several shocked seconds, I lay there like an old dog, an old dog that wants its old belly stroked. Now how's this going to look? I got to my feet. I rubbed my nose.

'You okay, Slick?'

'Yeah. I'm cool,' I murmured. I bent down for my racket, and straightened up. Behind the glass wall the sea-creatures watched from their pool. Sharp faces. That's right, get your staring done with.

And so it went on. I won about half-a-dozen points—from Fielding's double-faults, from net-cords and shots off the wood, and from telling lies about a couple of the calls. I kept wanting to say: 'Look, Fielding, I know this is costing you a lot of money and everything. But do you mind if I stop? Because *I think I might* DIE if I don't.' I didn't have the breath. After five minutes I was playing with a more or less permanent mouthful of vomit. It was the longest hour of my life, and I've had some long hours.

The first set went six-love. So did the second. We were about nine-love in the third when Fielding said, 'You want to play or you just want to hit?'

'Let's hit.'

Finally a bell rang, and Sissy Skolimowsky appeared with her coach. Fielding knew this chunky, white-skinned girl, whose face and body showed the price of the athletic life, not its glow.

'Hi,' she said.

'Hey, Siss,' said Fielding, 'is it okay if we watch?'

She was already on the line, starting work. 'You can watch,' she said, 'but you can't listen. Shit!'

But I was staggering off by this time. Ten minutes later, I was still slumped wheezing on a canvas chair in the ante-room when Fielding trotted up the steps. He squeezed my shoulder.

'I'm sorry, I....'

'Relax, Slick,' he said. 'You just need to sink a couple of thou into your backhand, maybe a grand on your serve. You should quit smoking, drink less, eat right. You should go to high-priced health clubs and fancy massage studios. You should undergo a series of long, painful, and expensive operations. You ought to–'

'Look, shut the fuck up, will you.'

'Your funeral, Slick. I just want you to stay alive, stick around for a while. You'll be a rich man by the time I'm done. I just want you to *enjoy*.'

Pretty soon, Fielding jogged off back to the Carraway. I went and sat next door in the changing-room. I stared at the pimpled tiles. I thought if I could just stay completely still for the next half hour, then maybe nothing too bad would happen. One twitch, I reckoned, one blink, and the changing-room was in for some Restricted special effects.... Then six huge guys came in—I guess from the squash courts, down the passage somewhere. These gleaming, stinging jocks were all shouting and swearing and farting as they stripped for the shower. I never saw their faces. I couldn't raise my head without copping an open-beaver shot of some armpit or scribble-haired backside; once I opened my eyes to see a great raw dick dangling two inches from my nose, like a pornographic reprisal. Then they had a ten-minute towel-fight. The chick in the smock even poked her head round the door and hollered at them through the steam.... I couldn't take it any longer. I weepily gathered my street clothes and crammed them into the duty-free bag. I hit Sixty-sixth Street in sweat-looped tank-top, knee-length Bermudas, black socks, and squelchy gyms. Come to think of it, I must have looked exactly like everyone else. My body craved darkness and silence, but the sun's controls were all turned up full blast as I screamed for cabs in the yellow riot of Broadway.

There is only one way to get good at fighting: you have to do it a lot.

The reason why most people are no good at fighting is that they do it so seldom, and, in these days of high specialization, no one really expects to be good at anything unless they work out at it and put in some time. With violence, you have to keep your hand in; you have to have a repertoire. When I was a kid, growing up in Trenton, New Jersey, and later on the streets of Pimlico, I learned these routines one by one. For instance, can you butt people (i.e. hit them in the face with *your* face—a very intimate form of fighting, with tremendous power to appal and astonish)? I took up butting when I was ten. After a while, after butting a few people (you try to hit them with your rugline, hit them in the nose, mouth, cheekbone—it doesn't much matter), I thought, 'Yeah: I can butt people now.' From then on, butting people was suddenly an option. Ditto with ball-kneeing, shin-kicking, eye-forking, etc: these were all new ways of expressing frustration, fury, and fear, and of settling arguments in my favour. You have to work at it, though. You learn over the years, by trial and error. You can't get the knack by watching TV. You have to use live ammunition. So, for example, if you ever tangled with me, and a rumble developed, and you tried to butt me, to hit my head with your head, you probably wouldn't be very good at it. It wouldn't hurt. It wouldn't do any damage. All it would do is make me angry. Then I'd hit your head with my head extra hard, and there would be plenty of pain and maybe some damage too. See?

Besides, I'd probably butt you long before it ever occurred to you to butt me. There's only one rule in street and bar fights: maximum violence, instantly. Don't pussyfoot, don't wait for the war to escalate. Nuke them, right off. Hit them with everything, milk bottle, car tool, clenched keys, or coins. The first blow has to give everything. If he takes it, and you go down, then you get all he has to mete out anyway. The worst, the most extreme violence—at once. Extremity is your only element of surprise. Hit them with everything. No quarter.

Well that tennis game really fucked me up good, I tell you. For seventy-two hours I just lay in my pit at the hotel. The tinnitus was on the scene more or less full time, and the toothache got much more complicated: it would wake me with sirens of pain, loud, inordinate, braiding, twisting, like currents in a river. I'd fucked my back, too, out on the court; and there was this incredible welt up the rear of my thigh where I'd fallen and tobogganed across the Astroturf on my can for a few yards, wrong-footed by Fielding. Last but not least, I seemed to have developed a severe gastric condition, maybe from all those frazzled junkfurters. For the first day I was pure turbo power, just a human hovercraft over the bowl. Oh, I had lift-off. The maid lurked but never got a look in, and soon the room was really showing its age.

Mike, the bellhop, turned out to be a good pal to me here. He ran errands to the pharmacy and liquor store. With his quick presence he punctuated the grey wastes of the afternoons. He even bawled me out when he found me shitfaced in front of *The Money Game* at ten-thirty one morning, and looked as though he might prove difficult about ferrying in the booze. I bawled him out back. 'Fuck it,' I said, 'I'll use room service.' So he did my bidding, restlessly, with dropped eyes. I was touched. Mike was getting money for this, naturally; but he'd be getting a lot more if I'd been liquored up all the time. In my frail state, I couldn't take much of his disapproval, and I tried to take it pretty easy on the whole.

I had fever. And I had Serena fever too. Lying in that heavy zone where there is neither sleep nor wakefulness, where all thoughts are cross-purposed and yet the mind is forever solving, solving, Serena came at me like pink smoke. I saw her performing flesh in fantastic eddies and convulsions, the face with its smile of assent and the complicit look in the flattered eyes, the demonology of her underwear suggesting spiders and silk, the muscular back tanned and tuned, the arched creature doing what that creature does best—and the thrilling idea, so rich in pornography, that she does all this not for passion, not for comfort, far less for love; the idea that she does all this for *money*. I woke mumbling in the night—yes, I heard myself say it, solve it, through the dream-babble—I said, 'I love it. I love her... I love her corruption.'

The telephone was a one-way instrument, an instrument of torture. How do I get all this poison out of my ears? Lorne Guyland called. Caduta called. That mad fucker, that really mad fucker, he called again, three times, four times, son of a *bitch*. He's got me worried, I admit it. I am starting to be afraid. I go hot now when I hear the empty sound at the end of the line, just before he starts his spiel. I don't want to be the centre of attention like this. I just want to lie here in my rust.

He knew about the tennis, and crowed at length over my humiliation. I assume he was glaring down from the glass gallery, having tailed me to the court. 'Man, did you look sick,' he said. His general theme? His theme was that I had ruined his life. I had traduced and humbled him many times. I was a bastard, a rotting monster of booze and hate. I didn't argue. I didn't say much at all. I kept wishing he would ring when I had a decent drunk on: then I'd give him a piece of my mind. Sometimes he sounded big, sometimes he sounded small. If it came to it...who knows? With a few brandies down me, maybe I could handle him with my weight and my brief but nasty repertoire of sudden street stunts. You never can tell, though, with mad guys. I once got bopped by a mad guy and it was like no blow I have ever felt—qualitatively different, full of an atrocious rectitude. Their internal motors are all fucked up. They can lift buses and things if they're feeling mad enough.

My producer Fielding Goodney rang several times too. He was concerned and solicitous, and apologized for having run me ragged on the court. I don't know about you, but I like that kid.... It was my own fault. He wasn't toying with me; he was just playing his natural game. Why did I play along? Why did I push myself so hard? I mean, my body must have been seriously near its brink. Fielding offered to send round his personal physician to take a look at me, but I saw no good reason to put the doc through that ordeal.

And on the third morning I awoke to find the sheets were dry. My head was silent, and in no pain. Cautiously I opened my eyes and sat up straight. Yes, it had gone, it had passed over, it had moved on to another place and was now active somewhere else. I thought: Home, go home.

I hopped out of the cot and rang room-service. For over a minute I jogged on the spot. Was it my fancy, or had I lost a little bit of weight? I showered. I shampooed my rug. I shaved off the itching mask of my three-day beard. I took a swig of disinfectant. I did a press-up. I rang the airline.

Halfway through the first pint of coffee, I torched a cigarette. Mmm, tasted good. Fags and fever don't mix, and, during my sickness, it had taken a hell of a lot of will power to keep my snout-count up to the mark. There was a slight shortfall on the second carton, but nothing I couldn't handle.

I touched my toes. I lit another cigarette and poured more coffee, popping the fifth carton of half-and-half. Well then, I asked myself, how about a hand job?

I flipped a couple of nude-mags out of my suit-case and returned to the sack to check them out. (You prop up the second pillow, like a lectern.) The whole idea was obviously a very serious mistake. I had an unbelievable neck-ache for about ten minutes afterwards. Besides, pornography is habit-forming, you know. Oh yes it is. I am a pornography addict, for instance, with a three-mag-a-week and at-least-one-movie habit to sustain. That's why I need all this money. I've got all these chicks to support. While I ruefully rubbed my neck in front of the bathroom mirror, and withstood the gaze of my pocked, parched face, I also received a memory from the gibber of my nights of fever in hot New York. Someone had come to the end of the long passage outside Room 101, once, twice, perhaps many more times, someone had come and mightily shaken the door, and not with the need for entry but in simple rage and warning.... Did it happen, or did something like it happen, or was it just a new kind of dream. I'm getting new kinds all the time now—sadness dreams, boredom dreams with me or someone else just going on and on, and dreams that I can liken only to the strains of search that poets must feel as they wait for their lines to form. I say this tentatively. I don't know what it's like to write a poem. I don't know what it's like to read a poem: I've forgotten—I haven't done it for twenty years.... About me and reading (I don't really know why I tell you this—I mean, do you read that much?—but it seems important under the circumstances): I can't read because it hurts my eyes. I can't wear glasses because it hurts my nose. I can't wear contact lenses because it hurts my nerves. So you see, it all came down to a choice between pain and not reading. I chose not reading. Not reading—that's where I put my money.

Half-dressed, I rang Fielding at the Carraway.

'Lorne wants humouring,' he told me.

'Yeah, well you humour him for a while. I'm going home.'

'Slick! So soon!'

'I'll be back. I've got to sort some things out.'

'What's the problem? Women or money?'

'Yeah, that's the problem.'

'When's your flight?'

'Ten.'

'So you leave for the airport at 8.45.'

'No, I arrive at the airport at 8.45. I'm flying Airtrack.'

'*Air*track? What do you get on Airtrack, Slick? A spliff, a salad, and a light show?'

'Well, that's,what I'm doing.'

'Listen... I want you to meet Butch Beausoleil before you wing out. Can you get to my club around seven? Leave your bags at the door and just stroll on through.'

Now this was turning into a busy day. Noon saw me queueing at the stall on Fifth Avenue, queueing with the studs and lumberjacks for a cheap thin seat on the wide-bodied, crash-prone aircraft. This is the people's airline: we are this airline's people. This airline brought the prices down across the board and now only the abject fly Airtrack. A uniformed girl with tomato-red hair and an incredible gobbler's mouth disappeared for an ominous few minutes to check out my US Approach card, then bustled back, her moist teeth refreshed by my sound credit rating. How old was she? Nineteen? Forty-two?

'What's the movie?' I asked.

She tapped out the query with her red nails. *'Pookie Hits the Trail, II,'* she said.

'Really?.... Who's in it?'

The tolerant computer knew this too. 'Cash Jones and Lorne Guyland.'

'Who'd you like best?'

'I don't know,' she said. 'They both suck.'

I had a drink in a shadowy bar on Fifty-fifth Street. For a while I read my ticket. On the next stool along a trembling executive drank three dark cocktails quickly and hurried off with a dreadful sigh.... White wine, me—trying to stay in shape here. Then I barked my sore tooth on a pretzel, my tinnitus joined in the fun, and suddenly I knew beyond all question that Serena had some other prong on her books. Of course she has. He'll be some property developer or spaced-out rich kid, some money man. She might not even be fucking him yet, just keeping him quiet with the odd spangled glimpse of her underwear, the odd audience at the bathtub—yeah, and the odd hand job too, no doubt. After all, this was how she processed me to begin with, when she still had her sugar-daddy, plus a twenty-year-old location researcher on the side. Yes, she knows how to fend them off gently, she knows how to keep them stacked above her tarmac—she is an old hand at air-traffic control. Then, one day, I got the lot.... Where is she now? It is six o'clock over there, when the dark comes down. She is getting dressed for the night somewhere, yet she is worried. She is worried. The night is young over there, but Serena Fox is not so young, not any longer. You know something? I've got to marry her, marry Serena Fox. If I don't, probably no one else will, and I'll have ruined another life.

h yeah—let me tell you this before I forget. Someone else rang. Someone else rang me here in New York. In my fever, out of the babble, one day, came a human voice.

By now I had begun to think of the telephone as something hysterical and malevolent in itself, this dumb doll with its ventriloqual threats and demands. Do that, think this, pretend the other. Then came a human voice.

I was lying hugely, malely, in my underpants on the bed. What does a guy do about underpants? Faggot jockeys, baggy shorts, winded Y-fronts? They all look like hell. I just lay there sighing and sweating and searching for sleep. Then the telephone did its number, its act. One of my big beefs about Serena was that her disappearance obliged me to answer this thing whenever it rang. And it also might be Fielding, I supposed, trying to feed me even more money.

'John?' said the voice.

'...Serena?'

'Bad luck. It's Martina. Martina Twain? So you're in town.'

I felt—I felt several things at once. I felt the squeeze of shame. I smiled, and felt my facial flesh ease out of its recent mould. I felt my abscess for a second, lightly tickled by the strange creasing of my cheek. And I felt too that I couldn't really be bothered with all this, not now, maybe never.

She laughed at my silence. The laugh somehow established me as a waster or gadabout—but not unkindly, I thought.

'Yes, I'm in town,' I said. 'How did you know?'

'My husband told me.'

'Oh really?' I said sadly.

'He's in London. He just called this minute. So. Why are you here?'

I drew breath. The usual paragraph formed in my throat. But I said, 'That's a good question. I'm supposed to be making a film but it all looks like crap to me. Plus my girl's run out on me, and I'm incredibly ill.'

'Poor you. I was going to ask you to dinner. But perhaps I should come over with some toys or magazines or whatever it is that boys like best.'

This was pretty well enough to set me bawling. I had the homeward tug by now, though, and also felt the full sprawl of my slurred state. I said, no, you're kind, next time, and told Martina Twain good-bye. I rolled over with a grunt, and for a while I tried to think seriously about that serious girl.

I finished my wine and settled the tab—surprisingly high. But then it seemed I had had six glasses, or vases, of the cool Californian cordial. I walked back to the hotel through the crowds (here they come again) of Manhattan extras, walk-ons, and bit-part players, these unknown Earthlings. I had worked a deal with the guy behind the desk: I'd given him ten bucks and as many minutes' chat about Lorne Guyland and Caduta Massi; in return, he'd given me my room until five o'clock without charging me an extra day's whack. (He was a lifelong Caduta fan, and also had a lot of time for old Lorne. 'He's been at the top for thirty-five years,' he explained. 'That's what he's got my respect for.') The unloved room looked on in quiet martyrdom as I packed my stuff. There was a half-empty fifth of Scotch on the table, and so, finding myself in provident mood, I started drinking it up. I tried Serena a few times, with no luck. What was I going back to? What was I leaving here?

Orderly at first, my packing became brutal and chaotic. Under the bed I found an unopened pint of rum—hidden there by Mike, probably—and started to tackle that too. Sometimes it seems as though the day's work is never done. My head was twanging—I flopped down on to the bed and must have dozed off for a few minutes. The telephone woke me. I took another slug of rum and lit a cigarette in my own good time.

'Oh Christ. You again.'

'You fuck-up,' said the voice. 'So you're running back home. Wreck some more lives there.'

Now this was a break. He'd really caught me in the mood. I held the receiver tight by the throat, leaned forward, and said,

'Okay, blow-job, now you just listen to me. Get some help, all right? Go down to the neighbourhood wacko project—or crazoid programme or scumbag clinic—and turn yourself in. You're a sick fuck, is all. It's your chemicals, they're all fucked up. They'll give you some pills and then you'll feel all right for a little while.'

'Big man,' he said. 'We'll meet one day.'

'Oh I hope so. And when I get through with you, pal, there'll be nothing left but hair and teeth.'

'We'll meet—'

'We'll meet one day. And when we do, I'll fucking kill you.'

I smacked the receiver down on its hook and sat there panting on the bed. I needed to spit. Uch, I hate making these threatening telephone calls.... Now how did all that go down? That's it: get him really mad.

I looked at my watch. Jesus, I must have gone to sleep for an hour or more—though 'sleep' might be putting it a bit high. *Sleep* is rather an exalted term for what I get up to nowadays. These are blackouts, bub. I up-ended the bottle of rum over my mouth, finished my packing in the sour, twanging room, marshalled my travel documents, and buzzed down for the boy.

In the end I had ample time for my farewell to New York. First off, I gave Mike a fifty. He was embarrassed but pleased, I hope. I love giving money away. If you were here now, I'd probably slip you some dough, twenty, thirty, maybe more. What would you give me, brother, sister? Would you put an arm round my shoulder and tell me I was your kind of guy? I'd pay. I'd give you good money for it.

Next, I bought a joint, a popper, a phial of cocaine, and a plug of opium from a spade in Times Square, and snuffled it all up in a go-go bar toilet. Apart from any other consideration, this is a dumb thing to do, because they say the spades mix in strong stuff like devil dust with the dope, and your head explodes or your face drops off. But where's the economics in that? What they really do is mix in *weak* stuff with the dope, so that in effect you're only buying a roll-up, a dime-store thermometer, some ground aspirin, and a dog turd. Anyway I snuffled it all up, as I say—and felt a distinct rush, I think, as I came bullocking out of the can. I wouldn't really know with drugs. I only ever take them when I'm so drunk I wouldn't really know about anything.

Urged on by the cars and their brass, I crossed the road and hit a porno emporium on Forty-third and Broadway. How to describe it? It is a men's room. These 25-cent loop cubicles are toilets, really: you enter your trap, putting money in the slot, you sit down, and do what you need to do. The graffiti is written in black magic-marker on yellow cards, to which curious pin-ups are attached. This bitch has a gash so big. Watch the fuckpigs frolic in torrents of scum. Juanita del Pablo gets it in the ass. Who writes these things? Clearly someone on cool terms with the opposite sex. Meanwhile, the black janitoriat stroll with jinking moneybags.... First I sampled an S/M item in booth 4A. They got the chick on her back, bent her triple, and wedged a baseball bat in the tuck behind her knees. Then they gave her electric shocks. It was realistic. Was it real? You saw a writhing line of white static, and the girl certainly screamed and bounced. I split before they gave her an enema, which they were billed to do in the scabrous hate-sheet tacked to the door. If the girl had been a bit better-looking, a bit more my type, I might have stuck around. In the next booth along I caught a quarter's worth of a film with a sylvan setting; the sex-interest of the piece focused on a girl and a donkey. There she was, smiling, as she prepared to go down on this beast of burden. Ay! The donkey didn't look too thrilled about it either. 'I hope you're getting good money, sis,' I mumbled on my way out. She wasn't bad, too.... Finally I invested twenty-eight tokens' worth of my time in a relatively straight item, in which a slack-jawed cowboy got the lot, everything from soup to nuts, at the expense of the talented Juanita del Pablo. In the instant before the male's climax the couple separated with jittery haste. Then she knelt in front of him. One thing was clear: the cowboy must have spent at least six chaste months on a yoghurt ranch eating nothing but ice cream and buttermilk, and with a watertight no-hand-job clause in his contract. By the time he was through, Juanita looked like the patsy in the custard-pie joke, which I suppose is what she was. The camera proudly lingered as she spat and blinked and coughed.... Hard to tell, really, who was the biggest loser in this complicated transaction—her, him, them, me.

Now I come jerking and burping up the portalled steps of Fielding's university club, having stopped off for a drink or two on the way. You'd think I'd be in pretty terminal shape by now, what with that rum and dope and all. But not me. No sir, not this baby. You recognize the type by now? Some people get sleepy when they drink a lot, but not us. When we drink a lot, we want to go out and do things.... *Never do anything* is the rule I try and stick to when I'm drunk. But I'm always doing things. I'm drunk. 'Never do anything': that's a *good* rule. The world might be a better place—and a lot safer for me—if nobody ever did anything.... So, as I say, I was in capital fettle when the revolving doors hurled me into the hall—to meet Fielding Goodney, and Butch Beausoleil, the real Butch Beausoleil.

There was a white-haired old robot at the desk, and we shot the breeze for a while as he checked me out on the intercom. I told him a joke. How does it go now? There's this guy and his car breaks down and he—No, hang on. There's this farmer who keeps his wife locked up in the—Wait, let's start again.... Anyway, we had a good laugh over this joke when I'd finished or abandoned it, and I was told where to go. Then I got lost for a bit. I went into a room where a lot of people in evening dress were sitting at square tables playing cards or backgammon. I left quickly and knocked over a lamp by the door. The lamp should never have been there in the first place, with its plinth sticking out like that. For a while I thrashed around in some kind of cupboard, but fought my way out in the end. Skipping down the stairs again, I fell heavily on my back. It didn't hurt that much, funnily enough, and I waved away the appalled footman who tried to help me to my feet. I then had a few pretty stern words with the old prong at the desk. He made sure I got there this time all right, personally escorting me to the door of the Pluto Room and saying with a bow,

'This okay now, sir?'

'Fabulous,' I said. 'Look, take this.'

'No thank you, sir.'

'Come on. What's a five?'

'We have a no-tips policy here, sir.'

'Just this once won't harm anyone. No one's looking—come on...Okay then—fuck off!'

Well that sorted him out. I chugged into the Pluto Room loosening my tie and craning my neck. Boy, was it dark and hot in here! The bent backs of women and the attentive angles of their men stretched down the bar away from me. I took a bit of a toss on a stool-leg and sprinted face-first into a pillar, but stumbled on until I made out my friend Fielding down at the far end. Dressed in a white tux, he was whispering into the nimbus cast by a miraculously glamorous girl. She wore a low-cut silk dress in a razzy grey that rippled like television. Her ferocious russet hair hung in solid curves over the vulnerable valves of her throat and its buzzing body-tone. Giving Fielding no time to intercept me, I swanned straight up to the girl and kissed her lightly on the neck.

'Hi, Butch,' I said. 'How you doing?'

'Well *hi*. John Sleep. An honour,' said Butch Beausoleil.

'How goes it, old sport,' said Fielding. 'Hey, Slick, you look really lit. Now before I forget, here's a present for you.'

He handed me an envelope. It contained an air ticket, New York-London return, first class.

'The flight's at nine,' said Fielding, 'but you'll catch your plane—I guarantee it. Now, John, you look like you could use a drink.'

The kids were on champagne and I soon hollered for another bottle. I spilt a lot of that and hollered for another. Butch was a million laughs—and an obvious goer: you should have seen the way she helped me dab her lap with the napkin. Whew, the stuff that hot fox was giving out, all miming so fluently with the pornography still fresh in my head. Heat, money, sex and fever—this is it, this is New York, this is first class, this is the sharp end. I was one happy yobbo up there in the Pluto Room, and then another bottle appeared, and my nose was fizzing with the stuff, and there was another room and terrible confusion, and someone turned me by the shoulder and I felt wetness and could see Fielding's face saying....

The yellow cab shouldered its way through the streets of New York, a caged van taking this mad dog home. The driver with his flexed brown arm gouged the car through the lights on amber and gunned us out on to the straight. Never do anything, never do anything. I watched his brown arm, the skin puckered and punctured by its lancing black hairs. I watched unfamiliar city acres surge past in their squares. Eventually the flat signs and white lights of the airport began to swish by my face.

'Wha you fly,' said the driver, and I told him.

I was lying. So far as I could tell—from my watch, and from the red streamers of the ticket-books—both my flights had flown. But a squad of surprises awaited me in the expo aviary of the terminal. The departure of the 9 o'clock flight had been delayed, thanks to a timely bomb hoax. They had just started reloading the baggage, and expected to be in the air by eleven. I strolled to the first-class check-in bay. First class, they treat you right.

'How many bags, sir?' asked the chick.

'Just the one,' I said, and turned with an obliging flourish. 'Oh, you poor fucking moron.'

'Sir?'

'No, no bags. Just me,' I said with a dreadful smile....

I rang Mike at the Ashbery. He would store my stuff with no sweat. I'd be back.... Under the hot dental lights I traversed the building in search of a bar, having developed the idea of toasting my deliverance from New York. Far and wide did I roam. 'Ten o'clock and you're closed?' I heard myself yelling. 'This is fucking JFK, pal!' By that time I had a couple of navy-blue serge lapels in my fists. The guy reopened the duty-free counter and sold me a pint. I sat drinking it in the departure lounge. Boarding began, first class first. I stood up and entered the tube.

And continued to travel deeper into the tubed night—to travel through the night as the night came the other way, making its violent sweep across the earth. I drank champagne in the wide red throne, friendless in the plane's eye, tastefully curtained off from the coughing, snoring, shrieking, weeping, birth-giving innards of Business, Trimmer and Economy. How I hate my life. I called for divining cards. I've got to stop being young. Why? It's killing me, being young is fucking killing me. I ate my dinner. I watched the film—I caught *Pookie*: it was terrible, and old Lorne looked like shit. What happened out there, with Fielding and Butch? Ay, keep it away! Don't let it touch me. I can't give it headroom. I've got to grow up. It's *time*.

GRANTA

PAT BARKER
BLOW YOUR HOUSE
DOWN

Pat Barker was born on Teesside in 1943. Her father was killed in action during World War Two, and she was brought up mainly by her grandmother. She was·educated at Grangefield school, Stockton, and at the London School of Economics. *Union Street* is her first novel. This is an extract from a novel, *Blow Your House Down,* to be published by Virago. It is set in a northern industrial town, at a time when women are being maimed and killed.

Brenda and Audrey ran the last hundred yards down Northgate and arrived at the Palmerston, flushed, wet, and out of breath. 'I'll have to go for a pee,' said Audrey, hopping from leg to leg.
'You've only just been.'
'It's the rain,' said Audrey, and ran.
'What'll you have?' Brenda shouted after her.
'Anything. Lager and lime.'
That wouldn't help much when she was stood out in the rain again. Brenda went into the back room, waved to a group of women in the far corner and stood at the bar, waiting her turn to be served.

The Palmerston was crowded, as it always was by this time of night. Other pubs were livelier, with music and strip-tease shows; and more comfortable, too, for the Palmerston's dingy lino and balding plush had been there as long as anybody could remember. But to the women who drank in the back room, the Palmerston was special. It was their pub in a way that the others were not, and what drew them back to it was the personality of its owner: Beattie Miller.

Last Christmas one of the girls had suggested holding a raffle with a bottle of gin for whoever came closest to guessing Beattie's age. Too hard, everybody said, and it was, too. Her hair was red, incredibly red, and there was make-up on her face an inch thick, cracked and flaking into the lines around her eyes and mouth. She moved with great caution on her thin legs, as though venturing out onto icy ground. In spite of which Brenda wouldn't 've put her much past fifty.

'You looked drowned, love,' said Beattie, as she handed over the drinks. 'Is it still as bad?'
'Awful. And there's a nasty wind getting up as well.'
The group in the corner parted to make room for her. Elaine was back.
'How are you, cock?' Brenda asked.
'Oh, I'm smashing now, thanks.'
Elaine didn't look it. There were deep shadows round her eyes. If they *were* shadows. Brenda bent forward to look more closely and

intercepted a warning glance from Jean.

'Hello!' said Audrey, coming up behind Brenda. 'I thought you were gunna pack it in?'

'Oh, I decided I'd give it a bit longer.' Elaine brought her upper lip down over her slightly prominent front teeth in a way that was both rabbit-like and touching. 'Seems a pity to pack it in when I'm still feeling alright.'

The women looked at each other.

'Wait till you start showing,' Audrey said. 'You'll be raking it in.'

'Will I?'

'Why, aye,' said Jean. 'There'll be no trade left for the rest of us.'

'Oh, well, if I'm gunna be doing you all out of a job, I'd better buy the next round, hadn't I?' She smiled and stood up.

'That's right,' said Jean. 'I'll have another gin.'

Audrey sat down. 'Is that mine?' she asked, picking up a pint glass and turning to Brenda. 'I meant a half. Cheers, love.' As she lowered the glass she noticed a pair of sunglasses on Elaine's side of the table. She shook the raindrops from her sleeve and mimed amazement. '*Costa del Sol,* was it?'

'No,' said Jean, crisply. 'Costa del thump-in-the-eye.'

Audrey stopped smiling. There was a long silence.

'And there's no use sitting there like a load of wet week-ends. Elaine's just got to toughen up, that's all.'

You couldn't help wondering what experiences had toughened Jean up. There was a scar at the base of her throat, the worst scar Brenda had ever seen. Oh, she wrapped scarves round her neck to try and hide it, but she had a habit of throwing her head back when she'd finished speaking and then the scar showed. She couldn't be more than twenty-two or three, but she'd made herself respected and with none of the effing and blinding that some of them went in for. With Jean it was the blow first.

'You heard from Carol?' Brenda asked.

'Not a sausage,' said Jean. 'I just can't understand it. I mean, I know she was getting frightened about this bloke and all, but she'd never've gone off without telling me.'

'Didn't she say anything?'

'No. She was always on at me to go to London.'

'No point,' said Maureen, a dark, heavy-featured woman with

the beginnings of a moustache.   'If you're gunna meet one, you'll meet one anywhere.'

There was a general murmur of agreement.

'Stick to your regulars,' said Audrey. 'That's your best bet.'

'That's what I used to tell Carol,' said Jean. 'She said, "He *is* somebody's regular."'

Silence.

'Well, I don't know about the rest of you,' said Brenda, 'but I could do with that drink.'

'I'll see if Elaine needs a hand,' said Audrey.

'It's OK,' said Jean. 'She's got a tray.'

Elaine handed the drinks round and sat down to a chorus of 'Cheers' and 'Thanks, love'.

There was another brief silence.

'Anyway,' said Jean. 'She was right, wasn't she? You can go with somebody ten, twenty times, then some little thing'll happen and he'll flip.'

Elaine had gone very white.

Brenda said, 'I don't know what you're all on about. There hasn't been a squeak out of him for months. You don't even know he's still in this area. Or perhaps he's just stopped.'

'I wish I had a fiver for every time I've heard that,' Maureen said.

The others looked at her.

'I was in Bradford.' She waited for it to sink in. 'Oh, there was a lot of girls moved on, but there was a lot more stayed. And they were always on: "He's given up, he's topped himself." (Like bloody hell!) And they were full of ideas. "Stop in the car. Get out of the car. Don't turn your back. Don't bend down. Don't suck." Load of bloody codswallop. I never did any of it. I did carry a knife for a bit and then I thought, Well, you dozy cow, you're just handing him the weapon.'

'I couldn't 've stood it,' said Audrey. 'I'd 've had to get out.'

'That's easier said than done. I had a council flat and two bairns. Where the hell could I go?'

'But you must've been beside yourself!'

'No. Oh, I suppose once or twice. I remember one night I was stood on the corner and there was this little alley just behind me, and a bloke jumped out. And he says, "I'm the Ripper." Only of course he didn't say it like that.' Maureen waggled her fingers on either side of

her face and repeated slowly in a grave-yard voice: ' "I'm the Ripper." '
I don't know what he thought I was gunna do. I just looked at him
and says, "Oh, aye?" '

'What did he do?'

'What do you mean, "What did he do?" What they all do.'

'You never went with him?'

'Of course I did. You had to. If you listened to them, every stupid
little sod with a few pints inside him was the Ripper.' She paused.
'They were the ones that used to get me. They can all say what they
like. A bloke what'll murder thirteen women he's never clapped eyes
on before in his life has gotta be mad. But *them*. They'd scare the shit
out of you and then stand back and have a bloody good laugh.'

This was the longest speech Maureen had made since she had
first showed up in the Palmerston a couple of months before. Usually
she seemed a morose, rather phlegmatic girl. She didn't seem to want
to talk about anything much. Once she'd shown them a photograph
of two little boys on a beach.

There was a long silence after she'd finished. Brenda cleared her
throat and tried to think of a way of changing the subject.

Then Jean leaned towards her across the table. 'You see that
bloke sat over there? In the corner. No, don't let him see you looking.'

Brenda directed a carefully casual glance across the room. 'Him
on his own? Yeah, I've got him.'

'He's the one....' Jean's voice wobbled so much that she had to
stop and try again. 'He's the one pays her...forty quid a week to piss
on him.'

'It isn't a week,' said Maureen. 'It's more like three.'

'It's the *rent*,' said Brenda. 'Bloody near.' She turned to Audrey.
'Where do they find these men?'

'I don't know,' said Audrey. 'It's never been my luck.'

'And look at her,' said Jean. 'She has the nerve to sit there
supping gin.'

'And what am I meant to sup?'

'Beer. *Beer!* Give the poor sod a run for his money.'

'She's mebbe afraid of drowning him,' said Brenda. 'Forty quid
a time? I know I would be.'

'He's a real gentleman,' said Maureen. '*He* doesn't say "piss".
He says "wee-wee".'

Jean, who had just taken a mouthful of gin, released it in a fine spray all over the table.

Maureen looked at her in astonishment. 'Now what have I said?'

The door opened and Kath Rogerson walked in. She stopped just inside the room, and looked round. There was a moment of complete silence, one of those inexplicable, simultaneous pauses in conversation that come over groups of people in a crowded room. You could hear the wind howling outside. Then a woman laughed and the noise rose up again, higher than before, as if some communal, unconscious decision had been taken to exclude whatever lay outside.

Brenda stood up. 'I'm gunna go and buy Kath a drink.'

'All right,' said Audrey. 'But go easy. She's tanked up to the gills already.'

Brenda pushed and jostled her way to the bar.

'Now then, Kath.'

Kath turned round, a drunk's turn, moving from the hips to keep her head steady. When she saw Brenda, her face split open into a gummy smile. 'Now then.'

'What'll you have?'

'A pint of cider.' She spoke in a hoarse whisper and the sentence ended in a burst of coughing.

'That doesn't sound too good.'

'No. Me chest's bad.' Her eyes were on the bottle in Beattie's hand. 'You keeping all right? And the bairns?'

'Oh, I'm all right. Sharon's not too....'

Brenda stopped. Kath wasn't ready to listen yet.

The drinks arrived. Kath drank deeply, only coming up for breath when the pint was more than half gone. She wiped the bubbles shakily from her upper lip. 'Sorry, Brenda, what were you saying?'

'I was just saying our Sharon isn't so good.'

'Aw dear. What's wrong with her?'

'Cystitis.'

'Surely not. Why, how old is she? Eight?'

'Eleven.'

Kath looked shaken by the passing of so much time. 'It's still no age. There was once over I had a real run of it. Couldn't shift it and at the finish the doctor said that was what was doing me kidneys. It'd all spread up the tubes.'

'Yeah. That's what they're frightened of with her. I had to take her up the hospital to get her X-rayed.'

'You want to make sure she drinks plenty. That'll clear it up quicker than anything.' As if to demonstrate her faith in her own advice, Kath downed the second half of the pint.

'Will you have another?'

The hesitation was only momentary. 'Thanks, Brenda. I'd buy you one, only I'm a bit....'

'It's all right.'

'I think I'd better go and make room for it. Here, save me place.'

Beattie Miller, filling Kath's glass again, raised her eyebrows expressively. She didn't need to say anything. She and Brenda were probably the only two people in the room who could remember Kath as she had once been.

This time Brenda waited until Kath had taken the first few gulps. 'How are your bairns, then?'

'Oh, they seem to be getting on all right. The boys are in Whitley Bay now, you know. They send them up there when they get into their teens. David's going on fine. They're on about getting him a job looking after the golf course. I says to him, "Is that what you'd like, son?" He says, "Oh, yes, Mam." You know what I mean, Brenda? I've no worries about them. But it's our Julie. You know she's in this foster home. Anyway, I got a bit upset once or twice when I went to see her and they said I hadn't to go no more. Like, I could still see her, but it had to be in the office. Well, it was awful. You know you're just sat on this bench together and you can't talk and there's this stuck-up cow wandering in and out with her ears flapping, and everybody looks at you as if you're muck. Anyway, at the finish, I give 'em a right mouthful. I says, "What do all yous know about bringing up kids? You've never bloody had any!" And do you know when they come and tried to get her off me she clung on, she didn't want to go.'

Kath lapsed into silence. Brenda continued to sit beside her, not even trying to speak. It was like sitting by the bedside of a very old woman, so old that memory and mental faculties have all decayed, and even the personality is gone, and yet you go on sitting there for the sake of what they once were, and what they meant to you. And yet Kath wasn't old. What would she be? Thirty-three? Thirty-four?

'Well, Kath, I'm afraid I'll have to love and leave you. Here, buy yourself another.' Brenda pushed a pound note into Kath's hand.

Kath looked up and smiled and just for a second you could see the woman she'd once been. 'Oh, are you going, love?' she said. 'Well, so long.'

'So long, Kath. Take care of yourself.'

'I don't know what you want to buy her more for,' said Audrey. 'She'd had more than enough.'

'She's got nowt else.'

They were in the corridor between the bars, putting their coats on.

'Jean was knocking it back a bit, wasn't she?' Andrey said.

'She can afford to.'

'Oh, I know, and doesn't it make you sick? I've seen bigger tits on a fella.'

'Ah, but she's got what it takes.'

'I know she's got it, dear. I'm just trying to work out what it is.'

'Well, don't ask me. If I knew I'd be charging double.' Brenda'd got her coat collar well turned up. 'Do you know I've seen the time I'd 've gone out in that with nothing on me chest? "Show 'em what they're getting!"' She threw her arms wide. 'It's as much as I can do now to wash the Vick off.'

Audrey opened the door. The wind blew in, lifting a corner of the thin carpet and sending an empty cigarette box skittering across the floor. 'You'll wish you'd kept it on tonight. My God!'

It was a struggle to close the door after them, but they managed it at last, and then, heads held sideways to save their breath from the wind, they began to walk towards the viaduct.

B renda had been standing in the doorway for about twenty minutes when the car drew up. She bent down expecting to see a strange face, but it was only George.

'Got rid of your other car, then?'

'No. It's gone in for a service. The garage give us a lend of this'n.' He was pulling on the gear stick. 'I haven't got the hang of it yet.'

Poor old George, his car was his God—and he was a lousy driver. 'God knows what it'll cost this time.'

He sounded really down. Brenda sighed: down meant down in every sense.

'Walker's yard, all right?' he asked.

'Yes. Long as you don't mind dropping me back.'

He didn't answer. He seemed to be in a funny mood tonight. Normally he was quite chatty. Perhaps he was worrying about the bill for his car. Anyway, all he ever talked about was the coloured people in his street and how much noise they made and how, if it hadn't 've been for them, his wife'd still be alive.

She could feel him looking at her. She turned and smiled a quick, stiff little smile, but he only looked away.

Oh well, sod him. She peered out of the window, trying to work out where they were. Normally they just went and parked in one of the boarded-up streets near the river. Perhaps he wanted to go to Walker's yard because he wanted to get out of the car. In this weather. Take her all her time to find it.

The silence was starting to get on her nerves.

'Had a bad week?'

'Yes.'

She turned to look at him, but there was only the faint, orange glow from the street lights.

'Yes,' he said. 'They were having a party till three o'clock. They wouldn't have the energy for owt like that if they had to get up and go to work, but they don't, of course. It's only mugs like me work.'

It was on the tip of Brenda's tongue to point out that anybody with a job was lucky, but she didn't. She didn't know what his job was. And, anyway, it paid to agree with them.

They slowed down to turn the corner into Walker's yard, but hit the kerb anyway. At least his driving hadn't changed.

'I'd forgotten it gets like this,' he said.

'It's dry over there, if you want to get out.'

'No, it's OK. We'll stop in the car.'

He did want to get out, she could feel it, but she was blowed if she was going to argue with him this weather. She was only just starting to thaw out.

She opened her bag and waited. He took the hint at once and handed over, without a word having to be said. There was never any trouble that way. Only trouble was bringing the bugger off....

'I'm afraid he's not quite ready,' he said, tensing his thighs.

An understatement. Brenda got to work on his cock, but it was no use. After a while she looked up.

'Is anything the matter?' she asked.

'No. No.' He pushed her head down again. 'Don't stop.'

She tried everything she knew: stroked, rolled, pulled, licked, nibbled, nuzzled, guzzled, flicked, swirled, kissed, sucked, hoovered it in, popped it out....

Finally he had the beginnings of an erection.

Then, just as she thought they were really getting somewhere, the tension in his thigh and stomach muscles relaxed. 'It's no good,' he said. 'I can't come with me knees bent.'

Brenda stifled a sigh.

'I think we'd be better in the back of the car,' he said. 'There's a bit more room.'

He'd never suggested that before. Brenda turned to look. There was more room. There were also child-proof locks on the doors.

'There's not a lot more room,' she said. 'Wouldn't we be better getting out of the car?'

Where at least I can run.

He took his time getting out, and even then stood for a while looking all round the yard and up at the windows on the right-hand side. Factory windows. Blank.

'You seem a little bit jumpy tonight,' she said, keeping her voice steady.

'Do I?'

They picked their way between the puddles to a patch of dry ground by the far wall.

'Look, it's dry here,' she said.

'I'm afraid he's not quite ready,' said George.

His voice and his hands were shaking.

Brenda knelt, though the skin at the back of her neck crawled. Don't be so bloody stupid, she told herself. *It's George.* She unzipped his trousers and got another cloud of talcum powder up her nose. Waste of a rubber putting one on George: you'd more like get silicosis than VD.

All he ever really wanted was mouth. She knew—though he'd never say—that he actively disliked cunt. But then he wasn't alone

Pat Barker

in that. It was surprising how many of them did.

Progress? Could be. She went on sucking—but then his hands came down, gripping the top of her head and forcing her mouth down over his cock until she gagged. She fought to get her head free.

'I'm sorry I'm taking so long.'And it was only George, blinking down at her.

'I think we're making progress,' said Brenda, and got back on the job quick, before any of it could be lost.

A few minutes later, he came, a weak trickle that hardly seemed to justify the groans coming from his open mouth.

Brenda stood up, brushing bits of gravel from her knees, and thinking, *Christ,* there've gotta be easier ways of earning a living than this.

He was still breathless. She waited for him and they walked back to the car together.

He was quite chatty on the way back. Grateful. He didn't mention the moment when he'd rammed his cock down her throat and half-choked her, but then she didn't expect him to. Men were funny.

'Back to the viaduct?' he asked.

'Yeah. Back to the viaduct. That'll do fine.'

58

GRANTA

JULIAN BARNES
EMMA BOVARY'S
EYES

Born in Leicester in 1946, Julian Barnes was educated in London and Oxford, and, and after reading for the bar, he began work as a freelance journalist. Under the pseudonym of Edward Pygge, he wrote the 'Greek Street' column of The *New Review*. It is possible that under other pseudonyms, he may have written a novel or three. It is likely that under the name Julian Barnes, he has contributed to the *Times Literary Supplement*, the *New Statesman*, and the *Observer*. He is the certified author of two novels, *Metroland* and *Before She Met Me* (witnesses were present).

The narrator, about sixty, is a retired doctor, a widower, who has developed a mania for Flaubert....

Let me tell you why I hate critics. Not for the usual reasons: that they're failed creators (they usually aren't; they may be failed critics, but that's another matter); or that they're by nature carping, jealous, and vain (they usually aren't; if anything, they might be better accused of over-generosity: inflating reputations so that their own fine discrimination thereby appears more special and important). No, the reason I hate critics—well, some of the time—is that they write sentences like this:

> Flaubert does not build up his characters, as did Balzac, by objective, external description; in fact, so careless is he of their outward appearance that on one occasion he gives Emma brown eyes (14); on another deep black eyes (15); and on another blue eyes (16).

This precise and disheartening indictment was drawn up by the late Dr Enid Starkie, Reader Emerita in French Literature at the University of Oxford, and Flaubert's most exhaustive English biographer. The numbers in her text refer to footnotes in which she spears the novelist with chapter and verse.

I once heard Dr Starkie lecture and, in a way, I'm glad to report that she had an atrocious French accent: one of those deliveries full of dame-school self-confidence and absolutely no ear. Naturally, this didn't affect her competence to teach at the University of Oxford, because until quite recently the place preferred to treat modern languages as if they were dead: this made them more respectable, more like the distant perfections of Latin and Greek. Even so, it did strike me as peculiar that someone who lived by French literature should be so calamitously inadequate at making the basic words of the language sound the same as they would have done when her subjects, her heroes, (and her paymasters, too, you could say) first pronounced them.

You may think this a cheap revenge to take on a dead lady critic simply for pointing out that Flaubert didn't have a very clear notion of Emma Bovary's eyes. But then I don't hold with the precept *de mortuis nil nisi bonum* (I am a doctor, after all); and in any case it's hard to underestimate the irritation when someone points out something like that to you. The irritation isn't with Dr Starkie, not at first—she was only, as they say, doing her job—but with Flaubert. So that painstaking genius couldn't even keep the eyes of his most famous character a consistent colour? *Ha.* And then, unable to be cross with him for long, you shift your feelings over to the critic.

I must confess that in all the time I read *Madame Bovary, I* never noticed the heroine's rainbow eyes. Should I have? Would you? Was I perhaps too busy noticing things that Dr Starkie was missing (though what they might be I can't for the moment think). Put it another way: is there a perfect reader somewhere, a total reader? Does Dr Starkie's reading of *Madame Bovary* contain all the responses which I have when I read the book and then add a whole lot more, so that my reading is in a way pointless? Well, I hope not. My reading might be pointless in terms of the history of literary criticism; but it's not in terms of enjoying the book. I can't prove that lay readers get more pleasure than professional critics, but I can tell you one advantage we have over them. We can forget. Dr Starkie and her kind are cursed with memory: the books they teach and write about can never fade from their brains. They become family. Perhaps this is why some critics develop a faintly patronizing tone towards their subjects. It's as if Flaubert or Milton or Eliot were some tedious old aunt in a rocking chair, who smelled of stale powder, talked of nothing but the past, and hadn't said anything new for years; it's her house, of course, and everybody's living rent free in it, but even so, surely it was, well, you know...*time*?

Whereas the common but passionate reader is allowed to forget; he can go away, be unfaithful with other writers, come back and be entranced again. Domesticity need never intrude on the relationship; it may be sporadic, but when there, it is always intense. There's nothing settled and bovine about it, none of the daily rancour which develops when people live together. I never find myself, fatigue in the voice, reminding Flaubert to hang up the bathmat, or use the lavatory brush. Which is what Dr Starkie can't help herself doing. Eyes of brown? Eyes of blue? Look, writers aren't *perfect,* I want to cry; any more than husbands and wives are perfect. The only unfailing rule is, if they seem perfect, they can't be. I remember an occasion in Matlock shortly after I was first married.... But no, I'd better keep that for another time.

I'll remember instead another lecture I once attended, a few years ago, at the Cheltenham Literary Festival. It was given by a professor from Cambridge, Christopher Ricks, and it was a very shiny performance. His bald pate was shiny; his black shoes were shiny; and his lecture was very shiny indeed. Its theme was 'Mistakes in Literature and Whether They Matter'. Yevtushenko, for example, apparently made a terrible error about American nightingales in one of his poems; Pushkin was quite wrong about the sort of military dress worn at balls; John Wain was wrong about the pilot who dropped the bomb on Hiroshima; Nabokov was wrong—rather surprising, this—about the phonetics of the name Lolita. There were other examples: Coleridge, Yeats, and Browning, I recall, were some of those caught out not knowing a hawk from a hand-saw, or not even knowing what a hand-saw was in the first place.

Two examples particularly stuck in my mind. The first was a remarkable discovery about *Lord of the Flies*. In the famous scene where Piggy's spectacles are used for the rediscovery of fire, William Golding got his optics all wrong. Completely back to front, in fact. Piggy is short-sighted, and the spectacles he would have been prescribed for this condition simply could not have been used as burning glasses. Whichever way you held them, they would have been quite unable to make the rays of the sun converge.

The second example concerns Tennyson's 'Charge of the Light Brigade'. 'Into the valley of Death/Rode the six hundred'. We all remember that. But in fact, what Tennyson initially wrote, as the newspaper reports came in from the Crimea and he pondered his public response to them, was 'Into the valley of Death/Rode the five hundred'. This was how many troops he thought were involved in the charge. Then, a few days later, the official figure was revised upward, and so five hundred became six hundred. Tennyson had caught a Mistake in Literature in the nick of time.

Well, he did and he didn't. I mean, how many troops actually took part in what Camille Rousset later called '*ce terrible et sanglant steeple-chase*'? Six hundred and seventy-three. It's nearer six hundred than five hundred, to be sure; but six hundred is still a mistake of some mathematical significance, if that's what interests you. 'Into the valley of Death/Rode the six hundred and seventy-three.' Not quite the same swing to it, is there? Though I suppose it might present a novel metrical challenge.

Not putting six hundred and seventy-three instead of six hundred hardly seems to me to qualify as a 'mistake'. The shakiness of Golding's optics, on the other hand, must definitely be put down as an error. The next question is, Does it matter? As far as I can remember Professor Ricks's lecture, his argument was that if the factual side of literature becomes unreliable, then ploys such as irony and fantasy become much harder to use. If you don't know what's true, or what's meant to be true, then the value of what isn't true, or isn't meant to be true, becomes diminished. This seems to me a very sound argument, though I suppose I wonder to how many cases of literary mistake it actually applies. With Piggy's glasses, I should think that (a) very few people—apart from oculists, opticians, and professors of English—would notice; and (b) that when they do notice, they merely detonate the mistake—like blowing up a small bomb with a controlled explosion. What's more, this detonation (which takes place on a deserted beach, with only a dog as witness) doesn't set fire to other parts of the novel.

Errors like Golding's are 'external mistakes'—disparities between what the book claims is the case, and what we know the reality to be; often they merely indicate a lack of specific technical knowledge on the writer's part. The sin is forgiveable. What, though, about 'internal mistakes', when the writer claims two incompatible things within his own creation? Emma's eyes are brown, Emma's eyes are blue. Alas, this can only be put down to incompetence, to sloppy literary habits. I read the other day a well-praised first novel in which the narrator—who is both a virgin and an amateur of French literature—comically rehearses to himself the best way to kiss a girl without being rebuffed: 'With a slow, sensual, irresistible strength, draw her gradually towards you while gazing into her eyes as if you had just been given a copy of the first, suppressed edition of *Madame Bovary*.'

I thought that was quite neatly put, indeed rather amusing. The only trouble is, there's no such thing as a 'first, suppressed edition of *Madame Bovary*'. The novel, as I would have thought was reasonably well known, first appeared in serial form; then it was prosecuted for obscenity; and only after the trial was it published in book form. I expect the young novelist (it seems unfair to give his name) was thinking of the 'first, suppressed edition' of *Les Fleurs du Mal*. No doubt he'll get it right in time for the second edition; if there is one.

Eyes of brown, eyes of blue. Does it matter? Not,Does it matter if the writer contradicts himself, but, Does it matter what colour they are anyway? I feel sorry for novelists when they have to mention women's eyes: there's so little choice, and whatever colouring is decided upon inevitably carries banal implications. Her eyes are blue: innocence and clarity. Her eyes are black: passion and depth. Her eyes are green: wildness and jealousy. Her eyes are brown: reliability and ordinariness. Her eyes are violet: the novel is by Raymond Chandler. How can you escape all this without a toiling parenthesis about the lady's character? Her eyes are mud-coloured; her eyes changed hue according to the gaze of the beholder; he never looked her in the eye. Well, take your pick. My wife's eyes were bluey-green. And so I suspect that if the novelist is any good, he probably admits the pointlessness of describing eyes. He slowly imagines the character, moulds her into shape, and then—probably last thing of all—pops a pair of glass eyes into those empty sockets. Eyes? Oh yes, she'd better have eyes, he reflects, with a minimum of interest.

Is it that much of a surprise if they sometimes get it wrong? Graham Greene has a sea-captain in one of his novels who appears first with blue eyes, and then, one hundred pages on (I count in the Tennysonian manner), turns up again with brown ones. This seems to me a trivial offence; it's a trifle tossed to the reviewers, the way that cross-Channel ferry passengers toss bits of gristle from their sandwiches to the hovering gulls.

I don't know what colour Enid Starkie's eyes were; all I remember of her is that she dressed like a matelot, walked like a scrum-half, and had an atrocious French accent. But I'll tell you another thing. The Reader Emerita in French Literature at the University of Oxford and Honorary Fellow of Somerville College—who was 'well known for her studies of the lives and works of writers such as Baudelaire, Rimbaud, Gautier, Eliot, and Gide' (I quote her dust-wrapper; first edition, of course), and who devoted two large books and many years of her life to the author of *Madame Bovary*, chose as a frontispiece to her first volume a portrait of 'Gustave Flaubert by an unknown painter'. It's the first thing we see;

it is, if you like, the moment at which Enid Starkie introduces us to Flaubert. The only trouble is, it isn't him. It's a portrait of Louis Bouilhet, as everyone from the *gardienne* at Croisset onwards and upwards will tell you. So what do we make of that once we've stopped chuckling?

Perhaps you still think I'm just being vengeful towards a dead scholar who can't answer for herself. Well, maybe I am. But then, *quis custodiet custodes?* And I'll tell you something else. I've just reread *Madame Bovary,*
    on one occasion he gives Emma brown eyes (14); on another deep black eyes (15); and on another blue eyes (16).
And the moral of it all, I suppose, is Never take fright at a footnote. Because here are the six references that Flaubert makes to Emma's eyes in the book. It is clearly a subject of some importance to the novelist:

(1) *Emma's first appearance*: 'In so far as she was beautiful, this beauty lay in her eyes: although they were brown, they would appear black because of her lashes....'

(2) *Described by her adoring husband early in their marriage*: 'Her eyes seemed bigger to him, especially when she was just waking up and fluttered her lids several times in succession; they were black when she was in shadow and dark blue in full daylight; and they seemed to contain layer upon layer of colours, which were thicker in hue deep down, and became lighter towards the enamel-like surface.'

(3) *At a candlelit ball*: 'Her black eyes appeared even blacker.'

(4) *On first meeting Léon*: 'Fixing him with her large, wide-open black eyes.'

(5) *As she appears to Rodolphe when he first examines her—indoors*: 'Her black eyes'.

(6) *Emma looking in a mirror, indoors, in the evening; she has just been seduced by Rodolphe*: 'Her eyes had never been so large, so black, or contained such depth'.

How did the critic put it? 'Flaubert does not built up characters, as did Balzac, by objective, external description; in fact, so careless is he of their outward appearance that....' It would be interesting to compare the time spent by Flaubert making sure that his heroine has the rare and difficult eyes of a tragic adulteress with the time spent by Dr Starkie in casually selling short this maniacally careful novelist. What magisterial negligence towards a writer who, one way and another, had paid quite a few of her gas bills. Quite simply, it makes me furious. Now do you understand why I hate critics? I could try and describe to you the expression in my eyes at this moment; but they are far too discoloured with rage.

The Letters of GUSTAVE FLAUBERT, 1857–1880

Selected, edited and translated by
FRANCIS STEEGMULLER

Belknap, January 1983, £12.00

Francis Steegmuller's first volume of Flaubert's letters culminated with the publication of *Madame Bovary* in 1857. Now, in the second volume, we see Flaubert in the years of his fame—the years in which he wrote *Salammbô, L'Éducation sentimentale, The Temptation of Saint Anthony, Three Tales,* and the unfinished *Bouvard and Pécuchet.* In writing the novels, Flaubert followed his precept, "An author in his book must be like God in the universe, present everywhere and visible nowhere," but in these letters of his maturity he gives full scope to his feelings and expresses forceful opinions on matters public and private.

We see Flaubert travelling to Tunisia to document the exotic *Salammbô,* then calling on his own memories and those of his friends to bring to life the Revolution of 1848 and the loves of his hero Frédéric Moreau in the pages of *L'Education sentimentale,* which many today consider his greatest novel. Flaubert is taken up by the Second Empire Court of Napoleon III and Eugénie, and becomes a lifelong friend of Princess Mathilde Bonaparte. But the most powerful feminine presence in this volume is the warm, sympathetic George Sand, with whom he maintains a fascinating correspondence for more than ten years. This dialogue on life, letters, and politics between the "two troubadours," as they called themselves, reveals both of them at their idiosyncratic best.

The deaths of Flaubert's mother, of his closest friend and mentor, Louis Bouilhet, and of Théophile Gautier, Sainte-Beuve, and other intimates, and Flaubert's financial ruin at the hands of his beloved niece Caroline and her rapacious husband, make a somber story of the post-war years. Despite these and other losses, Flaubert's last years are brightened by the affection of Guy de Maupassant, Zola, and other younger writers.

Together with Francis Steegmuller's masterly connecting narrative and essential annotation, these letters, most of which appear here in English for the first time, constitute an intimate and engrossing new biography of the great master of the modern novel.

The Letters of Gustave Flaubert, 1830–1857, also edited and translated by Francis Steegmuller, is still available at £12.00. Hailed by the New York Times as "brilliantly edited and annotated...a splendid, intimate account of the development of a writer who changed the nature of the novel", it went on to garner widespread critical acclaim and to win an American Book Award for Translation.

HARVARD UNIVERSITY PRESS
126 Buckingham Palace Road, London SW1W 9SD

GRANTA

URSULA BENTLEY
FOREIGN BUDDIES

John Adams

Ursula Bentley was born in Sheffield in 1945 and was educated at the Ursuline Convent School and at Manchester University. She has travelled extensively in the United States and Europe, and is currently living in a small village outside Zurich with her husband and two children. She is the author of *The Natural Order*.

BJ was fascinated to observe that everyone who got on to the train took off their outer coat and hung it up on the hook provided. She agonized for a moment or two and then took off her own jacket and hung it up too, a little reluctantly, because it was a suit she had bought the day before at Löw and taking the jacket off was like sawing the lady in half. But still, she dreaded arriving overheated for an appointment and feeling the sweat cool slightly as she got out of the car. It was sunny, and she could be lightly broiled by the time she got to Winterthur, for her seat was directly by the window. Relaxing from the hassle of catching the train, she reached for her cigarettes. As she drew them from her bag, the man sitting opposite tapped her on the hand and pointed to the No Smoking sign.

'Shit,' muttered BJ.

The man giggled.

BJ was not used to well-dressed, middle-aged men giggling; she did not know how to deal with them. She considered going to the next carriage for a smoke, but that would mean putting on her jacket again, so she steeled herself to wait. It was a great relief that Michael smoked. She was so excited at the prospect of his coming to dinner it would be difficult to get through it without smoking. Of course Philip disliked her smoking, but one could not start deferring to one's husband's preferences or who knows where it would end. At the moment it was not hard not to smoke: BJ was in an expeditionary mood, ready to be fascinated by the smallest idiosyncrasy of Swiss behaviour.

BJ's train journey was meant to take twenty minutes, and most of it was spent watching a small human drama that stirred her interest in a possible Swiss underground culture. In the next section of the carriage was a young man with a stud through his nostril, a razor blade through one ear lobe, tight jeans on pipe-cleaner slim legs, and a grey vinyl jacket with orange acrylic and sheepskin lining. He sat with his hands tucked into the jacket pockets, his pale face inscrutable. It remained inscrutable when the ticket inspector came round and asked to see his ticket, although he did not have one. During the inspector's tirade on the subject of abusing public facilities and undermining the state, the young man did not bother to remove his hands from his pockets, except to hand the inspector some kind of identity card. The young man won BJ's admiration for his

71

cool. It was particularly touching in view of his fragile physique: BJ imagined that, if it were not for the razor blade and the pierced nostril, he might be the type that would appeal to Michael—vulnerable yet defiant; a body scarcely a man's, yet perfect in every detail. After the inspector had moved on, BJ's thoughts dwelt pleasantly on a conjunction of this man's body and Michael's and she closed her eyes to give her daydream more privacy.

The train was soon slowing down to a rhythmic chunt, orchestrating BJ's fluttering orgasm as she came round from a sun-drenched reverie. Outside she saw serried back gardens at an almost vertical tilt down to the railway line and neat rows of vegetables tipping downhill as if trying to imitate *art naïf*. BJ blinked as the houses blotted out the sun. Now, damn it, her knickers were damp. It could not possibly show, but still it would affect her concentration. And where her skin had been hot it was now cold and clammy; the doors were opened while the train still moved and a draught went through the carriage and up her skirt. BJ felt nervous. She regretted now that she had arranged to have lunch with Geraldine and Christina before her appointment. Psychologically it was better to get the business over before socializing. And pre-occupied with finding the right office on time and then having to stem the flow of negative comments long enough to finish her pitch—a problem she encountered here much more often than in the States—she was not really in the mood to cope with Geraldine's rôle-related aggression.

So it was with a sense of relief that she saw Christina standing alone on the platform, although the sight of her genetically slim body—that no amount of fashionably disfiguring knickerbockers could make other than stunning—produced its own aggressive twitch. Christina wore no make-up and had casually bundled her long hair behind her head with a huge buckle.

They shook hands.

'Hi. Where's Geraldine?'

'She is not feeling well today. We go there perhaps later in the afternoon for the tea.'

'Oh. Good. Wonderful.' No doubt Geraldine had not wanted the aggro of having to amuse herself like a good little *hausfrau* in the town while BJ was doing business. Further proof of Geraldine's competitive discomfort with BJ. After all, here she was, a foreigner, effectively doing business with the locals as soon as possible after the plane touched down, and there was Geraldine simply—let's face it—going to pot or seed or any number of other possible bio-degradeable fates. Christina was much more fascinating than Geraldine, anyway: BJ was not averse to spending time with her. Furthermore, the outlines of an idea were forming (perhaps as a result of thinking about Michael's sexual preferences): BJ had so far repressed her own homosexual interests and, really, it was about time she faced up to them and did something. These interests had been of a totally theoretical nature so far. She had never met a woman who turned her on, but that had not deterred BJ from thinking of herself as ripe for total encounters of any sexual kind. Philip called her an armchair Lesbian: she would like to prove him wrong, even if she might not particularly enjoy the proof itself. But why shouldn't she, if it were with someone as physically perfect, as sweet natured and biddable as, say, Christina? She was the perfect solution in one way, in that she was a natural for the passive rôle. BJ was accustomed to that kind of submissive stuff in her heterosexual life, and a rôle reversal would be entirely appropriate as she was deliberately setting out to broaden her experience. She did not anticipate emotional involvement and by preference would have been quite happy to stick to men, but the pressure was relentless and was being built up constantly from articles on 'How To' in *Cosmopolitan* and on the evidence of best-selling feminist novels that suggested a Lesbian relationship was simply *de rigueur* for today's woman.

It would be amusing to have a lover in this remote spot, who by virtue of being female would never be suspected. However, if half the point was to prove to Philip that she really went to bed with a woman, there would then be no object in burying the affair in The Country. Although Winterthur was an industrial town, she understood that Christina and Geraldine lived outside it, in The Country. And if The Country was what she had seen from the train, it was a little disappointing. There were few stretches between Zürich and Winterthur unmarred by pylons or blocks of flats or gravel pits. BJ was used to The Country of New England—miles and miles of thick forest and cute villages of white or yellow or blue clapboard houses with lace-edged cotton curtains at the window. BJ had never even seen a concrete house before. It was certainly a shock to see them in The Country.

The time it took to get from the station to halfway down the Marktgasse was easily charted with exchange of information on their respective journeys. Christina apologized for her appearance, she had been in such a hurry. BJ said it was all right, that Christina was the type where a little superficial scruff only emphasized the underlying order. She had to explain this, and the thought crossed her mind to dwell on this personal note, to put out a feeler to test Christina's reaction to the idea of sexual experiment. After all, one could not go into this sort of thing cold. But Christina seemed distracted as well as dishevelled and had said nothing since the transport theme gave out. She was still smiling, but at the same time her eyebrows were drawn together in a frown, hitching her smile up into a wince. It made BJ wonder if her husband, the so-called beast Max Baumann, had been giving her a hard time, and she thought that that at least would be a subject that Christina might be glad to talk about when she warmed up.

'You know you remind me of someone,' said BJ, running out of comments on the shops, the paving stones, the street entertainers, and crêpes-sellers which had kept her going for a few minutes. 'I can't think who.'

'Is it Princess Alexandra? Geraldine always makes joke of Princess Alexandra.'

'How's that?'

'It's a royal person, isn't it? The same as in German.'

'Okay, forget it.' They sauntered on, BJ stopping to look into a gift shop that had a lot of white china objects in the window, all with white doves stuck on them. 'But you know, there is something princess-like about you,' she said seriously, swinging her heavy attaché case into the other hand. 'Don't be embarrassed'—for Christina had blushed— 'I don't necessarily mean that as a compliment. I just mean you seem to be the type who's accustomed to a high quality environment. You look like you'd feel comfortable in very expensive clothing.'

'I do not wear expensive clothing.'

BJ gestured her objection aside. 'That's not the point. Your body would not be embarrassed by it.'

Christina stopped. 'I am sorry, I am not understanding. My clothes, they is embarrassing to you?'

'Oh no. Shit. Forget it. This looks like a decent place for lunch.' They had stopped outside a restaurant on the corner of a crossroad. It had many bull's-eye windows, and looked warm and full of people eating plastic food. BJ was starving, having skipped breakfast, and looked forward to the equivalent of steak, French fries, and a chocolate sundae.

'Er—do you mind not? I do not go here.' She did look a little embarrassed now. 'I make boycott. You understand?'

'Really? That's fascinating. Are you politically active, Christina? That's wonderful. You must tell me all about it.'

Christina looked pleased. 'My action does make no difference, perhaps, but one must do as one thinks right. Anyway, there is a much nicer place with tablecloths around the corner.'

'Tablecloths. Boy. That's fascinating.'

BJ followed Christina to the place with tablecloths, which was faintly demi-monde, carpeted, and upholstered in cerise velvet, and full of businessmen whose eyes fell out and bounced along the carpet after Christina as she edged her way through to a table in a dark corner. The tablecloth and plated silver cutlery glimmered of intimacy. BJ's spirits somewhat sank as she took in the details. Although the place was essentially dressed-up down market, it still raised anxieties in her. She was the type who would get the tablecloth stuck in her bag and take the whole thing with her when she went to the bathroom. A low gasp from Christina distracted her.

'What's wrong, Christina? The plastic vine a little strong?'

'No, no. Nothing. I only am recognizing someone over there.'

'Oh? Who?'

'My doctor, actually.'

'So what? Did he just order you to stay in bed for a month, or something? Why do you look so scared?'

At the mention of the magic word 'bed' Christina blushed.

'No, no, I am not afraid. But this morning I am making an appointment to see him. He must think I am following him around the town. I was only surprised to see him.'

'Well, where is he?'

'Please don't stare at him. He is sitting under that small barrel on the wall. Now he has seen us. Ay, ay, ay.'

'I hope it doesn't fall on him. He looks cute.'

BJ had located the doctor, a boyish-looking man in his early forties, with a ready smile—not quite as ready as Christina's but more natural. He had regular, macho features, a jaw lightly clenched when not in use and eyebrows drawn together as if to play down the aura of *joie-de-vivre* given off by his fitness and general vigour. He wore rimless glasses tinted blue and a grey roll-neck sweater which revealed the contours of a compact, muscular body. He was sitting with two other men in grey suits and blue ties.

Despite the confusion of smoke, noise, and black-clad waitresses—their aprons bulging obscenely over their money-bags—BJ felt the vibrations from the doctor's well-kept body and guessed at once the reason for Christina's confusion. Lust. BJ was sympathetic. Personally she did not respond to types like the doctor, who had every thing in the shop window, so to speak. She thought he would turn in a pretty routine performance for her taste. But still, he and Christina together complemented each other in looks and condition in a way that BJ used to rate as rateable. Some people, like Geraldine, were off the scale altogether, at least as long as they continued on the long slide into the pear-shaped masses. But she took considerable pleasure in imagining the union of Christina and her doctor. It would be pretty natural and healthy and probably make both of them feel good. She turned to Christina with a knowing smile, offering her a cigarette, which, to BJ's surprise, Christina accepted.

'Listen, Christina, I think I understand the problem, okay? I think he's very attractive. I hope you get together, I really do.'

'Of what are you talking, BJ?'

'You know—your friend over there. I think he's very attractive and you obviously do, too, so I hope you get to sleep with him, that's all.'

Christina gasped and looked around, agonized, to see if anyone was listening. 'Please! Don't say this! Please!'

'Oh? Oh. I get it. You've already slept with him. I'm sorry—'

'No! Also not. I don't want to. That's not the problem. Let us please talk of something else, please.'

'Okay. Sure. Listen, have I come on a bad day for you? You seem a little tense.'

Christina blew smoke inexpertly in BJ's direction. As she had taken the last cigarette, BJ discreetly motioned to the waitress to bring some more. This gesture gave her a little thrill of protectiveness towards Christina—the Provider. Of cigarettes, of sex—it was much the same.

'Yes, you are right. Today is not so good for me.' Her troubled face—mobile with sadness as she concentrated on turning the cigarette tip round and round in the ashtray—reminded BJ of a medieval madonna bending over the body of Jesus that she had seen in the home of her college president. Or was it a Modigliani madonna? No matter, it was the quintessence of life being a pain in the neck that they had in common.

'Do you want to talk about it?'

'It is very difficult.'

'Well, think of it this way. I'm a complete stranger, really, and likely to remain so'—unless we end up in bed under Plan A, reflected BJ—'so you can trust me if you want. I mean, we have no mutual friends or anything.'

'I would like to talk of it, BJ, but it is a question of the marriage bond. You, I am sure, would not tell me bad things of your husband.'

'Oh sure I would. I think that's all nonsense, anyway—unswerving loyalty no matter what and all that. Of course, Philip and I are pretty open about everything and when it comes right down to it, he doesn't do anything that I'd be ashamed to talk about. But if he beat me up or anything, I'd talk about it. With my feet, probably, but I'd talk.'

Christina smiled. 'Max does not beat me. He is a pacifist.'

'Sweetheart, don't believe it. There are some areas where no man is a pacifist. This Max character sounds to me like the type who'd get a real kick out of whipping you occasionally. Of course I can see that his socio-economic hang-ups would tend to inhibit him. But that doesn't change his preferences; it just modifies his behaviour.'

Unfortunately for the dynamics of her statement, BJ had to clarify parts of it that Christina could not understand. When it was all clear, she sat back and looked at BJ with gentle pity.

'BJ, I must tell you, I think you are crazy.'

'That's okay. People tell me that all the time. I just say what I think, that's all.'

'But your husband—does he whip you occasionally, as you say?'

'Philip? Oh no. Oh my, no. No, Philip and I are real good friends. We have an arrangement that's somewhat commercial in nature, but—oh no, that kind of thing would be quite inappropriate for Philip and me.'

'But I think most husbands and wives are good friends.'

'Yeah. That's the trouble, see—oh, thank you.' The waitress handed them menu cards, firing off a round of Swiss German in BJ's direction.

'She says do you know you must have lunch—not coffee only.'

'Okay, okay, I want lunch. Isn't that typical? I suppose she thinks because I don't speak the language I have to have everything explained to me. Does she think I'm Turkish or something? Do I look Turkish? I mean, have you ever seen a blond Turk?'

'Yes. Actually I think Kemal Ataturk was blond.'

'Who's that?'

'He was a famous leader.'

'Oh. Well I'm sorry if I over-reacted. I guess I'm a bit paranoid because of what happened on the bus the other day.' BJ had already related this incident to Christina over the phone when she called to confirm their appointment. Christina had been puzzled to know what BJ was getting at. In Max's opinion, BJ was hoping that Christina, being Swiss, would offer to lead a demonstration down to the bus company. 'Did I tell you what happened to me on the bus the other day?'

'Yes,' said Christina, a little too eagerly, BJ thought.

'Yes. Well the Swiss have this thing about telling you what to do all the time, don't they? I mean, I put a chocolate wrapper in an ashtray at Bellevue the other day, and this guy in a pork-pie hat comes up and starts yelling at me about something or other. I mean he didn't even stop to find out I couldn't understand a word he was saying.'

'They are nervous, perhaps, at Bellevue because of the riots. But anyway it is always worse than here. Zürich is a stuffed-up town in some ways. It is full of stuffed-up people.'

'Yes. Your vocabulary is excellent, Christina. But here's me going on about myself as usual. Tell me about yourself, Christina. Quite frankly I'm somewhat fascinated by you.'

'Me? I think you must be making fun. Why do you say these things? Is it not because it is making you more fascinating actually?'

'Huh? Oh no. Oh God, no. I'm really quite dull. I guess I must seem patronizing, and if so I'm sorry, but I was quite sincere. I am genuinely interested in you, Christina.'

'But I am just a housewife. You—you are full of courage like a man. You go to the offices of Sulzer and Aluswiss and Sprüngli and so, and you make men with important jobs listen to you. This I could not do.'

BJ pulled a face and writhed a little, feeling for her words. 'Be that as it may, what I actually do is just bull-shit. It isn't difficult. I do it because I do it well and I'm preparing myself for higher things, but quite frankly selling software to the planning manager of a chocolate company isn't a particularly dynamic assignment in my opinion.'

'You over-estimate yourself,' said Christina warmly. She ignored BJ's frantic attempt to correct her English. 'Even for a man it must be difficult to go to a manager in his own office where he feels himself so'—she raised her hand above her head—'And the visitor feels himself so'—she lowered it to just above the carpet. 'But as you are a woman I think it must be terrible. At least here in Switzerland. I am imagining if you go to my husband, for example, in his office. He would not be so nice, I think. No, no, you are full of courage.'

'God, I'm dying to meet your husband. As a matter of fact I could very well go call on him quite legitimately. What's his business?'

'Machines that make office furniture. But no, please, BJ, if he thinks I have sent you he will be angry.'

'Don't worry. I'll make it quite clear it was my idea.'

'He will not believe you.'

'Jesus, you *are* scared of him, aren't you? What does he do to you? Come on, you're hiding something interesting there aren't you, Christina?'

'No! No. He is not unkind to me. He does not hit me. Nothing. But he must always work so hard, and he is having big responsibilities. He becomes easily tired and makes critic then, because he is tired.'

'U-huh. Well, I guess I know what you mean. On the other hand, if I considered that he was a legitimate potential sale, you wouldn't expect me to give that up, would you?'

'No. But I don't think he is buying stuff from you. Honestly.'

'We'll see. Anyhow, I've met a whole lot of bastards in my time and thank God I'm not married to one, but a bastard is a bastard is a bastard, to quote, and I guess your husband is no different to the others in a sales situation.'

'Please, what is a bastard?'

BJ explained. Afterwards Christina's face dipped into furrows of shame and regret.

'If you think that Max is like that,' she said, 'you really have—what is the word? Ah, thank you.' The waitress had brought their soup.

'Balls, probably.'

'Are you sure?'

'Pretty much.'

'Well then, you really have balls to go and sell him stuff.'

BJ loved Christina's use of 'stuff', with its connotations of surreptitious sales of white powder outside the Singer sewing machine store in Central Square, Cambridge. But Christina had whetted BJ's appetite to meet Max Baumann, and plans for an eyeball to eyeball with him began to form. She was quite serious when she said she was used to dealing with bastards as she did it all the time. Even if she did not sell him anything, which seemed likely, it would prove to Christina that BJ did indeed have balls. Well, why not? BJ was beginning to fill in the scenario that would culminate in sleeping with Christina, and what more natural preamble than proving herself to be of equal weight with the dreaded M. Baumann? BJ did feel herself superior to Christina, more capable, more courageous, as she said. Her brownie points, however, were balanced by Christina's sophistication, her ease in expensive clothing and in restaurants with tablecloths, and very probably, her intelligence. Considering she had not lived in an English-speaking country, Christina had a command of the language that was impressive. BJ, despite the oft-repeated German I and II and two months with a nodal family in Munich, still felt lost for words when speaking German. She had been very disappointed that the Munich visit had failed to convince her that German was a real language used daily by millions, rather than a kind of Lego for grown-ups that had to be assembled with laborious

exactitude each time. She had put part of the blame on the diet
provided by the host family, which consisted, in memory at least, of
cornflakes, white sausage, and Coca-Cola. It was in Munich that she
had turned in desperation to gourmet food.

The waitress brought BJ's *cordon bleu,* a huge slab of veal that
flapped over either side of the plate, the hot cheese inside dripping
towards the tablecloth, but just air-cooled in time to be arrested in an
arty droplet. BJ's mouth ran with saliva. Five hundred, six hundred
calories—but what the hell? After dinner she could bicycle up
Zürichbergstrasse, an almost vertical hill near the apartment. After
going without dinner, of course. Philip was used to eating alone in
dieting emergencies. Christina was brought a plate of paper thin
smoked beef with a baby gherkin in the middle. BJ's saliva was turned
to ashes of remorse. No wonder Christina was thin, and BJ had to
spend every waking minute fighting fat, like a horse swatting flies.

'You should be eating this,' she said. 'I'm so fat. I disgust myself.'
She pushed the plate away.

'No, of course you are not fat. Usually I eat a lot, but today, I
told you, it does not go so well with me.'

'You didn't say why.'

Christina gave a little smile and a shrug, letting her eye slither for
a second on to the doctor's table, where he was taking a glass of black
tea. Then she told BJ about the letter from the *Baukommission,* the
plan for the new houses and the road, the rapist, and the visit from the
policeman. BJ fell into a rapt silence, fascinated by the unfolding
drama, hitherto unimagined, that was spreading out in bright colours
from the grey areas of Christina's life. Her silence was broken only by
helping out with vocabulary and the occasional expletive where
appropriate. She particularly took to heart the prospect of a battle
with the planning authorities, typifying in little the struggle of the
proletariat against The System. Despite the fact that the Swiss voted
for something every other week, it seemed to BJ that their personal
freedoms were everywhere in chains. She was excited at the prospect
of interesting an underground newspaper in the case. Surely
Winterthur was large enough to have an underground newspaper? In
comparison with the prospect of large-scale political aggro, the case
of the inept rapist seemed trivial. But Christina was disturbed about it
and had clearly been shaken by the visit from the policeman, though

it seemed to have been quite routine. When all had been revealed BJ lit a politely ruminative cigarette and applied herself to finding out why.

'Policemen, in America anyway, are considered to be educationally sub-normal. I mean, that's an exaggeration, but you know this image you get on television where this young guy about six-foot five is standing there with his hands on his hips, with these short sleeves showing his muscles.' She demonstrated the pose. 'Beautiful body with all these shiny medals and guns and stuff, and he stands there saying, "Yes, ma'am, no ma'am, glad to help you, ma'am." That's all bull-shit. I mean they are dangerous, seriously, especially on the West coast. You know there was a federal investigation in LA recently that concluded that a member of the public approached a policeman at his own risk. Is that what upset you about this guy who came to see you? I mean, did you feel more in danger from him than you would from the rapist actually?'

'In danger from him? Oh no, I think the Swiss police are not criminals themselves.'

'Well neither are the American. I just know I'd rather deal with a criminal: at least they're not under the protection of the law.'

'I'm sorry, I am not believing you. I think if you are frightened you go to the police at once, just like me.'

'Maybe. As I said, I'm exaggerating somewhat, of course. As a matter of face'—BJ smiled a wry smile —'there was this patrolman in Cohasset—oh well, I guess you don't want to know about that.' The fact was that the patrolman in Cohasset was one of BJ's success stories, but she did not want to introduce Christina to her highly personal mores all at once. She had shocked her quite enough by wishing her luck seducing the doctor.

'No, I was not afraid of the policeman,' said Christina, anxious to uphold the image of the Swiss constabulary. 'But you know, when someone asks you—*oder anklagen.* Was is "*anklagen*"?'

'Accuse, I guess.'

'That's right. When one is accused, it makes guilty feelings, if you are or not.'

'It does? But you can't have done anything wrong.'

'No. But he is asking me if I go to this place or that place, as if, perhaps, he thinks I am not careful enough.'

'That you were leading the guy on? He must be real stupid if he thinks you're that type. Of course, they have to be sure because rape is notoriously difficult to prosecute because men always assume it's a gift at the price—'

'Excuse me?'

'Oh shit. What I mean is, if there are no witnesses it's hard to prove the woman wasn't willing—legally. Unless they're beaten up badly. Is that the case with the one in your village?'

'No. He does not hurt them really.'

'Then how do they know the women didn't consent?'

'Because they came home crying and upset and the clothes in a mess and so. They are all young girls. They were very shocked, of course, but not really hurt.'

'Hmm. Sounds weird. It sounds to me as if they know him.'

'To me also. And I also wonder if the police know who it is and they are only waiting for the man to show himself.'

'Hmm. But what's interesting is....' BJ broke off to shake hands with the doctor who, passing their table, had stopped to say goodbye. Christina was thrown into an orgy of confusion, speaking in High German and confusing them all, for the doctor spoke English and wanted to practise it. He shook BJ's hand warmly and spoke of his joy in meeting her. He was really very cute. Then he was gone, leaving Christina in a state that might have been justified if she had been trampled by a wart-hog, but to BJ seemed overdone to the point of hysteria. She realized that the half litre of Chianti was partly to blame, and quietly lit the cigarette that Christina had ripped from BJ's packet after the doctor had left. She murmured more reassurances as to his being cute. Christina wondered if BJ really thought so. BJ was sure she really did.

'What's interesting is,' she repeated, returning to the subject of the rapist, 'why they wouldn't give the guy away. That must be a big clue. I mean, suppose the girls got pregnant. If they were Catholic, say, they'd have to go through with it, wouldn't they? And then it might be important to know who the father was for medical reasons.'

'But they did not. I think in only one case of the three happened—oh dear, how does one say this....'

'Penetration?'

'Yes. The others were not successful attempts.'

'The girls got away?'

'Yes.'

'But was that checked out? See, I'm imagining this guy to be someone they perhaps arranged to meet. Perhaps, you know, some respectable, quote, married man they shouldn't have been messing about with anyhow, so that's why they didn't say anything. That happens. I mean, it's somewhat unusual for people to jump out on passing victims. They'd have to be pretty psychotic to do that, and if that were the case you'd think the girls would want to see him put in prison.'

Christina had gone very pale. 'Why should a married man need to do a thing like that?'

'Lots of reasons. It's not usually because they can't get enough at home. It's much more likely to be because they're in a stress situation at work, which expresses itself like that. Rape is a crime of violence.'

'But if this were a married man—as you say, respectable—would they not, out of kindness for the wife, say something to her, so that she is not shamed by the police?'

'I doubt it. Perhaps she's a really nice woman, and the girls feel sorry for her because she seems to love her husband. Nobody wants to be responsible for breaking up a marriage.'

'Excuse me. I must to the bathroom.'

'Oh. Okay. Are you all right?'

'Yes.' Christina smiled a vestigial smile and hurried away.

Perhaps she's pregnant, thought BJ, her eyes lingering on the old-fashioned baize curtain that veiled the exit to the toilets. She was going to see the doctor the next day. BJ wondered how Max would react to the pregnancy. He did not sound like the type who would rush home to give the baby its 6 o'clock feed. In fact, he would probably use the baby as another stick to beat Christina with. Not literally, if Christina were to be believed, but whatever he used in place of physical violence was just as effective. BJ, in her fledgling rôle as masterful protector, could even sympathize a little with Max the Beast as regards Christina's limitations. She was doubtless somewhat ladylike in bed and had not given much thought to her sexual identity. She probably thought the clitoris was somewhere between Sentis and Glarus. Max the Beast would surely have other women on the side. He might not go so far as to waylay them in the woods—or might he? BJ suddenly perceived another reason why Christina was so agitated. What if the policeman had questioned her about Max? To someone as wedded to the status quo as Christina, the idea of her husband being a small-time criminal of a peculiarly distasteful genre would be enough to make her throw up.

When Christina came back from the toilet she had recovered her poise. BJ was relieved to see her in control of herself.

'Listen, Christina, when I was talking about it being a married man there, I didn't mean to imply your husband. Did you think that? I was just speculating very generally. I have no reason to think it might be him and I'm sure you don't either.'

'Please let us go, BJ.' She called the waitress and asked for the bill.

'Okay, but I really think it would help if you talked about it, you know.'

'Perhaps, but not here.'

When the bill was paid, Christina went outside quickly, pursued by BJ, who was embarrassed to see her rush up to the hood of the nearest BMW for support and burst into a kind of shuddering sob.

'Hey, come on, now, Christina. Oh God, why can't I keep my mouth shut. Come on, take my arm. It's okay.'

She led Christina around the parked cars in the centre of the square, muttering words of consolation and desperately trying to memorize the layout of the streets for when they would have to go back to the car and her appointment.

Christina soon calmed down and began to pour out her fears of Max being the rapist, frequently drawing analogies to the multi-murdering Yorkshire Ripper who had, moreover, such an innocent wife. Christina said that she could not protect Max if she thought he was guilty, nor could she give him up. What could she do? What could she do? BJ had no idea, but after ascertaining that there was no evidence against him, only a vague doubt as to his whereabouts on the relevant days, and that he had never come home wild-eyed and/or dribbling and with bits of fir tree stuck to his clothing, she managed to convince Christina that he could not be involved. It was only an extension—syllogism-wise—of her own fear of Max. Therefore he must be someone to be afraid of, i.e. the rapist. On the home stretch to the car park BJ emphasized that someone in Max's position would have to be really nuts to go after girls in the woods, and if he wanted raw sex he would probably go to a prostitute. In fact BJ was somewhat sure he did, but equally sure that he could not be the rapist.

'You think he would go to a prostitute?' Christina stopped in her tracks. 'But you have never even met Max, BJ.'

BJ made a dismissive gesture with the hand that was not through Christina's arm. 'That's irrelevant. I deal with people like him all the time. And when you think about it, somebody goes to them, they do a brisk trade. Admittedly Max is in the kind of bracket where he wouldn't have to prowl the streets. They'd probably come to him in the hotel massage parlour.'

'Perhaps you are right. It is true, I don't think I am very good at sex any more.'

'Were you better at it before you were married?'

'I think so. I don't know why.'

'Might I suggest it's because he has given you such an inferiority complex that you can't act for yourself.'

'But you know, I think he prefers it that way.'

'That's what I figured.'

Christina stopped just as BJ was approaching the cashier's window under the car park. She took BJ by the arm and turned her round.

'BJ, do you despise me too? Max I know has contempt for me. Do you think I deserve it?'

'Huh? Of course not, Christina. You're okay, really. It's just that Max is obviously the kind of guy who isn't comfortable unless he's making everyone else feel inadequate. You're just brainwashed. I've seen it happen a lot: normal, well-adjusted kids who develop this, like, slave mentality within a year of the marriage. Naturally it affects their sexual identity if their total identity is crushed. Do you have the ticket, by the way? I'll get it.'

Christina let go of BJ's arm to look for the ticket. 'You are very wise, BJ. You must be very good at sex. Your husband is lucky.'

'Well now. listen....' Fortunately BJ had to break off for a minute to pay the parking ticket, which gave her time to think up an appropriate reply. She was flustered that what had been meant merely as supportive chat had given Christina the idea that BJ knew what she was talking about. She suddenly had a vision of Christina ringing up Philip at work to find out what BJ did in bed. Preposterous, of course. Or was it? Christina seemed very nervous and people in that mood were apt to act strangely.

'Listen, if I seem to understand your experience it's because I somewhat share it. Of course Philip and I respect each other totally, but where sex is concerned he is somewhat conventional, and I've come to find that rather inhibiting. Though with others....' she smiled, intending to suggest limitless resources of sexual fireworks in store for the right person. She wanted to leave Christina with the idea that her original assumption had been correct, but with certain modifications. There had to be the thrill of anticipation, or their encounter would be as exciting as a coupling of railway carriages.

The short drive to BJ's appointment was one of the hairiest that she had ever experienced. Christina was in a deep funk and nearly flattened two traffic wardens, despite their sun-glo raincoats. BJ decided to keep her eyes averted, and concentrate on the coming appointment. The man she was to see was a smaller cheese in the planning department than she had hoped to get to. But it had told her one useful thing about the firm: that it had a very high opinion of itself. It was as well to know these things. In this case an expanded smattering of well-informed flattery might be helpful; it was everything to be well-informed.

GRANTA

WILLIAM BOYD
EXTRACTS FROM THE
JOURNAL
OF FLYING OFFICER
J

William Boyd was born in 1952 in Accra in Ghana, where he lived for nine years. He made his first acquaintance with life on a Tuesday morning in 1961. He was then sent to a boarding school in the far north of Scotland. He now lives in Oxford where, when he is not writing for the *New Statesman* or the *Sunday Times,* he is winning prizes for the novels he writes. These include *A Good Man in Africa* and *An Ice Cream War.*

Ascension

'The hills round here are like a young girl's breasts.' Thus Squadron Leader 'Duke' Verschoyle. Verbatim. 4.30 p.m., on the lawn, loudly.

Rogation Sunday

Last night ladies were invited into the mess. I went alone. 'Duke' Verschoyle took a Miss Bald, a friend of Neves. At supper Verschoyle, who was sufficiently intoxicated, flipped a piece of bread at Miss Bald. She replied with a fid of ham which caught Verschoyle smack in his grinning face. A leg of chicken was then aimed at the lady by our Squadron Leader, but it hit me, leaving a large grease stain on my dress jacket. I promptly asked if the mess fund covered the cost of cleaning. I was sconced for talking shop.

Verschoyle liverish in morning.

June 4

Sortie at dawn. I took the monoplane. Flew south to the Chilterns. At 7,000 feet I felt I could see every trembling blade of grass. Monoplane solid as a hill. Low-level all the way home. No sign of activity anywhere.

Talked to Stone. Says he knew Phoebe at Melton in 1923. Swears she was a brunette then.

Friday. Lunch-time

Verschoyle saunters up, wearing a raffish polka-dot cravat, a pipe clamped between his large teeth. Speaks without removing it. I transcribe exactly: 'Msay Jks, cd yizzim psibly siyerway tklah thnewmn, nyah?' *What?* He removes his loathsome teat, a loop of saliva stretching and gleaming momentarily between stem and lip. There's a new man, it appears. Randall something, or something Randall. Verschoyle wants me to run a routine security clearance.

'Very well, sir,' I say.

'Call me "Duke",' he suggests. Fatal influence of the cinema on the service. Must convey my thoughts on the matter to Reggie.

Stone is driving me mad. His shambling, loutish walk. His constant whistling of 'My Little Grey Home in the West'. The way he breathes through his mouth. As far as I can see he might as well not have a nose—he never uses it.

Sunday a.m.

French cricket by runway B. I slope off early down to The Sow & Farrow. The pub is dark and cool. Baking hot day outside. Slice of joint on a pewter plate. Household bread and butter. A pint of turbid beer. All served up by the new barmaid, Rose. Lanky athletic girl, strong looking. Blonde. We chatted amiably until the rest of the squadron—in their shouting blazers and tennis shoes—romped noisily in. I left a 4*d.* tip. Strangely attractive girl.

MEMO. Randall's interrogation

1. Where is the offside line in a rugby scrum?
2. Is Kettner's in Church Street or Poland Street?
3. What is 'squegging'? And who shouldn't do it?
4. How would you describe *Zéphire de Sole Paganini?*
5. Sing 'Hey, Johnny Cope'.
6. Which is the odd one out: BNC, SEH, CCC, LMH, SHC?
7. Complete this saying: 'Hope springs eternal in the—'.

Dominion Day (Canada)

Randall arrives. Like shaking hands with a marsh. Cheerful round young face. Prematurely bald. Tufts of hair deliberately left unshaved on cheekbones. Overwhelming urge to strike him. Why do I sense the man is not to be trusted?

Verschoyle greets him like a long-lost brother. It seems they went to the same prep school. Later, Verschoyle tells me to forget about the interrogation. I point out that it's mandatory under the terms of the draft constitution. 'Duke' reluctantly has to back down.

NB. Verschoyle's breath smelling strongly of peppermint.

Wednesday night

Sagging, moist evening. Sat out on the lawn till late writing to Reggie, telling him of Verschoyle's appalling influence on the squadron—the constant rags, high jinks, general refusal to take our task seriously. Started to write about the days with Phoebe at Melton, but kept thinking of Rose. Curious.

July —?

Sent to Coventry by no 3 flight for putting their drunken Welsh mechanic on a charge. Today, Verschoyle declared the monoplane his own. I'm left with a lumbering old Ganymede II. It's like flying a turd. I'll have my work cut out in a dogfight.

P.M. Map-reading class: Randall, Stone, Guy, and Bede. Stone hopeless, he'd get lost in a corridor. Randall surprisingly efficient. He seems to know the neighbourhood suspiciously well. Also annoyingly familiar. Asked me if I wanted to go down to The Sow & Farrow for a drink. I set his interrogation for Thursday, 15.00 hours.

Bank Holiday Monday

Drove down to the coast with Rose. Unpleasant day, scouring wind off the ice caps, grey-flannel sky. The pier was deserted, but Rose insisted on swimming. I stamped on the shingle beach while she changed in the dunes. Her dark blue woollen bathing suit flashing by as she sprinted strongly into the breakers. A glimpse of white pounding thighs, then shrieks and flailing arms. Jovial shouts of encouragement from me. She emerged, shivering, her nose endearingly red, to be enfolded in the rough towel that I held. Her front teeth slightly askew. Made my heart cartwheel with love. She said it was frightfully cold but exhilarating. Her long nipples erect for a good five minutes.

July 21

Boring day. Verschoyle damaged the monoplane when he flew through a mob of starlings, so he's temporarily grounded himself. He and Randall as thick as thieves. I caught them leering across the bar at Rose. Cleverly, she disguised her feelings on seeing me, knowing how I value discretion.

Randall's interrogation

Randall unable to complete final verse of 'Hey, Johnny Cope'. I report my findings to Verschoyle and recommend Randall's transfer to Movement Control. Verschoyle says he's never even heard of 'Hey, Johnny Cope'. He's a deplorable example to the men.

Note to Reggie: in 1914 we were fighting for our golf and our weekends.

Went to the zoological gardens and looked at the llama. Reminded me of Verschoyle. In the reptile house I saw a chameleon: repulsive bulging eyes—Randall. Peafowl—Guy. Civet cat—Miss Bald. Anteater—Stone. Gazelle—Rose. Bateleur Eagle—me.

475th day of the struggle

Three battalions attacked today, north of Cheltenham. E. went down in one of the Griffins. Ground fire. A perfect arc. Crashed horribly not two miles from Melton.

Dawn patrol along the River Lugg. The Ganymede's crude engine is so loud I fly in a perpetual swooning migraine. Struts thrumming and quivering like palsied limbs. Told a disgruntled Fielding to de-calk cylinder heads before tomorrow's mission.

Randall returned late from a simple reconnaisance flight. He had some of us worried. Claimed a map-reading error. It was because of his skill with maps that he was put on reconnaisance in the first place. Verschoyle untypically subdued at the news from Cheltenham. Talk of moving to a new base in the Mendips.

RANDALL: Did you know that Rose was a promising young actress?
STONE: Oh yes? What's she promised you, then?

As a result of this flash of wit, Stone was elected entertainments secretary for the mess. He plans a party before the autumn frosts set in.

63rd Wednesday

On the nature of love. There are two sorts of people you love: there are people you love steadily, unreflectingly; people who you know will never hurt you. Then there are people you love fiercely; people who you know can and will hurt you.

August 1. Monday

Tredgold tells me that Randall was known as a trophy maniac at college. Makes some kind of perverse sense.

August 7

Luncheon with Rose at The Compleat Angler, Marlow. Menu: *Oeufs* Magenta; Mock Turtle Soup; Turbot; Curried Mutton *au riz*; Orange Jelly. Not bad for these straitened times we live in. Wines: a half bottle of Gonzalez Coronation Sherry.

Sunday

Tea with the Padre. Bored rigid. He talked constantly of the bout of croupous pneumonia his sister had just endured.

Suddenly realized what it was that finally put me off Phoebe. It was the way she used to pronounce the word 'piano' with an Italian accent. 'Would you care for a tune on the *piano*?'

Aug. 15, 17.05

Stone crash-landed on the links at Beddlesea. He was on the way back from a recce. of the new base in the Mendips. Unharmed, luckily. But the old Gadfly is seriously damaged. He trudged all the way back to the clubhouse from the 14th fairway, but they wouldn't let him use the phone because he wasn't a member.

Rose asked me today if it was true that Randall was the best pilot in the squadron. I said, don't be ridiculous.

Read Reggie's article: 'Air power and the modern guerrilla'.

500th day of the struggle

It's clear that Verschoyle is growing a beard. Broadmead and Collis-Sandes deserted. They stole Stone's Humber. It's worth noting, I think, that Collis-Sandes played wing three-quarter for Blackheath.

Wed. p.m.

Verschoyle's beard filmy and soft, with gaps. He looks like a bargee. The Padre seems to have taken something of a shine to yours truly. He invited me to his rooms for a drink yesterday evening. (One Madeira in a tiny clouded glass as big as my thumb, and two *petit-beurres*.) Croupous pneumonia again....

On the way home, stopped in my tracks by a vision of Rose. Pure and naked. Harmonious as a tree. *Rose!*

Mendip base unusable.

71st Monday

Verschoyle shaves off beard. Announcement today of an historic meeting between commands at Long Hanborough.

6th Sunday before Advent

Working late in the hanger with young Fielding (the boy is ruined with acne). Skirting through the laurels on a short cut back to the mess, I notice a torch flash three times from Randall's room.

Later, camped out on the fire escape and well bundled up, I see him scurry across the moonlit lawn in dressing-gown and pyjamas with what looks like a blanket (a radio? semaphore kit? maps?), heading for the summer-house.

The next morning I lay my accusations before Verschoyle and insist on action. He places me under arrest and confines me to quarters. I get the boy Fielding to smuggle a note to Rose.

Visit from Stone. Tells me the autogiro has broken down again. News of realignments and negotiations in the cities. Drafting of the new constitution halted. Prospects of Peace. No word from Rose.

3rd day of captivity

Interviewed by Scottish psychiatrist on Verschoyle's instructions. Dr Gilzean; strong Invernesshire accent. Patently deranged. The interview keeps being interrupted as we both pause to make copious notes. Simple ingenuous tests:

Word Association

Dr Gilzean		*Me*
lighthouse	–	a small aunt
cave	–	tolerant grass
cigar	–	the neat power station
mouth	–	mild
key	–.	kind
lock	–	speedy vans
cucumber	–	public baths
midden	–	the wrinkling wrists of gloves

Rorschach Blots

Dr Gilzean

Me

'A queer nun'   'A new trug'   'A fucked hen'

Dr Gilzean pronounces me entirely sane. Verschoyle apologizes.

First day of Freedom

Stone's party in the mess. Verschoyle suggests the gymkhana game. A twisting course of beer bottles is laid out on the lawn. The women are blindfolded and driven in a harness of ribbons by the men. Stone steers Miss Bald into the briar hedge, trips and sprains his ankle. Randall and Rose are the winners. Rose trotting confidently, guided by Randall's gentle tugs and 'gee-ups!' Her head back, showing her pale throat, her knees rising and falling smartly beneath her fresh summer frock, reminding me painfully of days on the beach, plunging into breakers.

At midnight Verschoyle rattles a spoon in a beer mug. Important news, he cries. There is to be a peace conference in the Azores. The squadron is finally returning to base at Bath. Randall has just got engaged to Rose.

St Jude's Day

The squadron left today for the city. The mess cold and sad. Verschoyle, with uncharacteristic generosity, said I could keep the monoplane. There's a 'drome near Tomintoul in the Cairngorms which sounds ideal. Instructed Fielding to fit long-range fuel tanks.

First snows of winter. The Sow & Farrow closed for the season. A shivering Fielding brings news that the monoplane has developed a leak in the glycol system. I order him to work on through the night. I must leave tomorrow.

P.M. Brooding in the mess about Rose, wondering where I went wrong. Stroll outside, find the snow has stopped. *Observation:* when you're alone for any length of time, you develop an annoying inclination to look in mirrors.

A cold sun shines through the empty beeches, casting a blue trellis of shadows on the immaculate white lawn.

Must write to Reggie about the strange temptation to stamp on smooth things. Snow on a lawn, sand at low tide. An overpowering urge to leave a mark?

I stand on the edge, overpoweringly tempted. It's all so perfect, it seems a shame to spoil it. With an obscure sense of pleasure, I yield to the temptation and stride boldly across the unreal surface, my huge footprints thrown into high relief by the candid winter sun....

GRANTA

BUCHI EMECHETA
HEAD ABOVE WATER

Val Wilmer

Buchi Emecheta was born in 1944 in Lagos in Nigeria, and moved to London with her student husband when she was eighteen. Her marriage broke up when she was twenty-two, and with five children, she began writing. She has a degree in sociology at London University. As well as writing numerous novels, she has written plays for television and radio, and has worked as a librarian, teacher, and community worker. In the last two years, she has lectured at eleven American universities.

I was late leaving my dormitory again, so that by time I had reached the Methodist High School, the Assembly had already begun. They were singing. The voices echoed along the Assembly Hall, and reverberated against the grey walls between the front of the school and the yard opposite. Everywhere there were young voices; everywhere there was the determined military tune, the tune that was making the khakied uniformed girls inside into pilgrims of Christ.

It was a little odd—a little nostalgia-making—standing outside, late, listening to an orthodox church hymn. The girls sang in tune—Miss Davies, their Welsh Music Mistress, saw to that—but you could tell that the voices were African. You could hear in these voices something of their grandparents: the grandparents who had once used their voices in village music—singing ballads or stories—or possibly in forest calls to accompany the rhythms of the cone-shaped talking drums. These girls, the modern girls of twentieth-century Africa, still possessed their grandparents' voices. They were voices full of strength and vigour, but they were also voices full of hope and pride. It was the hope and pride of believing that they were going to be the new women of the new Africa. They had been told that they were special, that one day they would be rubbing shoulders with the likes of Miss Davies from Wales, Miss Osborne from Scotland, Miss Humble from Oxford, Miss Walker from Australia, plus many, many other white missionaries who had left their own countries to come to Lagos to teach the girls here to value their own importance. There were a few black mistresses—one in the needlework department and the other in the domestic department—but you could tell that they really didn't count.

I, though, was not really among these new women. In part it was because I was shy and sensitive—too shy and too sensitive to be able to forget myself among a crowd of people. Even though I craved company, I always seemed to act like a fool when with people. And so I lingered or walked alone or read or memorized what I read. In part, it was because I was different. Although I could recite works by Shakespeare or Keats or Rupert Brooke, I was the daughter of parents who had scant education, who had simply emerged out of their innocent (and yet exotic) bush culture. They were innocents in the so-called civilized world. Maybe a little crude. But in their world—in terms of communal caring and support, in expressions of language and in the making of music—they could not be surpassed in

101

their sophistication. But they had to leave all this, my parents, in search of this New Thing. They left their village homes which had been the homes of their ancestors for generations and generations, and they came to the city. And it was in the city that they had me, and they said I was clever. They said I was clever because I won something called a scholarship and which my mother called 'sikohip'. I was to be brought up in the new way. That was why instead of being in the village—claying the mud floor of my ancestors—I had to stand in front of this school compound feeling guilty for having read too late into the morning, hearing the voices now of my already assembled school friends singing.

I often gave the village life a good deal of thought. My people made sure I never lost touch with it. I had to go through all the rituals: tribal marks on my face, clitorization at the age of eight so that I would have sexual self-control as a young adult and would be kept on the straight and narrow. Even so, even then, I knew that, like my parents, I was already trapped in this New Thing. But of course to all my friends and even to me, it wasn't a New Thing any more. It was becoming a way of life.

However much I may have admired or thought about village life, I knew that, just to survive, I had to make a go of the education I was being offered. I was at a school where all the girls had to pay, but I was going for free. And because I was not paying for my education I ended up spending more and more time by myself, without friends. I was not of course given a scholarship out of charity but it made no difference. Although I was also aware that my parents could not have paid the high fees if they had been asked to do so. How could they? My father had been dead for some time. And my mother even though a Christian, had to return to being a native in our village town Ibuza. She had to return for survival. So I was, in a funny way, guilty for being on a scholarship, and grateful for being on a scholarship.

That morning I was late, and I knew that I was in trouble. I was a Christian girl of fourteen behaving like an irresponsible 'bush' girl. But inside, I knew it was more complicated: I knew I was both—a 'bush' girl and a civilized Christian. I could also play both to perfection. That morning, it was obvious that the humble, quiet Christian was called for.

I ran in, stopping by the door, my eyes lowered, my fat navy blue

Methodist hymn book clasped to my flat chest. But then I walked straight into my form Mistress, Mrs Okuyemi.

This morning Mrs Okuyemi sat on the outside of our row. She made way for me, but not immediately, keeping me waiting just long enough for all the subject teachers to see me. That stupid Ibo girl, with the marks of '10' on her face, had done wrong again. I stared at the cement floor. I would not look at anybody's face. The other girls were pretending to be disturbed by my lateness. Then I collided with Bisi, and her chair clattered on the floor, and Miss Davies stopped the piano, and the Head, Miss Walker, lowered her glasses, and Miss Humble, a giant of a woman, always in sneakers, stood on tiptoe. She was the physical education Mistress and also the head of English and literary studies. I tumbled to the end of the row, making for the empty seat. Why didn't they allow the empty seat to be near the door?

The morning service resumed, after Miss Davies had put her glasses back on and tossed her head back. We soon knelt in prayer and finished the morning assembly by singing the school hymn.

Lord grant us like the watching five,

To wait thy coming and to strive,

Each one her lamp to trim...

I always felt this hymn was having a go at me. I was the foolish virgin who did not trim her lamp and was late and unprepared for the wedding feast.

Some people said this story of the foolish virgins in the Bible was symbolic; some of us believed it was real. I remember during one of my school holidays I was explaining the meaning of our school hymn to a distant cousin in Ibuza. She was at school too, but not in a 'big school' like mine. At the mention of the virgin she gasped. 'You mean Jesus Christ refused women, even though they were virgins, simply because they did not trim their stupid lamps?' she asked.

'Not just their lamps, Josephine. They were not ready for the wedding....'

'I wish I was there. I can trim and fill twenty million lamps if that is all it will take to be a good woman. Not like this rotten place. You have to be a virgin, a virgin all the time.'

I looked at her, too scared to say a word. We were coming to that age when we were not allowed to say everything that came into our heads. But I suspected that my cousin Jo would be in a big trouble on her wedding night. She did not say it: she did not need to. But as if to make me sorrier for her she did say, 'You can kill a fowl and pour it on the white cloth you use on your first night with your husband.'

I shook my head. I did not know, but went on, 'My mother said that any other blood would go pale before morning. But the real thing would always be red.'

After an uncomfortable silence, Jo said, 'I can trim lamps. I think Christianity is better. Think of all the beatings and humiliations one would have to go through otherwise. Trimming lamps is easier.'

Jo and I were clitorized on the same day, when we were eight, because we belong to the same age group. That was now years ago, and here she was saying this.

I was asking about her the other day, twenty years after this conversation. And I was told she was a nun. Jo went into a nunnery because she probably thought God would accept girls who, by mistake or curiosity or sheer ignorance, had become rather adventurous. That it needed two people to become adventurous but that it was the girl who was penalized makes you think sometimes. But it was just this kind of adventurousness which they said clitorization was supposed to prevent. I'm not so sure. But I am sure that, even with a clitorization, I managed to have five children in five years and all before I was twenty-five. Imagine how many I would have—imagine what I'd be!—if I hadn't had one.

Like my cousin Jo, I was taking the school song literally.

It was, as I think about it, a rather strange life I had then, and it is no surprise that I had a number of escapes. My greatest escape was into literature, or, if not literature, into stories. I remember the first English story I read by myself: Hansel and Gretel. I used to imagine myself lost, like them, in the bush, and imagined then that my relatives would be kinder to me and stop beating me. I believed that my mother would return and stay with me and my younger brother—as she did before my father died. And I dreamed that she would leave her new native husband, who was living with her only because he inherited her, not because he married her, as my father had.

I used to live for stories. During the school holidays, we used to come home to Ibuza. And there I virtually drank in everything the old ladies told us in the village.

Later I used to dream stories, and this was when my work began to suffer. It was because of one of these dream stories that I got into so much trouble on the day that began so badly with my showing up late at the Assembly.

I had always guessed that Miss Humble did not like me. There was nothing to like about me, anyway. I was always too serious looking, with formidable glasses, and was not particularly clean or clever. My class work was steadily going down, and this was making life more difficult.

Anyway, the tall and broad Miss Humble never liked me. But because I wanted her to like me as she liked my friend Kehinde Lawal, I used to really try in her literature lesson.

But it didn't help: Miss Humble did not like me and that was that. On this particular day, a rather strange thing happened. Miss Humble was reading Coleridge's 'Christabel', when she reached the part that goes,

Tu - whit! Tu - whoo!
And hark, again! the crowing cock,
How drowsily it crew.

I did not understand what I was hearing. My mouth was agape in wonder. I was no longer looking at a young English teacher with an MA in English from Oxford, but I was back in the village land of my ancestors. I was listening to the voice of my father's little mother, with her big head covered in white woolly curls, and saliva trickling down the corner of her mouth, and her face sweating and shining in the sweat, and me sitting by her feet, and the Ukwa tree shading from the bright moon, and the children who would not sit still for stories because they wanted to play Ogbe. I was there in Ibuza, in Umuezeokolo, in Odanta, where all my people came from. I was there in that place and I was no longer hearing the young English woman born in the Lake District and trained at Oxford, calling me, calling me. Suddenly somebody nudged me. Then Miss Humble's voice came through. Sharp. Angry.

'Florence! Florence! What are you going to be when you grow up?'

'A writer,' I replied.

Silence.

She stretched herself, standing on her toes as if she was determined to reach the ceiling, and pointed stiffly at me. Then she said in a hoarse voice, her protruding teeth looking as if they were going to fall out: 'Pride goes before a fall!'

I was now fully awake. 'I said I would like to be a writer,' I began again, just in case she did not hear me at first.

'Go out, out, and straight to the chapel. Go there and pray for God to forgive you.'

'Eh?' I said.

'And take a bad mark!'

I then knew this was serious. I was by the door, ready to run for it. Bad marks were added up and shown in one's school report. Nevertheless, I was confused. I did not know what I had done. I hesitated, my eyes not leaving her face. I saw that her mouth started to make the shape of another 'bad mark'. It was then that I ran and did not stop until I was sure Miss Humble could see me no longer. I started to walk slowly up the stairs towards the chapel.

My mind was at first blank, with only Miss Humble's voice ringing in my ears. The voice of authority. Then as I neared the chapel, my own voice, little and insecure, started to express some doubts. 'What are you going to tell God, eh? What, Florence, are you going to tell Him, when you go inside there to ask His forgiveness? Are you going to say, "Please dear God, don't make me a writer"…. And then at the same time say, "But, dear God, I so wish to be a writer, a story-teller like our old mothers at home in Ibuza. But unlike them, I would not have to sit by the moonlight because I was born in an age of electricity, and would not have to tell my story with my back leaning against the Ukwa tree. I have learned to use a new tool for the same art; I have learned a new language, the language of Miss Humble and the rest of them. So where is the sin in that?"'

My voice suddenly grew increasingly more bold until it covered up the voice of Miss Humble, and by the time I reached the chapel door, I decided to walk past it. God had more important things to do than punish me for saying my dream aloud. I have thought about this episode for many nights, and I have finally come to the conclusion that Miss Humble probably felt that her language was too pure for the likes of me to use it to express myself. Hence to her it was a matter not just of pride but arrogance to say what I said. But why—I keep asking myself—did she take the trouble to leave her island home and come and teach her language to us in the first place? It makes my head ache so much whenever I try to puzzle this out.

GRANTA

MAGGIE GEE
ROSE ON THE BROKEN

Maggie Gee was born in Dorset in 1948. She was educated at Oxford, and has a M.Litt. and a Ph.D. in modern literature. *Dying, in Other Words* was her first novel to be published (1981), although it was the fourth she had written. In 1982, she was appointed Eastern Arts Fellow at the University of East Anglia. She has just completed a second novel, *Dying in Formation*. Of her work, Maggie Gee writes: 'I believe in the importance of making new things and making things new. Britain has had its fair share of artistic eccentrics but that is a quite different thing from the kind of respect for originality and innovation which is inbuilt in the critical values of parts of contemporary Europe and the United States. The attempt to crack existing formal modes is still regarded in this country as an aberrant act rather than the proper concern of restless creativity. Contemporary British writing will be richer and more exciting if and when we change this attitude of mind.'

We all know windows are pictures, in towns, outside looking in. And especially at tea-time in winter, lit curtains making a frame. Each window hints at a drama, a hand which lifts like a sign. Heads burn from the shadows and vanish. The figures circle and dance. There is sacrament and romance about food half-glimpsed on a table.

One day I was far from home, in a town where I lived as a child. Nothing looked quite the same, but I cut up through a back alley. I wanted to see the allotments before the sun had quite set. A back gate had been left open, and through it a pink-lit garden...the window looked out on the garden, and a dim world glowed behind glass.

I could see there were children. A cake. A woman stared out with wild hair. Dirty glass made her cheeks wild roses. Her hand on the pane was a sign. For a moment we stare straight in. The picture opens. We enter.

A cake, nine inches across, with white icing, not quite set, and piped edges of brilliant chemical pink, and two roses of pink whirled sugar, and six pink candles which fail to match. Underneath the wet icing is yellow sponge in three layers. Between the layers is chemical strawberry jam. But you have to admire the roses.

The children admire the roses. A child with a round yellow face like a lemon and small sweet eyes like Smarties. Another has round red cheeks and brown eyes like the toffee on apples. And the third has a long curved face with a long curved sneer of a nose. One thinks of a sour banana, unripe, cut down too soon.

The roses were hard to do. Only two (and Lorna tried dozens) had come out looking real roses. She hoped that Henry would notice. He did, but he didn't speak. They met fourteen years ago, one long-dying day in the park. He had seen her a lot in the shop, and he took her a walk by the river. *You silly, it's not a canal.* There were dog-roses on a grey wall. He dragged her some down and his hands got fretted with blood. *They're only wild flowers. I wish I could buy you real roses.* But to her they became the real roses, frail petals, each centre a sun. And they smelled of sun and beginnings, as clear and thin as the water.

She has copied those roses in sugar, not knowing what she has done. Her pride in them is intense. Is it right the others should eat them?

The children are sitting at table. They shine in the light of the candles and swell like fruit in summer. They sit round the glistening cake, and their heads are stuffed sick with the sticky wet whiteness and pinkness and yellowness, jammy and creamy deliciousness of it, *oh Mummy*. They do not say much because they are waiting for Jimmy to blow out the candles. For Jimmy is six today, for today is the lemon-faced child's happy birthday, *oh Jimmy sit up dear and blow out the candles Jimmy, oh go on Jimmy.*

And this is Daddy. Daddy is stunted and thin and his limbs appear woody. Daddy has thin grey hair, very short, with a yellowish tinge like lichen. It crawls on the wall of his head like lichen. Daddy has glasses of steel which gleam. When the candles are lit there are six points of flame in his glasses. But Jimmy will blow them out, *oh go on then Jimmy.*

Daddy wears trousers of black cloth rubbed at the knees and the seat and dully gleaming, and Daddy wears his best striped shirt with wide stripes (dark green) then thin stripes (dark green) like sunlight falling on bright green leaves behind bars. He is glad they are all together, for blood is thicker than water.

Through the smudgy panes of the small bay window the sun goes down. It is heavenly pink with the pink of the sunsets of sweetshop artists and cinema screens and the pink of Mummy and Daddy meeting that late June day in the park and the rock-pink that bled behind thin black piers on their seaside honeymoon eleven long years ago. It is chemical lipstick pink and the melting pink of cheap dreams. It is pink as the little boy's cake, and it fills the room. Yet the dirt on the window protects them.

And this is Mummy. She sits on the leatherette armchair next to the pane for a moment and pulls at her hair with her back to the sun. Her hair grows out with the light behind it like fire. She has curled her hair with cheap tongs and by daylight the ends are all broken and split and the curls uneven.

But there for a moment she sits and as time stays still behind glass she pulls at her hair and thinks as that second coils and uncoils of the state of her nails and her husband's arthritis which runs in the family and him in his thirties and thinks of the bumps on her straight slim legs which she loved (they are veining, veining) and thinks of the trifle she drowned with some old sherry essence she happened to find

to make up for the cream which she spilled and had cried and cried on
the floor of the kitchen and knelt there, sobbing, hurting her knees as
she scrabbled to get it all up before Henry noticed and said they must
have some more, it was Jimmy's birthday, but birthday or not she
could not *afford* any more: and she sits and pulls at her hair, and there
with the sun behind her and one pale leg still girlishly slender tucked
up underneath her and one foot swinging and sun-frayed hair spread
to bushes and birds' nests and clouds, her husband can stare for a
second and stare and beauty burns him like fire...but the dirt on the
window protects him.

She made the cake and she moves on her flat-soled shoes like her
mother to cut it *her mother* he thinks and the pain of seeing her
mother growing inside and already around her and trying to bulge
from her slim girlish legs, were those bumps he had never
acknowledged her mother?—makes him forget that he thought of her
mother, and sharply dig George in the ribs for eating his fourth
marshmallow when Mummy had not had any.

And George is too fat. He has round red cheeks and his eyes are
as soft and unhealthy as toffee, though he is the bright one, they say
up at school, he is top of his class. He is careful and kind and if left
alone he invents things. Now he is busy. His tummy is churning with
soft white bread and tinned salmon and margarine. His tummy is full
of fizzy and ice-cream foamed into waterfalls of pure sugar where
sausage rolls tumble and leap like snouted fish and the bad dreams
snap at him later.

George eats too much and his knees are all dimpled with fat. He
cries in the night. There are dogs which bite him and monstrous birds
which peck at his cheeks which are pink as peckable apples, the
windfalls dropped from the branch in the heavy wetness of dawn. He
feels so cold in the grass and the heads of the worms and the brutal
blue beaks of the birds and the fear of the hour before sunlight is real
and shakes him awake just before she can save him...he wakes and the
cold sweat soaks him. She reaches the table and picks up a long sharp
knife and he smiles. Two teeth are quite rotten.

The child with the long curved face and the smile like the split in
the skin of a fruit is the eldest. Guy is eleven. Above all the world he
detests his preposterous film-star's or hero's name (and it doesn't
sound English: Guy wants to be normal and English, but Guy is

called Guy). He is tortured after his uncle, the one who grew rich selling lawn-mowers, handsome and tall and appalling with black greasy hair and moustache.

His uncle has a machine for making you strong, a terrible *Bullbreaker* thing which he once brought along to show Junior (as he calls him) how to grow strong. *It doesn't matter how funny you look*, he would say, et cetera. And Guy never heard any more. His uncle has bulging muscles under his shirt and his thighs bulge under his trousers. His face is a fine bronze bulge and his wallet bulges with money. *It matters how funny they show that they think you look.*

For instance, though Guy does not know this. His Mummy has pale silver stretch marks like lines of long camouflaged fish just under the flesh, and her breasts have been pulled too much and they want to rest. They hang near her waist in her sad pink faded pink floor-level nightie, for warmth though a husband might well complain and what else can she do when there isn't a fire in the bedroom.

His Mummy has networks of fine crimson veins in her nostrils and high on her cheeks which she tries to conceal with a greenish foundation and powder, as counselled by magazines. She cannot afford magazines, but on bad days buys them and hides them under the sink, though no one is looking. She cannot afford the foundation, buys in a sweat of confusion and guilt and fear of the sharp-nosed salesgirls, *Green, Moddom? Is Moddom sure? Yes, green, so it said. It's for veins. I've only just got them...*voice shrivelling, drying, defeat. They twitter like birds.

She does not wear make-up at bed time. At bed time her face is shiny and washed and the texture minutely crumpled in close up like leather or maps of lost countries, the travellers dying of thirst and the spiteful red-and-green birds pressing in on her, chattering, circling. At bed time the veins grow out clearly, a network of fine crimson roots reaching out towards water or love, *can he see me and love me?*—silence.

They grow of themselves, are no longer hers, as in childhood. And also the muscles. After three children they feel they have done too much, with the pulling and pushing and twisting before one more tiny red head and a howl of anger emerges, not her anger, theirs. (Where is hers? Inside her, inside her.) And then you are empty, and used, and the first time you stand your belly comes out like a soft white balloon which will always go with you, *not yours.*

She thinks that she catches him looking. He sees how it sags now in skirts, he must do, her skirts are all tight on the hips now because they are old and as she grows older hide nothing. She thinks that she catches him looking. He never says much but he puts out the light now, in bed. *It matters how different they show that they think you look.*

She comes to the table and picks up the long sharp knife. If he can no longer watch her with pleasure, then she becomes dark. They are all the same in the dark she thinks and she laughs, a dark bag for his sperm. She laughs in the morning bathroom, painting her morning face, the bright mourning. *He loved me once, by the sea, after breakfast, and I was too young and afraid. But I let his hand go where it wanted, the light diamond-white on the sand, then everything, maybe the best time, the first time, although there was pain. Then we ran like kids in the sea.* Now love for him is a knife: it has pierced the ageing skin of her, left her limp and collapsing, passively letting him work, something rubbing, dark woman of rubber.

Now everything happens inside her. A pain which cannot get through. And it changes as you grow older. Once everything was outside. You looked at the world from outside, you belonged with the dark on the pavement. The wind raised hairs on your skin. You were cold and afraid, but alive. She used to walk home after school and stare in through the lighted windows. They were pictures of magic and love, of things she would never possess. She continued the plays she had glimpsed as she went through the dark allotments. But now she has got inside and the play inside is quite different. And so she must go further in, she must hide from her disappointment.

She picks up the long sharp knife and smiles her love at her children. Her three lovely children, who stare all their love at her cake. It is round like a face, and as palely gleaming. She made it. She made it with hours of love and a splitting headache. She smiles at the children. She made them. She made them with all the give in her muscles and miles of fine pale unstretched skin, *her own, her own.* She made them with all that she had of Henry, his sweating and strenuous passion and babble of love when coming, *I'm coming,* now gone.

And this is Daddy. He sits in the lessening glow of the sun in his striped green shirt like leaves, and his limbs are as cramped and craggy and dark as the thin knotted limbs of a tree, and his face as impassive. His father went mad, and sometimes she worries. It can't be right for a man to go quiet for days. Behind his glasses you cannot tell what he is thinking. His father also was quiet but his thoughts were wild. He fled in the end, and from strange addresses wrote terrible shaming letters.

Dear Lorna,

You will be wondering whether we haven't seen through your game. I have also seen all the filth which you hide in your knickers. It will not be long before all these things are revealed. His mother has also seen through you and seen you at it. You spend all his money on painting and padded bras and his children have to have bottles....

When Henry read this he went white and he wept, it ran under his glasses. She was more ashamed of his weeping than all the rest. But her breasts did run out in the end and the last two had to have bottles. She sometimes thinks this is why George gobbles and has bad dreams and Jimmy looks just like a lemon, already gone dry. But kind Nurse Potter assures her that this is nonsense. So Lorna is snappy with Guy when he sneers and calls her Old Rotter.

That boy was born with a frightening old man's sneer, and though people said that the first was always your favourite, she never quite managed to like him. He wasn't as good at his books as George, but at home he was far too clever. The thing she hates most is his habit of calling her *Mother*, not meaning it straight but as if to remind her that she is too common for *Mother*.

Don't call me Mother—not once but a thousand times. And she hears her voice with the years drying up and the same tiny ridges and veins coming in it, dried out and worn out like her who had always been told by the vicar and teachers at school that her voice was lovely, *sing up.*

And Henry had also said it, a long time ago. *I do like to hear you calling my name,* he said once on the pier when she called him to look at the lines of blown pink on the water before they were gone. *Come on then. I'm coming.* Now gone, now gone...*oh come on....*

And the foaming pink on the sea was the same as tonight's low sun, but also so different, when we were...yes. You go out and face it and drown in it, when you are young. The cold doesn't bother you,

only love bothered her then, freezing and laughing. Nor do you fear
for your children lost in the blaze, or falling and drowning. *When we
were young.*

They stood on the edge of the spray and watched it together, the
deepening pink on the waves which the wind blew wild and the lines
of brightness, of bright lines breaking and briefly kissing again till her
whole body tingled with brilliance and cold and trying to tell him
(already so distant at times and as stiff as a tree and now freezing and
wanting to go back inside for a drink) that she wanted to drink the
sea, something beat like wings at her breastbone....

Now dirt on the inside pane of the window and dust on his
glasses and darkness outside the pain creeping down on the tiny
garden protect him, *I'm sorry, what's that?* The wind on the pier blew
that bleeding impossible pink into waves of wild pain, *come back in.*
But eleven years later the sweet round face of the cake and the rounds
of the children's faces and darkness coming round kindly will surely
protect him.

He watches. He loves all his children, but who will protect them?
He feels his limbs locking, and something is lost or was never quite
there in his brain, or he does not know how to explain it and now he is
too far off to explain. But he knows he is going away, and that
something which should have held him is lost and is getting more
hopelessly lost every day and the half-thoughts circle and day is
darkening, closing. He does not like light now so *Go on Jimmy* he says
as she waits for the little lemon-faced boy to blow out the candles.

His only regret for the light is his wife's lost beauty, her lovely
long breasts and her pale slim legs in the night which he dimly
imagines like beautiful deep-sea fish through the deepest and
darkening waters gracefully swimming. He fears to make love in the
light because light is fearful. He fears to tell her he thinks she is lovely.
He tries, but he finds her too far or himself too far so she cannot hear
what he is thinking. He wonders if fishes can hear and he horribly
fears he will lose her, swimming away.

She stands by the table, the knife in her hands and her face to the
flames. This is Mummy and here are her children, their faces as solid
and heavy and concentrated as fruit, with a single purpose. And this is
the cake and the last pink display of the candles which just fail to
match the whirled sugar roses, one slightly crooked and all of them

115

pinkly leaking, but each with its neat bright pennant of flame, now dipping and dying as Jimmy's small thin mouth purses and shrivels much further than lemons and blows, *ooh Jimmy, oh Jimmy!*

This is Mummy, her bulk printed black on the drowning pink of the window, between her child and the drowning pink of the sun. This is Jimmy, who blows out the six little flames on the cake she made him and crows, I did it, I did it! He smiles with his small shrivelled face which is suddenly sunny and clear as the juice of young lemons and smiles and the smile hangs briefly, a question-mark, smoke hangs briefly, *can't see*—time for a second stands still and *could they be happy, could this end happily?*—

smoke hangs briefly   and dies

and the black blank bulk of the mother bends nearer and nearer the moist round face of the cake she has made or the child she has made *oh no* or the cake she made him with candles and jam and time or the trifle *no*—*not her fault he wasn't normal, no* and remembers the tears she had wept for the cream she had spilt from the trifle or cake that she made with the last of her youth and her looks and her tears and she chooses the round moist face of—*the child,* not normal, his thin scared face and she raises the long sharp knife to his rind and she cuts it, she cuts it, she cuts and she cuts and they all fall down with the helpless bumping and falling and splitting and bruising of fruit as they fall from the tree and the long sharp blade pursues them, they fall with the helpless squawking and flapping of terrified birds and fall over each other and turn on each other in panic as birds peck fruit when it falls too near and panicking birds become fruit and quite heavy and solid and still and one bleeding vegetable bruise as the strong worn maternal hand for the last time securely holds them and cuts and cuts at their flesh with the long sharp blade.

This is Daddy. He sits like a tree, with the rigid black limbs of a tree in a red and black landscape of horror. The red is inside the pane and inside the window. The tiny bay of the window in thick brick walls, the thick brick walls and the tiny fenced square of the garden behind them, the tiny back garden protected by ramshackle fencing of board and the regular rows of allotments behind them where sooty-leaved turnips and cabbages reach to the last dark blaze of the sun and the black stakes of factory chimneys behind them—his deafness and blindness and all the dark layers of patient construction behind them, cannot protect him. The pain is inside him.

His children lie hacked at the foot of the tree like fruit. You fear for your children falling and drowning or lost in the gathering dark...you fear for them horribly severed and falling, here in the kitchen, falling like bird-pecked fruit, *I can't hear you,* calling him, *help me.* He loved all his children, but could not protect them. He feels his limbs locking and cruel birds cover the sun and are hacking and pecking, *please help me.* He cannot express it and now he is too far off to explain, though she brings the blade nearer. He fears to tell her he thinks she is lovely, and now she is anyway wild-haired and strange and her fingers are sticky and crimson and suddenly claw at his eyes and his steel-framed spectacles cannot protect them, the dirt on his lenses cannot protect them, her blank black shape for the last time comes between him and the lost wild end of the sun *to protect him, surely* but cuts him, cuts at him, cuts him....

This is the family on Jimmy's birthday. Jimmy was six, and he blew out the candles bravely. He had eyes like Smarties, but not smart enough to protect him. Now gone. This is George. He was top of his class, but now fallen. And this is Guy Junior, now with his smile lopped off but still looking funny.

And this is Mummy. Mummy is painting her face. She has eaten her cake very carefully, breaking the roses of whirled pink sugar. But she has left space for her children, who she will eat later (she made them). Now she is painting her face with green foundation and powder, to hide the red veins which are blooming. *You do not want too much blood.* The salesgirls pecked at her pride. *Yes, I do want green, you old parrot!* She answers them back too late, and is rocked with silent laughter. The powder is green but the fingers which hold the pale puff are all sticky and crimson. Red-and-green, green-and-red circling birds flash crazy warnings in neon.

This is Daddy. His glasses are broken. His hair is like blood and lichen. His shirt is like sun between bars upon blood on the broken leaves. Though Mummy is talking and smiling, Daddy is already gone. She smears one hand on the dirty window, a sign. She need never go out again, now the beauty has leaked back in. It is sad, perhaps, in a way, that she still has no one to talk to. And yet, there is blood to talk to, and blood is thicker than water (raising the blade to her wrist: too much blood to be kept inside her). Thicker than water, yes, though it rises thinly as laughter.

Thicker at last than (sun like love, wild rose on the broken) water.

Thicker than (light on their love's first tracks breaking) water, now lost, now gone.

But the children call her. *Oh cut it, Mummy, oh go on, cut it, go on...oh Mummy, I'm starving.* She smiles at Henry. They watch the long blade glide.... Smoke from the candles veils them: the happy ending has come. I walk away and I wonder.... The bright glass bleeds in its frame. The curtains close on their picture. Her shadow is still outside.

KAZUO ISHIGURO
SUMMER AFTER THE
WAR

Kazuo Ishiguro was born in Nagasaki in 1954. He came to Britain with his family in 1960. He was educated at the University of Kent in Canterbury and subsequently did a Masters degree at the University of East Anglia under the supervision of Malcolm Bradbury. He is the author of one novel, *A Pale View of Hills,* and a number of short stories that originally appeared in Faber's *Introduction 7.* Ishiguro lives in London, where he sleeps during the day, and eats enormous quantities of food at night. He is of samurai descent.

Something like a torn blanket—I could not see clearly through the evening gloom—had caught high in the limbs of a tree and was billowing gently in the wind. Another tree had fallen and tumbled over the shrubs. Leaves and broken branches lay scattered everywhere. I thought of the war, of the destruction and waste I had seen throughout my earliest years, and I stared at the garden, saying nothing, while my grandmother explained how a typhoon had passed through Kagoshima that morning.

Within a few days, the garden had been tidied, the broken tree piled against a wall together with all the branches and dead foliage. Only then did I notice for the first time the stepping stones which wound a passage through the shrubs towards the trees at the back of the garden. Those shrubs bore a few signs of the assault so recently endured; they were in full bloom, their foliage rich and strangely coloured—in shades of red, orange, and purple unlike anything I had encountered in Tokyo. In all, the garden ceased to hold much resemblance to that defeated place I had glimpsed on the night of my arrival.

Between the veranda of the house and the start of the stepping stones was a flat area of turf. There, each morning before the sun had fully risen, my grandfather would lay out his straw mat and exercise. I would awake to the sounds coming from the garden, dress quickly, and go out onto the veranda. I would then see my grandfather's figure, clad in a loose kimono, moving in the early light. He would bend and stretch with some vigour, and his step was light when he ran on the spot. I would sit waiting quietly through these routine movements. Eventually, the sun would have risen high enough to fall over the wall and into the garden, and all around me, the polished planks of the veranda would become covered in patches of sunlight. Then at last, my grandfather's face would turn stern, and he would begin the judo sequences: swift turns, frozen postures, and—best of all—the throwing motions, each throw accompanied by a short shout. As I watched, I could see vividly the invisible assailants who came at him from all sides, only to fall helplessly in the face of such prowess.

At the end of each session, my grandfather would follow the stepping stones to the back of the garden to confront the largest of the trees that grew by the wall. He would stand before the tree for several seconds, absolutely still. Then, with an abrupt shout, he would pounce on it and attempt to throw it over his hip. He would repeat the attack four or five times, beginning each time with those few seconds of contemplative silence, as if that way he would catch the tree by surprise.

As soon as my grandfather had gone inside to change, I would go into the garden and attempt to reproduce the movements I had just seen. This would end with my constructing elaborate scenarios around the movements—scenarios which were always variations on the same plot. They always began with my grandfather and I walking home at night, along the alley behind the Kagoshima railway station. From out of the darkness would emerge figures, and we would be obliged to stop. Their leader would step forward—a man with drunken, slovenly speech—demanding we hand over money. My grandfather would quietly warn them they should let us pass or they would come to harm. At this, voices would laugh in the darkness all around us—dirty, leering laughs. My grandfather and I would exchange an unworried glance, then take up positions back to back. Then they would come, an unlimited number from all sides. And there in the garden I would enact their destruction; my grandfather and I, a smoothly co-ordinated team, rendering them harmless one by one. Finally, we would survey with gravity the bodies all around us. He would then nod, and we would go on our way. Of course, we would show no untoward excitement about the matter and continue home without discussing it.

There were times midway through such a battle, when Noriko, my grandparents' housemaid, called me in to breakfast. But otherwise, I would conclude my programme as my grandfather did; I would go to the tree, stand before it silently for those vital few seconds, then embrace it with appropriate suddenness. I did at times act out a scenario in which, before my grandfather's startled gaze, I would actually uproot the tree and send it tumbling over the shrubs. But the tree was infinitely more solid than the one broken by the typhoon, and even as a boy of seven, I accepted this particular scenario as unlikely, not of the same realm of possibility as the other.

I do not think my grandfather was an especially wealthy man, but life at his house seemed very comfortable after the conditions I had known in Tokyo. There were shopping expeditions with Noriko to buy toys, books, and new clothes; and there were many kinds of food—though commonplace enough today—which I tasted for the first time in my life. The house too seemed spacious, despite a whole side of it being so damaged as to be uninhabitable. One afternoon soon after my arrival, my grandmother took me around it to show me the paintings and ornaments which adorned the rooms. Whenever I saw a painting I liked, I would point and ask: 'Did my grandfather do that?' But in the end, though we must have inspected each of the many paintings displayed around the house, not one turned out to be an example of my grandfather's work.

'But I thought Oji was a famous painter,' I said. 'Where are his paintings?'

'Perhaps you would care for something to eat, Ichiro-San?'

'Oji's paintings! Bring them at once!'

My grandmother looked at me with a curious expression. 'I wonder now,' she said. 'I suppose it was Ichiro's aunt who told him about his grandfather.'

Something in her manner caused me to become silent.

'I wonder what else Ichiro's aunt told him,' she continued. 'Yes, I do wonder.'

'She just said Oji was a famous painter. Why aren't his paintings here?'

'What else did she say, Ichiro-San?'

'Why aren't his paintings here? I want an answer!'

My grandmother smiled. 'I expect they've been tidied away. We can look for them another time. But your aunt was saying how keen you were yourself on drawing and painting. Most talented, she told me. If you were to ask your grandfather, Ichiro-San, I'm sure he'd be honoured to teach you.'

'I don't need a teacher.'

'Forgive me, it was merely a suggestion. Now, perhaps, you would care for something to eat.'

As it was, my grandfather began helping me to paint without my having to ask him. I was sitting on the veranda one hot day, trying to compose a picture with my water paints. The picture was going badly, and I was about to screw it up in anger when my grandfather came out onto the veranda, placed a cushion near me, and sat down.

'Don't let me stop you working, Ichiro.' He leaned over to see the picture, but I hid it with my arm. 'All right,' he said, with a laugh. 'I'll see it once it's finished.'

Noriko brought out some tea, poured it, and left. My grandfather continued to sit there with a contented air, sipping tea and looking out onto his garden. His presence made me self-conscious, and I made a show of working at my picture. After some minutes, however, the frustration overtook me again, and I hurled my paint-brush across the veranda. My grandfather turned to me.

'Ichiro,' he said, quite calmly, 'you're throwing paint everywhere. If Noriki-San sees that, she'll be very angry with you.'

'I don't care.'

He gave a laugh and once more leaned over to look at my painting. I tried to hide it again, but he held my arm aside.

'Not so bad. Why are you so angry with it?'

'Give it back. I want to tear it up.'

He held the picture beyond my reach and continued looking at it. 'Not so bad at all,' he said, thoughtfully. 'You shouldn't give up so easily. Look, Oji will help you a little. Then you try and finish it.'

The brush had bounced across the floor boards to a point some distance from us, and my grandfather rose to retrieve it. When he picked it up, he touched the end with his fingertips as if to heal it, then came back and sat down. He studied the picture carefully for a moment, dipped the brush into the water, then touched it against two or three of the colours. And then, in one smooth movement, he passed the dripping brush across the surface of my picture, and a trail of tiny leaves had appeared in its wake: lights and shades, folds and clusters, all in one smooth movement.

'There. Now you try and finish it.'

I did my best to look unimpressed, but my enthusiasm could not help being rekindled by such a feat. Once my grandfather had returned to sipping his tea and looking out at the garden, I dipped the brush in paint and water, then tried to emulate what I had just witnessed.

I succeeded in painting a number of thick wet lines across the paper. My grandfather saw this and shook his head, believing I had been erasing my picture.

Initially, I had assumed that the damage to the house had been caused by the typhoon, but I soon discovered that most of it originated from the war. My grandfather had been in the process of rebuilding that side of the house, when the typhoon had demolished the scaffolding and ruined much of what he had achieved over the past year. He showed little frustration over what had occurred, and during the weeks after my arrival, continued to work on the house at a steady pace—perhaps two or three hours each day. At times, workmen would come to assist him, but usually he worked alone, hammering and sawing. There was no sense of urgency about the matter. There was plenty of room in the rest of the house, and, in any case, progress was necessarily impeded by the scarcity of materials. Sometimes, he would wait days for a box of nails or a certain piece of wood.

The only room in use on the damaged side of the house was the bathroom. It was very bare; the floor was concrete, with channels cut into it to allow water to flow out under the outer wall; and the windows looked out onto the rubble and scaffolding outside, so that one felt one was standing in an annex of the house rather than within it. But in one corner, my grandfather had built a deep wooden box into which could be poured three or four feet of steaming water. Each night before going to bed, I would call to my grandfather through the screen, and sliding it back, would discover the room filled with steam. There would be a smell, like that of dried fish, which I thought appropriate to the body of a grown man, and my grandfather would be in his bath, up to his neck in hot water. And each night, I would stand in that steam-filled room and talk to him—often of matters I would never mention elsewhere. My grandfather would listen, then answer me with sparse, reassuring words from behind the clouds of steam.

'This is your home now, Ichiro,' he would say. 'No need to leave until you've grown up. Even then, you may want to stay here. No need to worry. No need at all.'

On one such evening in that bathroom, I remarked to my grandfather: 'Japanese soldiers were the best fighters in the war.'

'Our soldiers certainly were the most determined,' he said. 'The most courageous, perhaps. Very brave soldiers. But even the finest of soldiers are sometimes defeated.'

'Because there's too many of the enemy.'

Kazuo Ishiguro

'Because there's too many of the enemy. And because the enemy
have more weapons.'

'Japanese soldiers could fight on even when they were badly
wounded, couldn't they? Because they were determined.'

'Yes. Our soldiers fought even when they were badly hurt.'

'Oji, watch!'

There in the bathroom, I began to act out a scenario of a soldier
surrounded by enemies, engaged in unarmed combat. Whenever a
bullet struck me, I would halt briefly,then continue fighting. 'Yah!
Yah!'

My   grandfather   laughed,   raised   his   hands from the
water and applauded. Encouraged, I fought on—eight, nine, ten
bullets. When I stopped for a moment to catch my breath, my
grandfather was still clapping and laughing to himself.

'Oji, do you know who I am?'

He closed his eyes again, and sank deeper into the water. 'A
soldier. A very brave Japanese soldier.'

'Yes, but who? Which soldier? Watch, Oji. You guess.'

I pressed a hand painfully against my wounds and recommenced
the battle. The large number of bullets I had received in my chest and
stomach obliged me to forego my more flamboyant techniques. 'Yah!
Yah! Who am I, Oji? Guess! Guess!'

Then I noticed that my grandfather had opened his eyes and was
staring at me through the steam. He was staring at me as if I were a
ghost, and a chill went through me. I stopped and stared back at him.
Then his face smiled again, but the strange look remained in his eyes.

'Enough now,' he said, reclining again in the water. 'Too many
enemies. Too many.'

I remained standing still.

'What's the matter, Ichiro?' he asked, and gave a laugh.
'Suddenly so quiet.'

I did not reply. My grandfather closed his eyes again and sighed.

'What an awful thing war is, Ichiro,' he said, tiredly. 'An awful
thing. But never mind. You're here now. This is your home. No need
to worry.'

One evening at the height of the summer, I came in to find an extra
place set for supper. My grandmother said in a low voice: 'Your
grandfather has a visitor. They'll be through in a moment.'

For some time, my grandmother, Noriko, and I sat waiting around the supper table. When I began to show impatience, Noriko told me to keep my voice down. 'The gentleman's only just arrived. You can't expect him to be ready so soon.'

My grandmother nodded. 'I expect they have much to say to each other after all this time.'

At last, my grandfather appeared with the guest. He was perhaps around forty—I had little sense of adults' ages then—a stocky man, with eyebrows so black they looked as if they were inked in. During the meal, he and my grandfather talked much of the past. A name would be mentioned, and my grandfather would repeat it and nod gravely. Soon, a solemn atmosphere hung over the table. Once, my grandmother began to congratulate the visitor on his new job, but he stopped her.

'No, no, madam. You're most kind, but too hasty. The appointment is by no means certain.'

'But as you say,' my grandfather put in, 'you have no real rivals. You're by far the best qualified for the post.'

'You're much too kind, Sensei,' the visitor said. 'But it's by no means certain. I can only hope and wait.'

'If this were a few years ago,' said my grandfather, 'I could have put in a good word for you. But I don't expect my opinion carries much weight these days.'

'Really, Sensei,' said the visitor, 'you do yourself a grave injustice. A man of your achievements must always be respected.'

At this, my grandfather laughed rather oddly.

After supper, I asked my grandmother: 'Why does he call Oji "Sensei"?'

'The gentleman was once your grandfather's pupil. A most brilliant one.'

'When Oji was a famous painter?'

'Yes. The gentleman is a very splendid artist. One of your grandfather's most brilliant pupils.'

The visitor's presence meant I was deprived of my grandfather's attention, and this put me in a bad mood. During the days which followed, I avoided the visitor as much as I could and spoke barely a word to him. Then one afternoon, I overheard the conversation which took place on the veranda.

At the top of my grandfather's house was a Western-style room with high chairs and tables. The balcony of the room overlooked the garden, and the veranda was two floors below. I had been amusing myself in the room, and had been conscious for some time of the voices below me. Then something caught my attention—something in the tone of the exchange—and I went out onto the balcony to listen. Sure enough, my grandfather and his guest were in disagreement; as I understood it, the matter involved some letter the visitor wished my grandfather to write.

'Surely, Sensei,' the man was saying, 'it's hardly unreasonable of me. For a long time, I believed my career to be at an end. Surely, Sensei wouldn't wish to see me burdened down by what happened in the past.'

There was silence for a while, then the visitor spoke again: 'Please don't misunderstand, Sensei. I'm as proud as ever to have my name associated with yours. It's merely for the purpose of satisfying the committee, nothing more.'

'So this is why you've come to see me.' My grandfather's voice sounded more weary than angry. 'So this is why you've come after all this time. But why do you wish to lie about yourself? You did what you did with pride and brilliance. A mistake or not, a man should not lie about himself.'

'But, Sensei, perhaps you've forgotten. Do you remember that evening in Kobe? After the banquet for Kinoshita-San? You became angry with me that night because I dared to disagree with you. Don't you remember, Sensei?'

'The banquet for Kinoshita? I'm afraid I don't. What did we quarrel about?'

'We quarrelled because I dared to suggest the school had taken a wrong direction. Don't you remember, Sensei? I said that it was no business of ours to employ our talents like that. And you were furious at me. Don't you remember that, Sensei?'

There was silence again.

'Ah yes,' my grandfather said, eventually. 'I remember now. It was at the time of the China campaign. A crucial time for the nation. It would have been irresponsible to carry on working as we once had.'

'But I always disagreed with you, Sensei. And I felt so strongly about it, I actually told you to your face. All I'm asking now is simply that you acknowledge that fact to the committee. Simply state what my view was from the beginning, and that I went so far as to disagree with you openly. Surely, that's not unreasonable, Sensei.'

There was another pause, then my grandfather said: 'You benefited much from my name while it was revered. Now the world has a different opinion of me, you must face up to it.'

There was silence for some time, then I could hear movement and the sliding shut of screens.

At supper, I searched for signs of conflict between my grandfather and the visitor, but they behaved towards each other with perfect politeness. That night, in the steam-filled bathroom, I asked my grandfather: 'Oji, why don't you paint any more?'

At first, he was silent. Then he said: 'Sometimes, when you paint your pictures and things don't go well, you get angry, don't you? You want to tear the pictures up and Oji has to stop you. Isn't that so?'

'Yes,' I said, and waited. His eyes remained closed, his voice slow and tired. 'It was rather like that for your grandfather. He didn't do things so well, so he decided to put it aside.'

'But you always tell me not to tear up pictures. You always make me finish them.'

'That's true. But then you're very young, Ichiro. You'll get so much better.'

The next morning, the sun was already high when I went out to the veranda to watch my grandfather. Shortly after I had sat down, there was a sound behind me, and the visitor appeared, dressed in a dark kimono. He greeted me, and when I said nothing, laughed and strode past me to the edge of the veranda. My grandfather saw him and stopped exercising.

'Ah! Up so early. I didn't disturb you, I hope.' My grandfather reached down to roll up his straw mat.

'Not at all, Sensei. I slept splendidly. But please don't let me stop you. Noriko-San was telling me you do this every morning, summer or winter. Highly admirable. No, please, really. I was so impressed, I promised myself I'd get up this morning and see for myself. I'd never forgive myself if I were the reason for Sensei breaking his routine. Sensei, please.'

In the end, my grandfather continued his exercises—he had been running on the spot—with an air of reluctance. He stopped again almost immediately and said: 'Thank you for being so patient. Really, that will do for this morning.'

'But Sensei, the little gentleman here will be disappointed. I heard how much he enjoys your judo training. Now isn't that so, Ichiro-San?'

I pretended not to have heard.

'It will do no harm to miss them this morning,' said my grandfather. 'Let's go inside and wait for breakfast.'

'But I too would be disappointed, Sensei. I was hoping to be reminded of your prowess. Do you remember you tried to teach me judo once?'

'Really? Yes, I seem to remember something like that.'

'Murasaki was with us then. And Ishida. At that sports-hall in Yokohama. You remember that, Sensei? However I tried to throw you, I'd end up flat on my back. I was so dejected afterwards. Come, Sensei—Ichiro and I would like to see you practising.'

My grandfather laughed and held up his hands. He was standing rather awkwardly at the centre of his mat. 'But really, I gave up serious training a long time ago.'

'You know, Sensei, during the war I became quite an expert myself. We trained a lot in unarmed combat.' As he said this, the visitor glanced towards me.

'I'm sure you were very well trained in the army,' my grandfather said.

'As I say, I became quite an expert. Still, if I were to take on Sensei again, I'm sure my fate would be no different from before. I'd be flat on my back in no time.'

They both laughed.

'I'm sure you had excellent training,' my grandfather said.

The visitor turned towards me again, and I saw his eyes were smiling in an odd way. 'But against a man of Sensei's experience, all that training would be of little use. I'm sure my fate would be just as it was in that sports-hall.'

My grandfather remained standing on his mat. Then the visitor said: 'Please, Sensei, don't let me disturb you. Exercise as if I weren't here.'

'No, really. That will do for this morning.' My grandfather

dropped down onto one knee and began rolling up his mat.

The visitor leaned his shoulder against the veranda post and looked up at the sky.

'Murasaki, Ishida....That seems a long time ago now.' He appeared to be talking to himself, but he spoke loudly enough for my grandfather to hear. My grandfather's back was turned to us as he continued gathering up the mat.

'All of them gone now,' the visitor said. 'You and I, Sensei. We seem to be the only ones left from those days.'

My grandfather paused. 'Yes,' he said, without turning. 'Yes, it's tragic.'

'That war was such a waste. Such a mistake.' The visitor was staring at my grandfather's back.

'Yes, it's tragic,' my grandfather repeated, quietly. I could see him gazing at a spot on the ground, the straw mat half-rolled before him.

The visitor left that day after breakfast, and I was never to see him again. My grandfather was reluctant to talk about him and would tell me only what I knew already. I did, however, learn something from Noriko.

I often accompanied her when she went shopping for groceries, and during one such outing, I asked: 'Noriko, what was the China campaign?'

She obviously assumed I had asked an 'education' question, for she replied in the pleased, patient manner she adopted when I asked her such questions as where frogs went in winter. Before the outbreak of the Pacific War, she explained, the Japanese army had undertaken a campaign of some success through China. I asked her if there had been something wrong about it and for the first time she looked at me curiously. No, there had been nothing wrong about it, but there had been a lot of argument at the time. And now, some people were saying there would not have been a war if the army had not pressed on into China. I asked again if the army had been wrong to invade China. Noriko said there was nothing wrong as such, but there had been a lot of argument about it. War was not a good thing, everyone knew that now.

As the summer went on, my grandfather spent more and more

time with me—so much so that he had almost ceased to work on the repairs to the damaged side of the house. With his encouragement, my interest in painting and sketching grew into a genuine enthusiasm. He would take me on day outings, and on reaching our destination, we would sit in the sunshine while I sketched with my coloured crayons. Usually, we would go somewhere far away from people—perhaps to some hill slope with tall grass and a splendid view. Or we would go to the shipyards, or the site of some new factory. Then on the tram going home, we would look through the sketches I had done that day.

Our days would still begin with my going out to the veranda to watch my grandfather exercise. But we had by then added a new feature to the morning's routine. When my grandfather had completed his round of exercises on the mat, he would call up to me: 'Come on then. Let's see if you're any tougher today.' And I would step down from the veranda, go to his mat, and hold his kimono as he had shown me—one hand gripping the collar, the other the sleeve close to the elbow. I would then try to execute the throw he had taught me, and after several attempts would succeed in getting my grandfather onto his back. Although I realized he was allowing me to throw him, I would nonetheless be overcome with pride when he finally went over. My grandfather would see to it though that I would have to try a little harder each time before succeeding. Then one morning, however much I tried, my grandfather would not oblige by going over.

'Come on, Ichiro, don't give up. You're not holding the kimono correctly, are you?'

I readjusted the grip.

'Good. Now try again.'

I turned and tried once more.

'Nearly. You have to put your whole hip into it. Oji is a big man. You won't do it with just your hands.'

I tried yet again; my grandfather still would not go over. Disheartened, I let go.

'Now, come on, Ichiro. Don't give up so easily. Just once more. Do everything right. That's right. There, now I'm helpless. Now throw.'

This time my grandfather gave no resistance and tumbled over my heel and onto his back. He lay on the mat with his eyes closed.

'You let me do it,' I said, sulkily.

My grandfather did not open his eyes. I laughed, deciding he was pretending to be dead. My grandfather still gave no response.

'Oji?'

He opened his eyes, then noticing me, smiled. He sat up slowly, a puzzled expression on his face, and rubbed a hand over the back of his neck. 'Well, well,' he said. 'Now that was a proper throw.' He touched my arm, but immediately his hand returned to the back of his neck. Then he gave a laugh and got to his feet. 'Breakfast now.'

'Aren't you going to the tree?'

'Not today. You've given Oji enough for one morning.'

A great sense of triumph was rising in me; for the first time, I thought, I had thrown my grandfather without his letting me.

'I'm going to practise with the tree,' I said.

'No, no.' My grandfather ushered me towards him, one hand still rubbing his neck. 'Come and eat now. Men have to eat or they'll lose their strength.'

It was not until the early months of autumn that I finally saw an example of my grandfather's work. I had been helping Noriko store away some old books in the Western room at the top of the house, when I noticed protruding from a box in a cupboard, several large rolled sheets of paper. I pulled one out and unrolled it on the floor. What I had found resembled a cinema poster. I tried to examine it more closely, but it had spent so much time rolled up, I could not hold it flat without it curling. I asked Noriko to hold one end, and I moved round to hold down the other.

We both looked at the poster. It showed a samurai holding up a sword; behind him was the Japanese military flag. The picture was set against a deep red background which gave me an uneasy feeling, reminding me of the colour of wounds when I fell and injured my leg. Down one edge were bold kanji characters, of which I only recognized those reading 'Japan'. I asked Noriko what the poster said. She was examining another section of it with interest, and read off the heading rather distractedly: '"No time for cowardly talking. Japan must go forward."'

'What is it?'

'Something your grandfather did. A long time ago.'

'Oji?' I was disappointed, for I disliked the poster and I had always imagined his work to have been of a quite different nature.

'Yes, a long time ago. See, here's his signature in the corner.'

There was more writing towards the bottom of the sheet. Noriko turned her head and began to read.

'What does it say?' I asked.

She continued to read with a serious expression.

'What does it say, Noriko?'

She released her end of the sheet, and it immediately rolled over my hand. I tried to spread it open again, but Noriko was no longer interested.

'What does it say, Noriko?'

'I don't know,' she said, returning to the books. 'It's very old. Before the war.'

I did not persist with the matter, but resolved to find out more from my grandfather.

That evening, as usual, I went to the bathroom and called to him through the partition. There was no reply, and I called more loudly. Then I put my ear to the screen and listened. Everything inside seemed very still. The thought occurred to me that my grandfather had discovered about my seeing the poster and was angry with me. But then a fear passed through me, and I slid back the partition and looked inside.

The bathroom was filled with steam, and for a moment I could not make things out clearly. Then I saw, over by the wall, my grandfather trying to get out of his bath. I could see through the steam his elbow and shoulder, locked in an effort to heave the body out of the water. His face was bowed over, almost touching the rim of the bath. He was absolutely still, as if he could go no further and his body had locked itself. I ran to him.

'Oji!'

My grandfather remained still. I reached out and touched him, but did so cautiously, afraid the shoulder would collapse and he would fall back into the water.

'Oji! Oji!'

Noriko came hurrying into the room, then my grandmother. One of them pulled me aside, and they both struggled with my grandfather. Whenever I tried to help, I was told to stand away. They lifted my grandfather out of the bath with considerable difficulty, then I was ordered out of the room.

I went to my own room and listened to the commotion around the house. There were voices I did not recognize, and whenever I slid open my door and tried to step out, someone would tell me angrily to return to bed. I lay awake for a long time.

During the days that followed, I was not allowed to see my grandfather and he did not emerge from his room. A nurse came to the house each morning and would stay all day. My questions always received the same reply: my grandfather was ill, but would be all right again. It was only natural that he, like anyone else, should fall ill from time to time.

I continued each morning to get up early and go to the veranda, hoping to find my grandfather recovered and exercising again. When he did not appear, I would remain in the garden, not giving up hope, until Noriko called me in to breakfast.

Then one evening, I was told I could visit my grandfather's room. I was warned I could see him only briefly, and when I went in, Noriko sat beside me as if she would take me away should I do anything out of place. The nurse was sat in the far corner, and there was a smell of chemicals in the room.

My grandfather was lying on his side. He smiled at me, made a small motion with his head, but said nothing. I sensed a formality about the occasion and became inhibited. In the end, I said: 'Oji, you're to get better soon.'

Again, he smiled, but said nothing.

'I drew the maple tree yesterday,' I said. 'I brought it for you. I'll leave it here.'

'Let me see it,' he said, quietly.

I held out the sketch. My grandfather took it and turned onto his back. As he did so, Noriko stirred uneasily beside me.

'Good,' he said. 'Well done.'

Noriko reached forward quickly and took the sketch from him.

'Leave it here with me,' my grandfather said. 'It'll help me get better.'

Noriko placed the sketch on the tatami close to him, then led me out of the room.

Kazuo Ishiguro

Weeks passed without my being allowed to see him. I still awoke each morning in the hope of finding him in the garden, but he would not be there, and my days became long and empty.

Then one morning, I was in the garden as usual, when my grandfather appeared on the veranda. He was seating himself as I ran up to him and hugged him.

'So what have you been up to, Ichiro?'

Somewhat ashamed of my show of emotion, I composed myself and sat beside him in what I considered a manly posture.

'Just walking around the garden,' I said. 'Taking the air a little before breakfast.'

'I see.' My grandfather's eyes were roving around the garden, as if to study each shrub and tree. I followed his gaze. It was well into autumn by then; the sky above the wall was grey, the garden full of fallen leaves.

'Tell me, Ichiro,' he said, still looking at the garden. 'What will you be when you grow up?'

I thought for a moment. 'A policeman,' I said.

'A policeman?' My grandfather turned to me and smiled. 'Now that's a real man's job.'

'I'll need to practise hard if I want to be successful.'

'Practise? What will you practise to become a policeman?'

'Judo. I've been practising some mornings. Before breakfast.'

My grandfather's eyes returned to the garden. 'Indeed,' he said, quietly. 'A real man's job.'

I watched my grandfather for a while. 'Oji,' I asked, 'what did you want to be when you were my age?'

'When I was your age?' For some moments, he continued to gaze at the garden. Then he said: 'Why, I suppose I wanted to be a painter. I don't remember a time when I wished to be anything else.'

'I want to be a painter too.'

'Really? You're very good already, Ichiro. I wasn't as good at your age.'

'Oji, watch!'

'Where are you off to?' he called after me.

'Oji, watch. Watch!'

I ran to the back of the garden and stood before my grandfather's tree.

'Yah!' I gripped it round the trunk and heaved my hip against it.
'Yah! Yah!'

I looked up and my grandfather was laughing. He raised both
hands and applauded. I laughed also, overcome with happiness that
my grandfather had been returned to me. Then I turned back to the
tree and challenged it once more.

'Yah! Yah!'

From the veranda came the sounds of my grandfather's laughter
and the clapping of his hands.

Faber's Best of Young British Novelists

ADAM MARS-JONES
Lantern Lecture
'So much page-by-page achievement . . .
Lantern Lecture may sometimes look
Waugh-like, even Wodehousian, but in the
end it feels solidly Modern. It remains
only to be added that the book is funny,
elegant and wonderfully clever.'
Martin Amis, New Statesman £6.95

KAZUO ISHIGURO
A Pale View of Hills
'A distinguished first novel . . . the writing is
as lucid as English can be,
wonderfully calm and elegant. Here is
a new writer of obvious gifts.'
Norman Shrapnel, The Guardian £6.25

CHRISTOPHER PRIEST
The Affirmation
'Extraordinary compulsion . . . altogether
an uncomfortable book that chips away
at certainties while enticing with story.
It is also an excursion into the nature of
creative writing.' *Janice Elliot,
The Sunday Telegraph* £6.25

ALAN JUDD
OBSESSIONS

Alan Judd

Jamie would not discuss why he was directing Middleton's and Rowley's *The Changeling* for the college dramatic society. The reason was Susan Hart. The play was an attempt to create an obsession that would take the place of his obsession with her. It worked as far as time was concerned since he had none left for anything else.

The production involved twenty characters, including servants and madmen. The publicity budget alone was greater than the entire budget for any of the other plays Jamie had directed. The play was difficult enough anyway and was complicated now by seemingly endless production problems: the set, which worked well on paper, had proved impossible to contain within even double the budget and had to be redesigned; the man who was to have organized the constructing of it had disappeared, and there was talk of a nervous breakdown in Fife; the lights firm had suddenly announced that it was double booked and its replacement had, for more money, fewer lights; the original Vermandero had glandular fever and his substitute was not good; and the madhouse scenes, which were under-rehearsed, were completely out of control.

More urgent, though, was the relationship between the two central characters, Beatrice and De Flores. The play stood or fell on this. Jamie believed—at least, often said—that great drama consisted in the creation of great moments, around which whole scenes should be constructed. The line between the dramatically intense and the embarrassingly ham was very fine, and was currently being lost. The wrong gesture or inflexion of voice at a crucial moment might normally ruin an entire scene but in the context of Beatrice and De Flores it could ruin the play. Beatrice had to loathe and love De Flores. What she most loathed was what she saw of herself in him and that was what he used to bind her closer to him. So far, however, their relationship lacked all conviction.

It was not only that this was central to the play, but also that it seemed to Jamie that it was central to himself and Susan Hart. He had no illusion that any relationship he might have could achieve the intensity or significance of the seventeenth-century stage but he did feel that Susan was both attracted to and repelled by him and that his knowledge of this was a source of potential power. So far, though, he had been unsuccessful in using this power in their relationship; at least on her side, the relationship, like the play, could be said to lack conviction.

140

Of course, no one concerned with the production knew of this abstruse connection. The obsession with Susan continued because like most obsessions it was based on the fact that there was no development in the relationship. There was hardly even any continuity. Brief spells of heady intensity alternated with long periods of no contact. A long period was a week or ten days and a brief spell was a few hours late at night, though one such spell had lasted nearly a week-end. He had known her since the end of the previous term.

The rehearsal that night was in a dark panelled room in Lincoln College. It was L-shaped and at one end the floor was raised by about six inches. With the armchairs and tables pushed back, there was just enough room to act on the raised part. The oak panelling, dimly lit by the wall lamps, suited the play. When Jamie arrived, late, only Alsemero and De Flores were present. De Flores was played by Malcolm, a slight man who had not been outstanding at auditions and whom Jamie had cast on the strength of an earlier performance as Mirabell in *The Way of the World.* Jamie had little faith in auditions since there are many actors who perform well in them while giving no indication as to how they can develop during rehearsal.

However, Jamie had to admit that he had made a mistake with Malcolm, and he believed that the others sensed it. There was something lightweight about Malcolm: he lacked the suppressed, brooding, dangerous quality necessary for De Flores. De Flores's bitter and ironical self-awareness was reduced by Malcolm to a nervous, jaunty, self-obsessed pirouetting. It was acting before a mirror and it lacked entirely the compelling quality that would make his attraction of Beatrice credible.

Jamie knew, though, that it was not merely a problem of miscasting. He had given less attention and guidance to Malcolm than he needed. Most of Jamie's energies had been directed towards Gina, who played Beatrice, though she needed them less. She was an exciting actress with a low strong voice and an emphasis and timing that were instinctive and sure. In herself she was abrupt, remote, difficult to know, but on stage she was fluent, malleable, and thrilling. When Jamie would demonstrate what he wanted of De Flores by feeding Gina the lines as he wanted Malcolm to deliver them, he could feel her come alive. She responded to him with a mixture of haughty refusal and a suggestive acknowledgement, a grudging yielding which

141

was what the play demanded. But when she played opposite
Malcolm, she was dull, mechanical, and flat—which further shook
his already unsteady confidence. Jamie was no actor, but the
temptation to take over Malcolm's part in rehearsals was almost too
strong. He found it impossible to exercise power without enjoying it
but he knew that if he indulged himself he would deny the cast and the
play any chance of independent life, and so he held back.

This made him all the more determined to improve De Flores, to
make him or to break him.

It was not to be a full rehearsal. He had told no one of his plan.
Disphonta and Jasperino had arrived but still no Gina. Jamie did not
suspect her of pursuing some vainglorious ideal of the leading lady's
prerogative; he believed she would have been the same if she had been
selling programmes. Not everyone thought so, however. She was
respected but was not universally popular.

For some time no one spoke. They all seemed tired. Jamie felt it
was going to go badly. Malcolm pulled a silver pocket watch and
chain from the pocket of his jeans, an affectation that seemed to give
him pleasure. 'Gina is determined to be as awkward off stage as on it,'
he said. 'Is it too much Stanislavsky or is she just making sure we all
notice her?'

The remark was obviously prepared and no one responded. A
few moments later, with an aptness that characterized nearly
everything she did, Gina pushed open the door and walked in without
closing it. She went straight to a chair by the empty fireplace and lit a
cigarette, as though she were alone. Jamie deliberately did not look
up from his notes.

Malcolm, who always seemed discomposed by Gina, put away
his watch, stood and stretched, self-consciously looking at his fingertips. 'Which bit are we doing?' he asked.

'All your major speeches,' said Jamie.

'All mine? Why?'

'To get them right.'

'But we've got...'

'And everyone here will play the opposite parts, reading them
dead-pan if necessary. No acting, no expression. They will sit in chairs
and say their lines like robots while you act your heart out before
them.'

There was a perceptible stir of interest. Malcolm looked at the others in bewildered appeal, then back at Jamie. 'I don't see the point. It's no good dead-pan. There's nothing for me to bounce off; there's no spark. It'll be like acting in front of Stonehenge.'

'Exactly. All the life and spark will have to come from you. De Flores has to be the motive force in the play. I want you to go right over the top and get so used to it that when everyone else is turning it on you'll still be predominant.' It would have been more truthful to say, 'I want to break you and remake you in the image I have chosen for you,' but that would not have worked.

'You don't need me, then,' said Gina.

'I do. I want you to respond very flatly.'

'Any of us can do that. It doesn't matter who responds. It doesn't have to be me doing my lines. Anyone can respond flatly.'

'You more than anyone.'

They had spoken quietly, without looking up. They glanced at each other, and Jamie then returned to pretending to be reading his notes. Out of the corner of his eye, he saw Gina stub out her cigarette in the fireplace and get up. He did not know whether she was going to stay or walk out. By a few words he had created a tension in everyone present that he felt would be decisive for the whole production. It was very easy. Although his heart was thumping against his ribs, he felt detached; he didn't care what happened.

Gina walked slowly to the chair on the raised floor. 'Let's get on with it, then.'

'I'll need a few minutes to warm up,' said Malcolm.

'No,' said Jamie.

Like many actors, Malcolm put great stress on physical and mental preparation, especially upon touching and exercising together. Jamie normally permitted it but it irritated him. He thought it forced and pretentious. He preferred a few minutes of old-fashioned PT which, so far as he could see, got the blood moving and warmed up everyone as well as anything. For the rest it was practice, discipline, repetition that made a production, given that the thinking behind it was sound. No actor could rely on precise mental attuning or empathy for every performance. To go on night after night he needed a hard core of technique and automatic but convincing responses that would carry him through no matter what his mental state. Acting was pretending.

Disbelieving at first, Malcolm appealed. 'I can't do it cold, Jamie. I can't go into it just like that.'

'You can. And it'll do you good to try.'

'But can't I have just a few minutes by myself? It won't take long.'

'No, just get on with it. Come on, you'll surprise yourself. Do it in front of Gina alone to start with.'

Jamie had discovered in other productions that in order to get people to do what they didn't want to do it was usually necessary simply to insist, and to be repetitive. He did not deny to himself that there was a certain pleasure in what was achieved in this way, but he felt confident now that he was doing it because the production needed it. The cast were becoming apathetic and bored. Malcolm in particular needed something radical, because he was the kind of actor who reacted to continuing sympathy and encouragement by slipping back into comfortable acting habits, none of which was right for De Flores. Jamie felt a keen and cruel determination to see De Flores as he would have him be. Also, he had to acknowledge to himself reluctantly a desire to show off in front of Gina.

When it is made a spectacle, cruelty is nearly always compelling. Malcolm began going through his speeches before the impassive Gina, who sat on a wooden chair and responded with the same expressionless indifference that characterized her social dealings with him. The rest of the cast sat by the dimly lit panelled walls, looking on.

Malcolm stopped after his first speech and turned to Jamie. 'It's no good, it doesn't work. You can hear it doesn't.'

'Go on with the next one,' said Jamie.

Malcolm gabbled through the second speech and then stopped halfway through the third. He turned again to Jamie, holding his hands open before him. 'Look, this is pointless. I can't act into a vacuum. It's not possible.'

'You're becoming precious.'

'Oh, come on....'

'Get on with it.'

Hurt, he carried on. Resentful, nervous and upset, Malcolm was unable to speak his lines with sincerity, and his timing and rhythm were haywire. He galloped through all his speeches scarcely able to look at Gina, despite Jamie's frequent admonitions. The result was so bad that Jamie could sense that everyone was looking at Malcolm as though he had some horrid and fascinating disease. He felt it wasn't going to work but it was too late now to stop. The moment Malcolm finished his last speech Jamie told the others to form with their chairs a semi-circle around Malcolm and to take it in turn to feed him his lines in the same expressionless way.

Malcolm stood with his arms folded and faced the far wall, so that he looked at no one. His back was towards Gina and Jamie. 'I can't do it. You'd better find someone else for the part. You're just trying to humiliate me and it's not going to work. You'd better find someone else.'

Jamie said nothing, having nothing to say. The others were all sitting on their chairs in a semi-circle, waiting.

'It will work,' he said quietly. 'You can do it and to prove it I'm going to make it even worse for you. Everyone will feed you your lines in unison so that you will act before a chorus. It will be awful for you at first but I want you to overcome your fear of the chorus so that you'll end up dominating everyone. They'll respond to you, not you to them. You can do it, Malcolm. It will work.'

Malcolm turned and faced them all, still with his arms folded. It was clear that he was near to tears but he did not walk out. Having the others round him inhibited that. Jamie wondered whether any of them would object but they did not. They seemed cowed and were no doubt secretly excited. Gina's expression was unaltered from what it had been when she first took the stage.

Malcolm began in a weak brittle voice. Jamie stopped him immediately, made him unfold his arms and told him to slow down. He began again and Jamie stopped him again. 'Stand in the middle,' he said. 'Face people when you're speaking.'

Malcolm began a third time and the threatened tears could be heard in his voice, but as he went on they turned into incipient rage, albeit a petulant anger that produced a frantic gallop until Jamie slowed him once more. Each time the chorus chanted their lines at him he flinched as though expecting blows. However, after ten or so minutes of stops and starts he acquired a desperation that lent some conviction to what he was saying.

'We're nearly there. You're beginning to do it,' Jamie told him gently. 'But you're now getting help from the chorus because you're carrying them along with you. Chorus, please keep all expression out of your voices.'

Malcolm was still upset but by now he was determined to prove something. He breathed deeply, trying to control himself, raised his voice and began to deliver his lines as though he were angry with the chorus. Soon he had developed a power and irony quite unlike his previous delivery. It did not sound like normal, nervous, touchy Malcolm. He had discovered a new part of himself.

'That is De Florès,' Jamie said at the end. It was an exaggeration but not too unreasonable under the circumstances. Malcolm looked drained but he was quiet now, absorbing his discovery.

The others were chastened and purged of apathy. Jamie rehearsed them in three short scenes involving everyone present. The acting was crisp and sharp. Gina listened to what he said and then reproduced his directions exactly, with no acknowledgement other than the doing of them. When the rehearsal was finished she left without speaking, though without appearing to go out of her way to avoid speech. She conveyed hostility as she conveyed sexuality, something she was aware of but could not be bothered with.

GRANTA

ADAM MARS-JONES
TROUT DAY BY
PUMPKIN LIGHT

Adam Mars-Jones is the author of *Lantern Lecture*. As a reviewer, he has written for the *Financial Times*, the *Sunday Times*, and the *Times Literary Supplement*.

Jim hardly sees the black and orange streamers which decorate the lobby for the costume ball, or the dish of pumpkin-seeds laid out in welcome on the table there.

There are three light-sources in the room he is approaching. Behind the beer-table at far left stands a traditional jack-o-lantern, carved and prepared by the Education Officer, who is now a purple dragon with only a beard and a paper cup showing beneath its papier-mâché snout. The Dragon-Officer scorns the low-caste pumpkins sold in town, piled outside the supermarkets like mis-shapen beach-balls. Every year he drives out into the country and prowls around pumpkin patches till he finds his phrenological ideal, every bump and lobe perfectly defined.

Back home he observes the simple rules of the operation:
1. Make sure you cut an irregular lid so that you can see right away which way it goes back on.
2. Hold the knife at a shallow angle when you cut the lid so it can't drop thru.
3. Carve the features on the bevel to help the light spread out.

The resulting jack-o-lantern is almost Apollonian, in spite of the carefully-etched scar and the thread of pumpkin-pulp dangling from the edge of its mouth. The mild golden light and the high pondering forehead make it a downright reassuring bogy. Similarly the ferocity of its maker's dragon-outfit is compromised by the soulful eyelash-fringes he has given it.

Placed at centre-left of the back wall is a day-glo midget of orange plastic, with a pumpkin instead of a head and a top hat perched above it, politely half-raised. He is lit up from inside and throws a miserly ellipse of orange-red against the wall.

Given pride of place on top of the TV is a second authentic jack-o-lantern, but this one's face is a crude piece of work, suggesting idiocy not menace. Mounted inside it, wedged into the flesh, is a strobe-light which gives off a bone-white flash several times a second—a lightning to match the thunder of the sound-system. The scooped-out skull, with its out-sticking pieces of metal and wire, looks like propaganda against electroshock therapy, so a sun-hat has been used to conceal them.

Stroboscopes have been known to trigger off petit-mal attacks, even in subjects with no history of epilepsy: the stuttering flashes interfere with the brain's own dance-rhythms. So the organizers of this event have instructions to look out for any jerks and seizures which go beyond permissible disco. No one pretends this will be easy.

Jim hardly sees the black and orange streamers which decorate the lobby for the costume ball, or the bowl of pumpkin-seeds laid out in welcome on the table there.

Pumpkin-seeds make a popular and tasty party snack: just soak a few hours in salted water, then dry off in the oven. The seeds Jim has been eating are less traditional, though by the standards of his friends they mark him as an anachronism.

The earth's metabolism turns pumpkin seeds, when planted in the normal way, duly into plants; but in the human body they act as mild psychotropics. They 'alter consciousness'. They screen an hour or two of eyelid movies. They rubberize a few perceptual grids. The US Government dislikes these effects, and arranges for the seeds to be sprayed with a preparation which multiplies their slight natural toxicity. They are then rejected by birds and bugs, and by the digestive systems of thrill-seekers.

Jim's source, though, has promised him a purity of one-hundred-per-cent.

Jim makes final adjustments to his head-dress. His handsome features, including green stupid eyes and a dark-blond moustache, are dimly visible through the coarse mesh of a veil which suggests both a vamp and a bee-keeper.

He is as old as sin, if sin is twenty-six.

Arriving at the desk, Jim pays the entrance fee and receives on his wrist a purple lambda in Magic Marker, which will qualify him for re-admission if he leaves and comes back. Lambda is the symbol of international gay liberation. T-shirts with a mock-fraternity logo, tri-Lambda, are currently in preparation. The faint-hearted opt for a more abstract wrist-mark, since the dye takes some days to wash out.

Here at the desk Jim receives the first of many routine compliments on his costume. He wears a pale-green jump suit, its sleeves short, a large corn-flower embroidered down one leg. His slightly convex stomach looms a little through the fabric, confident like Snoopy's of being liked for itself. Rustling wings are formed along his arms by wide feathers of tissue paper, in shades of green. An effect of ethereal vigor is achieved.

Once inside the Informal Lounge, Jim weaves his way across to the beer keg, though several drinks are already contributing to the impure flux inside him. The music *It's fun to stay at the YMCA* drowns out extended conversation, but there is much nodding and smiling.

A passing GI asks Jim whether he is Oberon or Titania. Jim shakes his head and leans across to shout 'Fellini-Satyricon', through his veil, into the military ear.

Maybe two dozen people are dancing. Twice as many watch them, or pretend to watch, while jockeying for position or edging up to each other. The secret is not to expect a welcome. Instead you should materialize just inside your target's peripheral vision as a rampant sex-object. Moments ago you were furniture; now you are sheer tantalizing Other. Keep saying this to yourself.

More people are arriving all the while.

The tape fades out 'YMCA' and starts on 'Fire Island'. A ripple of pleasure passes across the floor. This song has won many fans with its cheery out-chorus of 'Don't go in the bushes'.

Mighty Mouse, a correction officer from Harrisonburg, is the first to ask Jim for a dance. His costume—cape, T-shirt, shorts, running shoes, and super-hero tights—is designed to turn his littleness to good effect. Mighty Mouse asks all his acquaintances in turn for one dance, coaxes wallflowers out onto the floor, speaks well of everyone. He respects the Personal Space of those around him.

The community reels from his reckless good-mouthing.

There are several styles of dancing already competing on the floor. Dwayne, wearing the Dancing Queen T-shirt he premiered at last year's Marathon, leads a line of followers through an intricate routine. He is as grim as a commando barking telepathic orders, and resentful of anyone who gets in the way of maneuvres.

The guys with the wild elbow-language, doing the splits and high kicks, watched *Soul Train* this afternoon. They are hoping that natural-sense-of-rhythm will turn out to be their birthright too.

A hard-hat and a cowboy are ignoring each other at point-blank range. In butch dancing of this type, the priorities are strutting and stamping. The music's rhythm becomes something to be resisted and brought to heel. To surrender would be as bad as failing a chromosome test. Feet turned out, these masterful slobs rebut, second-by-second, the world's accusations of exquisiteness.

Established couples step and spin with practised smoothness. Issues of leading and following are settled by tiny signals, eye-sent and eye-caught, and tiny pressures of hand on waist or hand.

Unaccustomed pairs, like Jim and Mouse, bob and stride in each other's direction, free-style.

Jim's eyes close as he dances, and his lips shape themselves into a gruff pout. He appreciates his steps ungrudgingly.

Punk-rocker dances with Dracula, dragon with convict, Tin Man with Straw Man. Cowardly Lion has presumably backed out at the last moment, and will not find his Courage tonight.

Inexperienced and poorly-coordinated, Mighty Mouse moves his feet but not his body, as others on the floor immobilize their hips or arms or shoulders. He watches Jim, who is showing the ceiling a clenched fist, all the time they are dancing.

The GI is now dancing with an enigma in black tie and gorilla-mask. No one knows who is under the costume, only that it must be hell in there. Someone may be curious enough to go home with him.

When the song ends, Jim says, 'Wonderful,' and Mighty Mouse thanks him. Jim returns to the beer-table.

Mighty Mouse looks around him. The eyes beneath his ebbing hair-line are radiant with fun-hunger, but when he stays behind each week to help clear up he seems perfectly content to be escorting no more than a broom. Maybe drinking a few beers satisfies the animalistic outsider in him; for of course in Virginia, the statutes of the Alcoholic Beverages Commission prohibit the supply of alcohol to homosexuals. A little liquid wrong-doing may amount (in the mind of a correction officer) to a potent flirtation with his pariah status.

Notice the similarity to the Wild West, where the White Man—speaking with forked-tongue—kept the Red Man well away from the fatal fire-water. And the history of the Indian offers a cheering precedent. Survivors of purges can become wonderfully fashionable.

A glistening Indian, fresh from tangoing with a sheikh, nods to Mighty Mouse's smile and is asked to dance.

As Jim refills his cup from the keg, he notices a youth with a beautiful uninhabited profile standing awkwardly by the soft-drink cooler. He wears a Jacobethan doublet and hose. If this stranger hopes to stay within the law as a teetotaler, he is deluded. Alcoholic Beverages Commission statutes in any case forbid the serving of alcohol in a place where homosexuals 'congregate' (to plan their colour-schemes, hen-parties, orphanage-raids).

Jim smiles and gets going on a little small-talk: 'What's your costume?'

'Uh...Formal Faggot, I guess.' The boy smiles back. 'Hamlet in Act Two. You?'

'Fellini-Satyricon.' Jim's genital brain tells him a little more charm is called for.

This will be his last wholly conscious move of the evening.

'Reel Three,' he says. 'Like to dance?'

Jim's dancing is much more purposeful now that it is a matter of erotic reflex. His strategy is to follow, but aggressively; moulding himself to his partner's steps, but forcing him backwards. Hamlet is easily wrong-footed. When his steps are brought to his attention in this way, he remembers he has no idea what he is doing. In self-defensive embarrassment, he raises his hands to Jim's shoulders. Soon they are dancing close.

Jim's romantic involvements last three days on average. He blames biorhythms.

A premature slow-dance follows the fast one on the tape. Jim grips Hamlet firmly and sways to the new tempo.

Once we were lovers
Can't they understand
Closer than others, I was you
I was your man.

Without a deejay to bully them into cooling it down whether they want to or not, the masqueraders at first hold back from the floor. Then figures from the edges of the room move in for a provisional kill. Their smiles are a little more authentic than the letters-pages of magazines they hide at home.

Don't talk of heart-aches
I remember them all
And I'm checking you out one night
To see if I'm faking it all

Jim murmurs incoherently in Hamlet's ear through the beer-sticky webbing—listing and exploring the hiding-places of cuteness.

There is a species of mantis whose female bites off her husband's head during early foreplay, leaving him to administer the conjugals on Automatic Pilot. She has sound evolutionary reasons for this, but her lover can't hear them. He continues to go through the motions, and here among the higher primates, so does Jim.

So many others
So many times
Sixty new cities and what do I
What do I find?

As the dance goes on, more and more of Jim's weight is transferred to Hamlet's shoulders. By its end, Jim's knees are near the floor and Hamlet is barely able to move.

Devotees of the Latin Hustle have by now tracked beer across the floor in sticky swirls and arabesques. It is like dancing on fly paper. Torn-down streamers of orange and black get wet and bleed their dye. Broad fronds of green tissue from Jim's moulting wings are trampled, down among the cigarette-butts.

In his desperation, Hamlet catches the attention of a tall man standing nearby, who carries a fan and wears a kimono. Hand-painted characters adorn the panels of the fan and also his ethnic undergarment, not now on show. On his feet are the traditional wooden sandals, thick rectangles supported by four blunt wooden pegs: they look like little coffee-tables.

Between them, Hamlet and the stranger get Jim to a chair, and then the Kimono-Man brings him a cup of water. After a couple of sips he says, 'Bathroom.' Jim is supported along the corridor to the men's room. He pulls up his veil and is immediately, effortlessly sick into the consoling bowl. His escorts leave him propped up against a stall, taking it easy behind closed lids.

In these special circumstances the men's room is a DMZ. The fluorescent strips over the mirrors are no competition for the flash and glow of pumpkin light. No one would cruise here by preference.

The players come here to take time out from the game. Only a merry-maker left over from the Trout Day banquet down the hall, flushed with fine wine and the excitement of the fishing-tackle auction, makes eye-contact of any kind; and looks down at his feet for the rest of his visit.

Here away from the music, a little pure conversation is carried on. A sweet-faced Pierrot with a disconcerting crimson codpiece removes his make-up and murmurs 'Zit City next stop' to the mirror.

Two of the Andrews Sisters practise their cross-talk: 'All *David* wants is a husband.'

'Don't you believe it. He'll settle for two legs and a pulse.'

'Now isn't that the pot calling the kettle beige?'

But drag is wildly unpopular here in the late seventies, and the Sisters will have to work hard to get laughs. Forbidden minorities develop their own exclusion-principles. They catch on fast.

Jim gets up off the ground and washes his face. As he wanders along the corridor back to the Lounge, his way is blocked by a small group of people. Two blacks are interrogating a piratical figure who wears a delicate mask of feathers. This is Mother.

Mother is a veteran and a long-time spokesman for the group. He belongs to the Old Guard of zapping. This confrontation is kid-stuff for him.

Jim leans against the wall to give moral support.

'Thar women in thar?' asks one of the blacks.

'Gay women, yes,' Mother tells him.

'See what I mean,' he says to his friend.

Mother is used to more abrasive encounters. His latest suggestion for the group, roundly defeated when it came to a vote, involved a poster that read:

HEY STRAIGHT WORLD! HOMOSEXUALS IN CHARLOTTESVILLE GAVE X (a figure preferably in millions) PINTS OF BLOOD LAST MONTH. DON'T YOU OWE IT TO YOUR LOVED ONES TO DILUTE THIS FILTH BEFORE IT SAVES A LIFE?

The other members are happier Earning The Goodwill of the Community.

The second intruder tries his hand. 'Thar women in thar?' he asks.

'Gay women, yes,' Mother tells him.

'See what I mean?' his friend says.

Mother outstares the two of them without any trouble. It is a small triumph now that the great days of zapping are over.

Mother affects a truckeresque beer-gut which is hopelessly out of date. He is anachronistic enough to enjoy dope even now, and to own

155

the big bike his style of dress suggests.

Exponents of Zapping-à-la-mode are much too cosmopolitan to stay in town for this dance; they are up in DC on the week-end, where they can find the international set and a wide range of 3-D movies. Nouveau Zapping goes to a gym, keeps its hair and beard trimmed, and buys those tough hardwearin' clothes from specialty stores (Chez Gomorrah, The Dude Ranch) advertised in the Washington *Blade*.

Blocking the pass, the Old Guard relives old victories: days when society was brought up short. Face to face with its contradictions. Shocked into a new awareness. Days when the world stirred in its sleep. Days when men were men, and the future was pure Frontier.

Mother lays down the law. 'The women here don't go for what you've got,' he says with show-down flatness. The two blacks retreat to the end of the corridor.

'Nothing personal you understand,' Mother calls after them as he and Jim return to the music and the beer-table.

On the way they pass two Fat Schoolboys with Measles sitting nervously near the desk. These two have come here, where the wild things are, to get themselves an authentic frisson. A jack-o-lantern no longer gives them chills, so they have chosen a more advanced bogy. Right now they are too scared to go in any further. They have greatly over-estimated the candle-power of deviance. But if they are lucky a swaying hairdresser will accost them.

Back in the half-dark, Mother pats most of the bodies he passes. Old Zapping spreads itself just as thin as New, thin as fallout or gold-leaf.

Almost everyone is dancing now, responding to the plaintive aggression of the current anthem.

Mighty Mouse dances with Anonymous Gorilla, Straw Man with Tin Man, Hamlet with Gertrude Stein of all people. The Kimono-Man dances with Dracula, flinging his clogs about like a berserk geisha.

(I gotta be a) macho macho man
(I gotta be a) mucho macho man

The vocal group performing this piece was recruited by an advertisement in the San Francisco *Advocate*. The wording stressed looks (HOT HUNKS WANTED); singing voices (NO MUTES NEED APPLY) were not a priority.

I am (I am)
What I am (what I am)
What I am—I'll be.

You could filter out the music and concentrate on the complex soundtrack left behind. Synchronized handclaps and finger-popping on the beats. Regular stamping of feet, the Kimono-Man's wild clog-clatter above all. The raucous sniff of a nose flooding its tissues with fun, from a bottle marked Liquid Aroma. The tearing sound of soles pulled from a sticky floor. And a communal whisper of wish-fulfilment as the crowd sings softly along.

I did not choose the way I am
(but) I am what I am....

After a long fade-out the last dance is announced. Jim makes his way over to where Hamlet is standing. Hamlet shrugs, and they dance.

Soon poor Donna Summer is in the grip of an asthmatic orgasm on the tape. Couples rotate unsteadily, or lean against each other like tent-poles. Many of the dancers continue to drink over their partners' shoulders. Mighty Mouse slow-dances with La Verne Andrews, Tin Man with Straw Man, Gertrude Stein with Isadora, Patti Andrews with Maxine Andrews.

Again Hamlet seeks out the Kimono-Man for help with Jim. When they get back to him, he is sitting on the floor and can only gasp 'Difficulty breathing.'

In this crisis the Kimono-Man is suddenly Hemingway. Telling Hamlet not to worry, he staggers with Jim out of the lounge, into the cold air and across to his little Japanese auto. They are only a few minutes away from the hospital by car.

On the way Jim starts muttering something about kidneys. The Kimono-Man steps grimly on the gas. He jumps several sets of lights in his hurry.

Then he realizes what Jim is saying. Jim is searching weakly through his costume, the words are 'kidney donor card', and he is doing his best to distribute his body after death as extravagantly as he has been doing in his life. Jim falls silent for a few moments, but his breathing is easier. The Kimono-Man returns to obeying traffic-lights. Then Jim starts to speak again.

'If anything happens to me,' he says, 'tell my friends...my good friends at Unitarian Church....' At this point he falls silent again, and is snoring by the time they reach the hospital.

Nobody in the Emergency Room is surprised by the arrival of a towering Oriental supporting a bedraggled sprite. At Halloween, everything is weird, so nothing is weird. Why else would it be the major gay festival? This October is National Hobbies Month; November will be devoted to Mental Retardation. Poised between them is a mildly distracting, mildly deranged celebration; one in which the family has little or no stake. Strangeness goes briefly unnoticed and unresented.

Jim is detained overnight as a precaution. The man in the kimono returns to the Informal Lounge to help clear up.

The mess is astounding. Mighty Mouse, working wonders with a broom, sums up the feeling of the helpers. For a bunch of supposed interior-decorators, we do great demolition.

Next day, Jim is discharged from hospital in good time to round up some friends for an almighty brunch. They put themselves outside huge platefuls of Steak'n'Eggs. They have themselves more than a few beers. Because people are wonderful. And when it's people you want, nothing else will do.

GRANTA

IAN MCEWAN
THE WRITING OF
'OR SHALL WE DIE?'

Ian McEwan was born in 1948 and spent his first years in Aldershot where his father was a Scots Seargeant-Major. He later went to Sussex University and the University of East Anglia. He has published two novels, *The Cement Garden* and *The Comfort of Strangers*, and two collections of short stories. He has also written a number of plays and screenplays, and has just completed a new film, *The Ploughman's Lunch*, which opens later this spring. *Or Shall We Die?*, which McEwan discusses here, was first performed on February 6 1983 at the Royal Festival Hall. The complete text is published by Jonathan Cape in a beautiful (and beautifully old-fashioned) edition at £4.95.

Throughout 1980, along with many others, I found myself disturbed and obsessed by the prospect of a new and madly vigorous arms race. Russia had recently invaded Afghanistan and later in the year there was the possibility of intervention in Poland. In the United States public opinion, or media opinion—the two are sometimes hard to separate—was demanding a restoration of American might after the perceived humiliation of the Iranian hostage crisis, and by the end of the year a new president had been elected who promised a programme of weapon manufacture on a scale without precedent. In this country the government was committed to increasing and 'improving' our nuclear capability. The Russians meanwhile were steadily deploying their SS 20 missiles. The language of the nuclear apologists had taken a fresh turn: there was open talk of a limited and winnable nuclear war in which Europe would serve as a battleground for the two major powers. Weapons had been devised accordingly. The fragile concept of deterrence had been shaken by the determination on both sides to find ever more accurate missiles that could hit enemy silos—weapons that were only of use in a first strike, before the enemy could empty its silos.

One turned in vain to the history books to discover a time when nations prepared so extensively for war and none had happened. And yet between East and West there were no obvious territorial disputes. Despite scare stories to the contrary, there was no ruthless competition for diminishing resources. And the extent of the mutual dependence for new markets and new technology was so great as to undermine any pretence of a genuine ideological conflict. It was as if each side prepared for war because it saw the other doing the same. The governments of each side had much in common, as did their civilian populations who were united by the prospect of annihilation and—in attitude—by their indifference, or by their helplessness and fear. For all the complex discussion of nuclear strategy with its unique blend of logic and paranoia, at heart the situation had about it the aspect of very simple human folly. To call it childish would be to demean children, who would soon tire of such a game: I'm getting ready to hit you because you are getting ready to hit me. That this madness, which threatens not only human life, present and future, but all life on the planet, should be presented on our television screens as sanity, as responsible deliberation on 'defence' policy by calm, authoritative men in suits, gave the matter the quality of a nightmare; either they were completely mad, or we were. Ultimately, however, I believe their madness is ours, and the responsibility for survival is a collective one.

The widespread apprehension experienced in 1980 brought about large-scale public opposition in Europe and later in the United States. Now three-quarters of all Americans appear to favour some form of freeze on weapon construction, and peace movements can claim to have modified, at least, the rhetoric of politicians. For all that, the arms race continues. New weapon systems are to be introduced across Europe during 1983, and the Russians have continued to deploy their medium-range missiles. Public opposition has had only minimal effect on policy, but its importance is greater than its effect—that opposition represents all the hope there is.

Public opposition, of course, had its roots in private fears, and in 1980 I was struck by how deeply the lives of individuals had been shaken by the new cold war. It was precisely this that made me want to write about it. Those who were parents, or had children in their lives, seemed particularly affected. Love of children generates a fierce ambition for the world to continue and be safe, and makes one painfully vulnerable to fantasies of loss. Like others, I experienced the jolt of panic that wakes you before dawn, the daydreams of the mad rush of people and cars out of the city before it is destroyed, of losing a child in the confusion. People described the pointlessness of planning ahead, a creeping sense of the irrelevance of all the things they valued against the threat of annihilation. Helplessness generated anger, which in turn threatened friendships. Images of nuclear war invaded dreams. As in war itself, matters of public policy had profound consequences for private lives.

For most people the panic could not last. A kind of numbness descends, and we have a saving—or is it fatal?—ability to compartmentalize, to keep dread in one room, hope or indifference in another. The threat remains, we continue to deplore it, a few of us take action, but life goes on, thankfully, and most of us learn to sleep again without nightmares.

I wanted to write about those private fears while they were still fresh. I thought the subject matter was best suited to film. I wrote outlines and abandoned them. I sketched out the opening chapters of a novel—but in all these attempts I felt defeated by scale; the problem was at once so colossal and so human. How could it be made to fit?

It was about this time that the composer Michael Berkeley asked me to consider writing a libretto for an oratorio, and I felt certain that this could be a way of approaching the subject. Music would at once translate it to another realm, abstract, beyond definitions, and yet with direct appeal to feelings. Michael Berkeley's music, and especially his oboe concerto, had affected me enormously: though its textures and complexities were undeniably contemporary, his was also an accessible music, often rhythmically exciting, with expressive melodies. His music had the power to move. He belonged to a tradition of English composers who have drawn inspiration from their country's literature. He had written settings of poems by Donne, Herbert, Lewis Carroll, and Hardy, among others, and had composed a particularly beautiful piece for piano inspired by Wilfred Owen's poem 'Strange Meeting'. Above all, it turned out that he shared my feelings about the urgency of the subject matter. He introduced me to Tippett's oratorio *A Child of Our Time*, written in the thirties when another war in Europe was a growing possibility. The Mother in this work certainly influenced the presence of the Mother in my libretto.

One immediate attraction of an oratorio was purely formal: a man's voice set against a woman's, and both set against a choir, addressing a matter of moral and spiritual crisis by singing about it directly, without the complications of a dramatic setting, and in terms that could be alternately public or intimate. There was a purity about this that was appealing. No characters, no psychology, no actors pretending to be other people, simply voices articulating profoundest fears and some hope. There was too the challenge, as I saw it, of writing a singable English, simple and clear, that could express public themes without pomposity and private feelings without bathos.

Traditionally, an oratorio is a non-dramatic choral work that addresses a religious theme. Clearly it could be extended to include moral, political, or even private themes, and there is, in fact, a well-established secular tradition. The oratorio, rather like the novel, is more a term of convenience than of precise definition. At the

163

beginning of this secular oratorio I present the idea of a mother and child, and it is possible that this presentation may seem a deliberate and even too obvious an invocation of the form's religious tradition. Tippett was an influence, but often it is only in retrospect that one realizes how one's choices may be influenced by a particular work one admires, and powerfully shaped by archetypal forms.

The oratorio is divided into seven sections, and at the time of writing I thought of the woman who sings the first section as an exact contemporary of mine, someone I might know well—a woman not necessarily given to millennial thoughts, who delights in a clear summer's evening and remembers, precisely at the moment of her greatest joy, the threat of war. She may have heard of or read accounts of the bombing of Hiroshima. Mrs Tomoyasu was a young woman in 1945 whose nine-year-old daughter died in her arms. She told her story to Jonathan Dimbleby in his film *In Evidence: the Bomb.* Although Mrs Tomoyasu's terrible experience is almost forty years in the past, I thought of it as a ghostly prefiguration in section one, the starkest embodiment of what we most fear from nuclear strategy.

During the time I spent considering exactly how the oratorio should proceed, I speculated that if there was intelligent life elsewhere in the universe, it was likely that sooner or later it would discover that matter and energy are not distinct entities but lie along a continuum. For civilizations without high technology the discovery would pose no threat. Long before Einstein's theories, the Chinese term for physics was *Wu Li*, in which the word *Wu* can mean either matter or energy. The identification of the two has long been a feature of eastern religions. In the Mundaka Upanishad it says: 'By energism of consciousness, Brahman is massed; from that Matter is born and from Matter, Life, Mind, and the Worlds.' For those civilizations with technology, on the other hand, the means for total self-destruction would become available. It is as if nuclear energy is a kind of evolutionary filter. Of those civilizations who make the discovery, only those who do not build the weapons or, less likely, build them and do not use them, survive to evolve further. This is the argument of the second section.

Later I discovered that this speculation of mine was at least as old as nuclear weapons. I heard one scientist fantasize about speeding time up to such an extent that one could look out across the universe and see countless pinprick flares of intelligent civilizations destroying themselves because their cleverness had outrun their wisdom.

From this remote perspective, the existence of nuclear weapons not only threatens but also indicts us all. It is not simply a matter of what governments do to us, but of what we are, and what we could become. If there is to be no nuclear war it will be because a sufficient number of people, inside and outside governments, set about securing this end. In the final resort the responsibility is for the species as a whole. If our evolutionary test defeats us, it will defeat us all.

The first nuclear weapons were developed in the early 1940s and built for use against the Germans. By the time the first bombs were ready, Germany had surrendered, and instead the inhabitants of Hiroshima and Nagasaki became the first victims of nuclear attack. It was by no means an inevitable choice. Reading the minutes of the committees set up to advise the American President on the use of the bomb, and reading the accounts of the deliberations of various interested groups, I was surprised by the extent of the opposition to the use of the bomb against civilians, and by the humanity and far-sightedness of the arguments deployed. There were numerous proposals: dropping the bomb in the desert or the ocean with Japanese observers present was one line of approach, discounted for many reasons. The US Navy was convinced that a blockade would bring a Japanese surrender within months. Japan's industrial output was a fraction of its pre-war figure, and raw materials were virtually non-existent. There was one forcefully argued case for dropping the bomb on a huge forest of cryptomeria trees not far from Tokyo. The trees would be felled along the line of blast, and the power of a single bomb would be evident. Beyond all this, intercepted and deciphered radio traffic suggested that powerful figures in the Japanese military, with access to the Emperor, were convinced that Japan could not win the war and were seeking a surrender—albeit a conditional surrender that would salvage some degree of national dignity. There were those in the US administration who argued that in this instance the difference between conditional and unconditional surrender was little more than verbal, and that with some flexibility the war could be ended by diplomatic means.

165

However, the bomb seemed to have had its own momentum. It was a triumph of theoretical and technological daring. The scientists working on the project were so involved in solving countless problems, and so elated when they succeeded, that many of them lost touch with the ultimate goal of their labours—colossal destruction. The bomb was a pinnacle of human achievement—intellect divorced from feeling—and there appears to have been a deep, collective desire to see it used, despite all arguments. Opponents of its use were always on the defensive. Furthermore, at the beginning of the war, genocide had been the strategy of the Axis powers alone. By 1945 it had become acceptable to all combatants; fascism had to be defeated by fascism's methods, and the mass destruction at Hiroshima and Nagasaki had powerful precedents in the fire bombing of Dresden and Tokyo.

The nuclear bombing of these two cities, then, was not purely the responsibility of a handful of genocidally inclined military advisers; it was made possible by a general state of mind, by a deep fascination with technological solutions, by judgements barbarized by warfare and by nations which—rightly or wrongly—had organized themselves to inflict destruction. The public, when it heard the news of the bombing, though shocked, was by no means overwhelmingly critical. Ever since that time, attempts to prevent the proliferation of nuclear weapons have been a total failure. There are now more than sixty thousand nuclear warheads, primed and programmed for their destinations. The smaller of these are vastly more powerful than the Hiroshima bomb. If, as a species, we faced a simple test of wisdom, from the very outset we appeared to be intent on failure.

The Chorus's lines in section three of the oratorio reflect my conviction that whatever moral or spiritual resources are necessary for us to avoid destroying ourselves, they are unlikely to be provided by the world-weary bureaucracies of the established churches, or by any religious sect that claims that it alone has the ear of God. If, for example, the Church of England comes to accept, as is likely, the idea that within women as well as men there is a spiritual dimension that could enable them to become priests, it will be less from conviction than from tired capitulation to changes in the secular world. In the same way, the Church may follow the opposition to militarism but never—as an institution—lead it. This is not to deny, of course, that many exceptional individuals work within that and other churches. But centuries of mind-numbing dogma, professionalization, and enmeshment in privilege have all but annihilated the mystical and spiritual experience that is said to be at the heart of Christianity.

During the first thirty years of this century, there occurred a scientific revolution whose significance we are only now beginning to understand, for its repercussions are not confined to science. Space, time, matter, energy, light, all came to be thought of in entirely new ways, and ultimately must affect the way we see the world and our place within it. We continue, of course, to live within a Newtonian universe—its physics are perfectly adequate to describe and measure the world we can see; only the very large and the very small are beyond its grasp. More importantly, our habits of mind, our intellectual and moral frameworks, are consonant with the Newtonian world-view. The impartial observer of Newtonian thought is so pervasive a presence in all our thinking that it is difficult to describe this 'commonsense' world in anything but its terms. Detachment is a characteristic we value highly in intellectual activity, so too is objectivity. In our medicine we describe the human personality as a static structure (superego, ego, id) and the body as a vastly complicated clock whose individual parts can be treated in isolation when they fail. We conceive of ourselves moving through time in an orderly, linear fashion in which cause invariably precedes effect. When it appears not to, as in, say, a precognitive dream, we are quick to dismiss the experience, or ridicule as superstitious those who do not. We frequently describe the world as though we ourselves were invisible. Environments are planned—from tower blocks to new social orders—as though people en masse are utterly distinct from the planners, and can be acted upon and shaped like clay. Though we recognize the line of our descent, for the most part we consider other animals as little more than automata to be experimented on or destroyed as we require. We stand separate from our world—and from ourselves and from each other—describing, measuring, shaping it like gods.

The insufficiency of this paradigm—knowledge as 'mastery' of the unknown—is the topic of the final section of the oratorio, and in section four I use a kind of battle hymn to celebrate ironically the most aggressive form of this world-view. Logic, discipline, objectivity, thought unmuddied by emotion, are qualities traditionally associated with the male, and patriarchal values are celebrated here in the same manner. Because governments have never sought public opinion on nuclear policy until after that policy has been shaped, and because of the cult of secrecy that surrounds them, nuclear weapons are represented here as powerfully subversive of democratic procedures.

Only when I had finished a first draft of the libretto did it occur to me to insert stanzas from Wiliam Blake's 'The Tyger', 'A Divine Image', and 'The Divine Image'. This particularly pleased Michael Berkeley whose piece for Soprano and Orchestra, *The Wild Winds,* was a setting of Blake's 'Mad Song'. We came to think of these additions as chorales. Blake was a powerful opponent of Newtonian science, and his poetry returns again and again to the perils of divorcing reason from feeling; inseparable from these polarities were the male and female principles which take many forms in his writing. Since I could never aspire to Blake's density of meaning or the simplicity and beauty of his expression, I decided to draw on his strength by quotation and to think of him as the presiding spirit of the piece.

One can only speculate about a world-view that would be entirely consonant with the discoveries of the scientific revolution of this century. It hardly seems possible that what is now orthodox in science should continue for ever to be so much at odds with what we now hold to be commonsense. Objectivity does not exist in quantum mechanics. The observer is a part of what he observes. Reality is changed by the presence of the observer—he can no longer pretend to be invisible. Matter can no longer be thought of as being composed of minute, hard 'bits'; sub-atomic particles are now seen in terms of their tendency to exist, or as fields of energy. The stuff of matter has become the stuff of mind. As one commentator* has written, 'We are a part of nature, and when we study nature there is no way round the fact that nature is studying itself....' Physics could be regarded as 'the study of the structure of consciousness'. Niels Bohr's Theory of Com-

*G. Zukav, *The Dancing Wu Li Masters,* 1979.

plementarity—as far as I can grasp it—explains that we do not study the world so much as study our interaction with it. Without us the object of study (light, for example) does not exist. Conversely, without a world to interact with, we do not exist.

Increasingly, the talk of physicists has come to sound like theology. Their theories and experiments have caused them to place consciousness at the centre of their concerns, and in many sacred texts they find their new understanding eloquently mirrored or extended. Some physicists are speculating about the ultimate identity of thought and matter. The new physics finds itself in the realm of the ineffable. The supreme intellectual achievement of western civilization, and its most potent shaping force—science—has perhaps reached a point where it might no longer be at odds with that deep intuitive sense—which seems to have been always with us—that there is a spiritual dimension to our existence, that there is a level of consciousness within us at which a transcendent unity may be perceived and experienced. It would be arrogant of scientists to believe that they might now be able to give some credence to religious experience, or that it is for them to ratify or disprove in their laboratories the teachings of yogis. No one who takes his or her own thoughts seriously has not asked, in some form or other, Tolstoy's great question: 'Is there any meaning in my life that the inevitable death awaiting me does not destroy?' Previously scientists have claimed that the question lies outside their brief, or have been quick to answer in the negative. Now some physicists are claiming an openness and humility towards religious texts that their predecessors would have found extraordinary.

I believe there are signs that the new physics has begun to be paralleled in many of the ways we study ourselves and our world—the two are no longer so distinct. Whether these emergent signs will ever become dominant, whether they could coalesce into a world-view that could transform our perception of everyday reality, is an open question. To bind intellect to our deepest intuition, to dissolve the sterile division between what is 'out there' and what is 'in here', to grasp that the *Tao*, our science and our art describe the same reality—to be whole—would be to be incapable of devising or dropping a nuclear bomb. How paradoxical that a scientific revolution should now suggest ways in which we might outgrow our materialism and dualism. In the great resurgence of interest in mysticism, eastern philosophies, ancient forms of divination and healing, it would be wrong to see only a fashionable escapism from the orthodoxies of rational scepticism; whether sublimely or inarticulately expressed, this interest represents a sure sense of the limitations of these orthodoxies, and a certainty that not all private experience is explained satisfactorily in materialist terms. Belief in the untapped resources of consciousness is radically reshaping our psychologies and therapies. Holism is a powerful influence too in many fields; holistic medicine and many forms of healing that lie outside the mechanistic approach of conventional medicine stress the consciousness of the practitioner as well as that of the patient, and regard them as interpenetrating. The growing science of ecology places us firmly within the intricate systems of the natural world and warns us that we may yet destroy what sustains us.

One could characterize these two world-views—the Newtonian and that of the new physics—as representing a male and female principle, yang and yin. In the Newtonian universe, there is objectivity; its impartial observer is logical and imagines himself to be all-seeing and invisible; he believes that if he had access to all facts, then everything could be explained. The observer in the Einsteinian universe believes herself to be part of the nature she studies, part of its constant flux; her own consciousness and the surrounding world pervade each other and are interdependent; she knows that at the heart of things there are limitations and paradoxes (the speed of light, the Uncertainty Principle) that prevent her from knowing or expressing everything; she has no illusions of her omniscience, and yet her power is limitless because it does not reside in her alone.

'Shall there be womanly times, or shall we die?' I believe the options to be as stark as that. Could we dare hope that we stand on the threshold of rethinking our world-view so radically that we might confront an evolutionary transformation of consciousness? It may seem a remote possibility, but then it is no more absurd a hope than that we will somehow muddle through. Perhaps less so, for violence is so dominant a feature of our civilization that failing change it seems unavoidable that sooner or later these weapons—all the power of the new physics at the command of Newtonian ambition—will be fired. Nor is there anything in our recent history to make me believe that in great, compassionate schemes of planning and reorganization we could engineer social systems that would somehow make nuclear war unthinkable or unnecessary.

Ultimately the change must come within individuals in sufficient numbers. The dominant theme would have to shift from violence to nurture. Children, not oil or coal or nuclear energy, are our most important resource, and yet we could hardly claim that our culture is organized round their needs. Our education system alone, with its absurd elitism, is sufficient demonstration of our betrayal of their potential.

Could we ever learn to 'live lightly on the earth', using the full range of our technological resources, but using them in harmony and balance with our environment rather than in crude violation of it? To desire a given outcome is not sufficient reason for believing it will transpire. If we are free to change then we are also free to fail. My own belief in the future fluctuates. There are sudden insights into the love and inventiveness of individuals to give me hope for all humankind; and then there are acts of cruelty and destruction that make me despair.

GRANTA

SHIVA NAIPAUL
THE FORTUNE-
TELLER

Shiva Naipaul was born in 1945 in Port-of-Spain, Trinidad. He was educated at Queen's Royal College and St Mary's College, Port-of-Spain, and read Chinese and Literature at University College, Oxford. He is the author of three novels, including *Fireflies* which won the Jock Campbell *New Statesman* Award, the John Llewelyn Rhys Award, and the Winifred Holtby Memorial Prize of the Royal Society of Literature.

She paused at the familiar cave-like entrance. She had always hated coming here. It was a punishment, a humiliation, she periodically inflicted on herself and it imbued her with a brooding self-disgust. Each visit was a defeat for her and a victory for Madame; and, after each, she would vow never to return. But while she may have given up counting those broken vows, she had not given up making them. Even at that moment, standing there outside the cave-like entrance, being jostled by the crowds pushing past her on the narrow pavement, she had not conceded defeat. She could still turn her face away from that darkness, still triumph over the impulse that had brought her there. She remained where she was, relishing and investigating her freedom of will. The brick tunnel facing her was piled with sacks of charcoal—a charcoal merchant used it as his store-room. It reeked of the open gutter, coated with glaucous slime, running down its middle. It extended murkily for about twenty yards before opening out into a light-filled courtyard criss-crossed with lines of dripping washing.

She was in that section of the town dominated by the cavernous halls of the Central Market, by the warehouses of wholesale merchants and by crumbling, balconied tenements harbouring a vagrant and disreputable population. The surrounding network of streets and lanes was perpetually jammed with lorries, handpulled carts, and bicycles. A permanent miasma of putrefaction hung over the locality. The blending odours of rank fish, of rotting vegetables and fruit, of blood, of decomposing offal, of sweat, fused into a nauseous fog. This miasma not only irradiated the air but seemed to ooze out of the asphalt and brick. One had to walk with care: a permanent slick lubricated the pavements. In the stagnant heat of mid-afternoon, the dirt, the stench, the clamour of horns and bells and voices, became unbearable. Madame could, of course, have chosen a more wholesome spot in which to live and carry on her trade. She certainly did not lack the means to do so: all successful practitioners of her art made a lot of money.

Madame might even be reckoned a wealthy woman. But, pleading poverty with a sly leer, she refused to move; adding that she was perfectly comfortable where she was. She steadfastly turned down invitations to visit her clients in their homes. Not even the inducement of a handsome bonus could persuade her to do that. It had to be concluded that Madame derived a malicious satisfaction, worth more than money, from dragging her respectable clientèle to this pestilential quarter of the town.

Hesitating outside the entrance, a fresh surge of detestation and resentment welled up in her. Long ago she had sensed a sort of seething rancour in Madame, verging on hatred. 'You people,' Madame had once observed, 'come here and use me like a public convenience.' After which statement she had laughed. This memory made her wince. She thought also of the amount of money she had expended on the devilish woman. Over the years she must have squandered a small fortune. Fortunately, her husband was not the kind of man to inquire into the outlets of her expenditure. She could do exactly as she pleased with the generous amount he gave her every month. Not once had he called her to account. Perhaps he should have done. It might have helped in more ways than he could have imagined. But that was not his way. Kind, trusting, considerate man! What would he say if he could see her now, his cherished one, his Best Beloved, lurking outside this tunnel? There arose before her those big, dark, compassionate eyes of his. Again she winced. Her skin prickled and itched in the mid-afternoon heat.

It was not a fascination with the occult as such which led her to that tunnel; it was not a simple desire to know what was going to happen to her in the next month or two that brought her there—just as it is not always a simple desire for physical gratification that brings a man to a harlot's door. She came because it was only here, in the presence of this sneering, strangely hostile woman, into whose waiting palms she emptied her purse . . . it was only here that she was able, after a fashion, to expose and acknowledge herself to herself: a voluptuous self-surrender. Her need to do so was not entirely dissimilar in its imperative nature from the overpowering urge to sexual fulfilment. How could she have begun to explain this malign impulsion to her husband (who called himself a rationalist) or to those who considered themselves her friends? It was not possible for her to reveal an appetite so elemental and so squalid. They would never overstep certain limits. Their instinct of self-preservation ran true and ran deep. It was precisely this instinct that wavered in her, fomenting a black exhilaration, a black yearning. It might have been no good to her if Madame had consented to leave her lair and see her in her own house. Maybe she needed to make the journey to this quarter of the town, to inhale its suppurating odours. Lurking outside the entrance to the tunnel, unable to turn away, she was revolted by her condition.

More than two months had passed since she had last stood there. It was the longest interval she had managed to sustain between visits. To that extent, she could congratulate herself. On leaving the house she had not conceded it was here she intended to come. Just as, even while standing outside the entrance, she had not conceded that she was necessarily going to walk in there and climb the stairs to the top of the tenement. She stood there, debating with herself, testing her freedom and power of will.

From a little blue-painted bar on the opposite side of the narrow street poured the pounding rhythms of a juke-box. Its exterior was adorned with crude but colourful renderings of jiving blacks. However, the centrepiece, occupying almost a whole wall, portrayed an imagined African landscape. It showed an extensive grassland, bordered by hills, watered by many rivers, dotted with lions, giraffes, and hippopotamuses. Flocks of white birds populated the blue sky. These decorations were a recent refinement. They had not been there on her previous visit to Madame. Within the bar, she saw a large framed photograph of the President, wearing a tunic buttoned up to the neck. His face was smooth as lava and his sleepy eyes exuded a hibernatory potency of desire. Above it was affixed a printed exhortation: End Oppression and Exploitation Now! One Nation! One Party! One Redeemer!

She became aware that she was being scrutinized. A young black, bearded, hair plaited, a knitted cap clamped like a bowl on his head, was staring at her from the doorway of the bar. She realized, with sudden alarm, how conspicuous she must be, loitering there in her sleeveless, salmon-coloured dress, wearing dark glasses that hid nearly half of her face, a tasselled leather handbag hanging over one shoulder, her open-work shoes displaying shining, red-painted toenails. She looked away from the hostile face in the doorway. A man carrying a bulky load on his back bumped into her. The rancid odour of his sweat enveloped her. She swayed away from him, in the process almost losing her balance on the slippery pavement.

'Is something you looking for, Miss? Or somebody?'

Startled, she glanced down at the questioner, a wrinkled crone crouched a few feet away from her, selling little heaps of sunbaked fruit arranged on a tray. The creature regarded her dispassionately.

Abruptly, as if propelled by some outside force, she set off down the tunnel, making her way between the sacks of charcoal. She came to the wooden stairs. Again she hesitated. A woman, pegging out lines of dripping washing in the courtyard, paused to look at her. Some naked children, laughing and shouting, were splashing themselves at a stand-pipe. She started the ascent, her eyes fixed straight ahead of her. The stairway was poorly lit and encrusted with dirt. A faint smell of urine mingled with the stagnant odours of stale cooking. On the landings, doors leading into lightless warrens were thrown wide open. From within old women and children stared at her. She climbed swiftly to the top of the building.

She reached the familiar, green-painted door with its brass knocker shaped like a lion's paw. She stopped to catch her breath. Daylight seeped through a cracked window coated with grime. She looked down into the courtyard at the criss-crossing lines of washing. The children at the stand-pipe were still laughing and shouting, their bodies glistening in the sunlight. She lifted the lion's paw. Inside she could hear coughing, groans, reluctant stirrings—the unmistakable sounds of Miss Bertha. The door opened a crack, no more than its security chains would allow. Miss Bertha's rheumy eyes stared at her. A flannel cloth was wrapped around her head. She exuded medicinal vapours, compounded in the main of bay-rum and camphor. Miss Bertha's collapsed, toothless mouth worked ceaselessly, futilely, as she scanned the visitor.

Images of murderous assault nearly always presented themselves when she came here. She would think of Dostoievsky's Raskolnikov armed with his axe. How easy it would be to come in here one day with a machete and slaughter these two old women whose lives could hardly have mattered to anyone except themselves. She would imagine herself carrying out the deed—suddenly revealing the machete, raising it with a cry of triumph, bringing it down on their soft skulls; she imagined the expressions of helpless terror and disbelief that would contort their faces. Indeed, it was a cause for surprise that they had survived all these years without coming to any harm in their little eyrie. Madame must have an indecent fortune stashed under her mattress. She was an ideal candidate for Raskolnikovian attack. But this, alas, was not St Petersburg. Madame might very well be murdered one of these days, but there would be no Raskolnikovs involved. Her death, whether violent or peaceful, would have no redeeming qualities; no metaphysical glamour. Like everything else in this sun-stunned vacuum, it would have no meaning.

Miss Bertha, mouth ceaselessly working, scanned her face. At length, recognition dawned. After a spasm of fumbling, she succeeded in replacing the chains. The room was flooded with dusty sunshine. A strip of red carpet, mottled with threadbare patches, covered the floor. To the left was a wooden partition rising to the ceiling. Behind that was the cubby-hole of a 'studio' where Madame received her clients. Her insinuating buzz penetrated the partition. To the right was a curtained alcove. The room was crowded with furniture and bric-à-brac. A sofa of cracked leather and two matching armchairs were arranged around a low, carved table; there was a grandfather clock with only an hour hand; there were chests of drawers; there were footstools upholstered in faded velvet; there was a Bible lying open on a reading-stand. Paintings of flowers and ships decorated the walls. Ornaments of brass and glass and porcelain were haphazardly arranged on sagging shelves. Vases ornamented with Chinese dragons stood on the floor. Some of these were filled with bouquets of paper flowers, their petals and stems coated with dust.

Catching a spectral glimpse of herself in a gilt-framed mirror, she quickly looked away. Miss Bertha, exhaling camphor and bay-rum, spoke behind her.

'Is Sister expecting you?' she asked.

'No . . . .' She listened to the murmur coming from behind the partition.

'You didn't make an appointment?'

Appointment! Madame was certainly coming up in the world. Normally, you just turned up.

'No . . . I didn't make an appointment. If she's too busy to see me, I'll go.' She made a half-hearted move towards the door.

Shiva Naipaul

Miss Bertha stayed her. She shuffled across to the partition and knocked gingerly. Madame growled in response. Miss Bertha opened the door and poked her head within. Closing the door, she shuffled back towards the sofa.

'Sister will see you,' she whispered. 'But you going to have to wait.'

She was torn. Even now she could escape. But she let herself be led by Miss Bertha across to the curtained alcove. Miss Bertha pushed her in and drew the curtain. This alcove was one of Madame's few concessions to the sensibilities of her clients—who, on the whole, did not much like running into each other. If, for instance, they encountered each other on the stairs, faces would be averted as they sidled past. Madame and Miss Bertha did what was in their power to isolate their visitors. Accidents, though, did happen. To date, nevertheless, her luck had held.

The alcove was furnished in the style of a down-at-heel doctor's or dentist's waiting-room. Two or three chairs were grouped about a round, glass-topped table piled with out-of-date English and American magazines. Too often had she lurked in there, invisible behind its floral curtain, waiting to be summoned to Madame's presence. Now she went across to the window. The children had finished their bathing and disappeared from the courtyard. So had the washerwoman. She looked out across the jumble of rooftops, through the brassy glare of the afternoon, at the grey harbour which rippled with an oily, viscous swell.

She had spent all her life in this town. Looking out at its derelict perspective, it seemed to her that she was looking out on no more than an extension of herself. She and the city were one. When she ventured into it, it was like venturing into an inalienable part of herself. What she saw, what she heard, what she felt, held no revelations for her. All its perspectives were well-trodden pathways through her brain. She knew its rank odours when, after a heavy shower of rain, the glistening streets steamed under the raw blast of the sun breaking through the clouds. She knew the days—like today—when the humid air trembled and shimmered and the sky was white and dead at three o'clock in the afternoon. She knew its brief, purple dusks and its thick, starry darknesses. She felt she knew the shape of every leaf, the texture of every stone, the rustle of every

180

warm breeze. Each had impressed on her a fossilized trace. She knew the faces and voices of the government clerks, the shop girls, the secretaries, the schoolteachers, all of whom, at bottom, seemed to have one face and speak with one voice.

It was summed up for her by those Sunday afternoons when you lay in a darkened bedroom with nothing to do, drowned in the afternoon silence, mesmerized by the slow rotations of the ceiling fan, the mind ballooning with vacancy, stunned by its own emptiness. There came to her an almost forgotten image of herself sprawled on a bed, watching with torpid fascination a mosquito that had settled on her wrist. She had watched it feed on her, letting it grow bloated with her blood; until, sated, it had floated lethargically away and come to rest on the wall behind her.

The vacancy . . . you could not get away from it for long. Whichever way you turned, there it was, lying in wait for you. There was a time when she had yearned to separate herself from it; when she had yearned to sail in a big, white ship out of that harbour upon whose oily swell she now gazed, to escape forever the sun-stunned vacuum and live another kind of life somewhere else. Only misery and death had been exhaled in this vacuum imprisoned between ocean and jungle—the primeval miseries of the small bands of wandering aborigines, worshipping fierce gods, living on roots and berries and small wild animals, at intervals hunting each other's heads; the miseries of the second-rate conquistadors who had come looking for gold and, finding none, had gone mad with disappointment and blood lust; the miseries of the slaves and their terrible revolts; the miseries of a fabricated statehood. The history of this patch of earth was written in blood. Pain was the only thing that had ever flourished on its red soil. Only in pain had they been self-sufficient. But, gradually, recognising the impossibility of escape, the yearning had died. Somehow, it had oozed away until she could say, not without truth, that she no longer cared what happened to her. Yet, to say it had oozed away was not quite correct. It would be more accurate to say that she had let it go . . . let go of it . . . and allowed the vision of redemption—those fleeting intimations of richness, of possibility, which sometimes welled up in her—to recede from her and eventually die. Was she to blame for what had happened to her? She did not think so. She had had no alternative.

There had never been much chance of her escaping; of her sailing away in a big, white ship. For she had come to understand that this place, however much it appalled her, ran in her blood. There was no escaping the hurt and deformity it had inflicted on her. Its sterility and pain were part of her sterility and pain. She could not be made new and uncontaminated. She would always carry its hurt, its presence, within her.

Miss Bertha had drifted off to sleep again and was snoring. Now and again she emitted startled grunts and seemed to be on the verge of choking to death. At other times she would break into an incoherent babble. Then she would fall quiet and the cycle would start all over again. She picked up one of the magazines piled on the glass table. The pages were tacky and fraying at the edges. She paused at an advertisement which showed a group of elegantly dressed men and women sitting at a candle-lit table. To judge from the picturesque disorder of knives and forks, crumpled napkins, scattered crumbs, bits of cheese and half-empty bottles of wine, they had just finished eating. A bowl-shaped lampshade hung low over the centre of the table. Cigarette smoke coiled up towards it. There was laughter on every face. Someone had evidently made a witty remark. Beyond the table was a marble fireplace heaped with glowing coal. Above it hung a mirror reproducing the happy scene.

Next door Miss Bertha wheezed and coughed and babbled. She idly turned the pages, pausing at another of the advertisements. This one showed a man on a white horse riding through a misty, sylvan landscape. A half-clad woman, freshly risen out of the foam of her luxurious ablutions, watched him dreamily from a window.

Next door Miss Bertha wheezed and coughed and dreamed of demons.

Putting aside the magazine, she listened to Madame's honeyed murmurings leaking through the partition. She was herself close to dozing off, beginning to dream of her own demons, when she was suddenly roused by the irruption of Madame and her client into the sitting-room.

'If you do as I tell you,' Madame was saying, 'everything will turn out to your advantage. Have no fear.'

The man mumbled self-effacingly. No doubt he was aware of her presence behind the curtain. She suspected Madame of relishing these situations.

'Come back and see me in a month's time.' Madame spoke like a doctor now. 'Let me know how you've progressed.'

The man promised that he would; the door opened and closed. His footfalls faded rapidly down the stairs. Madame returned to her studio. She was not called immediately because Madame liked to rest a little between her consultations. She experienced the tingle of anticipation that nearly always accompanied these moments. The effect produced was like that induced by a quick intake of alcohol. She surrendered to the illicit warmth of the sensation. After a few minutes Miss Bertha parted the screen and announced that Sister was ready to receive her.

Madame was sitting at a table placed in the centre of the room. Her head was thrown back and her eyes were closed. Her stubby fingers were splayed out on the edge of the table. Without opening her eyes Madame indicated by a languid, downward sweep of her plump arm that she should take a seat opposite her. Miss Bertha drew out the chair. She sat down. Miss Bertha retreated, glancing with nervous deference at her sister as she did so.

The studio was dark and airless. Madame did not stir. The noises of the city were muted by the closed windows. Along one wall was a narrow bed where Madame, when she was especially exhausted, was sometimes to be found lying with a damp towel covering her face. On the other side of the room was a glass-doored cabinet in which she stored the tools of her trade—manuals on palmistry, astrological charts, a crystal ball. To divert herself, she studied Madame's double chin, her thick, short neck, the smooth mounds of her cheeks which shone as if they had been dipped in oil, the flattened, gaping triangles of her nostrils.

Presently, Madame opened her eyes and lowered her head. She blinked rapidly.

'Well, my dear,' she murmured, her shining cheeks swelling into a smile, 'how can I help you? Tell me.'

ANTHONY BURGESS

THE END OF THE WORLD NEWS

'A feast for the reader... a brilliant extravaganza... Anthony Burgess's energy and imagination continue to astound. I can think of few living writers with the same vitality and encyclopaedic vision, the same eagerness to tackle the largest themes.' J.G. Ballard, *Guardian*

'Shows the virtuoso in his finest form' Paul Bailey, *Standard*

'Brilliant word play and so many exuberant ideas... Buy, read, enjoy' Nina Bawden, *Daily Telegraph*

HUTCHINSON £8.95

GRANTA

PHILIP NORMAN
OL' BLACK ROCK

Philip Norman was born in 1943 and was brought up on the Isle of Wight where his father operated the Amusement Arcade and Skating Rink at the end of Ryde Pier. He has written widely about Rock and Blues music for *The Sunday Times* and *The Times*, and, during 1976, he wrote the *Sunday Times* Atticus page. He is the author of *SHOUT! The True Story of the Beatles* and *The Skater's Waltz* and *The Road goes on Forever*.

P.T. saw them long before they reached the cabin. There were two in the car, a red Pinto—the kind Englishmen liked to rent—bumping up the track around the ploughed hill, scattering dust, chickens, and the brighter red cardinal birds. At the top they drew in behind P.T.'s old pick-up truck. One of them got out, slowly, like a nervous cop, using the car door for cover: that one had the recorder. The other, with cameras, slung them behind him as he stooped to lock the car. P.T. heard his loud yelp to feel static electricity, carried from some big city motel, still burning far into the poor lands of Tennessee.

'This must be it,' they told one another uncertainly across the car. For the road stopped here, above a barren slope where lumps of torn newspaper leapt and somersaulted. There was nothing beyond the cabin, with its earth wall, its tin roof, its strong points of wire and matchboard, all poised at the summit by some whim of the weather. A long, singing moan reached their ears from the wind in the deep-rutted earth. Yet again they conferred, and agreed: this ought to be the place.

The cabin door, beaten on hesitantly, opened a fraction to reveal a child, no more than five years old, barefoot, with hair gathered into little beribboned stooks.

'Is—Ol' Black Rock in there, please?'

The child did not answer, but only smiled indulgently at the voice's timbre. The door pushed wider to disclose P.T., a figure altogether reassuringly of this world.

'We called from Memphis,' one Englishman said. 'Jim Tarbutton sent us—from Kazoo Music.'

'Sure. C'mon in.' P.T. said, turning away the child under his hand. Grizzled grey fringed his powerful neck within a raised black-and-white plaid lumberjack collar. Across his barrel-like T-shirt could be seen part of some printed slogan. He stood aside for them, fingering a metal chronometer that lay loose on one hefty brown forearm.

The cabin had one room and eight inhabitants. Three children played on the dirt floor; at a single post in the centre, two young men leaned, intensely dolled-up in patent leather shoes and velvet caps, chewing gum they had not the means to purchase, snapping fingers to a rhythm they only hoped to hear. A young woman in a long pink ballgown was clearing pots and dishes, helped by a girl. Home life was recognizable, though in fragments that could never form a picture.

'We just got through eatin' breakfast,' P.T. explained. He had sat down on a small bed along the inner wall. 'Where you all from, you boys?'

The Englishman with the tape recorder opened it briskly by unfastening two clasps. He had a warm, soft, vibrant, disinterested voice.

'I work for radio, P.T. In London—you know? We met before, if you remember, when you and Ol' Black Rock came over with the Blues Caravan. That was sure a *great* show.'

'Yeah?' P.T. said, on a rising note of indifference. Mostly they said they remembered some show or Blues Caravan someplace, which was more than P.T. could do. Bright lights, a big, cold stage, were all P.T. remembered of London. And getting money, and a bottle.

'I'm putting together a big radio special, P.T.—Blues and Country Blues, right from the beginning,' the Englishman said, unravelling a large microphone, with doubtful glances at the children whose six snowy eyes studied his every movement. 'Steve here works for *Radio Times*. You know *Radio Times*?'

'M-hm,' P.T. assented. 'You want to do interview with Ol' Black Rock?'

'Right.' The Englishman seemed relieved to find himself understood. 'Is that okay?'

'No problem: he be right with you,' P.T. said. 'He ain't been feelin' so good.'

At the end of the cabin was a curtained recess, from which Ol' Black Rock now walked, helped by the young men and children. He was nearly brown bones, both eyes stuck fast with a thick yellow blindness, yet he crossed the floor delicately, unaware of his helpers. The flesh on his skull had shrunk to expose veins in an intricate pipework that twitched and fluttered with secret, unaccountable life. He wore two parts of an ancient grey suit, made sleek by decay, and his clean white shirt cuffs, folded back with almost conscious elegance, revealed a hospital plastic identity-tag worn like a charm on one skeletal wrist. He was guided to a chair, near the door, whereon his limbs arranged themselves as from memory in an attitude of sitting. A cigarette groped its way between his lips.

And you knew Blind Blake, isn't that right?'

The Englishman cupped the microphone under Ol' Black Rock's face, closer still lest the tape spools fail to catch that eerie, croaking voice in which all fences between the words had been blown down.

'Yeah. Blind Blake. We knowed him.'

'And Blind Boy Fuller?'

'Yeah. Blind Boy Fuller. We knowed him, too.'

'—and Barbecue Bob?'

'Yeah, we knowed him. Barbecue Bob.'

One of Ol' Black Rock's teenage sons, meanwhile, sidled up to the photographer and inquired nonchalantly: 'What you all drinkin' today?'

'—he had a barbecue stand; isn't that right?'

'Yeah. Barbecue Bob. We knowed him.'

'—I could go git it down at the liquor store,' whispered Ol' Black Rock's son. 'Just a six-pack o' beers.'

The victim, understanding, groped behind his camera; a five-dollar bill changed hands. They took P.T.'s truck away to fetch the beer.

'And Blind Lemon Jefferson, you know?'

'Yeah. Blind Jefferson.'

'When you were on Beale Street?'

'Yeah. Beale Street—'

'But he came from Texas, didn't he?'

'Yeah. Texas. We knowed him....'

'He was good with that knife, you know,' murmured P.T. from the bed.

'Yeah.' Ol' Black Rock nodded. 'Yeah. We knowed him.'

'—he was blind, man,' P.T. said. 'But he could take that knife, man, and cut you all to pieces. He'd catch where your voice was. Take a knife, he could, and cut you all to pieces—'

'—sorry, P.T.,' the Englishman said. 'Could we try to keep the background noise down? Otherwise...you know...the recording....' He leaned forward again, through the children, to Ol' Black Rock, glancing timidly at the needle which registered sound-level.

'And you knew Memphis Minnie, too, didn't you? Isn't that right?'

This cat fooled me, P.T. thought, just as he thought most every day....

This cat fooled me good. I must have been 'leven years old, he was round thirteen, fourteen. He'd come down around Snake Hollow, playin' for our country picnics, gettin' round two dollars for the engagement. Playin' was awful cheap then. My mom, she'd take out the beds in our cabin to make room, and set a table 'cross the kitchen door. My mom would cook catfish an' sell it, and they'd sell that ol' moonshine whisky, maybe git to shootin' craps in the barn. Late at night, it'd start to git rough. Somebody'd go shoot out all the lights.

I seen this guy at early mornin', comin' 'cross the fields, swingin' that old guitar. He seemed to me like a big city man back there in '29. He heard me playin' that harmonica—I had one o' them that cost a dime.

He say, 'Look man, you oughta come to town with me. Hitch your mule to the fence, and let's go.'

I said, 'You got to ask my mom.'

She said, 'Okay, but you all gotta bring him back tomorrow.'

So we went on down to Memphis. Nex' thing I know, we was in Arkansas. And we bin runnin' ever since....

You and P.T. rode the freight trains, isn't that right?'

'Yeah,' Ol' Black Rock nodded. 'Rode the freight trains. Me an' P.T. rode the freight trains.'

'Riding the boxcars?'

'Yeah, ridin' the boxcars. Me an' P.T., we rode the boxcars.'

Best was when you'd get to ride top deck. On the roof, that means. You'd ride the bumpers, maybe, in between the cars. Some nights, man, 'f you was pressed, you'd ride them iron rods they had lyin' long underneath. Him an' me, we'd lie together, ridin' them boxcar rods.

O Man, we had us a time, runnin' all over with Jimmie Rodgers—he was a good hobo, you know: he could do the beggin'. Nights, we'd git in one them hobo jungles by the railroad side, and they'd have some big pot cookin' with ever' kind o' meat in there that could be named. Turtles, man, they'd cut up for the pot. They'd have some ol' tin cup, you know—pick up an' dip an' pour into your cup. We'd set there, man, in the hobo jungle, an' git snug, and someone'd go git a bottle that whisky, that ol' moonshine, poison whisky, and we'd git half juiced-up there.

This cat used to be awful bad 'bout fightin', you know, while we was gettin' round. Why they gave him the name Ol' Black Rock was 'cause of an ol' black rock he toted in his pocket. He'd git to drinkin' and goin' with some woman, and he'd want to bull-do her, then some other guy step in there. This cat'd chonk him with that ol' black rock—knock hell outa the other fellow, then take off. Man, he light on his feet, but he sho' hit you.

Memphis used to be awful bad 'bout stickin' you up, on Beale Street, there. Stick-ups and bank robbin'; armed robbery. Confidence. O man: one of the confidencest places in the world! Droppin' the pigeon, they done. Some guy come outa the bank, and you'd confidence him outa what he got. We see all that stuff worked. We was musicians—those smart guys, they thought we's on the sunny side. Some sharp guy, he'd come up and say, 'Here's twenty dollars, man, put it in your pocket.' Him an' me, we'd git half juiced-up, start playin' there on Beale Street, the people come gangin' round. That was what the sharp guys wanted, so they could clip them pocketbooks.

This cat—he could sure hide money! I'd always be gettin' my pocket-book clipped, but this guy hid his in his shirt-tails. This guy had money tied up in his shirt-tails.

O man, the drinkin' we done back there. The fightin' and the runnin', man! This guy been hoboin' six to eight months, and he 'spects his girl-friend to be the same thing. He say, 'Where's all them little clothes I bought you: where they at?' And some bad guy sittin' on the bed. He'd always push me in! He'd say, 'Go on, git the guy, P.T., go git him!' And I was astoundin' nimble at that time. I'd really catch the guy an' handle him pretty good, 'fore I do too much an' have to leave town.

I done time, man. Ain't nobody ain't done no time in the penitentiary. If people try to hurt you—maybe git to rap at you with a knife—I'd find me that ol' scattergun, man, and—*boom*! They try to hurt me: I boom. I musta boom three, four guys, man, that tried to hurt me.

Two children crossed the cabin bringing Ol' Black Rock's guitar. It was an instrument devoid of history: no Ultratone or Nick Lucas Special, only a cheap, flat, mass-produced Japanese model, wired to a splintered wooden frame in which an old radio loudspeaker kept loose company with some feebly-glimmering valves. They fed the guitar to Ol' Black Rock, who grasped it like a drowning man, blind eyes cast to Heaven, while his fingers staggered over the frets. Children clustered round, picking and testing; a tattered chord buzzed through the valves. P.T., on the bed, had tipped a small harmonica from his pocket.

'"Railroad Bull"—you remember that one? Made that record in 1937. Let's hit 'em a lick on it, Black Rock.'

The tape recorder was German, one of a type in general use by contributors to music programmes. It could record with the utmost clarity voices that discoursed together smugly or pompously; losing no cadence of a question purposed to ingratiate; faultlessly reproducing each half-formed sentence, each vain non-sequitur in the reply. But here, on a three-legged stool in Tennessee, the tape recorder faltered, as if at the behest of draughts, as if called on to register psychic disturbance. That was the effect of Ol' Black's voice, unearthly, metallic, from a long-dead tongue; of the guitar which furred and buzzed on one lone, crouching chord. P.T., over at the bed, blew intelligible Blues perkily into his cupped hands, one thick leg stamping time. And the tape spools made a show of doing their work. The photographer moved in closer to Ol' Black Rock's chair. Senses laboured yet could not see, as that blind yellow eye plainly saw, the bodies of rags in ragged firelight; the dreary land, with boxcars passing endlessly across it.

Light died in the amplifier valve. Ol' Black Rock's son pulled the ring from his fourth can of Schlitz.

Both Englishman, somewhat belatedly, clapped their hands and exclaimed, 'Yeah!'

The interviewer added a perfunctory 'whew!' then leaned forward again. '"Railroad Bull". That was your first record for Okeh. Isn't that right?'

'Yeah—on Okeh,' Ol' Black Rock repeated. 'We done that on Okeh Records.'

'In Chicago.'

'Yeah, in Chicago. We made that one in Chicago.'

'We done the jug, too,' P.T. said. 'Ol' guitar, we never did have but five strings on it. Man—when he starts goin' blind, I see this cat run outa' a saloon—with some shootin' goin' on in there, you know—he's near blind, but he done got outa there somehow and went straight through a man's cornfield. This guy musta run clean through a six-strand wire fence. Them little guitar strings, you know, would hit a cornstalk, and with ever' 'ping', he'd run that much faster.'

'What was the personnel?' the interviewer resumed doggedly. 'On those early sessions for Okeh.'

'We done the jug, too,' Ol' Black Rock said.

'People on the street that heared us, they'd fill that jug up,' P.T. said. 'They'd put quarters and half-dollars in there.'

'Yeah, right,' the interviewer said, in a tone that dismissed the jug and its contents. 'I'd like to ask you, Black Rock—'

'They'd put quarters in,' Ol' Black Rock said. 'Sometimes they'd put half-dollars in there.'

'Mm—right!' the interviewer said, firmly. 'But the personnel on those early Okeh sessions—'

'Mel Williams, he was Okeh manager,' P.T. said. 'Workin' for them in Chicago. He walked up. The jug was full. People put quarters and half-dollars in there. Mel Williams told us, 'You all come up to my office, 166 Lake Shore Drive, tomorrow—you too good to be messin' round here.' So we went up an' made a record. And from then on, New York City. But we never could give up that habit. All that money in our pockets, and we *still* rode the freight trains. Ever' time Okeh Records sent us the money to come over, we'd go buy ourselves a pair overalls and catch the freight.'

'Those early sessions for Okeh,' the interviewer said, leaping for his chance as if it were moving boxcars—'"Railroad Bull", "Sometime Baby", "Puttin' my House on Fire": they all give you and P.T. as joint composers. Was there any set pattern to the way you got into writing songs?'

'I didn't catch you,' Ol' Black Rock said.

'I said—maybe P.T. would like to come in here...how about "Railroad Bull"? Did you write that to any set pattern?'

'Railroad bull? That what they'd call the guy that rode the freight trains,' P.T. said. 'He was special agent for the railroad company.'

'So—many of these songs were the result of direct personal ex—'

'They had Winchester Slim,' P.T. said. 'He was the railroad bull, rode the train from Scarboro' to Efrin'ham, from Efrin'ham down into Cairo. He had that *bad* Winchester rifle.'

'Special agent,' put in Ol' Black Rock suddenly.

'He made us git off the train at Cairo, but we was 'terminated to go anyway, 'cause we had those people's money, you know, at Okeh Records.'

'Right,' the interviewer nodded, having ceased to pay attention some moments earlier. 'Can we break off a moment, fellas, while I turn the tape over?'

The photographer, who had grown steadily more fascinated, sat back on his cowboy heels and said, 'I bet they never paid you all that much.'

'A few bucks,' P.T. agreed. 'Jus' a few bucks and—boom. Gone. Drink and foolishness like that. At Okeh, man, they got rich off of us. They musta made a couple million dollars off that "Railroad Bull", the one we just quit playin'. A couple million dollars.'

Ol' Black Rock's fingers collapsed on a different chord. Opening his gums, he sang, 'I'll be Glad When you Dead, you Rascal you', by way of a spectral grin. P.T. joined him on kazoo. The song, full of misplaced joy and buoyancy, faded before adjustments to the tape recorder were complete. P.T. looked at Ol' Black Rock, who remained grinning after the last echoes.

'This here is *the* you-rascal-you, man,' P.T. said fondly. 'This cat ruin me. I can't go to tell howsomany times he come along and say, "I got me a trailer, P.T., let's go." I'd say, "I just got married, man, I cain't leave. I done messed up so much." I been married ten times—Ol' Black Rock take me 'way from all on 'em. And I'd do same for him when he got himself a good woman. We'd take off together down them dusty roads.'

'Friends, eh?' the photographer said, holding up his light meter.

'I'd get mad ever' so often when we was paid off, and we'd git to cussin' each other. Once, while we was cussin' each other, this guy,' P.T. said with admiration, 'this guy fell plumb in one them big vats they cooks whisky in! He was steppin' too high, I guess. 'Cause I saved this cat's life, you know, when he was like to git drownded one

time. Some big Model A car run us right in the Mississippi River. This
guy's floatin' in there like a drownded rat. I save his life, man. I bust
the windshield an' bring him out. His eyes swelled up like that with
water. We'd raise devil once in a while.' P.T. guffawed under the
ogling lens. 'Buckin' 'gainst one another—I'd git mad at him, he cuss
a while, we threaten each other. He done took away my best
woman—Lord, I hated him back there for a while. Wanted to cut him
an' see some of his blood.'

'Don't you have a family, P.T.?'

'Well...yeah.' He glanced round the cabin, at the children who
were mothers, at the mothers almost children still. 'Yeah—I'm gettin'
me a family. A-all the time. I got Black Rock's oldest girl now. Maybe
I stick with her—*maybe*. We both sick, tired ol' men now. 'f I take off,
man, I know this cat be right behind me, tho' he so old and blind. I'd
take off at night but he find me at mornin'. We always run into a good
break, you know, 'soon as we get off on our feet. 'Soon as we start
playin', why then we always hit. Only trouble's the freight trains they
got today. Them ol' coal-burners, all you had to do was run along and
git on there. These here diesel engines jerk one plumb off the track.'

The photographer leaned forward, peering into the glutinous
yellow eye. 'You still feel the Blues the same, Black Rock?'

His face turned, comprehending. 'The same.'

'Is it a sad or a happy feeling?'

'Happy feelin'.'

'When I gets to playin' this harmonica,' P.T. said, 'I'm like to feel
pretty full o' the Blues at times. Then him an' me, we puts the Blues on
each other. That makes both on us feel good.'

The interviewer sat back at last from his tape recorder, the spools
of which remained motionless.

'No joy,' he said. 'I'm afraid it's all gone phut somewhere inside.'
He began, quite cheerfully, to rewind the microphone lead. 'Hey, well
thanks anyway,' the interviewer said, again cheerfully, for
incompetence brings its own kind of relief. 'It was really great
meeting you, Black Rock...P.T.'

'Glad you all came over,' P.T. said.

Ol' Black Rock sat with fingers stuck to the last chord, still
studying a vista no one else had seen.

'Listen, I'd still like very much to have you on the programme. It just means we'll have to get by with archive material. P.T.—before I forget—you wouldn't happen to have any of your old Okeh recordings, would you, that I could take back? They'd be great to use on the programme.'

'We ain't got no phonograph,' P.T. said.

'Okay—no sweat. Only, we may have to feature your stuff by other artists. B.B. King's done a lot, hasn't he?'

'B.B. King, sure. He done plenty our things.'

'And Tina Turner even! She did a great version of "Puttin' my House on Fire". I'll have a good look around in Memphis at the Blue Light. It's a great record store, that. And anyway'—the interviewer laughed—'it's all on expenses. Well—goodbye, Black Rock...P.T., thanks...and Black Rock's lady, is this?' He extended an almost Royal hand. 'Goodbye. This is a really nice place you've got.'

The young woman, in her pink-ribboned ballgown, lifted up fierce and injured eyes.

'It's a no 'count place,' she murmured.

'You all see that dress she's wearin'?' P.T. said. 'That dress was made a hun'ed years ago.'

P.T. accompanied them outside, shook hands firmly with each, and inquired, 'Where you all stayin' at Memphis?'

'The Rivermont.'

'Oh.' He came in closer, looking worried and sliding the chronometer along his wrist. He seemed about to warn them off The Rivermont. 'Folks usually pay us, you know,' he said. 'After we done played a little set for 'em.'

The interviewer was entirely taken aback by this. He had forgotten the warning that black people always try to rip you off. He glanced into his wallet, but saw only a ten-dollar bill. His colleague, meanwhile, handed over fifty dollars. The bill vanished, without undue thanks, into P.T.'s plaid coat.

They drove in silence—for they were starting to hate each other—back down the ploughed hill, where wings of old newspaper still fluttered and gambolled in the wind. At the bottom, by a corrugated liquor store, they regained the Brownsville highway.

Two miles on, the interviewer gave a yelp: 'I left the bloody mike back there!'

The cabin remained clinging to the hilltop, but P.T.'s pick-up truck no longer stood outside.

Inside they were washing clothes. Ol' Black Rock's young wife, in her hundred-year-old ballgown, glanced up at the Englishman without surprise. The microphone lay where he had left it, on a chair.

Beyond the raised curtain, Ol' Black Rock had been arranged along the edge of a grey blanket. His skull's cheek rested pensively on joined fingertips. The Englishman drew near, as one brought to view a corpse.

'So long, Black Rock. I just came back for...'

An arm arose suddenly, like a cobra. A wrist, in its hospital identity tag, gripped the Englishman's white one with unusual strength. The blind yellow eyes glared into his, then, suspiciously, towards the door.

'How much?' Ol' Black Rock whispered. 'How much was it you give P.T. to gimme? I don' trust that sonofabitch.'

EASTERN ARTS ASSOCIATION

The Regional Arts Association for the East of England:
Norfolk, Suffolk, Cambridgeshire, Bedfordshire, Essex
and Hertfordshire

Support for Literature

Visiting Writers Scheme:
The largest scheme in the country for visiting writers in schools and
community workshops.

Creative Writing Courses:
Up to 20 courses a year at residential colleges in the region.

Festivals:
The Cambridge Poetry Festival and Essex Festival of Contemporary
Literature.

Support for Literary Groups and Societies.

Writing Fellowships in Community and University
Including the University of East Anglia Fellowship.

Small Press Distribution Scheme
At St Mary Arts Centre, Colchester.
First Scheme of its kind.

Financial Assistance for Literary Magazines
Including GRANTA.

Literature Officer (Laurence Staig)
Eastern Arts Association
8/9 Bridge Street, Cambridge CB2 1UA
Cambridge (0223) 67707

GRANTA

CHRISTOPHER PRIEST
THE MIRACULOUS
CAIRN

Wolfgang Suschitzky

Christopher Priest was born in 1943 in Cheadles, a suburb of Manchester. He was educated at Manchester Warehouseman, Clerk's Orphan School, and, after leaving school, held a wide variety of jobs. Since 1968, he has lived entirely from his writing, which includes six novels, two story collections, and one children's book. His work has been translated into a number of languages including Hebrew, Japanese, Russian, and Bulgarian.

The island of Seevl lies like a dark shadow over my memories of childhood. It was always physically there, sprawling across the horizon opposite Jethra Harbour, blurring sometimes into the low clouds of storms, standing out at other times as a black, rugged outline against the southern sky. Its landscape was not unlike that of the mountains around Jethra, but there was a saying among us that the rocks and soil our ancestors had no use for had been thrown out to sea to make Seevl.

The closeness of Seevl to Jethra had created an inevitable bond—family ties, trading agreements, old alliances—but although to the Jethrans it was just an off-shore island, politically it was a part of the Dream Archipelago. Journeys between mainland and island were forbidden, except with official permission from the Seigniory, but a ferry still ran every day in defiance of the ban, openly and commercially. Officialdom turned a blind eye, because trade was important to Jethra, and crucial to Seevl. I myself travelled to Seevl many times, three or four times a year, for several years of my childhood.

It was twenty years since I had visited Seevl, and sixteen years since leaving Jethra. The last time I saw the city was when I left to go to university in Old Haydl, and I had never returned. Twenty years of mixed fortune, with most of the success on the surface, misleadingly. I had a passable education, an interesting career. I had avoided war-service so far, and was now probably too old to be caught up in it, except incidentally. Many friends of my own age (I was thirty-four) had volunteered, but it was not for me. As a teacher I was officially exempted, and if I searched my conscience I knew that the work I was doing was more useful than any war-work might have been. I had done well in teaching, or well enough to have self-esteem and the respect of my colleagues.

In my private life, though, those twenty years had been less successful, and it was returning to Jethra, with Seevl looming on the horizon, that brought it to mind.

Jethra was the old capital of our country, but because of the war and the need for decentralized government, there had been an exodus to the newer, ·less exposed cities inland. There was still a token government presence in Jethra, but the Seignior's Palace was unoccupied, and the Senate House had been bombed at the outbreak of war. Now there was just the fishing, and a certain amount of light industry, and Jethra had become a large, desolate ghost of a city.

A return to the place of childhood is a gathering of reminders. For me, Jethra was life with my parents, schooling, old friends with whom I had lost contact...and Seevl. Not an uncommon grouping of memories, perhaps, but between them they had the effect of reminding me of what I had become. This became clear as I sat on the train going to Jethra, thinking of the past. I had not actually chosen to make this journey—because there was family business I had to resolve—but neither did I make it unwillingly. I was curious to see Jethra again, and nervous of travelling to Seevl, but I felt it was time, after twenty years, to confront the past.

When I was a child, the closeness of Seevl had a foreboding quality for everyone, and certainly for the other children at school. 'Send you to Seevl,' was the ultimate childish threat, with unstated connotations of eternal damnation and terror. In our alternate world of invented myth, Seevl was populated by bogeymen and creeping horrors, and the actual landscape of the island was thought to be a nightmare terrain of crevasses and volcanic pools, steaming craters and shifting rocks. This vision was as true for me, in an imaginative sense, as it was for all Jethran children, but with a child's unconscious ability to see the world from a number of different viewpoints, I also knew Seevl for what it really was.

It was no less horrifying to me in reality, but its horrors were acutely personal.

I was an only child. My parents, both Jethrans, had had another child before me, but she had died a year before I was born. I came into a world where my life was guarded, for reasons I could not begin to understand until I had almost grown up. In some ways I can now sympathize with the protective way my parents brought me up, but it meant that when I was more than just a child: in my early and middle teens, I was still being treated as some precious object that had to be guarded against all the possible dangers and threats of life. While youngsters of my own age were hanging around in gangs, and getting into scrapes, and learning about sex, I was expected to be at home, sharing my parents' friends and interests. These were numerous, and although some were not uninteresting, they were hardly the normal activities of a teenager. Other filial duties, though, I entered into with a sense of duty and numb acceptance, suppressing the urge to evade them. The most unwelcome of these was to go with my parents on their regular visits to see my father's brother on Seevl.

My Uncle Torm was a few years younger than my father, but had married at about the same time: there was a photograph in our living-room of the two young men with their brides, and although I recognized the youthful versions of my father, mother, and uncle easily enough, it took me years to realize that the pretty young woman holding Torm's arm in the photograph was my Aunt Alvie.

In the picture she was smiling, and I had never seen Alvie smile. She was wearing a gay, flowery dress, and I had never seen Aunt Alvie in anything except an old nightgown and a patched cardigan. Her hair was short and wavy, cut attractively about her face, and Aunt Alvie's hair was long and greasy and grey. And the girl in the picture was standing beside her new husband, raising one leg to show her knee coquettishly to the camera, and my Aunt Alvie was a bedridden cripple.

Torm and Alvie had moved to Seevl soon after their marriage just before the war started. He had taken a clerical job at a catholic seminary in the remotest part of the Seevl mountains; his reasons for this I do not understand to this day, but I do know that it caused a bitter, if short-lived, row between him and my father.

They were there with their new baby on Seevl when war broke out, and were unable to return to Jethra. By the time the war had settled into its interminable routine of attritional skirmishes, in which a certain amount of movement between Seevl and Jethra was possible, Aunt Alvie had been taken ill and was not to be moved.

It was in this climate that my parents made their occasional week-end visits to Seevl to see Torm and Alvie, taking me with them. For me, they were week-ends of unrelieved dreariness and depression: a voyage to a bleak, windswept island, to a cramped and dark house on the edge of a moor, a house where a sickbed was the centre of attention, and where the conversations were at best about other adult relatives and at worst about sickness and pain and false hopes of a miraculous recovery. The only distraction from all this, and the ostensible reason for my being there, was Torm and Alvie's daughter, my cousin Seri. She was a few months older than me, plump and rather stupid, and we were the worst kind of companions to each other. The prospect of her company did nothing to relieve those long days of dread before a visit, and afterwards the memory of it did nothing to help me recover from the profound moods of depression that always followed.

As I left the station, a young woman in Seigniorial uniform opened a car door and walked across to me.

'Are you Lenden Cros?' she said to me.

'Yes.'

'I am Serjeant Reeth. I am your escort.'

We went to the car, and I placed my bag on the back seat. She held the door open for me, like a chauffeuse, but before I was properly seated she walked around to her own side. She started the engine.

'Where are we going?' I said.

'The ferry does not sail until the morning. We will stay overnight at the Grand Shore Hotel.'

She drove out of the station square, and turned into a main road leading towards the centre. I watched the buildings of the city through the window. We had lived in the suburbs, and I knew the centre only superficially. I recognized buildings, names of streets; and some had vague but poignant associations for me. As a child, I had known Jethra's centre as the place where my father worked, where my mother sometimes went shopping; and the street names were landmarks from their territory. The city now looked disused and unloved: there were office blocks, shops, civic buildings, but many of them were boarded up and litter blew across the steps. There was not much traffic in the streets: several cars in various stages of decay, a few trucks, a surprising number of horse-drawn vehicles.

We were held up for a few seconds at a large intersection.

I said: 'Are you from Jethra?'

'No.'

'You seem to know where you are going.'

'I arrived this morning. I've had time to explore.'

The traffic moved on, and the conversation ended.

I had never stayed at the Grand Shore Hotel, had never even

been through its doors. It was the largest, most expensive hotel in town. In my childhood it had been the scene of society weddings, business conferences, and many glittering civic occasions. We drew up in the car park outside the main entrance, with its imposing and solid fâcade of smoke-dirtied red brick.

Serjeant Reeth stood back as I registered. The clerk pushed across two pieces of white card for my signature. One was for a room in my own name, the other, an adjacent number, was for Serjeant Reeth.

A porter took my bag, and led us up the wide, curving staircase to the next floor. There were mirrors and chandeliers, a plush carpet on the stairs, gold paint on the plaster ceiling-mouldings...but the mirrors were unpolished, the carpet was worn and the paint was peeling. The hotel's grandeur was inherited from the days before the war. The muted sounds of our climbing seemed like memories of those famous parties of the past.

The porter opened the door to my room, and went in ahead of me. Serjeant Reeth went to her own door and inserted the key. For a moment she glanced back at me, and something in her expression took me by surprise: I detected a curiosity, a quick interest?

I tipped the porter, and he left. He had placed my bag on a low table by the door, so I took out my clothes and hung them in the wardrobe. I went to the basin, washed off the grime from the train journey, and put on clean clothes. Then I sat on the edge of the bed and looked around at the dingy room.

It was an unexpected position from which to contemplate my past; I had imagined that we would go straight across to Seevl, and had not realized that we were, of course, dependent on the ferry. How were we to spend the evening? I supposed the policewoman would have arranged that, too.

I recalled the look that Serjeant Reeth had given me, as we went into our rooms. She reminded me of someone I had once known, a girl of about the same age, with similar build and colouring. She was one of many lovers I had had at one time, when a succession of young women had passed through my life. Perhaps if I had met Serjeant Reeth then, she would have been one of them, but I was older now. I knew that such affaires almost always ended in emotional disaster; I had had no casual pick-ups for years, preferring the less intense discontents of sexlessness. Serjeant Reeth was the same sort of reminder of the past as Jethra itself had become, and she induced in me much the same quality of depression....

I was thirsty, so I left my room and went towards the staircase, thinking I would visit the bar. When I reached the head of the stairs I thought I should, out of politeness, see if the policewoman wanted to join me.

She answered my knock at her door after only a moment's delay, as if she had been standing there, waiting for me.

'I'm going downstairs for a drink,' I said. 'Will you join me?'

'That would be nice. Thank you.'

We went downstairs and found the bar. It was locked, and there were no lights on inside. We went into the lounge, rang a bell, and in a moment an elderly waiter came to serve us.

When he had taken our order and left the lounge, I said, making conversation: 'Have you worked as an escort before, Serjeant Reeth?'

'No...this is the first time.'

'Does the work come up very often?'

'I'm not sure. I have only been in the Seigniory for a year.'

Just then the waiter returned with our drinks.

'Will you be dining in this evening?' he said to me.

'Yes.'

When he had gone, I looked around the lounge; we were the only people there. I liked the airy, gracious feeling in the room, with its big windows and long velvet drapes, the high Consortship light shades, and the broadbacked wicker chairs grouped around the low tables. There were dozens of potted plants, great spreading ferns and tall parlour-palms, lending a feeling of sedate livingness to an otherwise decaying hotel. All the plants were green and alive, so someone must still be looking after them, dusting them, watering them.

We sat in silence for several minutes, and I had plenty of opportunity to try to assess my companion of the next day or two. I placed her age at about twenty-four or five. She was no longer wearing her cap, but the uniform—stiff, sexless, and unflattering—effectively neutered her. She wore no make-up, and her hair was drawn back into a bun. She seemed shy and uncommunicative, and unaware of my regard.

At last, it was she who broke the silence.

'Have you been across to Seevl before?'

'I was taken there several times as a child,' I said. 'What about you?'

'No.'

'Do you know what it's like there?'

'I'm told it's bleak. Is that how you remember it?'

'More or less. It's twenty years since I was there. It won't have changed much.' I tried my drink, swallowing much of it, hoping it would ease the conversation. 'I used to hate going across there. I always dreaded it.'

'Why?'

'Oh...the mood of the place, the scenery,' I said vaguely, avoiding specific memories. The seminary, Alvie, the open moors, and the dead towers. 'I can't describe it. You feel it as soon as you land.'

'You sound like my brother. He says he can always tell if a house is haunted.'

'I didn't say the place was haunted,' I said, quick to the defence. 'It's a question of the landscape. And the wind...you can always hear the wind.'

Jethra itself was built in the shadow of the Murinan Hills, but beyond these, to the west, was a wide, straight valley that led northwards into the foothills of the northern range. For all but a few short weeks at the height of summer, a polar wind came down the valley and escaped out to sea, whining across Seevl's treeless fells and moors. Only on the eastern side of the island, nearest to Jethra, were there villages of any size, and the only port, Seevl Town, was there. One of my clearest childhood memories of Seevl was seeing it in the springtime. I could look out to the south from my bedroom window, and see the blossom shining pink and white and bright red on the trees along the boulevards in Jethra, and beyond, out in the blue Midway Sea, there would be Seevl, still with its wintertime crust of snow.

Serjeant Reeth's mention of a brother had given me, for the first time, a little information about her background. I asked her about him. He was also in the Seigniory, she told me, serving with the Border Police. He was hoping for promotion, because his unit was soon to be shipped across to the southern continent. The war was still confused and confusing: neither side would admit to being the first to send an expeditionary force to the south—claims and counter-claims came from both sides—but almost every week there was news of more troops being sent out. That very morning, before setting out from home to catch the train, I had heard government claims that the enemy was building a transit-camp on one of the islands in the Dream Archipelago. If this was true, it marked a new stage in the war, because the political status of the islands was controlled by a Covenant of Neutrality.

It was a precarious state of the neutrality that had involved me with the Seigniory: the request from the Father Confessor that I should visit my uncle's house to sort out his belongings had been channelled through the Seigniorial Visa Department. If it had come direct to me, if the priests at the seminary had had my address, I could have slipped across unofficially. But that was not to be. Thus my need to be escorted, thus Serjeant Reeth.

I was telling her the reason for my trip—the need to sign papers, to permit furniture to be burned or given away—when the waiter returned. He was carrying two menus, discreetly implying that the dining-room staff were ready for us. While we perused the menu, the waiter drew the curtains, then led us down the corridor to the dining-room.

My last visit to Seevl. I was fourteen.

There were examinations at school and I was trying to concentrate on them, but I knew that at the end of the week we were going to see my uncle and aunt and cousin. It was summer, and Jethra was dusty and windless. Sitting by my bedroom window, distracted from my revision, I looked frequently out to sea. Seevl was green then, a dark, tough green; a coloured lie, a deceit of lushness. Day followed day, and I thought about feigning illness: a migraine attack, a sudden bout of gastro-enteritis, but at last the day arrived and there was no avoiding it. We were out of the house soon after dawn—in the cool, lovely light of summer, when no one else is about—and hurried down to the stop to catch the first tram of the day.

What were these visits for? Unless my parents spoke in some adult code I have never been able to decipher, they went out of a combination of habit, guilt, and family obligation. I never heard anything of interest discussed, in the way I now know educated adults can discuss matters (and both my parents were educated, and so was my uncle, although I cannot be sure about Alvie); there was news to impart, but it was stale news, trivial events in the family, not even interesting when fresh. Everything that passed between the four adults was familial or familiar: an aunt or cousin who had moved house or changed jobs, a nephew who married, a great-uncle who had died. Sometimes, photographs were passed around Alvie's sickbed: Cousin Jayn's new house (hasn't he done well?), or this is us on holiday, or isn't she a lovely baby? Family banality it was; it seemed so when I was a child and it seems so now. It was as if they had no ideas they could externalize, no sense of the abstract; or, if they had, it was deemed dangerous, not to be spoken of. News of the family and old conversations revisited were a levelling device: it was almost as if they were instilling a sense of mediocrity into Alvie, to bring her to their level, to make her, that is, no longer ill. Mediocrity as medicine.

And where were their recollections? Did they have no past together that they could reminisce about? My only hint of this forgotten past was the photograph taken before I was born, the one in our living-room. I was genuinely fascinated by it. When was it taken, and where? What were they doing that day? Who took the photograph? Was it a happy day, as seemed from the picture, or did something occur later to mar it? Why did none of them ever mention it?

It was probably Alvie's sickness. It suffused everything in past and present: her pain, her discomfort, her doctor, and her pills. Death surrounded Alvie's sickbed, and occupied it. The disease was creeping through her. Every time we visited her she was a little worse. First her legs lost all sensation; then she became incontinent; then she could not take solid food. But if her decline was steady, it was also slow. News of further deterioration came by letters, so that whenever I saw her I did so with the prospect of seeing her arms withering, or her face decaying away, or her teeth falling out; the ghoulish imagination of childhood was never satisfied, disappointed even, once I had resigned myself to having to visit her again. There was always an inverse surprise: how well she looked! Only later, as the depressing news was exchanged, would we hear of new horrors, new agonies. Yet the years dragged by and Alvie was still there in her bed, propped up by eight or nine pillows, her hair in a lank skein over one shoulder. She grew fatter and paler, more grotesque, but these changes would happen to anyone who never got exercise, who never went outside. Her spirit was unfailing: her voice was always pitched on one note, sounding sad and dull and dreary, but the things she said were self-consciously normal. She reported her pain and setbacks; she did not complain about them. She knew the disease was killing her, but she talked of the future, even if it was a future of the narrowest vision (what would I like for my next birthday,what was I going to do when I left school?). She was an example to us all.

Whenever we made our visits, one of the priests would come in to see Alvie. I always suspected that no one ever came from the seminary unless there was someone there from the outside world to witness it. Alvie had 'courage'; she had 'fortitude'; she 'bore her cross'. I hated the priests in their black clothes, waving their white hands sanctimoniously over the bed, blessing not only Alvie but my family, too. I sometimes thought it was the priests who were killing her; they were praying not for a cure but a lingering death, and they were doing it to make a theological point to their students. My uncle was godless, his job was just a job. There was Hope in religion, and to prove it to him the priests were killing Alvie: no one works in the service of the Lord as one toils in the vineyards. We shall save.

The last visit....

The boat was late; the man in the harbour office told us the engine was being repaired, and for a joyous moment I thought the trip would have to be cancelled...but then the ferry appeared in the harbour, coming slowly to the quay to collect us and the handful of other passengers who stood with us.

It seemed, as soon as the boat was outside the harbour, that we were almost upon Seevl: the grey, limestone cliffs were dead ahead; but it was an hour's voyage to Seevl Town, the boat swinging far out to sea to avoid the shoals beneath Stromb Head, then turning in again to take the sheltered passage beneath the cliffs. I stood apart from my parents, staring up at the cliffs, watching for occasional glimpses of the high fells beyond, and feeling the onset of the real, stomach-turning dread I always felt as we arrived. It was cold at sea, and though the sun was rising quickly, the wind came curling down on to the passage from the cliffs above. My parents were in the bar with the other passengers, and I shared the deck with crates of livestock, packing-cases, newspapers, cases of drink, two tractors.

The houses of Seevl Town, built up in terraces on the hills around the harbour, were constructed from the grey rock of the island, the roofs whitened around the chimney-stacks with bird droppings. An orange lichen clung to the walls and roofs, souring the houses, making them seem not warm, but crumbling. On the highest hill, dominating the town, stood the derelict remains of a rock-built tower. I never looked directly at this, fearing it.

As the boat glided in on the still water my parents came out of the saloon and stood beside me, one on each side, like an escort, preventing flight.

There was a car to be hired in Seevl Town; an expensive luxury in Jethra, but a necessity for the wild interior of the island. My father had booked it a week before, but it was not ready and we had to wait an hour or more in a cold office overlooking the harbour. My parents were silent, trying to ignore me as I fidgeted and made fitful attempts to read the book I had brought.

Around Seevl Town were the few farms on the island, rearing their scrawny animals and growing their hybrid cereals on the barren soil of the eastern side. The road climbed up through these small holdings, following the perimeters of the fields, and turning through sharp angles and steep climbing corners. The surface had been metalled once but now it was decaying, and the car lurched uncomfortably in the potholes and the wheels often spun on the gravelly sides. My father, driving, stayed silent, trying to master not only the dangerous road but also the controls of the unfamiliar vehicle; my mother sat beside him with the map, ready to direct him, but we always got lost on Seevl. I sat in the back, ignored by them both, except when my mother would turn to see what I was doing; I always did nothing, staring out of my window in mute suspension of thought.

It took nearly an hour to reach the first summit of the fells, by which time the last farm, the last hedge, the last tree, were miles behind us. There was a last glimpse of Seevl Town as the road went over the crest, and a wide view of the gun-metal sea, flecked with islets and the indistinct shape of the mainland coast.

On the moors the road rose and fell with the whim of the country, winding through the scrub-covered land. Sometimes, the car would come out from a high pass, where on each side great crags of limestone loomed over the scree slopes, and the blast of wind from the north would kick the car to the side. My father drove slowly, trying to avoid the loose rocks on the road and the potholes; the map lay unconsulted on my mother's knee, because Father knew the way. Yet he always made mistakes, took the wrong turn or followed the wrong fork, and then Mother would sit quietly at his side until he realized. The map would be taken from her, the car would be reversed, and we would go back the way we had come to the place where we went wrong.

I left all this to them, although, like Mother, I usually knew when we went wrong. My interest was not with the road, but the landscape it passed through. I never failed to be appalled by the gigantic emptiness of Seevl, and Father's wrong turnings had for me the double advantage of not only delaying our eventual arrival at the seminary, but also of opening up more of the island to my eyes. The road often passed the dead towers of Seevl. I knew the islanders never went near these, but I did not know why; whenever the car passed one, I could scarcely look towards it for fear, but my parents never even noticed. If we passed slowly, I would cower in my seat in anticipation of some ghoul of legend making a rush for the car.

Later in the journey the road itself deteriorated into a rough track, consisting of two gravel paths divided by a strip of long, coarse grass that scraped against the floor of the car.

Another hour passed, and then the road went down into a shallow valley where four of the dead towers stood like sentinels along the ridge. The valley was treeless, but there were many sprawling thorn-bushes, and in the lowest part, beside a wide stream, was a tiny hamlet with a view of the sea and the mainland. A part of Jethra could be seen: a black spread against the side of the Murinan Hills, and it seemed close and foreign. Outside the village we climbed the high fells again, and I looked forward to one of the scenic surprises of the journey: the island was narrow for a distance and crossing the moors the road touched on the southern side. For a few minutes we had a view of the Midway Sea beyond Seevl, with island after island spreading across it as far as the horizon. I never really considered Seevl to be a part of the Dream Archipelago. That was a different place: a lush, tropical maze of islands, hot and tranquil, forested or barren...but always dozing in the equatorial sun, and peopled by a strange race with customs and language as bizarre as their food, clothes and homes. But this fleeting glimpse, from the window of a car lurching along an unmade road on a cold grey island, was as close as I would ever be. The rest was dream.

Another valley; another hamlet. I knew we were approaching the seminary, and in spite of myself I was staring ahead, looking for the first sight of it.

After dinner, Serjeant Reeth and I returned to our rooms, she because she said she wanted a bath and to wash her hair, and I because I could think of nowhere else to go. I sat for a while on the edge of my bed, staring at the carpet, then went to my suitcase and found the letter from the Father Confessor at the seminary. It was strange to read his ponderous, circumlocutionary sentences, full of a stiff intent—meant not only to engage my sympathies, but also to intimidate me—and to try to reconcile this with my adolescent bitterness about him and his priests. I remembered one occasion of many: I had been walking on a lawn at the seminary, innocently close to one of the flowerbeds, and a priest had appeared and reprimanded me severely. They could never leave it at that, because they had insights into the universe and I did not, and so I was warned of hell and my imminent and inevitable destiny. That priest was possibly now this reverend father, and the same implied threat was there: you must attend to your uncle's affairs, or we will fix the fates for you.

I lay back on the bed, thinking about Seevl, and wondering what it would be like to return. Would it depress me, as Jethra had done in the afternoon? Or would it scare me, as it had done in childhood? The priests and their heavenly machinations held no terror for me; Alvie was dead, and now so was Torm, both joining my parents, and a generation was gone. The island itself—as scenery, as a place—interested me, because I had only ever seen it with child's eyes, but I did not look forward to its emptiness. The dead towers...they were another matter, one I put aside. I had never come to terms with those, could only shun them as the islanders did. The difference, though, the factor that wrenched me into adult perspective, was the presence of Serjeant Reeth.

Her name was Bella; this she told me during dinner, and I, with wine inside me, had been unable to stop myself smiling. I had not

213

known that policewomen had names like Bella, but there it was. She had an innocent quality to her, a certain wide-eyed ingenuousness; I liked it, but it made me feel my age. It seemed during the meal that our roles were reversing—that I, being older, was becoming her guardian for the journey. It had been too easy to forget that she was a member of the Seigniory, that if I spoke too freely or took her into my confidence, what I said might go into her report, might find its way on to a file.

Now I was alone again, it became a matter of personal reassurance. However much I might rationalize my fears, I did feel considerable trepidation about visiting Seevl again. If my Seigniory escort had been someone else—a man, perhaps, or someone older than myself—I might have indulged in psychological dependence on them...but because Bella was who she was, I felt differently. It would be I who took her to Seevl, not the other way around.

It was still too early to go to bed, so I found a book in my case, and lay on the bed to read it. Some time later, I was subconsciously aware that Bella must have returned to her room, because I heard her moving around.

Then, making me start a little, there was a tap on my door.

'Yes?' I called.

'Are you asleep, Lenden?'

'No...come in.'

The door opened, and she put her head round. She had a towel wrapped about her hair.

'I'm sorry to be a nuisance, but I'm trying to dry my hair. The plug on my drier is the wrong one. You haven't got an adapter, have you, or a screwdriver so I can change the plug?'

She came into the room, closing the door behind her. I stared at her in surprise. She had changed out of her uniform, and was wearing a loose, silken wrap. Her face was pink, and where her robe was open at the neck I could see her skin had that glowing cleanliness that follows a hot bath. The wrap was thin and white, and I could not help but see that she was full-breasted, dark-nippled. Damp ringlets of hair fell from under the towel.

'I've got a penknife,' I said, trying not to reveal my reaction. 'We can take a plug off something in here.'

She stood by the door, holding her electric drier as I looked around for some appliance I could plunder. There was an electric radiator by the wall, but it had no independent plug. Then I saw the bedside lamp.

'Turn on the central light,' I said. 'I'll use this.'

'I know it sounds stupid,' she said, and gave me a little embarrassed smile. 'I have to dry my hair like this, otherwise it goes frizzy.'

I found my penknife, and started to unscrew the plug. She made me feel capable.

'Sit down, Bella. It'll only take a couple of minutes.'

She sat on the edge of the bed, folding one knee over the other, while I knelt on the floor, picking at the screws of the plug with the knife-blade. I did not look up at her; I was suddenly too conscious of her presence, her young body, her casually revealing wrap.

At last I got the plug off.

'Give me the drier,' I said, looking up at her. The towel had loosened, and more hair was falling free. I wanted to reach up and stroke it. She put a hand to the towel, rubbed it gently against her head with an up-and-down motion.

She said: 'Do you think we're the only people staying in the hotel?'

'It's very quiet. I haven't see any other guests.'

The closed bar, the silent lounge. We had been alone at dinner, the lights on around our table, but the rest of the room in darkness. The attentive waiter, standing by the serving-door, had been responsive to every move we made, every request. And the menu had been a full one; the food had been freshly cooked, and was attractively served.

'I looked in the register this morning,' Bella said. 'No one else has booked in for more than a week.'

I looked up at her, but quickly bent my head over the plug. She was still towelling her hair; as she raised her arm she stretched the thin fabric of the robe across her body. The garment was working loose.

'It's the quiet season,' I said.

'I tried room-service just now, to see about the plug. No one answered.'

I screwed the back on the plug, and passed the drier up to her.

'That's fixed it,' I said.

'Do you mind if I dry my hair here? It won't take long, and I'd like company.'

I sat opposite her, in the one easy-chair in the room. She leaned down to connect the drier, then unwound the towel and played the warm stream of air over her. She swung her head, loosening the hair, then combed it through, playing the heat across it.

She was awakening things in me that had been dormant too long; I wished she had not come, yet I could not resist the feelings in me. With her hair loose, she looked so young! As she dried her hair she was looking directly at me, with her head cocked on one side. She combed out several strands, holding them away from her head in the hot current, and as the hair dried it fell in a light cascade about her shoulders.

'Why don't you have your hair like that during the day? It's much more attractive.'

'Regulations. The collar must be seen.'

'Isn't it a strange job for a girl to have?'

'Why?' she said. 'The pay's good, and it's a secure job. I get a lot of travel, and meet people.'

'It just seems unfeminine.'

She was fingering the vee of her wrap, where the fabric crossed loosely above her breasts. 'Do I seem unfeminine?'

I shook my head, knowing that I had not meant it that way.

Her hair was dry. She bent down to unplug the drier, and for an instant, as her wrap fell forward, I caught a glimpse of her breast.

'Would you like me to stay?' She was sitting erect on the bed, looking at me.

I turned away, not knowing what to say. She got up from the bed, gathering the robe around her, and walked across to me. She gripped my arm lightly, just above the elbow. Her face was close to mine, and she was breathing quickly. I wanted to stroke her breasts, wanted to kiss her.

Still not meeting her gaze, I said: 'I'd like you to, but—'

I willed her to interrupt me before I had to invent an excuse but she stayed silent.

'Do you find me attractive?' she said.

'Of course I do.'

She released my arm and picked up the drier, coiling the flex around it. She walked slowly towards the door.

'Please don't go!' I said.

'I thought you wanted me to.'

'Not yet...I want to explain. It's not your fault, and please don't be hurt.'

'I made a mistake,' said Bella.

'No...I'm not ready, that's all. I can't say why.'

She paused, with her head down, then turned and came back to me. For a moment her fingers twined themselves around my arm, and she kissed me quickly on the cheek. Before I could put my arm around her she stepped back.

'Goodnight, Lenden.'

She went quickly from the room, closing the door quietly behind her. I stood where I was, my eyes closed, deeply ashamed of myself. I could hear Bella in her room: a drawer opening and closing, water running, then silence. At last, when I could bear to, I went to the mirror and stood looking at myself for a long time, stretching the skin around my eyes, smoothing the tiredness.

I undressed and went to bed. I awoke at intervals through the night, straining to hear some sound of Bella, urging her mentally to come back to my room...for that, at least, would have resolved an uncertainty. Through it all, the nearness of her, the little glimpses of her young body, I had been attracted to her as I had not been attracted for a long time. Even so, deep down, I was terrified she would return. This struggle between attraction and repulsion had dogged my life. Ever since Seri.

The ticking clock by Alvie's bed, and the gusting wind rattling the window in its loose frame; these were the only sounds in the pauses between conversation. I sat by the draughty window, looking down into the gardens outside and watching a black-robed priest tending one of the flowerbeds with a rake. The lawns and beds of the seminary's grounds were brightly incongruous on Seevl, an island within an island, constantly watered and fertilized and prodded. When we went in the winter months only the lawns survived, but today there were clusters of tough-looking flowers, gripping the paltry earth with shallow roots. If I craned my neck I could see the huge vegetable garden where the students were made to work, and on the other side of the grounds, invisible from Alvie's room, was a small livestock farm. The seminary tried to keep itself, but I knew that food was brought in from outside, because it was part of my uncle's job to organize this. Why had the priests lied about it, when I was shown around the seminary once? They must have known my uncle ordered food and fuel-oil from Seevl Town, so what was the point of maintaining the fiction that they were entirely independent of the world?

The priest at the flowerbed had glanced up when I first sat by the window, but since then he had ignored me. How long before he, or one of the others, came to see Alvie?

I looked across to the rising ground beyond the seminary walls. The skyline was a long, straight crag, with sloping scree beneath it, and below that the rank wild grass of the moors. There was one of the dead towers out there, a short way from the seminary, but it was one of the less conspicuous ones on Seevl, standing not against the sky, but against the duller background of the crag.

My parents had started to discuss me: Lenden was taking examinations; Lenden had not been studying properly; Lenden was not doing well. I sometimes wished I had the sort of parents who boasted about their child, but their method, at least with relatives, was to try to embarrass me into making greater efforts. I loathed them for it: the embarrassment I felt was the sort that made me resentful, even less willing to apply myself. I looked over at Seri, who was sitting by herself at a table in the corner of the room, apparently reading a book. She was listening, of course, while pretending not to, and when she saw me turn in her direction she looked back with a blank stare. No support there.

'Come here, Lenden,' said Aunt Alvie; it was the sort of moment I always dreaded.

'Go to your aunt, Lenden,' said my father.

Reluctantly I left my seat by the window, and went to stand beside the head of the bed. She stretched out a palsied hand, and took mine.

'You must work harder,' said said. 'For the sake of your future. For me. You want me to get well, don't you?'

'Yes,' I said, although I did not see the connection. I was acutely aware of my parents watching me, of Seri's feigned indifference, and my embarrassment intensified.

'When I was your age,' Aunt Alvie said, 'I won every prize at school. It wasn't as much fun as being lazy, but in the end I was glad. You do understand, don't you?' She wanted my future to be like her present; she wanted to inflict her illness on me. I shrank away from her, as if her disease were contagious, but the pressure on my hand increased. 'Now kiss me.'

I was always having to kiss Alvie: when we arrived, before and after every meal, as we departed. It was part of the dread. I leaned forward, presenting my cheek to her cyanotic lips, but my reluctance held me back and she pulled my hand towards her. As her lips touched coldly against my skin, I felt her pressing my hand against her breast; her coarse cardigan, the thin nightdress, the flaccid flesh. In turn, I kissed her cold white cheek, then tried to move away, but my hand was still clasped against her chest.

'Promise me you'll try harder from now on,' Alvie said.

'I promise.'

I tugged my hand away and, so released, stumbled back from the bed and returned to my chair. My face was hot with the indignity of the interview, and I saw a satisfied look on my father's face. We had endless rows at home about the marks I got at school, and now he had recruited an ally. Sitting by the window, staring sightlessly out across the lawns, I waited for them to find another topic to discuss. But they would not leave me.

'Why don't you go out for a walk, Lenden?'

I said nothing.

'Seri, take Lenden, to see your den.'

'I'm reading,' Seri said, in a voice that tried to convey preoccupation.

'Seri!' said Uncle Torm. 'Take your cousin for a walk. You'd like to see Seri's den, wouldn't you, Lenden?'

'Yes,' I said. We were being dispatched; something adult and perhaps interesting was going to be discussed. Medical treatment, no doubt, details of bedpans and suppositories. I should not have minded hearing about those.

Seri and I looked at each other with mutual resignation, and she closed her book. She led me out of the room, down the gloomy and must-smelling corridor and out of the house. We crossed the garden, and came out through a gate in a brick wall into the main grounds of the seminary. Here Seri hesitated.

'What do you want to do?'

'Have you got a den?'

'That's what *they* call it. It's my hide-out.'

'Can I see it?' I sometimes climbed a tree in the garden at home, to be by myself, but I had never had a proper hide-out. 'Is it secret?'

'Not really. But I don't let anyone in I don't want there.'

'Will you let me in?'

'I suppose so.'

We walked along a gravel drive edging one of the lawns. From one of the open windows there came the sound of voices chanting a psalm. I walked with my feet scuffing up the gravel, to drown the sound, because it reminded me of school.

We came at last to one of the long wings of the seminary building. Seri led me towards some railings beside the base of the main wall, beyond which were some narrow stone steps leading down to a basement. A priest, hoeing a flowerbed, paused in his work to watch us.

Seri ignored him, and went down the steps. At the bottom she got down on her hands and knees and crawled through a low, dark hatchway. When she was inside she turned around and stuck out her head to look at me. I was still waiting at the top of the steps.

'Come on, Lenden. I'll show you something.'

The priest was working again, but glancing back over his shoulder to look at me. I went quickly down the steps, and crawled in through the hatchway.

Seri's hide-out had once been some kind of store or cellar, because there were no windows and the hatch was the only way in or out. The ceiling was high enough for us to stand erect. It was dark and cool, and Seri was lighting three or four candles placed high on a shelf. The tiny cell smelled of match phosphor and candlewax and soot. There were two up-ended boxes to sit on, and from somewhere Seri had found an old mat for the floor.

'What do you do in here?' I said enviously, thinking at once of all the fantasies I could live out if it were my own.

'That's what I'm going to show you.'

The candles cast a weak yellow light, although now that my eyes had adjusted from the bright daylight it seemed perfectly adequate. I sat down on a box.

I had been expecting Seri to sit on the other box, but she came and stood in front of me.

She said: 'Do you want to know a secret, Lenden?'

'What sort of secret?'

'The special sort.'

'All right,' I said, without much interest, still very much under the cloud of Aunt Alvie and the others, and so assuming it was going to be something to do with that.

'How old are you, Lenden?'

'Fourteen.'

'I'm fifteen. Have you got any hair yet?'

'Hair?' Of course I had hair; it was constantly falling in my eyes, and I was always being told to cut it.

'This is a dead secret. Just between you and me.'

Before I realized what she was talking about, Seri quickly raised the front of her skirt, and with her other hand pulled down the front of her pants. I saw a tangly black bush of hair, at the junction of her legs.

I was so surprised that I almost fell off the box. Seri let go, and the elastic in her pants snapped them back into place, but she did not release the skirt. She held this high against her chest, looking down at herself. Her pants were dark-coloured and woollen, and the elastic bit into the plump flesh of her stomach.

I was acutely embarrassed—my own pubic hair had started growing some months before, and it was a matter of mystery, astonishment, and shame, all mixed up together—but I was also compulsively interested.

'Let me see again, ' I said.

She stepped back, almost as if she were uncertain, but then came forward again.

'You pull it down,' she said, thrusting her abdomen towards me.

Nervously, I reached forward, took the top of her pants in my fingers, and pulled the cloth down until I could just see the first growth of hair.

'Further!' she said, knocking my hand out of the way. She pulled the pants down, front and back, so that they clung around her thighs.

Her triangle of hair, curling and black, stood unambiguously before me. I could not stop staring at her, feeling hot and prickly, and with a sudden and quite unmistakable stirring of arousal. I said nothing.

'Do you want a feel?' Seri said.

'No....'

'Touch me. I want you to feel.'

'I'm not sure I should.'

'Then let me have a look at you.'

That, by presenting an awful alternative, resolved my doubts. I was too shy to let anyone see me. I reached out and put my fingers on her hair. It was coarse and wiry, and I recoiled in surprise, mentally but not physically. Seri moved her body against my fingertips.

'Lower down, Lenden. Feel lower down.'

I turned my hand, so that it was palm up, and reached for the junction of her legs. It felt different there: less hair, a fold of skin. I snatched my hand away.

'What's the matter?'

'I don't know,' I said, looking away. But I looked back, and Seri had moved much closer.

'Touch me again. Go right inside.'

'I...can't.'

'Then I'll touch you.'

'No!' The thought of anyone, anyone at all, exploring my body; it was unimaginable. I was still growing; there was too much unexplained. I was ashamed of my body, of growing up.

'You can put your finger right inside, if you want to,' Seri said. 'I don't mind.'

She seized my wrist and brought my hand up against her. Her body was warm, and the hairs curled against my palm. She pressed herself on my hand, encouraging my fingers to explore the cleft beyond. I felt the soft damp flaps of skin, and my fingertip played on the warm recess behind. I was in a heat of excitement, eager to do anything. I wanted to slip into her, sink my fingers, my hand into her. But then, just as I was going into her, she stepped back and let the skirt fall.

'Seri—'

'Ssh!' She crouched by the square of daylight that was the hatch, and listened. Then she straightened, and hoisted up her pants with a sinuous movement of her hips.

'What are you doing?' I was distressed by her sudden withdrawal.

'Keep quiet,' she said, softly. 'I think there's someone outside.'

'You're just teasing me, making an excuse!'

'No...really. I heard something fall. Did you hear a clattering noise?'

'No. Let me touch you again.'

'Not now. I'm frightened.'

'Then when?'

'In a minute. We'll have to go somewhere else. Do you still want to?'

'Of course I do! Let's go now!' I was excited beyond anything in my previous experience. And this was Seri! My stupid cousin!

'I know somewhere safe. Outside the seminary...a short walk.'

'And then I can...?'

'Anything you like, Lenden.'

She made me crawl first through the hatch, and she blew out the candles as I did so. I stood up at the bottom of the steps, then jumped with surprise. The priest we had seen earlier was standing at the top of the steps, leaning down with one hand on the railings, as if listening. He backed away as I looked up. I went up the steps, and saw him hurry across to where he had dropped his hoe on the path. By the time Seri had joined me at the top he was back at work, hoeing the soil with quick, sharp movements.

He did not look up as Seri and I walked hurriedly along the gravel path, but as we passed through the gate I looked back. He was standing with the hoe in his hand, staring towards us.

'Seri, that priest was watching us.'

She said nothing, but took my hand and led me, running, through the long wild grass outside the seminary grounds.

A hired car was waiting for us in Seevl Town, with a Seigniory pass attached to the windscreen. I sat in the front seat beside Serjeant Reeth as she drove slowly up the narrow streets towards the hills.

I was in a complex state of emotions, and this revealed itself by a forced exterior calm and an unwillingness to talk. She needed me to direct her, so I sat, as once my mother had sat, with the map on my knee, wondering if we should need it.

Last night had not been mentioned. Bella had appeared at breakfast, crisp in her uniform, once more the policewoman. Her straightforward proposition, my embarrassed refusal; I could hardly bear to think of them, yet how I wanted to speak of them! I did not want Bella to think she had made a mistake, but still I was incapable of explaining. I wanted some formula by which we could bring the incident forward into today, in an acceptable form, but by her silence and mine we were simply pretending nothing had happened.

She had, however, awakened my awareness of her sexuality, and that could not be pretended away, by either silence or her starchy uniform. Waiting on Jethra dockside for the ferry, sitting together in the saloon of the boat, walking through Seevl Town to collect the car: I could not ignore her physical presence, could not forget that young body in the loose silk wrap.

Now we drove, and sometimes, as she shifted gear in the antiquated car, her hand or her sleeve would brush lightly against my knee; to see if it was as accidental as it seemed I moved my leg away, unobtrusively, and it did not happen again. Later, I let my leg move back, for the touch excited me.

Once, at a junction on the higher slopes of the moors, we went to the map for guidance. Her head bent down beside mine: another moment of physical nearness, but it ended as soon as we found the correct turning.

Watching the sombre green of Seevl's fells, my thoughts moved imperceptibly away from that intrigue to the other, the larger: the island and the seminary. My recollection of the road was unreliable, but the mood induced by the scenery was a familiar companion, twenty years absent. To someone seeing it for the first time, as Bella was seeing it, Seevl would seem wild, barren, grossly empty. There was the roundness of line that betrayed the millennia of harsh winters and unrelenting gales; where the rock was exposed, no plant life clung to it except in the most sheltered corners, and then it was only the hardiest of mosses or the lowliest of lichens. There was a violent splendour to it, a scenic ruggedness unknown in our country. Yet to me, who had been along this route before, actual and mental, the scenery was merely the context. We passed through it as a hand, reaching through luxuriant grass, passes into a snake's nest. The moors were neutral, but contained a menace, and for me, they were always coloured by it.

As Bella drove unsteadily along the narrow road I was already imagining ahead, seeing that valley at the other end of the island, with the cluster of grim buildings, the lawns, and the incongruous flowerbeds.

Seevl was an island made for night. Although on this day the sky was clouded, the sun broke through from time to time, casting for brief periods a bright, unnatural radiance on the windscreen of the car. We had the windows closed and the heater on, yet the cold reached us. I shivered every now and then, shaking my shoulders, pretending to be more cold than I really was, because it was the island chilling me and I did not want Bella to know.

She drove slowly, steering more cautiously over the rutted track than ever my father had. The car was in low gear for much of the time, the engine's note changing continually, making me irrationally irritable. Still, we said nothing to each other, beyond intermittent directions. I watched for familiar landmarks—a cluster of standing stones, a fall of water, the dead towers—and sometimes I could direct her without referring to the map. My memory of the landscape was partial: there were long sections of the road that seemed new to me, and I was sure we had lost our way; then something I remembered would appear, surprising me.

We stopped for lunch at a house in one of the little hamlets, and here some preparation was revealed: we were expected; a meal was ready. I saw Bella sign a document, a form that would recompense the woman for her services.

When we reached the narrow part of the island and travelled along the road above the southern cliffs, Bella pulled the car on to the side and stopped the engine. We were shielded from the wind by a high, rocky bank, and the sun warmed us.

We stood outside, looking across the glistering sea-scape, the view that, as a child, I had only been able to glimpse from my parents' moving car.

'Do you know any of the islands' names?' I said.

Bella had removed her cap, left it on the driver's seat in the car, and wisps of hair blew lightly around her face.

'A few. Torquin is the biggest; we have a base there now. My brother will probably pass through Torquin. And one of them must be Derril, where the Covenant was made. I'm not sure which one that is, though.'

'Have you ever been in the Archipelago?'

'Only here.'

Only Seevl, the offshore island.

The islands we could see were different shades of green, some dark, some light. It was said that of the ten thousand inhabited islands no one was like any other, that a true islander, if planted blind in a foreign island, would know its name by smell and sound alone. All I, a mainlander, knew was that the islands we could see from here were a part of the Dream Archipelago known as the Torqui Group, that they were primarily dependent on dairy-farming and fishing, and that the people spoke the same language as my own. This was school knowledge, half-remembered, all but useless.

'Did you ever want to run away to the islands?' Bella said.

'When I was a kid. Did you?'

'I still do, sometimes.'

'At least you have come to Seevl.'

'At least.'

Talking about something outside ourselves had eased the tension between us; it was as if we had slipped unconsciously into another language. It came naturally to speak in the same tongue, so I said: 'Bella, about last night—',

'Lenden, I'm sorry about that.'

'That's what *I* was going to say.'

'But it is I who should say it. I shouldn't have come to your room. I made a stupid mistake.'

I found her hand, and squeezed it quickly. 'No, not mistake. I wanted you...but I just wasn't ready.'

'Can we forget it?'

'That's what I want.'

Yes, to forget the misunderstanding, and the shame that followed...but not to forget what still might be. I thought about that for a while, as we leaned together against the side of the car, watching the sea.

I said: 'We'll have to stay at the seminary tonight. You know we can't get back to Seevl Town?'

'Yes, I know.'

'They'll probably give us rooms in the college.'

'That's all right. I went to a convent.'

She went around to the driver's door, and opened it. We drove on. I knew it would take at least another hour from there, and the afternoon was drawing on. Bella said nothing, concentrating on the difficult drive, and I surrendered to my memories and the oppressive mood of the island.

Seri held my hand, and we leaped and ran across the rough ground, the coarse grasses whipping against our legs. It was the first time I had ever left the seminary grounds, and never until then had I recognized how the stout walls became a symbolic defence against the rest of the island. Out here the wind seemed stiffer and colder and we were more exposed.

'Where are we going?' I said, gasping because I was out of breath.

'Somewhere I know.' She released my hand, and went on ahead.

'Let's do it here.' Some of the tension that had built up inside her hide-out had been dissipated by our sudden escape, and I wanted to go on before she changed her mind.

'Out in the open?' she said, rounding on me. 'I told you this was a secret!'

'There's long grass,' I said lamely.

'Do you still want to do it?'

'Yes!' I said, sure of that if nothing else.

'Then come on.'

She set off again, leaping down a shallow slope towards a stream. I held back for a moment, staring guiltily towards the seminary. There was someone there, outside the walls, walking in our direction. I knew at once that it was the priest with the hoe, although he was too far away for me to be sure.

I ran after Seri, and jumped across the narrow stream to join her.

'There's someone following us. That priest.'

'He won't find us!'

It was not quite obvious where Seri was taking me. The ground sloped up steeply from the stream, rising towards the high crag in the distance. A short way from us, built with the limestone rock of the island, was the dead tower.

I looked back, and saw we were out of sight of the priest if he was still following us. Seri marched on, a long way ahead of me, scrambling up the hillside through the windswept grass.

The tower was not noticeably different from any other of its sort I had seen on Seevl: it was about as tall as a four-storey house, with window-frames higher up which once had contained glass, but which now were broken. There was a door in the base, hanging open on its hinges, and all around in the grass were pieces of broken brick and tile. The tower was not wide: perhaps fifteen feet in diameter, and hexagonal. There had once been a roof, built in candle-snuffer shape, but now it had all fallen in, and only two or three beams stood out to revel its former design.

Seri was waiting for me by the open door.

'Hurry, Lenden!'

'I'm coming,' I said, stepping over a heap of masonry, and looking up at the tower as it loomed over me. 'We're not going inside, are we?'

'Why not?' It's been here for years...it's quite safe.'

All I knew about the towers of Seevl was that no one went near them; yet Seri stood by the door as if it were just another hide-out. I was torn between my dread of the tower, and what Seri would offer me inside.

'I thought these towers were...dangerous,' I said.

'It's just an old ruin. Something to do with the college, when it was a monastery. Years ago.'

'But they're all over the island!'

Seri shrugged dismissively, and went through the door. I hesitated a few seconds longer, then followed her. She closed the door behind us.

Daylight came in through two windows set high under the ceiling, which was a bare skeleton: dusty joists and broken planking. A fallen beam lay at an angle across the room, propped up against the wall. The floor was littered with glass, plaster, and pieces of rock.

'See...there's nothing to worry about.' Seri kicked a few pieces of rock out of the way, to clear a space on the wooden floor. 'It's just an old dump.'

'Are you still going to let me touch you?' I said.

'If you want to.'

'I do...but that priest was following us. You said it was secret.'

Seri started to say something, but changed her mind and turned away. She opened the door, and peered out; I stood behind her, looking over her shoulder. We both saw the priest. He had reached the stream and was walking along the bank, trying to find somewhere to cross.

Seri closed the door again. 'He won't come here. Not to the tower.'

'But he is coming!' It was obvious that he was following us.

'Lenden, none of the priests will come here. They say the tower is evil. They're terrified of the place...that's why it's safe for us.'

I glanced around nervously. 'What's evil about it?'

'Nothing...it's just their superstition. They say something wicked happened. A long time ago.'

'But he's still coming,' I said.

'You wait and see what he does.'

I went to the door and opened it a fraction of an inch. I peered through the slit, looking down the hill for the priest. He was some way away, standing still, looking up towards me. I closed the door, and told Seri this.

'You see?' she said.

'But he'll wait until we come out. What then?'

'It's none of his business,' she said. 'He won't know what we're doing. I know him...it's Father Grewe. He's always poking around, wondering what I'm up to. I'm used to it. Shall we start?'

'If you want to.' The mood had left me.

'Get undressed then.'

'Me? I thought you—'

'We both undress.'

'I don't want to.' I looked at the rubble-strewn floor, shyly. 'Not yet, anyway. You do it first.'

'All right. I don't mind.'

She reached up under her skirt, and pulled her pants down her legs. She tossed them on the floor.

'Now you take something off,' she said. I hesitated then complied by taking off my pullover.

Seri undid two buttons on the side of her skirt, and it slid down her legs. She turned away from me to drape the garment over the beam, and for a moment I saw the pinkness of her buttocks, slightly dimpled. 'Now you.'

'Let me feel you first. I've never done...'

Some compassion softened her determination to make me undress at the same rate as her. She smiled, quickly, then sat down on the floor, keeping her knees together and reaching forward to clasp her ankles. I could see none of her secrets, just the pale curve of her thighs, rounding towards her buttocks. Her sweater finished at her waist.

'All right. But be very gentle. You were jabbing me before.'

She sat back, resting her elbows on the floor behind her, and then she parted her legs. I saw the black thatch of hair, the whorl of pink skin, revealed but mysterious. Staring at her, I moved forward, crouching down. I was suddenly as excited as I had been before; it switched on like a motor, compelling me towards her almost against my will. I felt a tightness in my throat, a sweatiness in my palms. That passive, lipped organ, lying between her thighs like an upright mouth, waited for my touch. I reached forward, ran my fingertips across the lips, felt the warmth of them, the moistness behind. Seri sucked in her breath, tensing herself.

Something small and hard whacked against the door, startling us both. Seri swung away from me, turning to one side; my hand brushed against the top of her thigh; then she was away from me.

'What was that!' I said.

'Don't move.' She went to the door, eased it open and peered out.

I heard, distantly: 'Seri, come out of that place. You know it is forbidden.'

She closed the door. 'He's still out there.'

She sounded surprised, as if she forgotten him. I had not, and I looked around for my pullover. 'Is he coming in?'

'I told you...he won't come near us. I'll have to go and talk to him.' She picked up her skirt and stepped into it, buttoning it again at the waist. 'Wait here, and don't let him see you.'

'But he knows I'm here. I'll come with you. We ought to be going back to the house, anyway.'

'No!' she said, and I saw the quickness of her temper. 'There's more to do, more than just touching. That's only the beginning.' Her hand was on the door. 'Stay here...keep out of sight, and I'll be back in a few moments.'

The door slammed behind her. I peeped through the crack, saw her running down through the long grass to where the priest waited. He seemed angry, but she was uncowed, standing near to him and kicking idly at the grasses while he spoke.

There was a faint, musky fragrance on my fingertips, where I had touched her. I drew back from the door, and looked around at the filthy interior of the tower. Without Seri I felt ill at ease in the old ruin. The ceiling was sagging; what if it fell on me? The constant wind of Seevl blustered around the tower, and a piece of broken wood, hanging by the window-frame, knocked to and fro.

Minutes passed, and as the aroused excitement faded for the second time, I began to wonder guiltily about the possible consequences of being caught here. Suppose the priest told Torm and Alvie that we had been up to something, or that we were gone long enough for them to guess anyway? If they knew the truth, or even a part of it, there would be a terrible scene.

I heard the voice of the priest, in a freak silence of the wind; he was saying something sharply, but Seri's response was laughter. I returned to the door, put my eye to the crack and looked out at them. The priest was holding Seri by the hand, tugging her, but she was pulling back from him. To my surprise, I realized that I was not witnessing a conflict, but what seemed to be a game. Their hands slipped apart...but it was an accident, because they joined again immediately and the playful pulling went on.

I stepped back, very puzzled.

We were in a part of the seminary I had never seen before: an office just behind the main entrance. We had been greeted by a Father Henner, thin, bespectacled, and younger than I had expected; condolences on the death of my uncle, a tragic loss, a servant of God. He handed over the key to the house, and we went for a meal in the refectory. Father Henner did not eat with us; Bella and I sat alone at a table in one corner of the room. Night was falling beyond the stained-glass windows.

I could hear the wind, made louder, it seemed, by the airy space above us, the high, buttressed roof.

'What are you thinking, Lenden?' Bella said, over the sounds of the students clattering their dishes at the other end of the hall.

'I'm wishing we didn't have to stay. I don't like this place.'

Afterwards, Father Henner took us across to the house, leading the way through the grounds with a battery flashlight; our feet crunched on the gravel pathway, the trees moved blackly against the night sky and the vague shape of the moors beyond. I unlocked the door and Father Henner turned on a light in the corridor. A dim, low-wattage bulb shed yellow light on the shabby floor and wallpaper. I smelled damp rot and mould.

'You'll find that much of the furniture has already been removed,' said Father Henner. 'Your uncle bequeathed the more valuable pieces to the college, and some of the effects belonged to us already. As you know, we have been unable to trace the daughter, so with your permission the rest may be destroyed.'

The daughter...ah, Seri. Where are you now, Seri? She left the island soon after Alvie died, but no one knew where she went. My parents would never mention her, and I never asked. Today she would be somewhere in the Archipelago.

'What about my uncle's papers?' I said.

'They're still here. We can arrange for them to be incinerated, if you will separate the valuable ones.'

I opened a door into a room off the corridor. It had been my uncle's office, but now it was empty, with pale squares on the walls where pictures had been; a dark patch of damp spread up from the stone floor.

'Most of the rooms have been cleared. There's just your dear aunt's room. And the kitchen. There are utensils there.'

Bella was standing by the door to my aunt's room. Father Henner nodded to her, and she turned the handle. I experienced a sudden compulsion to back away, fearing that Alvie would still be there, waiting for me.

Father Henner went back to the main door. 'Well, I'll leave you to your work. If there's anything you need, I shall be in my office during the day.'

I said: 'We need somewhere to stay.'

Father Henner opened the door, and his black habit blew in the sudden wind from outside. 'You may use the house, of course.'

'We were expecting you to give us rooms,' Bella said.

'In the college?' he said to her. 'I'm afraid that would not be possible. We have no facilities for women.'

Bella looked at me questioningly; I, stricken with a dread of spending a night in the house, shook my head.

'Are there proper beds here?' Bella said, pushing open the door and peering into the room, but my aunt's folding screen was there, making it a temporary corridor into the room and blocking the view of the rest.

Father Henner was outside. 'You'll have to make do. It's only for one night, after all. God be with you.'

He went, and the door slammed behind him. Quietness fell; the thick walls effectively muted the wind, at least here in the centre of the house, away from the windows.

'What are we going to do, Lenden? Sleep on the floor?'

'Let's see what's in there.'

Aunt Alvie's room; my dear aunt.

Pretending to Bella that it was just an ordinary room, pretending to myself, I went past her and walked in. The central light was beyond the folding screen, so the way was shadowed. At the end, facing us, someone from the seminary had stacked two huge piles of old documents; tomorrow I would have to go through them. Dust lay in a gritty film on the top sheets. Bella was behind me; I looked beyond the screen to see the rest of the room. The double bed, Alvie's bed, was still there, dominating everything. Tea-chests had been brought in to the room, two extra chairs were crammed against the wall, books lay in uneven piles on the table beneath the window, picture-frames rested on the mantelpiece...but the bed, piled high with pillows, was the focus of the room, as ever. By its head was the bedside table: dusty old pill-bottles, a notebook, a folded lace handkerchief, a telephone, lavender-water. These I remembered.

Alvie still lay in the bed. Only her body was missing.

I could smell her, see her, hear her. Above the bed, on the wall behind the top rail of the brass-fitting, were two dark marks on the wallpaper. I remembered then: Alvie had had a characteristic gesture, reaching up behind her to grip the rail with both hands, perhaps to brace herself against pain. Her hands, years of her hands gripping like that, had left the stains.

The windows were black squares of night; Bella drew the curtains, and dust cascaded down. I could hear the wind again, and thought: Alvie must have known this wind, every night, every day.

'Are you all right, Lenden?'

'Of course.'

'Well, there's a bed, at least.'

'You have it,' I said. 'I'll sleep on the floor.'

'There'll be another bed somewhere. In one of the other rooms.'

'Father Henner said they had been cleared.'

'Then...will you share? Or I could go on the floor.'

We stood there in awful indecision, each for our own reasons. At last we came to silent agreement, changing the subject, pretending to look for enough space on the floor for me to lie down, but it was inevitable we would share. We were both tired, and chilled by the cold house. I let Bella take charge, and she tidied the bed, shaking out the old sheets to air them a little, turning them over. Spare pillows went on to the floor, extra covers were found. I busied myself, trying to help, distracting myself from the thought: Alvie's bed, Alvie's bed.

At last the bed was ready, and Bella and I took it in turn to use the bathroom upstairs. I went first, and when Bella went after me I sat on the edge of Alvie's bed listening to the sounds of her footsteps on the bare boards above. Here, in this room, my fears were conjoined: the shadow of my past and how it barred me from Bella, the memories of Alvie, and the winds and darknesses of Seevl that surrounded the house. I heard Bella above me, walking across the room, and she started down the wooden staircase. I made a sudden decision, stripping off my outer clothes and sliding in between the sheets.

Bella switched off the central light as she came in. She saw that I was in the bed, but her expression remained neutral. I watched, and did not watch, as she undressed in the glow from the table-lamp. The blouse and skirt of her uniform; suspender-belt and stockings; black pants and a sensible bra. She stood naked, looking away from me, finding a tissue to blow her nose on.

As she lay down beside me I felt her skin cold against mine, and realized she was shaking.

'I'm freezing,' she said, and turned off the light. 'Will you hold me?'

234

My arm went easily around her; she was slim and her body shaped itself naturally against mine. I could feel the plump weight of her breast on my arm, the prickle of her hair against my thigh. I was getting excited, but did not move, hoping to conceal it.

She ran a hand lightly over my stomach, then up to my breasts. 'You've still got clothes on.'

'I thought—'

'Don't be frightened, Lenden.'

She slipped her hand inside my bra, caressed my nipple, kissed me on the neck. Pressing herself to me she unhooked the bra and slid it down my arms. Her head ducked down, and with her hand cupping me she took a nipple in her mouth, sucking and pulling on it. Her hand crept down, went beneath the fabric of my pants, and her fingers slipped expertly between my legs. I stiffened, excited and terrified.

Later, Bella sat astride me, her hair falling loose and touching my face. I caressed her beautiful breasts, playing with the small firm nipples, licking and kissing them. She guided my hand to her sex, but as soon as my fingers felt the bristle of hair, I snatched away. Again I was guided there, again I pulled back.

'Touch me, Lenden, oh, touch me....'

Bella was kissing my face, my neck, my shoulders, but I could not touch her. I shrank from her as once before I had shrunk from Seri, but Bella took my wrist in her hand, thrust my clenched fingers between her legs, clamped down on me, thrusting herself against my knuckles in repeated spasms. Afterwards, she sprawled across me, her sweat dripping down from her temples and into my open mouth.

I left her in the bed and stood, shivering, by the window. I leaned against the wall by the frame, staring out into the gusty night. The dark was impenetrable. There were no lights, not even the subdued glow of a cloudy night, and I could not see the bulk of the moors.

Bella turned on the table light, and after she had lit a cigarette I turned to look back at her. She was lying with the cigarette between her lips, her hands gripping the brass rail of the bed above her head. Her hair fell down across her shoulder, partially covering one breast.

'You do prefer men, don't you?' she said.

I simply shook my head, and waited by the window until she had finished her cigarette and turned out the light. In the darkness I returned to the bed. Bella did not stir, and I curled up against her, resting my head on her shoulder. I started to drift towards sleep, and I laid my hand gently on her breast. The bed smelled of bodies.

While Seri was outside the dead tower with the priest, something happened to me, and I cannot explain it. There was no warning of it, and I had no premoniton of fear.

My main preoccupations were intense sexual frustration and curiosity about what Seri was doing. She had suddenly and unexpectedly illuminated an area of my life I had always kept in the shade. I wanted the knowledge that she was offering, and I wanted the consequent knowledge of myself.

But she had told me to wait, to stay out of sight....I was prepared to do both, but not for long. I had expected her to get rid of the priest somehow, but instead she was out there apparently playing with him.

Thus preoccupied, I barely noticed a low, snuffling sound that came to me over the noise of the wind. I was picking up my pullover, retrieving Seri's pants. I was going out to join Seri, because I wanted to know what she was doing.

I was stuffing her pants into the pocket of my skirt when I heard the noise again. It surprised me: because I had heard it the first time without really thinking about it, I had subconsciously ignored it, but when it came again it was both strange and half-familiar. It was like nothing I had ever heard before. It was animalistic, but there was a human quality to it, too, as if some beast had managed to form half a word before reverting to its usual grunt. I still felt no fear, only a sense of curiosity. I suspected that Seri had returned, and was playing a joke on me. I called her name, but there was no answer.

Something about the animal quality of the noise had made me hesitate. I stood in the centre of the crumbling tower, looking around, thinking for the first time that perhaps some predatory beast was in the vicinity. I listened, trying to filter out the persistent noise of the wind, trying to distinguish the sound again. Nothing.

A beam of Seevl's bright cool sunlight was striking in through one of the high windows, illuminating the wall beside the door. This, like the rest of the tower, was decaying; and, a short distance from the door-post, the plaster and brickwork had fallen away, leaving a jagged hole about the size of a man's head. Beyond, the cavity of the wall was revealed, with the great, grey bricks of the main structure dimly visible behind. It was one of several holes in the wall, but it caught my attention because some instinct told me that this was the source of the noise. I stepped towards it, still suspecting Seri of some complicity; perhaps having got rid of the priest she had returned quietly to the tower, and was fooling around outside the door.

Something moved inside the cavity, and although I was staring straight at the place I saw only a dark, quick movement. The sun went in, as one of the low clouds covered it, and it seemed suddenly much colder. Moments later the sun came out again, but the chill remained; I knew then that it was in me.

I placed my hand on the brickwork, leaning slightly towards the hole, trying to see down into it. I did not want to go too close, yet I was convinced someone, or something, was in there, and I wanted to know what it was. There were no more movements, no more noise, but an almost tangible sense of presence remained.

I was no longer alone in the tower.

'Is that you, Seri?' I said, and the sound of my voice seemed too loud and too feeble, simultaneously. I cleared my throat, noisily, giving Seri a chance to declare herself...but there was no response.

I moved my hand further into the hole, until I touched the bricks on the far side of the cavity. There was something warm in there, because I could feel a gentle heat, as of a living body. I reached down, into the dark.

There was a violent noise, a movement that I felt without seeing, and something grabbed my hand.

It pulled, dragging my arm down into the hole until my shoulder scraped painfully against the bricks. I screamed in surprise, gasping in terror. I tried to pull back, but whatever it was that had taken hold had sharp claws or teeth and they were biting into my skin. My face was jammed sideways against the wall, the skin of my bare upper arm was grazing against the rough bricks.

'Let go!' I shouted, helplessly trying to tug my arm away.

As the thing had grabbed me I had instinctively balled my hand into a fist, and I could feel it contained in something wet and very warm, hard on one side, soft on the other. I pulled again, and the grip of the teeth tightened. Whatever it was in there was no longer dragging me down, but was holding me. Whenever I pulled back, the sharp teeth tightened around me. They were backward-pointing, so that to pull against them dragged my flesh against their edge.

Christopher Priest

I unballed my fingers slowly, painfully aware that to loosen them was to expose them. The tips pressed against something soft, and I clenched my fist reflexively. I shuddered, wanting to scream again, yet lacking the breath.

It was a mouth that had seized me. I knew that from the moment it had taken hold, yet it was too horrible to believe. Some animal, crouching in the wall, some huge, rank animal had taken my arm in its mouth, and was holding me. My knuckles were jammed against the hard roof of the mouth, my tightly balled fingers were against the coarse surface of the tongue. The teeth, the fangs, had closed about my arm, just above the wrist.

I tried turning my arm, attempting to twist it free, but the instant I moved, the teeth closed more tightly on me. I shouted in pain, knowing that the flesh must have been torn in many places, and that I was surely bleeding into the animal's mouth.

I shifted my feet, trying to balance, thinking that if I could stand firmly I could pull harder, but as the animal had dragged me down it had pulled me over. Most of my weight was on the shoulder jammed against the bricks. I moved a foot, shifted some of my weight on to it. The fangs tightened on me again, as if the animal sensed what I was doing.

The pain was indescribable. The strength that held my fingers closed was draining away, and I could feel my fist loosening. Again my fingertips touched the hot, quivering surface of the tongue, and drooped down towards the throat. Miraculously, I still had the sensation of touch, and I could feel the hard gums, the slick sides to the tongue. It was the most disgusting thing I had ever felt in my life: wild, bestial.

The animal, having firm hold of me, was trembling with some kind of incomprehensible excitement. I could feel the head shivering, and the breath rasped in and out over my arm, cold against the wounds as it inhaled, wet and hot as it exhaled. I could smell its stench now: sweet with the saliva of gross animalism, rancid and fetid with the smell of carrion.

I tugged once more, in desperate, disgusted terror, but the agony of the biting teeth redoubled. It felt as if it had almost bitten through me; I had a ghastly, flashing image of withdrawing my arm at last, and seeing it severed through, the sinews dangling from the stump, the blood pumping away. I closed my eyes, gasping again with horror and revulsion.

The tongue started moving, working around my wrist, stroking my palm. I felt as if I were going to faint. Only the pain, the intense, searing agony of torn muscle and crushed bone, kept me conscious to suffer longer.

Through the veils of pain I remembered Seri was outside. I shouted for help, but I was weakened and my voice came out as a hoarse whisper. The door was only a few inches from me. I reached over with my free hand and pushed at it. It swung outwards, and I could see down the slope, across the long grass. The brilliant cold sky, the dark rising moors...but no sign of Seri. I was alone.

Staring through tear-filled eyes, unable to focus, I stayed helpless, leaning against the rough brickwork as the monster in the wall slowly ate my arm. Outside the wind made light-coloured patterns on the thick, waving grass.

The animal began to make a noise, a reprise of the first sound it had made. It growled deep inside its throat, and beneath my helpless fingers the tongue was quivering. It sucked in breath and the head tensed, and then there came a second growl. Somehow, the sound made my fevered imagining of the animal more detailed: I saw a wolf's head, a long snout, flecks of foam. The pain intensified, and I sensed the animal's increased excitement. The throat-noises were coming regularly now, in a fast rhythm, faster and faster as its hold on my arm tightened. The agony was so acute that I was sure it must have almost bitten through, and I tried once more to pull away, quite ready to lose my hand for the sake of release. The animal held on, chewing more viciously, snarling at me from its hidden den below. My head was swimming; unconsciousness could not have been far away.

The animal noises were now coming so quickly that they seemed to join into one continuous howl; the pain was intolerable. But then, unaccountably, the jaw sagged open and I was released.

I slumped weakly against the wall, my arm still dangling inside the cavity. The pain, which surged with every heartbeat, began to diminish. I was crying with relief and agony, and with terror of the animal which was still there below. I dared not move my arm, thinking that one twitch of a muscle would provoke another attack, yet I knew my chance had come to snatch away what was left of my arm.

My tears stopped, because I was afraid. I listened carefully: was the animal breathing, was it still there? I did not know if my arm had lost all sensation, but I could not feel the animal's foul breath moving across me. The pain was almost indiscernible; my arm must be numb. I imagined, rather than felt, the fingers hanging uselessly from the mangled wrist, blood pulsing down into the animal's open snout below.

A deep revulsion stirred me at last, and, not caring if the animal should attack me again, I stood away from the wall, withdrawing my shattered arm from the cavity. I staggered away, and rested my good hand against the low-lying beam. I looked at the damage done to me.

The arm was whole, the hand was undamaged.

I held it before me, disbelieving what I saw. The sleeve of my blouse had been torn as I was dragged through the brickwork, but there were no marks on the skin, no lacerations, no teeth-marks, no blood. I flexed my fingers, bracing myself against the anticipated pain, but they moved normally. I turned my hand over, looking at it from all sides. Not a mark, not even a trace of the saliva I had felt running across me. The palm was moist, but I was sweating all over. I touched the arm gingerly, feeling for the wounds, but as I pressed down on the sore areas the only sensation I could feel was of fingertips squeezing against good flesh. There was not even a ghost of the pain I had suffered. There was a faint, unpleasant odour on my hand, but as I sniffed at the backs of my fingers, at my palm, it faded away.

The door was open. I snatched at my pullover, which lay on the floor, and lurched outside. I was holding my wounded, undamaged arm across my chest, as if I were in pain, but it was just a subconscious reflex.

The long grass swept around me in the wind, and I remembered Seri. I needed her then: to explain, to soothe, to calm me. I wanted another human being to see me, and give me the reassurance I could not give myself. But Seri had vanished, and I was alone.

At the bottom of the slope, near the stream, a good distance from the tower, a figure in black stood up. His habit was caught in the band at his waist, and as he turned he was pulling at it, making it hang normally. I ran towards him, rushing through the grass.

He turned his back on me as soon as he saw me, and strode away quickly. As I dashed towards him he reached the brook, leaped over it, and hurried up the slope beyond.

'Wait, Father!' I shouted. 'Please wait!'

I came to a place where the grass was flattened, and in its centre lay Seri. She was on her back, with her skirt rolled up above her waist. Her sweater had been pushed up to her neck, revealing plump little breasts, pink-tipped. Her eyes were closed, and her arms lay on the ground above her head. Her knees were raised, and her legs were wide open.

'Seri!'

'Do you still want to touch me, Lenden?' she said, and giggled.

I looked at the place; a pale, creamy fluid trickled from the reddened lips.

A wave of nausea came over me, and I backed away from her, unable to look at her. She was still laughing, and as she saw my reaction her laughter became shrill and hysterical. She rolled around in the flattened grass, writhing as she must have writhed before.

I kept a distance between us, waiting for her to sober. I remembered that I had her pants in the pocket of my skirt, and I found them and threw them at her. They landed on her naked belly.

'You're...' I tried to find a word forceful enough to convey the revulsion in me, but failed. 'You're *filthy*!'

Her crazy laughing stopped, and she lay on her side to look at me. Then, deliberately, she opened her legs in tacit invitation.

I turned from her and ran away, towards the seminary, towards the house. I sobbed as I ran, and the torn sleeve of my blouse flapped around my arm. I stumbled as I crossed the stream, drenching my clothes; I tripped many times, cutting my knee, tearing the hem of my skirt. Bloodied, hysterical, bruised, and soaked through, I ran into the house and burst into my aunt's sickroom.

My uncle and my father were supporting Alvie above a chamber-pot. Her white, withered legs dangled like bleached ropes; drops of orange liquid trickled from her. Her eyes were closed, and her head lolled.

I heard my uncle shouting. My mother appeared, and a hand was slapped over my eyes. I was dragged, screaming, into the corridor.

All I could say, again and again, was Seri's name. Everyone seemed to be shouting at me.

Later, Uncle Torm went out on to the moors to find Seri, but before they returned we had got back into our car and were driving, through the evening and night, towards Seevl Town.

It was the last time I went to Seevl. I was fourteen. I never saw Seri again.

We burned my uncle's papers in the yard behind the house: black charred ashes floated up, then were whisked away by the wind. There were also some clothes, and some chairs and a table the priests did not want. They burned slowly, and I stood by the fire, watching the flames reflectively.

Bella, standing by the doorway, said: 'Why do you keep staring at the moors?'

'I didn't know that I was.'

'There's something out there. What is it?'

'I was watching the blaze,' I said.

'Have you ever been out on the moors?'

'No.' I kicked a chair leg that had rolled from the fire, and sparks flew. Something in the fire spat, and a cinder shot across the yard.

Bella came towards me, took my arm tenderly.

'It doesn't matter, about last night.'

I said nothing because I knew she was right, but also that it did matter.

'Was that your first time?' she said.

'Of course not.'

'I meant, with someone like me?'

'No.'

What was she like, that was so different? She meant perhaps: was she my first female lover? I smiled sadly, thinking of the men I had loved, the women too. More women than men, over the years, because I only went to men in desperation. I, always the passive lover: excited and slightly appalled by their relish in caressing my body, envying them their lack of inhibition, and determined with each new partner that *this* one would be different, *this* one would find me active. No, in that sense, Bella was no different. I had not changed. I had thought a few years' abstention, a gaining in maturity, would cure me of the irrational fear. I should not have put it to the test; I had been weak, thinking that the return to Seevl would, in itself, be some kind of exorcism. I had fallen for Bella's youth, her hesitancy, her pretty body; these had drawn me, once again, to failure. I had not known that I had dried up, become a husk.

'I'm only trying to understand,' Bella said.

'So am I.'

'We're alone.' Bella, speaking softly. 'Be frank with me.'

'I am, I think.'

'Will we see each other again? After this?'

'Yes,' I said, postponing.

'I can travel freely. Let me visit your home.'

'All right. If you'd like to.'

It seemed to satisfy her, but she stood with her hand on my arm as we watched the fire.

I wondered what it was she saw in me; surely she had other friends? I was several years older than her, and she made me feel it, with her economical body, her youthful mannerisms. I had my first grey hairs, my breasts had started to sag, my waist was full, my thighs were thick. I was the older woman, more mature and presumably more experienced, yet it was she who pursued. I found it very affecting and flattering.

If it had been anywhere else: not Seevl, not Alvie's room and Alvie's bed. Would it have been any different?

The inevitable failure...but also the inevitable seeking for an excuse.

The real excuse, if there was any at all, lay out there under the crag of Seevl's moors.

That morning I had risen before Bella, and climbed from Alvie's bed to go to the window. From there I had been sure I would be able to see the tower where it all had happened, but I looked and I had not been able to see it. The seminary gardens were just as I recalled them—although less well tended than I had thought—and so was the view across to the high, limestone crag. But there was no sign of the tower.

Bella was right: all that morning, as I worked through my uncle's papers, I had looked frequently towards the moors, wondering where the tower had gone.

There must have been a rational explanation: it had become unsafe; it had been demolished.

There must have been a rational explanation that it was not there, that it had never been there. I shied away from that, unable to face the consequences.

Bella was still holding my arm, resting her cheek lightly against my shoulder.

She said: 'I've a confession, Lenden.'

I was lost in my own thoughts, and barely heard her.

'Is it important?' I said.

'I don't know. It might be. There's a file on you, in the Seigniory. Does that surprise you?'

'No, not really.' There were files on everybody; we were at war.

'I read your file. I know a lot about you.'

'What sort of thing?' A tremor of concern.

'Nothing political.'

No surprise; my isolation was almost total. 'What then?'

'About your private life. I suppose that's worse really.' I had drawn away from her, to face her. 'The file told me the sort of person you are...the fact that you have had women lovers. There was a picture of you.'

'When did you see this?'

'When the assignment was posted. I volunteered for this, I wanted to meet you. I thought...it's hard to say. I've been very lonely.'

'And it's hard to meet the right people,' I said. 'I've been through all that too.'

'You don't mind?'

'I object to it being on file. But I don't mind what you did.'

The fire was almost out. There was an old broom in the yard, and I used it to sweep the charred wood and ashes into a small neat pile. A few flames flickered, but they would not burn much longer.

There was nothing left for us to do at the house, and we had a long drive to catch the evening ferry. I took the key back to Father Henner's office, while Bella carried our stuff to the car. Walking back through the grounds, alone, I knew that this was my last chance to find the tower. I left the path and walked through the gardens until I came to the wall. I found a gate, went through, and stood looking across the rough ground.

I could not see the tower, could not even see where it might have been. I was standing there looking for it, when Bella found me.

She slipped her hand into mine.

'Something happened here once, didn't it?'

I nodded, and held her hand tightly.

'A long time ago?'

'Twenty years ago. I'm not sure what it was. I think I must have imagined it. It all seems different now.'

'I was just a child, twenty years ago,' Bella said.

'So was I.'

But thinking, as we drove back through the fells, it seemed different again. I was sure the tower was there, that it was simply that I had not seen it.

Bella talked, in the car, on the ferry, and we made our plans for future meetings...but we parted on the quay in Jethra, and I have not heard from her since.

GRANTA

SALMAN RUSHDIE
THE GOLDEN BOUGH

Salman Rushdie was born in Bombay in 1947 and lived in India until he was fourteen. Then he came to England where he wrote great books and won big prizes. He has just completed his third novel, *Shame,* which should be published in the autumn, and which is, Rushdie claims, his last piece of work 'set in the subcontinent'. He is, however, about to leave for a two month lecture tour in India.

As the interview progressed I became convinced that I would not get the job. My considerable experience of such events had made me almost preternaturally sensitive to the unspoken truths that lay behind their neutral formality, like snipers behind a battlement. In the early days, I had blamed myself for my failures: I must have been wearing an unacceptable jacket, there was a spot on my tie, I had interrupted a question on two occasions. I did my best to overcome my faults—careless dressing, over-eagerness, a certain insolent air of being too good for what was being offered. I became tidy, polite, humble. But the outcome of the interviews was still the same. So I decided to try arrogance. I went into the interview rooms with my hair deliberately unbrushed, my shoe-laces untied, the zipper on my fly left half-way down. I sneered at the suited, expressionless adversary across the desk, and told him what was wrong with his firm and what I would do about it, given two days and a free hand. Sometimes I snapped my fingers under his nose. My luck refused to change. Next I tried hypocrisy. I started making eloquent, testamentary statements to my inquisitors, vowing my eternal commitment to the great work of photocopying invoices, packaging bone-shaped dog biscuits, selling farm machinery, bottling a synthetic orange drink that, I was told, 'contained no harmful oranges.' My eyes goggling with sincerity, I pleaded for a chance to show my dedication to such work. It was never given to me. At length I despaired. I continued to go to the interviews, to prove that I was still alive, but I no longer expected anything. I was staring into the bland face of my latest interrogator—the same face I had seen behind a hundred such desks and above a hundred such blank white shirts—fully persuaded that I was about to fail yet again, when the reason for all my troubles came into my head. It was so simple that I was furious with myself for not having seen it before.

The same face. At every interview the same bland features. It could not be—but it was. I was sure of that. And finally, unable to conceal my triumph, I came right out with it. 'It is you, isn't it?'

'I beg your pardon?' Frostily.

But I had no intention of letting him off the hook. 'It has always been you,' I insisted. 'I'm right. I know I am.'

His face changed, acquiring a sly, contemptuous look. 'Yes,' he admitted, not in the least abashed. 'Most of you fools never realize.'

'But why?'

He ignored my question. 'I'll say this for you,' he said reflectively. 'You've given me a busy life. Some people make it too easy; I like a challenge. Look at it from my point of view. I have to know in advance where you're going to turn up next. I always have to be one jump ahead, to make the proper arrangements, so that I can be here, behind these desks, when you walk in. There are nights when I get no sleep. Oh, yes. Credit where it's due.'

I wanted to ask how the proper arrangements were made, and other things, but I was sure he would not reply. Instead I said, 'Now that I've unmasked you, I suppose you'll go away and....'

'Don't bank on it,' he snapped. 'It makes no difference at all.'

'You've failed,' I taunted him. 'You'll lose your job, you'll be out on the scrap-heap like me, they'll probably assign an interviewer to deal with you!'

'This interview is concluded,' he told me, his face smooth and meaningless once again. 'I'm afraid I don't think you would be happy here, Mr... Mr....'

'Good-bye,' I crowed, sure of his defeat, filled with insane joy.

On the day of my next interview, I was still in a state of elation. I dressed neatly (I had decided to revert to this strategy for a while), and whistled in the lift as it carried me to the room in which I would have to duel for a job. When I was called into the room, it was as if I had been punched on the nose.

'Next!' The voice came through the half-open door, and I knew that I was finished. He did not permit himself the luxury of a smile when I entered. Every inch the professional, he began to comment on my curriculum vitae. I think that was when I realized that I would have to kill him.

I planned the murder for weeks, weeks during which I attended four more interviews with my merciless antagonist. At least, I tried to plan; but I could not think of a single way of doing the deed and getting away with it. There were desk diaries, letters, files. Everyone would know who had been in the room with him, even if I did manage to kill and flee without being caught. There were moments when I considered abandoning the scheme, but they passed, because I knew that the only alternative to murder was suicide, and I liked being alive.

So one day I thought, 'To hell with it,' and went to my interview with a bread knife in my inside pocket. 'Next,' the voice called, and I went in and slit his throat. The blood went everywhere, and the receptionist, hearing his death-gurgles, came and stood in the doorway, blocking my escape route. I tried to decide whether or not I should kill her, too.

A door opened in the wall behind the interviewer's desk. I had never noticed such a door in any of the rooms before. A white door set in a white wall. But maybe it had always been there, because how could anyone have known that I would pick this day, this room? Yes, the problem was just my own stupid lack of observation.

The interviewer lay twitching, frothing, etc, on the floor with the bread knife stuck in his gullet. The new man stepped over this dying marionette and extended his right hand. I took it, automatically. I was covered in blood—not a pretty sight, I assure you.

'We are now in a position,' the man said, 'I'm happy to say, that is, if you're interested, to offer you a job.'

Orderlies came in and carried out the corpse. Two cleaning ladies entered and started scrubbing the walls and the carpet, which, being blood-red, would not show the stains. My new friend opened a desk drawer and got out some clean clothes and held them out to me. 'What job?' I finally managed to say.

The new man went to the interviewer's chair and stood behind it.

'A vacancy has arisen,' he said, in a regretful but resigned way. 'It is well-paid work.'

I sat down in the chair and composed myself. My face became bland, smooth, devoid of all expression. I wondered how long it would be before someone came to see me with a bread knife up his sleeve.

GRANTA

LISA ST AUBIN DE TERAN
THE FIVE OF US

Lisa St Aubin de Teran left the James Allen's Girls School to marry at the age of sixteen. She and her exiled Venezuelan husband travelled extensively through Europe for two years before returning to his family home in the Andes. For seven years, she ran her husband's sugar and avocado estate, the experiences of which form the background for her first novel, *Keepers of the House*. 'The Five of Us' is selected from her second novel, *Slow Train to Milan*, which is published by Jonathan Cape. She currently lives in East Anglia, and she and her husband, the poet George Macbeth, have recently bought a castle in the Fens.

I t's nearly ten years now since I left Italy, and three full years since I left the Andes, but strangers still come up to me sometimes in Paris or London or Caracas. And they say, 'You were one of the four, weren't you?'

And I know what they mean, and sometimes I nod, and sometimes I don't any more, but inside, I always think, 'We weren't really four; there were five of us: César, Otto, Elias, and me, and the slow train to Milan.' And the slow train was the slide rule of our existence, often our raison d'être. Our exile was aimless without it. I wonder if we would have survived the waiting, the tension, and the failure, but for the luxury of moving on.

I met César when I was sixteen. Like so many others, I was fascinated by him. I suppose that I could claim to know him better than anyone else, and yet he is still the same stranger of our first days, has still the same shy, cruel smile. Later people ask me why I did it. When I think it over, I can only come up with a kind of restlessness. I joined them out of boredom, and then just stayed on. It all began in London, and then we drifted to Italy, later travelling from Paris to Milan and back, and sometimes to Bologna.

I met César first, although I didn't really meet him as such: I just came upon him in my tracks. I had been doing some quick shopping for the week-end, and I was making my way home, carrying my mother's round wicker basket clutched to me with both hands as an improvised shield from the wind. As I went to turn the corner into my street, César loomed up in front of me, immensely tall, and directly in my path. I looked up, ready to dismiss any explanation that might be proffered, but before I could fully collect my thoughts, César, who was then a total stranger, said, 'South America'. And I said, 'Yes', and I still don't know exactly what he meant.

He took my basket and walked beside me. I waited for him to say something else, and it took me some minutes to grasp that that was all. I was living with my mother in a rambling flat in south London. She was away for the week-end, and I was preparing for my Cambridge entrance examinations. I stopped in front of the row of bare pollarded limes, hoping to disguise my home. But it was early January and very cold, so I moved back to the entrance to the flats. I tried to dismiss César at the outer gates, at the door, on the stairs, and finally at my door. But each time he nodded and followed me on. I realized that despite his appearance, he wasn't English, and his 'South America' made more sense. When all my farewells failed, I gave up and shut the door in his face, only to find that he had his foot wedged in the frame.

He forced his way into the flat without a word. I was physically blocking the way to the sitting-room, so he made his way in to the kitchen and sat down. Once there, he stayed very still and silent with his arms crossed. I made a few jokey attempts to get him to explain himself, and then asked him to leave. César took no more notice of me than of the specks of dust drifting over the stove. He would neither talk nor move.

I walked around him, as one might at a gallery. I viewed him from different angles. He was very beautiful in a strange passive way. I was reminded of Buster Keaton or of a Greek statue. His eyes were the golden brown of an eagle, and the line of his nose was perfectly straight. Later, I learned that he was very proud of that line and of his pride itself which he carried like a Siamese twin. I began to want him to speak. But he was silent. I tried tempting him with other languages, with French and Dutch and German; I even exposed my faulty Latin. He showed his good-will; he smiled indulgently. He was like a mountain towering over my table. I offered him food. He shook his head; then he pointed to himself, like Tarzan in corduroy, and said, 'C'est ça.'

I was delighted. I didn't realize that that was his name: César. He was silent again, and I left him so I could have a bath. I locked myself in, poured an extravagant quantity of my mother's bath salts into the water, and lay back to day-dream and think, in that order.

The next time I went back to the kitchen, he had gone.

César returned the next day with carnations. He was wearing a three-piece suit, and he made straight for the sitting-room and stationed himself beside the fire, where he remained for the rest of the day. I was most intrigued by his not eating. He turned down all my offers of tea and coffee and food, and yet stayed for the entire day. My mother would be returning from Loughborough on the following morning, and I couldn't quite make up my mind who to tell first, her or him. I decided that, in all decency, she should be the first to know that a strange man was keeping up some mysterious vigil in her sitting-room, so I telephoned her at my sister's house.

We exchanged our news and were about to ring off when I found a way of telling her about César. She seemed more alarmed than I had predicted. I couldn't keep up with her questions.

'What does he look like?'

'Old.'

'How old?'

'Very old.'

'Oh.' The last very disappointed but still keeping a brave face on it. 'And who is he, darling?'

'Well, I don't know.'

'But where did you meet him?'

'Just on the street.'

'Oh God. What do you mean just on the street? Where on the street?'

'In Abbeyville Road.'

'In Abbeyville Road!' This last was too much for her and her voice rose. Why that road should seem worse than any other I don't know.

'Well, never mind, darling.' She was brave again, in control. 'I'll be back tomorrow. Just wait until I get there, all right? Where is he now, anyway?'

'He's here.'

'What do you mean, here?'

'He's here, at the flat, in the room.'

'Oh my God. Why did you let him in?'

'Well, he just forced his way in, actually.'

'I see. You're alone in the flat with a very old Venezuelan man whom you have never seen before and who forced his way into the flat and has been there for two days and he doesn't eat anything and he's got rings under his eyes and he's started calling you Veta, but he doesn't say anything else—is that about right?'

'Yes, that's more or less it.'

'I see. Now, do you think,' my mother weighed her words very carefully, 'that he is going to attack you? I mean, I think that I should call the police.'

'Oh no, he's all right. He's very old-fashioned.'

'So was Jack the Ripper.'

'Why don't you come and take a look at him and then see what you think. He's not doing anything. He's just here.'

When my mother arrived home, cold and tired from her journey, and put out by having to come home a day early, she was in a mood for no nonsense. She was visibly relieved to see me in one piece and the furniture still intact. She was inside; the door hadn't been barricaded; I was not a hostage—all these things soothed her rage. She swept in to the sitting-room ready for a fight. César had moved towards the window when he heard the knock at the door, and he'd peered into the street to reassure himself. My mother stared at him for a moment and then said, 'But he's beautiful, darling,' and they shook hands. César clicked his heels like a Prussian officer, and they smiled as though at the signing of some treaty.

'Sit down, sit down,' she said, 'you must be tired.' All her own tiredness had fled. My mother has always had a passion for lame ducks, and a great respect for genuine sadness, and as a very beautiful woman herself, she admired the quality of beauty in others. César came like a sacrament to her house, both sad and beautiful. He was her world as it should be, the aesthete's dream.

On the third day after I met César, he asked me to marry him. We were standing at a bus stop on the edge of Clapham Common. I shook my head. His face was always very pale, but sometimes it became quite expressionless, almost ghostly. It did then.

'Why, no?' he asked me.

'I don't know you.' I laboured with his pocket dictionary and brought out a 'Maybe later, *tal vez luego.*' He said some words in Spanish that I didn't understand, but that I remembered later. He said, 'You will never know me.' And then again, 'Marry me, *vamanos a Italia.*'

We were married at the Lambeth Registry Office on October 2. I remember that we had some difficulty filling in the forms. First, the registrar took down our names. I had come to speak for César on most occasions, owing to his lack of English, combined with his natural reticence.

'Is that your full name?' the registrar asked.

César looked at him for a while, and then said, 'No, but it is enough.'

'Oh, I'm sorry,' said the offended registrar, 'but we must have your full name. All your names.'

César shrugged, and then took a long breath, and began, 'César Alejandro Diego Rodrigo...' and the names unfurled in a dull litany of Spanish vowels, repeating themselves over and over again until they came to a halt with a final '...de Labastida', and César took his breath.

The registrar looked at him very hard, and then from him to me and back again. 'Is he serious?' he asked.

I nodded, and we began to decipher the string of surnames that had just been reeled off. It was a revelation to me, as I had never heard them all before.

When we reached the column marked 'profession', we were held up again.

It occurred to me then, for the first time, that I had no idea what profession César had. I knew that his passport said 'businessman'. But previously, when I had asked him why, he had just looked away in his usual manner and said, 'Life is easier like that.'

'Shall we just put "businessman" then?' I asked him.

'No!' Short and sharp with the unleashing of his hands.

'It is very simple,' the registrar explained. 'Just put down your work.'

'He doesn't work, as such,' I volunteered.

'Well then, that's easy, he's unemployed.' The registrar prepared to write 'unemployed' in his careful copperplate.

'No!' César said. 'Unemployed' conjured up a layabout to him, and he maintained that layabouts should be lined up against a wall and shot, preferably by him personally. The fact that he spent most of his time literally lying about, sleeping, was somehow different.

'I see,' the registrar said, humouring him. 'What *do* you do then, sir?'

'I don't do,' César said, 'I am.'

'But what are you?'

'I am an *hacendado*.'

We looked up the word in my, by now, very frayed pocket dictionary; he was a landowner. This was news to me too, and I was

259

strangely reassured by it. I didn't know exactly what César's friends did—Otto, and Elias—but I was pretty sure that it was illegal. But César was obviously different. Now I would be able to tell my grandmother, and Bridie, our housekeeper who was coming back, and Jonah, my English tutor, what César was. People would be satisfied with the answer. For once, it wouldn't sound like an evasion.

My mother came as one witness, and David, my brother-in-law, came as the other. The wedding photographs drifted into the family album, and but for the carnations on our lapels, and the fact that I was wearing a fur coat and Russian hat on what was obviously a sunny day—they didn't look at all special, following all the other photos of my mother's four marriages. It didn't really feel like a wedding, not like my sister's had been.

Everything felt unreal that day. The weather had changed and become strangely warm. César had eaten his usual breakfast: a plate of fried eggs and half a pound of strawberry jam, and then he had insisted that we take a walk. We walked past the house where at the turn of the century an Indian prince had been stuffed in a mattress and left to rot, and outside which I had first met César, and we walked on through the winding backwaters of Clapham. It was eleven o'clock, and our wedding was fixed for one.

'We're not getting married,' he said, solemnly.

I stared into the window of the Indian shop on the corner, and said nothing.

'It's better that way,' he added, and then walked on. I could see that he was going to tell me something, and I thought that I'd do best just to let him get on with it. So I hurried to keep up with him, and waited for what was to come. I had a feeling that he was going to tell me something about himself that I wouldn't like. We were walking past the tall railings of the South London Hospital for Women.

'*Estuve preso,*' César told me, 'I have been in prison.'

I nodded. It had been easy enough to guess, over the months. His phobia about closed doors, the scars from bullet wounds in his neck and leg, his restlessness, his pacing, the way he groaned and shuddered in his sleep, gave him away.

'You don't mind?' he asked.

'I mind,' I said, 'but it doesn't matter.'

'Otto, Elias, and me, we believe.'

I didn't know what they believed in, but I was glad to hear that they believed in something. I had spent some time with all of them. I had no idea, however, what kind of time was in store for me. I nodded again, encouragingly.

'We rob banks,' he said.

I nodded again. 'And what else?' I asked, casually.

'Nothing else,' he said simply. 'There was the guerrilla; Otto was like our general, our speaker; Elias was the commando. I robbed the banks.'

Put like that, it all sounded very straightforward. They were all more scrupulous than I had thought.

'I am a rich man,' César continued, obviously determined to say his whole piece. 'All the money from the banks was for the guerrilla. You understand.'

I was understanding very clearly now, and I could feel a great wave of relief sweeping over me. I liked a man of principle.

'We are an army of three now. We are defeated. There is a price on Otto's and Elias's head and I am exiled. There is no reason why you should stay with us. You are young, Veta. If you marry me, you might never be safe again.'

'I would like to stay,' I told him, and he stared at me dully, as though in pain.

We walked along in silence for a while, past the scarred bunkers on the edge of the Common, and the gaping mouth of the Underground. Then César said, 'My father is dead.'

Everything else had been like some unburdening of his mind. He was offloading his conscience. I didn't feel that he really wanted to tell me the things he did; it was just that he didn't want me not to know them. What he had said last was what mattered to him most.

'My father would have liked you.'

The first weeks after the wedding we spent in Oxford, and they were by far the quietest I had known. The worst of the summer tourists had gone, and although the term had just begun, we saw little of the students. Some mornings we had the dining-room entirely to ourselves, which pleased César as he could have as much jam as he wanted without having to ask. It was turning cold again and most of the leaves had fallen and soaked into a mottled sponge underfoot. I spent a lot of time in the garden. Otto was absorbed in his study of linguistics and in long conversations with a girl-friend; Elias was studying aviation—he intended to take a flying certificate in Italy; César was deep in a mound of leather-bound volumes of sixteenth-century history that he had found in Blackwell's. And I had considerable status since my marriage. I now went out 'on business'. Every morning at ten o'clock, Otto and I walked to a phone box, and made a long-distance call to the Midland Bank in Gracechurch Street in the City.

'It is easier for you; you speak English,' he explained. 'Ask for a cable in my name. It is for $340,000 US. Nothing else, just ask if it has arrived yet.'

I dutifully telephoned each day, and each day I was told that there was no such cable.

By the end of the first week, I made them check, and double-check. Nothing came, and we waited after that and telephoned only on alternate days. Finally, after it had begun to seem like an entirely mythical sum, the mere routine of asking and nothing more, a young man said: 'Yes, there is a cable here.'

When I told Otto, he kissed me, and we bought a whole cardboard-boxful of cream pastries to take back to the hotel, and everyone got very drunk on aquavit mixed with whisky, rum and vodka.

'It's a Molotov cocktail', they said. 'You'll love it.'

I could hardly move for the hangover the next morning. My head had become icily heavy. 'We're going to London,' Otto said, and he left the room, returning shortly with a mug of cold beer. 'Here, drink that; it'll put you back into first gear.'

I felt very sick all day but I had been commissioned to go into the bank and see about the money.

'Just remember,' Otto kept saying, 'don't let them follow you out.'

We took a taxi to the city and Otto dropped me off in Gracechurch Street outside the bank. We had arranged to meet up not far away. I was feeling rather grand, wearing a great fox-fur hat. I asked by name for the young man I had last spoken to on the telephone. He came towards me, saying something as he walked. 'You're not listening,' he whispered.

I apologized.

'Have you spoken to anyone else at the bank?' he asked. I shook my head, and he seemed relieved. 'I've spoken to you on the phone,' he said. 'I could tell you were a child by your voice. '

'Thank *you*,' I thought, and wished I could look a bit older.

'I don't know what part you play in all this,' he continued, 'and I don't want to. But I'd like to give you a chance. I shouldn't tell you this, but whoever touches that money is in trouble. Do you understand me?'

I was beginning to, but I wasn't prepared to believe him.

'I just don't like to think of you getting involved,' he said, and then he looked slowly around the bank and then back to me. 'I'm afraid your husband's money is frozen—' he paused. 'No one knows who you are here. Please go now, and if you're wise, don't come back. There's a special instruction with that cable, and your husband is mentioned by name. I'm sorry,' he added.

I felt as though I was going to cry. I didn't really know why, except that what I was being told seemed to imply some kind of betrayal. I can't remember how I left the bank. I don't think I even thanked the man, and I had forgotten all about not being followed.

I wondered how I was going to break the news to Otto. It was my first assignment, and I felt personally responsible for its failure. Otto listened very carefully when I told him the news, and then he asked me to repeat what I had said, and then to repeat it again.

'What does it mean?' I asked.

'It doesn't matter,' he said, and we walked towards the Underground staring grimly at each other. After a few minutes Otto burst out laughing.

'Why are you laughing?' I asked.

'Sometimes things are that bad,' he said.

The freezing of the money signalled the beginning of virtual penury. It also signalled the beginning of our fame. We separated and then some time later Otto phoned us and asked to meet us at Domodossola, just inside the Italian border. 'Take the slow train from Paris on Tuesday,' he said, 'and I'll pick it up along the line.'

'What if you miss it?' I asked.

'Then we'll miss each other,' he said and rang off.

César and I took the boat train to France and began to make our way south via Paris. The train we took from there was worn, like a seaside hotel past its prime. It rattled along in a sort of bronchitic wheeze, lurching from time to time as it swung its long tail over the winding tracks. Occasionally an express train would burst past us, and its smug efficiency seemed to shriek 'rush of art, rush of art' as it sped out of sight.

Our train spoke in a different voice. It had a confident whisper as it rolled along, like a drunkard with money to spend. Everywhere there was a station it gasped into it and waited with its iron feet hunched up under the platform, and clouds of steam drifting along its sides. A handful of passengers got in or out. Soldiers on leave, a few tourists, a few teenagers, and a few quiet people on their own. Some of them drifted out into the corridor to smoke, or, like me, just to watch the night. Whenever the train jolted or braked everyone fell back a little. Only the ticket collector swung his way up and down the corridors as sure-footed as before. I began to practise, incorporating the train's lurching into a rhythm of my own.

One country distinguished itself from the next by the magazines and fizzy drinks that were offered through the windows in different languages and dialects, and in different flavours according to where we were. César slept and woke and slept, and he seemed brighter and younger after each bout. The food got worse as we went along. The rolls became even harder, the ham drier, and the apples and bananas more bruised. It was as though all the bread had been cut a week before our departure and carefully distributed to all the stations on our route, so that the nearer we came to Italy, the staler the rolls became. We had our own hard rations of chocolate and wine, and César had several jars of strawberry jam, which he ate with a teaspoon. Once a day we trekked along the train to the restaurant. It would take thirty hours to reach Milan and the best part of another day to get to Rome....

One morning, long after we had been in Italy, and met up with Otto and Elias, and then been separated again, I woke up, my legs rigid with cold, and every joint in my feet and hands stiff and cramped, and I whispered, 'Are you there?' to César, and was horrified to find that he wasn't. I extricated my fur coat from the blankets and put it on, noticing that César's was gone. I had fallen asleep convinced that I was rigid from malnutrition, but having found myself alone, I staggered out of bed and was on my feet in no time. I had hardly the time to consider how angry I was at this desertion when César appeared, laden with everything from hot food to letters from home, and even a minute cylinder of Calor gas.

I was so hungry that I couldn't face the pizzas César had brought, so I left them to him, and ate my way steadily through a whole box of cakes and pastries and a litre of pear juice. When I was about halfway through, I asked him how he had acquired such wonders, but he wouldn't tell me.

'We're going to Milan today,' he announced.

We packed a few books and clothes, and locked up the flat, and took our leave of the neighbours. They shook their heads sadly and one of them said, 'You don't have to pretend. We have seen you all come and go; the one with the beard and the one with the limp, the one with the child and the one with the rings. They never come back again, and nor will you.'

I hoped they were wrong about this, since I had left half my belongings in the flat, and I had every intention of returning once the weather changed.

When we reached the station I said to César, 'I've forgotten my rings.'

'No you haven't', he said, 'we ate them this morning,' and he handed me the pawnbroker's ticket.

No matter how awful Milan looks when you leave it, there is always a brightness under the grime when you return. The same thing applied to Paris and Bologna and all the other places where we stopped and stayed. No matter where, during our last days there, the very place would eat into us. We would come to believe that everyone was following us; the police were always reaching for their guns; other cars aimed at us; even the food would become tasteless and the wine sour. And we would leave, glad already, because we were getting away. And then the new place would begin to pall, and we would return, and see all the things we'd missed from the time before. So Milan became the prima donna once again.

We discovered Il Duomo, and we fed the pigeons at the foot of the monument in the Piazza del Duomo, and Otto climbed on to the horse of Victor Emmanuel II and declared himself Otto I, one night when he was drunk, and César told him that he would have to be Otto II, and Otto had pretended to cry, so loud that the carabinieri came, and we had to run, pursued by them down the cobbled backstreets. It took us till dawn to meet up again.

Elias had found us a place to stay in Milan. It was in the old quarter, near the Via Dante, and the trams rattled right past the windows. It was part of the mezzanine floor of a converted palace, and the panelled walls and floor-length shutters had an elegance that we were unused to. There was virtually no furniture, just beds and canvasses and a pair of easels and a makeshift kitchen and nothing else.

'We can stay here until June,' Elias told us. He obviously wasn't volunteering any more information, and he didn't like being asked, so we never knew whose flat it was.

The weeks went by very quickly in Milan—sightseeing again and visiting Elias's good friend Tito, who was planning some king of raid. It was Elias who financed us during this period, with a seemingly endless trickle of ready cash from one of his many mysterious bank accounts. Elias had, by now, grown so brash about 'shopping' in Standa that he used it as though he had an expense account there. He even asked the shop assistants to pass him things that were behind counters or out of his reach. He would ask for delicacies: 'Do you have eels' livers or Jackson's teas?' He moved in and out unchallenged, carrying away our every necessity and my every whim.

'All you need is confidence,' he'd say. 'If you take my advice, don't ever shoplift,' he told me, 'you blush too much, and you just haven't got that natural flair. You might do for something big, but it often takes more *sang-froid* to go for the little things. You see you have to go in like a big-timer, like the Aussie gang, and then nobody dares to stop you.'

Judging by his own success, I thought he must be right. There was nothing that Elias couldn't steal, however awkward or however large. If it took two people to take out a television set from a department store, then he would ask someone to help him, and wheel it out, so that César shouldn't be 'deprived'. If it was raining, he would dash into Standa and reappear with four umbrellas, one for each of us. Elias flouted danger for the fun of it, and we'd come to think he would never get caught. And then, one day in the middle of April, he was trapped in Standa.

He had been with Tito, and it was he who brought us the news.

'Couldn't he have run?' César asked.

'No,' Tito said, 'it was a trap from the start. He went down the escalator to the food store in the basement, but they were waiting for him. I had to buy a new plug, and I went upstairs to get it. The noise brought me back. It sounded as though the whole shop was screaming. Elias was downstairs: they'd stopped the escalator and cordoned off the food hall; there was a crowd of customers herded into one end, and Elias, with his clothes all torn, fighting like a madman. He had policemen on the floor, whole racks of food knocked down, and six men tackling him. I don't know who was the worse off physically but they got him in the end.'

Nobody wanted to say anything, but we all had the same thought. All evening we kept a vigil, hardly daring to break the silence. We kept the lights off, and sat on the floor under the window, listening to the rumbling of the trams and hoping that Elias would somehow escape, knowing that he would most likely die. Prisoners had a way of falling to their deaths in Italy; it had happened already that year to a friend of Tito's. As the night progressed, I felt again like an outsider, the neighbour attending Elias's wake.

We ran the risk of being arrested by sitting through the night in our flat, which was Elias's flat, and they must have known it, but they didn't seem to care. Tito was the first to move. He had wept, with his back against the shutters, and I had envied him his tears. I was too stunned even to cry. Theoretically, I had known that this could happen at any time. There had been occasional reminders; once, outside Oepli, the bookshop, a car had backfired like a gun, and thrown out a stone from the gutter which hit Otto in the leg, and I knew that when he moved, he did so believing that he was shot. And the greyness of César's face, reflected in the shop glass, was resigned grief. They were always ready for the one beside them to fall down dead, and ready for their own arrest. But they put it out of their minds, concentrating on their success. Every day was a success; for Elias, it was one more day of avoiding the warrant out for his death.

Tito rose to leave.

'It's just possible,' he said, 'that his cover will hold. If anyone is lucky, it's Elias.'

He squeezed César and Otto by the shoulder, picking his way over their legs as he went.

'I have friends with friends,' he said, 'I'll find out what I can.' The room was dark, and he turned the light on, by the door, and then thought better of it, and turned it off.

'You shouldn't be here, Otto,' he said. 'They were waiting for him in Standa; they could be waiting outside this door.'

'No,' Otto said, 'they haven't found this yet. I think it would feel stranger than it does.'

'This is no time for voodoo,' César butted in. 'Tito's right. Why don't you go with him and see what you can find out.'

Otto didn't answer but he stood up and left the room. He returned with his shoulder bag and a box of papers. He seemed glad to be on the move. He turned the light on and pointed to the papers.

'Burn these,' he told me. I nodded but didn't move. 'Now!' he said, 'and then scatter the ashes. Then stay here with César. If you're gone when I return, I shall assume that you are arrested.' He kicked a socket in the skirting-board lightly. 'If anything happens, put that switch down with your foot.' He was talking to me. César was lost in his thoughts, stone-faced on the floor. 'I'll be right back,' Otto added as a parting shot.

I began to rummage through the box of papers and then for something to burn them in. I wondered how long Otto would be. His 'right back' was no guide. They always said it, and I knew it bore no relation to time. I supposed that Tito would tell us if anything happened to him. He was more likely to be arrested than we were. I wished that we had all gone together. It was always fatal to split up. It was what happened in horror films. Ghosts only came to you when you were alone. But César was immovable in a calamity. It took time for him to react. Once he decided on a course of action, he was a strategic genius, but while he decided, he was cataleptic. As I picked over our papers, I wondered if he could even see me.

I burned all that we had except for clothes and books.

Otto returned alone; he looked at my blackened hands and the heap of charred evidence with indulgent approval. 'Good,' he nodded and then left me to talk to César.

I was surprised to see how alert César had become; I had thought that he was sleeping.

'What news?' he asked, and then before Otto could say a word, 'Tell me first, is it good or bad?'

'I don't know yet but it might be good,' Otto told him, and then turning to me he said, 'you can listen if you want to,' which I was, and then to César again. 'They took him down to a local station and they beat the hell out of him and then a chap from the *Immigrazione* was called in. Elias was carrying his Peruvian papers today. He's been moved to a central interrogation block.'

'How do you know?' César asked.

'Tito's friend knows someone in reception.'

'Did they see him?' César asked.

'Yes. They said he looked like one man going in and another coming out; they've beaten the shape out of his face.'

'Thank God,' César said.

'What do you mean?' I asked him.

'There's a chance they won't recognize him.'

'But what about finger-prints?' I asked. Even his passports had finger-prints on them; they all did.

'Elias has never been taken before,' Otto told me, 'they can only identify him from photographs and if he talks.'

'What do you think?' César asked Otto.

'I hardly like to believe it,' Otto said, 'but he could just get done for shoplifting and the brawl at Standa. He could just get out.'

César took out a cigarette and lit it.

'Will Tito come back?' he asked.

'If he thinks it's safe. If not, we're to meet him at the corner of the street where the tram stops, every two hours on the hour.'

'Has he got a friend in the new block?'

'Sort of, there's a cousin of that chap Marcello's. Tito says he's never been very forthcoming but he's O.K.' Here Otto turned to me and asked if I had finished burning the papers.

'Not really,' I said, and I knew I had said the wrong thing. He glared at me; there was only ever yes or no. I went back to the flowerpot, which was cracked.

'Use a saucepan,' Otto snapped.

When I came back from the mini-kitchen he and César were discussing something under their breath. As I drew near them, Otto stuffed two bundles hurriedly into his bag. I recognized them by their shape and bulk.

'Why the guns?'

'We might leave suddenly,' César said.

'Well, why hide the guns from me?' I asked indignantly.

'Are you good with one?' Otto demanded.

'No, but....'

'Then get on with what you are good at, and don't ask questions.'

Otto came and went twice more during the night, but he brought no news with him of any kind. César slept, leaning against the wall, and then moved to his mattress.

'Elias knows how much I love him,' he said, 'but I can't stay awake any longer.' He covered himself and curled up. 'Call me if you need me.'

Tito arrived at seven in the morning, haggard and unshaven. He brought a bag of fresh rolls with him.

'I have to go to work,' he said. He had an office job as a civil servant. 'I'm afraid there's still no news.'

'None?' Otto said, looking hard at Tito's hands. Tito was fiddling with a scrap of paper from the bread bag.

'Well...a man from Interpol went in this morning, and...Maurizio was seen to go in.'

Even I had heard of this Maurizio. He was the scourge of Milan, the most ruthless interrogator since the SS left the city.

'There's just a chance he's been called in for someone else,' Tito added. 'We don't know it was for Elias.'

The others weren't listening any more. Tito could see that. He picked up his hat and scarf, and said good-bye. He was reluctant to go though.

'It's all right,' Otto said, 'Elias won't talk.'

Tito looked relieved. 'I know myself,' he explained, 'with Maurizio, I might talk; I'm sorry.'

'No,' Otto said again, 'Elias won't talk, but Maurizio is an animal; if Elias doesn't pretend to talk, he might kill him for fun.'

'Elias isn't stupid,' César said. 'He'll say something; he knows.'

Tito returned at lunch-time.

'He is with Maurizio,' he confirmed. 'But Marcello's cousin says they don't know who he is yet.'

After he left, I asked Otto how long it would take before they discovered that Elias's passport was false.

'But it isn't false,' he said.

'That's not his name though.'

'No, but it is somebody's name, someone who has never had a passport, and who has agreed to lie low for a year or two. It has Elias's photo and Elias's fingerprints, and all the right seals and signatures.'

I hadn't realized before that a false passport could be real.

'Do you mean that if Elias doesn't talk, and they don't recognize him, they really can't trace him?'

'That's right,' Otto said, without much hope. 'If that bastard Maurizio leaves him alive, they could just call in the Peruvian consul, and deport him.'

'What if the Consul recognizes his accent?' I asked, doubtfully.

'Do you know, the man who shot Trotsky spoke a host of languages, and Elias is like that; he is just South American, from anywhere in the continent, always a stranger, always a native. He's been roaming since he was fourteen, and he has a brain like a computer.'

Tito returned in the evening with the news that Maurizio had been seen to leave the building.

Tito took back his guns, wrapped in the same clothes they had been in the night before. 'You won't need these now,' he said, 'they're more of a liability than a help at the moment.'

We spent the evening together with some of Tito's 'men'. We

didn't know most of them, but the events of the past twenty-four hours had drawn us suddenly close, with Elias as a common cause. As Elias's chance of escape grew, the air of reverence with which we had treated him in his absence slackened off. Everyone was struck by the absurdity of the situation. Here were the Milanese police holding an internationally wanted criminal, whom they were interrogating for information about far less significant people wanted for far smaller crimes, and they didn't know it. The very police had punched his face to an unrecognizable pulp. If only they could see under the bruises, they would see the man whose poster was in every police file in Europe, whose photograph would be in the hands of every casual hit-man whom Interpol had ever hired: Elias who said, 'I'm not a gangster, I'm a soldier.' Elias who had turned a pogrom into a civil war. I had seen a CIA photograph in Paris of Elias in action with a target dot on his chest in the angle between his arm and his machine gun. I found it impossible to believe that the police could really be so stupid as to catch him, question him, and still let him slip through their net.

Elias was finally taken from the central interrogation block on the following morning. We were kept closely informed by Marcello's cousin, who was kept informed by converging gossip and chance sightings of Elias himself. On one occasion he saw Elias being carried down a corridor. He was unconscious. Tito spared us the details, but we heard them later from Marcello's cousin, who described the scene with a wealth of gory Latin zest.

'He looked like a monster,' he said, 'a monster with no skin on his face.'

Elias was deported. He had a police escort to the Italian frontier. Ironically, they took the slow train to Simplon, the same that we had travelled on so many times together.

Our informant told us of the time of departure, and Tito drove us to the station. Elias was handcuffed to two uniformed guards. That was how we recognized him, and by the way he walked, because his face was swollen into a horrifying purple mess. They led him like a blind man; his eyes were so nearly closed.

'How will he manage when he arrives?' I asked.

'He'll manage,' Otto said.

I was the only 'legal' person of the group, the only one who had nothing to lose by being seen with Elias.

'Follow them on to the train, and then say good-bye,' Otto told me, 'let him know that we know he's all right.'

As I stood in front of Elias, facing him and his armed escort on the train, I suddenly didn't know what to say. I might never see him again; he might still die; and I had never told him how much I loved him, missed him, wanted him to stay. I needed one perfect phrase to sum up all the worry and goodwill. The whistle blew, and the train was about to leave. The police guards pushed past me, pulling Elias by the wrists. It was now or never, and no single sentence would do.

'Good-bye,' I said to him. He could just see me through his one half-open eye.

'Geronimo!' he croaked, and followed the guard.

I bit my lip and jumped off the train. The others were waiting for me.

'What did he say?' they all asked together.

I told them, and they laughed, but I felt miserable and depressed.

'Say something then,' Otto nudged to cheer me up.

But I didn't have the heart to.

'I bet you're upset because you couldn't think of what to say on the train,' Otto whispered to me in the car.

I nodded, and we let the matter drop. It was the second time in a year that I had been lost for words. In Venice, leaning over one of the minor bridges, I had seen an old man walking towards me in a haze of white hair. He was bowed and seemed more ancient than is usually possible. Something about him forced me to stare, and I recognized him. As he drew nearer, I told César, 'That's Ezra Pound.'

'Speak to him,' César said, 'you'll never have the chance again.' I stepped into the via, and all my language left me, looking at an old man with a wind-tanned wrinkled skin, enjoying his walk.

'Speak to him,' César urged, 'now or never.'

But nothing I could say could mean as much to him as to say nothing and let him pass and enjoy his ninety-year-old walk through Venice undisturbed. Again, cramped in the back of Tito's ravaged Fiat Cinquecenta, I felt cheated by the eloquence of silence.

GRANTA

CLIVE SINCLAIR
ANTICS

Clive Sinclair was born in London in 1948. He is the author of one novel, *Bibliosexuality,* and two collections of short stories, *Hearts of Gold* and *Bed Bugs.* On his current contribution to *Granta,* Sinclair writes: 'The phone rings. I answer. A quiet American voice says, "Got any new stories?" No, but I have an idea.... "'Antics", like many of its predecessors, has a central image which serves also as a metaphor taken from nature. I was watching a programme on Channel 4 about a tropical rain forest when the ghost of Franz Kafka suddenly hi-jacked the script. There is this ant, you see, which undergoes a metamorphosis; it is transformed by persuasive spores into a fungus. The problem was to write my own story, not Kafka's. That required a second image, anecdote, incident, or idea; the story emerging from the connections made. Fortunately, at about that time, I had a row with my wife about our respective household duties, and something one or other of us said set the story in motion. The feminist wasps also exist....'

No sooner had I opened my eyes than my intended coquettishly requested a deposit. An enviable invitation, you might think, coming from such a voluptuary, but I dallied. Later, after having supped upon a host of aphrodisiacs whilst sipping extranuptial nectar, my passionate inquisitor returned. Her musky scents turned my olfactory membranes into traitors, so I shook my head to clear my brain. This involuntary act was misinterpreted as a negative signal and thereby saved me.

'You cold-blooded bastard,' screamed my would-be spouse, 'you're no better than a neuter!' And up she went on a lonely nuptial flight, displaying her moist orifice to me, as she copulated with my invisible doppelgänger. My senses jigged and my nerve ends jingle-jangled; my instincts urged me to capitulate, and my brain was overcome with desire; but a disembodied voice advised me otherwise.

'Do you remember your father?' it demanded.

'No,' I replied.

'Hardly surprising,' it retorted. 'He gave in to your mother.'

'Obviously,' I replied, 'or else I wouldn't be here.'

'What's the euphemism females use for *fucking*?' it asked.

'They say they've lost their wings,' I replied.

'Males lose more than that,' it said. 'They die.'

I blanched as I heard the unspeakable truth. 'Who are you?' I demanded.

'Your mind,' it replied.

'Impossible,' I said. '*Hymenoptera* can't think.'

'You can!'

My nubile companion, assuredly no intellectual, continued to masturbate in front of me. 'You've got no alternative,' she whimpered, 'so why not enjoy it?' She was right, as it happened. For we were the last of the species. If I failed to impregnate her, it was extinction; if I did, it was death. Some choice!

Oh, if I could only find one reason to justify my existence! 'To reproduce,' say my genes. But surely there is more to life than that?

Long ago, when I was nothing but a grub, Nursey would transport me from my nocturnal recess into the ultra-violet light where I absorbed the vitamins concealed in sunshine. Even in the midst of this blissful slumber, I could let out a sudden wail, whereupon my canny nurse would summon one of Mother's domesticated aphids and milk its abdominal ducts with her antennae, drawing forth sweet droplets. Then it was salvation (not salivation) as the syrup invaded my impatient mouth and smothered my new-born ego. Satisfied, at last, I would demand a story; so Nursey told me about the ants of North India, as big as Egyptian wolves, who mined gold in the bowels of the earth. 'What else happened?' I cried. But my nanny didn't have an answer.

Now there are no more questions. All is silence. The inner sanctums of our cities are stuffed with the decomposing corpses of our babies, dead of hypothermia and starvation.

At first our scientists were complacent: they explained that matter cannot vanish but only change its form; therefore, the unexpected fate of the nurses—the cause of the trouble—was obviously the beginning of a fourth metamorphosis in our life cycle. Well, we were used to change, so this explanation was accepted, until it became apparent that the nurses had actually reached a terminal stage in their development. Without the nurses our slaves were neutralized, and Mother had acted the queen too long to be of service. So death began to feast upon us, and our future perished.

Unlike our unlamented boffins, however, I was an empiricist. But by the time I was big enough to conduct my own research, only my faithful old provider remained (insuring my survival, bless her).

I followed her as she scuttled along a familiar path, foraging among foliage to restock our larder, until I began to wonder if she were immune to the contagion that had carried off her sisters. She wasn't. The trail led to a particularly verdant patch in the heart of the jungle, where the nurses habitually gathered the juiciest leaves and exchanged gossip (about what?) before turning back to the city. Here the fumes from the decaying wood were all but intoxicating; drunkenness, however, cannot account for what I saw next. Having taken only a few homeward steps, Nursey seemed to lose all sense of direction, and began to climb the nearest tree like a creature possessed. Underdeveloped sexual organs went with the job, what did she want with the sky? Higher and higher she went until she was overwhelmed by exhaustion. I shouted at that formerly wise head, enumerating the advantages of terra firma, as if she were now the naughty boy; but she took no notice, probably wasn't even able to remember who I was. Anyway, with one last effort my nanny sank her mandibles into the bark and died. Nor was her fate unique; on the contrary, it was axiomatic.

My mind, hitherto quiescent, began to nag, no doubt encouraged by its recent success.

'Listen,' it said. 'I saved your life. Now do something for me. Go back to the jungle. See if you can work out why the nurses went haywire.'

For the first time, I experienced something profounder than curiosity; the desire for knowledge. Thus instead of ascending heavenwards, leaving my imprint within my mate en route, I trudged over rotten leaves in search of our nemesis. Her curses clung to me, but none came within a mile of the sights that awaited me in the odiferous glade where our keepers perished.

All the trees in that weird place were decorated with cadavers that had once borne a passing resemblance to me. But not any more. My erstwhile nurse, when observed at close quarters, had undergone a terrifying change. Her fragile carapace had cracked from within, letting out long tendrils that curved under the weight of their tumescent lobes. These dusty fruits looked malevolent, the fungoid excrescence of a nightmare. It was as if she had perished in order to give birth to some new deformity—an impossibility given her circumstances. Nor did the irony inherent in this possibility afford me any masculine satisfaction. Nevertheless, it was clear that something had taken root within, engendering itself in a more congenial place than her sterile womb. How?

'Think,' said my mind.

Even as I mused over-ripe globules, blown by puffs of hot air, dropped to the ground from the trees above and exploded, releasing a dust-bowl of spores. These scattered like ash, awaiting further disturbance. This was provided by an ant from a related species, which received a light coating from them. Sure enough, a few minutes later, she also began to climb a tree. What was going on?

'If you ask me,' replied my mind, 'some of those spores have affected that unfortunate's brain, wherein they are issuing new orders. You can see the result. In other words, she has been persuaded to give birth through a mind, once as moribund as her uterus, but obviously capable of resurrection. What a seductive patter that over-sexed mould must have! It would be fun to reproduce it.'

'Fun?' I said.

'Sorry,' replied my mind. 'I forgot that seduction isn't in your line.'

Even so, the idea began to fascinate me. Our society was based upon unquestioning obedience to instinct, in case my fiancée's impatience had left you in any doubt. As a rule, the males and females leapt from their cracked pupa-cases, flexed their hymenopterous appendages, and took off to satisfy their reproductive urges. Thereafter, the males went into a rapid decline while their widows snapped off the wedding wings, as if to remove the temptation of copulation without a purpose. These fertile ladies were then fussed over and treated like queens by the sadly deficient nurses, who grabbed us grubs as soon as we emerged from Mum's ovipositor. How on earth did that revolting fungus turn their dedicated heads and bring disaster to our civilization? That question became an obsession, helping me to forget about my connubial duties despite furious reminders from elsewhere.

I am, you'll agree, an imago with imagination, but it was still hard work finding an answer. Each time I thought I was getting close, the virago returned with the same demand, destroying my concentration completely.

'You're not yet a wife,' I said, 'why are you in such a hurry to be a widow?'

Now that I was enlightened, the thought of mating with such a prehistoric pest made me shudder. I had too much talent and too many ambitions to squander them upon family life. True, it would mean curtains for the species, but I was prepared to swap genetic immortality for self-realization: once you've had an inkling of an alternative existence there's no going back. Perhaps my nurse had been persuaded to abandon her responsibilities by a silver-tongued smoothie who promised her the world. But unlike mine, this was the false voice of a tempter, whose sweet hum led Nursey to a nauseating end and our species to the brink of oblivion. My mind, on the contrary, had guaranteed me a future (though—it must be confessed—the result is the same in terms of evolution). Certainly I am alive today and, what is more, able to address you in a fashion that is not unentertaining.

The genie leapt out of the ground my nanny had just traversed. 'Why are you doing this for another woman's offspring?' he whispered. 'Why not give yourself a little pleasure for a change?'

'I am doing my duty,' replied Nursey. 'It is why I was born.'

'Poppycock,' hissed the genie, 'that's just propaganda put out by the ruling classes.'

'True or not,' replied my nanny, 'the larvae will starve if I'm not back soon.'

'That is exactly why I have come to speak to you,' said the genie. 'I have news of a great famine sweeping across India. Soon the pestilence will reach your shores and there will be no more food for your babies.'

'What shall I do?' cried my nurse.

'Are you brave?' asked the genie.

'Look at my jaws,' she replied. 'I fear nothing.'

'Good,' said the genie, 'for at the top of that baobab lives a giant to whom ants are caviar. The famine that kills you will provide a feast for him. But if you can strike first, his treasure will be yours. Then, praise the Lord, your babes will never go hungry. Now climb the tree!'

Thus Nursey began the ascent I did my best to prevent. Just as she was about to expire, the genie yelled, 'There's the giant!' and Nursey sank her teeth into what she believed was the throat of her enemy. But all she bit was bark, of course.

'The moral being,' added my mind, 'that one gene's expansion is another's extinction.'

Don't get me wrong, I was genuinely upset by my nurse's demise, but at the same time I was exhilarated by my reconstruction. So much so that I was determined to do more. I saw at once that my nanny's case was exceptional, such altruism being too rare a motive to provide a useful model. No, my evil genius must have sensed an unconscious dissatisfaction amongst the nurse-ants; perhaps he had picked up a clue from listening to their gossip. Don't forget they had never been treated as individuals before, and probably never even considered themselves as such. Yes, the genie awakened their sense of self (how else could he have cajoled them into becoming selfish?), and having done so, sought out their weaknesses and played upon them. He peopled the treetops with giants, fairies, gods, dragons, paradises, and utopias. The shy or vain were assured that awaiting them among the branches of a tamarind was a fairy-godmother who would transform them from drudges into princesses, not forgetting to supply them with the requisite sexual organs. Megalomaniacs or those insignificant enough to possess inferiority complexes were told that power grows from the bole of a tree. So up they marched mistaking their increasing weakness for approaching strength until, in desperation, they sank their jaws into the bark in the vain hope of vampirizing the tree's potency. Ideologues were pointed in the direction of salvation and sent on their way. All (save my nurse) were carried aloft by the promise of self-glory, but their only achievement was to procreate a parasitic mushroom; their metamorphosis being a testament to the genie's poisonous tongue. So great became my admiration of the same (tempered, of course, by a self-knowledge denied his victims) as I reinvented tale after tale, that I feared my mind would burst from the effort of retaining them all. The only solution was to commit the stories to paper.

Now paper was not easily obtained in those days. It was only to be found in the houses of paper wasps; in fact it was the very stuff from which those homes were made. There were plenty of wasp settlements in our neck of the woods, but unfortunately since my refusal to consummate my marriage I was *persona non granta*. You see, the wasps had a similar set-up to us, though their menfolk were even unluckier than ours. Thanks to one of evolution's little quirks, sisters were more closely related to each other than mothers and daughters, as a result of which their cities were militant sororities, each sister being prepared to give her life for her contemporaries. Not a place for an uninvited intruder of the opposite gender, especially one whose name had been blackened by his dissatisfied bride. Lacking companions with whom she could bellyache, my intended had found another place wherein she was able to hive-off her discontent. The buzz of outrage that followed her recitation quickly spread from hamlet to townlet until it became a permanent part of the background, so much so that I began to fear for my chastity. But my need to write was greater than my fear.

Physically I was no match for the wasps; one sting would be enough to finish me off. But I had a mind, which I could use, unlike my adversaries. I calculated that I would require the walls of at least a dozen villages, which I would have to empty somehow. I considered burning out the inhabitants, but that could be self-defeating if the walls also caught fire.

'Try its abstract equivalent,' suggested my mind. 'Rumours spread like wildfire and can be no less devastating.'

The rumour itself was no problem; one word—insecticide—and a location—just beyond the horizon—would suffice. The real difficulty was in getting it started; I couldn't risk showing myself to a wasp. But how else could I pass on the word? Believe it or not, I still shared an apartment with my fiancée (I had too many things on my mind to be bothered with finding new accommodation, and my suitor was reluctant to let me out of her clutches). You can imagine her surprise when I said,

'Come on, then, let's spread our wings.'

'Oh darling,' she said, all smiles and blushes, 'you won't regret it.' I hoped not.

We took off, and warm terminals quickly carried us into the dusky sky where fireflies advertised their love. As the sun set, its rays illuminated several unusual smudges hovering on the rim of the visible world—exactly what I needed!

'Do you see those?' I asked. 'They are clouds of poison. Your friends, the wasps, are being gassed by the local patriarch. Serves 'em right.'

'That's terrible,' responded my wife dreamily.

She was fluttering ahead of me at an excruciatingly slow pace—deliberately, of course—so that I kept bumping into her abdomen. I'll tell you now, if it wasn't for my strength of mind, I would certainly have surrendered to the beauty of the evening and the open invitation of those sensuous undulations.

'Yes, sweetheart, yes,' she trilled, as we rubbed torsos yet again. 'Please don't stop.'

But I did. Just in time.

'You prick,' screamed my wife, as soon as she realized it wasn't her lucky day after all, 'who do you think you are?'

I was still learning the answer to that, but I knew what I had done. Her womb remained empty, but I had planted an idea in her head.

It bore fruit. The following night I watched in delight as the wasps left their homes in droves and swarmed across the sky to rescue their non-existent sisters, leaving the real danger behind. I knew it wouldn't be too long before my plot was twigged, but ants are industrious creatures and my heart was in the work. Without opposition it was almost too easy. I even felt a pang of remorse as I tipped the grubs out onto the ground and saw them devoured by predators who could hardly believe their luck. But the grubs were expendable, whereas my brain-child was unique. Moving swiftly, I demolished the walls by lapping up the honey-glue that joined them, until I considered I had enough paper to fill a book. Then I went into hiding, drunk with honey and success, and began to dream of my masterpiece.

Ink was less of a problem. You'll recall the aphids (now, alas, all feral) we once herded for their milk; well, they have slightly smarter cousins called gall-gnats (for reasons that will become apparent). These deposit their eggs in the local pistachios, along with a little misinformation left behind in the punctured foliage. The pistachios, as is their wont, attempt to produce nuts but, in these instances, are actually fooled into turning out galls, thus perpetuating the gnats rather than themselves, for the alien vessels are inhabited by growing larvae. As luck would have it, these oak-apples also contain tannin; gallic and ellagic acids; ligneous fibre; and water—the basic ingredients of ink. Having few enemies to worry about, the gall-gnats leave their young unprotected, trusting to the efficiency of their freakish citadels. But they had not reckoned on the ingenuity of a single-minded writer. In no time at all I had gathered sufficient of the galls for my purpose. Once again I felt sorry for the infants. But what is art without sacrifice?

My hide-out was on a bluff over-looking our deserted cities and the jungle beyond. In this solitary cell I wrote day and night until my eyes ached. I cannot deny that I had sexual longings, but these were rendered irrelevant by my literary endeavours. Sometimes, when I raised my head from the paper, I saw bands of unforgiving wasps still seeking vengeance for the destruction I had visited upon them. If only they could have appreciated the creativity that was born of that act.

There it was, growing upon the floor of my cave, an animate stalagmite, my pile of stories. As it increased, so did my self-satisfaction, for I knew that I had found a reason to live and a voice of my own.

'What use is that?' demanded my mind. 'When there is no one to hear it.'

Depression followed immediately. The next time I glimpsed my wife flitting around the entrance of my spartan lodgings, I was tempted to invite her to a recital: but—even if she weren't stupid—she would hardly applaud the enterprise for which she had been jilted. Nor was there any posterity to inherit my *oeuvre,* I had seen to that. So I wrote on, unrecognized—until the paper ran out.

There were, however, a few abandoned wasp residences that I still had not ransacked. These I stealthily raided. Returning from one such mission I noticed an aroma in the air far sweeter than my formica. Honey! Before I could flee, they were upon me. Awaiting the fatal thrusts of their stings, I cursed my folly. Instead, the wasps gently lifted me up by my wing-tips.

'As a matter of interest,' I said, 'how did you find me?'

'Look at your hands and feet,' said one of my kidnappers, 'covered in ink. We simply followed your footprints.'

Without another word they escorted me to my bride, also my executioner. She was in no mood for formalities, she grabbed my genitals—which, it turned out, had not atrophied—and forced my body to act in accordance with her will. Some ending!

GRANTA

GRAHAM SWIFT
ABOUT THE EEL

Tara Heinemann

Graham Swift was born in London in 1949. His books include *The Sweet Shop Owner*, *Shuttlecock*, and *Learning to Swim and Other Stories*. He writes by vocation and teaches from necessity. If not constrained to do either he would probably go fishing. 'About the Eel' is from a longer work in progress.

Of which the specimen dropped by Freddie Parr in Mary Metcalf's knickers in July 1940 was a healthy representative of the only, if abundant, freshwater species of Europe—namely, *Anguilla anguilla,* the European Eel.

Now there is much that the eel can tell us about curiosity—rather more indeed than curiosity can inform us of the eel. Does it surprise you to know that only as recently as the 1920s was it discovered how baby eels are born, and that throughout history controversy has raged about the still obscure life cycle of this snake-like, highly edible, not to say phallically suggestive creature?

The Egyptians knew it; the Greeks knew it; the Romans knew it and prized its flesh; but none of these ingenious peoples could discover where the eel kept its reproductive organs—if indeed it had any; and no one could find (and no one ever will) in all the waters in which the European Eel dwells (from the North Cape to the Nile) an eel bearing ripe milt.

Curiosity could not neglect this enigma. Aristotle maintained that the eel was indeed a sexless creature and that its offspring was brought forth by spontaneous generation out of mud. Pliny affirmed that when constrained by the urge to procreate, the eel rubbed itself against rocks and the young were formed from the shreds of skin thus detached. And among other explanations of the birth of this apparently ill-equipped species were that it sprang from putrefying matter; that it emerged from the gills of other fishes; that it was produced from horses' hairs dropped in water; that it issued from the cool, sweet dews of May mornings; not to mention the peculiar tradition of our own Fenland, that the eels are none other than the multiplied mutations of one-time corrupt monks and priests, whom St Dunstan, in a holy and miraculous rage, consigned to eternal, slithery penance for their sins, thus giving to the cathedral city of the Fens its name: Ely—the eely place.

In the eighteenth century the great Linnaeus, who was no amateur, declared that the eel was viviparous: that is to say, its eggs were fertilized internally and its young were brought forth alive; a theory exploded (though never abandoned by Linnaeus) when Francesco Redi of Pisa clearly showed that what had been taken for young elvers in the adult's womb were no more than parasitic worms.

Womb? What womb? It was not until 1777 that one Carlo

289

Mondini claimed to have located the miniscule organs that were, indeed, the eel's ovaries. A discovery which raised doubts in the mind of his countryman Spallanzani (a supporter of Redi *contra* Linnaeus) who asked the simple yet awkward question: if these were the ovaries, then where were the eggs? And thus—after much refutation and counter-refutation and much hurling to and fro of scientific papers—it was not until 1850 that Mondini's discovery was confirmed (long after the poor man's death) by a Pole, Martin Rathke, who published in that year a definitive account of the female genitalia of *Anguilla anguilla*.

Witness the strife, the entanglements, the consuming of energy, the tireless searching that curiosity engenders. Witness that while the *ancien régime* tottered, while Europe entered its revolutionary phase and every generation or so came up with a new blueprint for the destiny of mankind, there were those whose own intellectual destinies were inseparably yoked to the origins of the eel.

And yet in 1850, though the ovaries had been accounted for, the testes still remained a mystery—open to all claimants—and the obscure sex-life of the eel still unilluminated. Obscure or otherwise, it must have been healthy for, notwithstanding the universal ignorance as to their reproductive processes, large numbers of young eels continued every spring to mass at the mouths of their favoured rivers—the Nile, the Danube, the Po, the Elbe, the Rhine—and to ascend upstream, just as they had done in the days of perplexed old Aristotle and before. And it is worth mentioning that in that same year, 1850, though it can only be connected by the most occult reasoning with the researches of a Polish zoologist, the eel-fare, that is the running of elvers or young eels upriver, on the English Great Ouse was on a notably large scale. Two and a half tons of elvers were caught in one day, the numerical equivalent of which can be estimated when it is considered that over twelve thousand elvers make a pound in weight.

In 1874, when you will recall there was much flooding of that same River Ouse and my great-grandfather became not only a father but Conservative Member for Gildsey, another Pole, Anton Syrski, Professor at the University of Lemberg, made the long-delayed discovery of the eel's testes—a breakthrough for which he received more recognition than Mondini. For these same tiny eel's testes are sometimes known—no doubt at the cost of a certain jocularity—as Syrski's organs. This, however, did not prevent, in the same year, one Jacob Munter, Director of the Zoological Museum of Greifswald, examining some 3,000 eels, declaring that none of them was male and concluding that the species reproduced itself parthenogenically; that is, by immaculate conception.

Yet, given those two vital and most complementary organs—the ovaries and the testes—when, where, and by what method do they combine to do their work?

We have not yet come to the most remarkable episode in this quasi-mythological quest for the genesis of the eel. It must be understood that in its natural habitat, the freshwaters and estuaries of Europe and North Africa, the eel assumes two distinct forms. For most of its adult life it is olive-green to yellowish-brown and has a snub nose. But when it has lived for some years, its snout grows sharper, its eyes larger, its sides acquire a silvery sheen, its back becomes black, and all these changes signal a journey back to the sea. Since this journey occurs in autumn and young elvers come upstream in spring, it is not unreasonable to infer that the latter are the offspring of the former and that spawning occurs in winter in coastal regions. Yet (to repeat) who has ever found a ripe female, let alone an eel's egg or a newly-hatched larval eel in the inshore waters of Europe?

In 1856—after Rathke and before Syrski—in the warm currents of the Straits of Messina, a tiny fish was caught one day, quite unlike an eel, and it was claimed as a new genus. Forty years later a similar specimen, caught from the same Straits of Messina, was reared in captivity and demonstrated to be, despite its uneel-like form, none other than the larva of the European eel. Yet if adult eels abounded in such vast numbers, why were their larvae such elusive rarities?

It is time to introduce into the story the figure of Johannes Schmidt, Danish oceanographer and icthyologist. Who has heard of Johannes Schmidt? It is said that modern times do not have their Sinbads and Jasons, let alone their Drakes and Magellans, that the days of great sea-quests went out with Cook. Johannes Schmidt is an exception. There are those who fashion history and those who contemplate it; there are those who make things happen and those

who ask why. And among the latter there are those who regard the
activities of the former as a mere impediment to their aims; who,
indeed, consigning history to the background, turning their backs on
its ephemeral compulsions, set out on the most fairy-tale searches
after the timeless unknown? Such a man—such a votary of
curiosity—was Johannes Schmidt.

In 1904, when the European powers were scrambling for
colonial loot, Johannes Schmidt set out to discover the breeding
ground of the European Eel. He voyaged from Iceland to the Canary
Islands, from North Africa to North America, in ships which,
because of his inadequate funds, were ill-suited to his purpose and ill-
equipped. Catching his first specimen of larvae west of the
Faroes—the first recorded outside the Mediterranean—he proceeded
to catch younger and younger specimens at various stations in the
Atlantic. At the same time, he examined and statistically classified
large numbers of mature eels and was able to confirm—which had
never been demonstrated before—that the European Eel was indeed
one single homogeneous species, *Anguilla anguilla*, as distinct from its
close relative, the American Eel, *Anguilla rostrata*.

In 1908 and 1910, while a crisis flared in Bosnia, Italy turned
covetous eyes on Tripoli, and the British people, impatient with only
four Dreadnoughts a year, began to chant 'We want eight and we
can't wait', Schmidt cruised the length and breadth of the
Mediterranean, collecting eel larvae even from such contentious
waters as those off Morocco and around the excitable Balkans. He
found that the larvae increased in size as he passed from west to east
of the Mediterranean and concluded that the eels of the countries
bordering the Mediterranean did not spawn in that sea but
somewhere in the Atlantic. The larvae taken from the Atlantic, in
almost all cases smaller than those from the Mediterranean,
confirmed the hypothesis of an eastward migration of larvae and
pointed to a breeding-ground in the western part of the ocean.
Schmidt realized that to locate this elusive region it was necessary to
hunt for still smaller larvae, plotting their position, until at length he
would have inevitably closed in on the long-sought Birthplace of Eels.

In 1911, when a German gunboat steamed into the port of
Agadir and my grandfather, whose brewery had burned down in
extraordinary circumstances, was winding up his affairs to live in

rumour-nurturing seclusion in Kessling Hall, Johannes Schmidt persuaded various ship-owners with vessels on the transatlantic route to co-operate in the collection and classifying of larvae samples. No less than twenty-three ships were thus enlisted. Not content with this, Schmidt voyaged ceaselessly himself, in his schooner the *Margrethe,* from the Azores to the Bermudas, from the Bermudas to the Caribbean.

Alas, that curiosity must allow history its way. Alas, that Schmidt has no choice but to hold up his search, furl the sails of the *Margrethe,* and fret impatiently while the world embarks on a four-year bout of carnage. Alas, that from 1914 to 1918 it is not the origins of its own homogeneous species of eel that concerns Europe, but the heterogeneous disposition of its national interests and armed forces. Alas, that it is not the presence in the Atlantic of minute eel larvae migrating dauntlessly eastwards which is uppermost in the minds of European seafarers, but rather the presence of German U-boats migrating westwards, out of Wilhelmshaven and the Kiel Canal.

And yet it must be said that this catastrophic interval, to which such dread words as apocalypse, cataclysm, Armageddon have not unjustly been applied, does not interrupt the life cycle of the eel. In the spring the elvers still congregate in their millions at the mouth of the Po, the Danube, the Rhine, and the Elbe, just as they did in Alexander's day and Charlemagne's. And even at the very epicentre of the slaughter, on the infamous Western Front itself, as my father Henry Crick was able to vouch, they are not to be dissuaded. If eels, indeed, were born out of mud, here they should have teemed; if eels sprang from putrefying flesh, here should have been a bumper crop.

Nor does this four-year intermission inhibit the determination, if it tries the patience, of Johannes Schmidt. For soon after war's cessation, glad that history has got its business over, he once more takes to the seas. Once more he is scooping up eel larvae—this time in the western Atlantic. And by the early twenties, so tirelessly has he worked, he is able to declare his findings; to affirm that, taking the area where the largest number of smallest larvae have been collected to correspond to the breeding territory of the eel, then this same, long unimagined, let alone undiscovered spawning ground is to be found between latitudes 20° and 30° North and longitudes 50° and 65° West—that is to say, in that mysterious region of floating weed known as the Sargasso Sea.

So it was that when my father became keeper of the Atkinson Lock in 1922 and began, as his forefather Cricks had done, to trap eels in the River Leem and its adjacent drains, human knowledge, after 2,000 years and more of speculation, had only just assembled the facts which might have shown him where those eels came from. Not that he ever learned, then or later, the truth of the matter. For what did he know, in his English Fens, about a Danish biologist? Yet assuredly, had he been informed on the subject, had he been told that those same eels he lifted from his traps had got there by way of a 3,000 to 4,000 mile journey from a strange marine region on the other side of the Atlantic, his eyes would have widened and his lips would have formed a distinct O.

But that is not the end of the story of the eel. Curiosity begets counter-curiosity, knowledge begets scepticism. Even granted, say the doubters of Schmidt, that the larval eel makes its way 3,000, 4,000, or even 5,000 miles to the haunts of its sires; even granted that the young elvers, undeterred by weirs, waterfalls, and lock-gates, travel up rivers and even wriggle over land to reach ancestral ponds and streams; are we to believe that the adult eel, after years of life in fresh water or brackish shallows, is suddenly both compelled and enabled to undertake this journey once more in reverse, with the sole purpose of spawning before it dies? What evidence can Schmidt produce of adult eels travelling in a westerly direction in the mid-Atlantic? (Alas, Schmidt can produce virtually nothing.)

Put the case that Schmidt is wrong in his conclusion that the European Eel is a peculiarly European species distinct from its American relative. Put the case that the differences between the so-called European Eel and the so-called American Eel are not genetic but physiological and determined by different environmental factors. Might it not then be possible that the European Eel, having separated itself by so many miles from its breeding ground, does indeed perish without progeny in continental waters, but its stocks are maintained by the American Eel (so-called) which is not faced with nearly such arduous distances? And that what determines that some eels will become denizens of the new world and some of the old is merely the exact point of spawning within the breeding ground and the prevailing currents thus brought to bear?

But why should nature have permitted such a wasteful mistake? Can Europe be the graveyard of orphaned and childless eels? Are the natural environments of America and Europe so different as to create a physiological contrast sufficiently pronounced to lead to speciological error? Can it be denied—for here centuries-old observation bears witness—that adult eels, adopting their silver costume, do indeed in the autumn make to the sea? And supposing, to offer a compromise, that these adult eels fail to reach Schmidt's critical lines of longitude and latitude, might they not spawn and die somewhere, let us say, in the eastern or mid-Atlantic; and might not their eggs, given seasonal and climatic conditions, still drift, just as the seaweed drifts, towards the vortical Sargasso; so that that marine nursery is, if not a breeding ground, still a hatching ground?

Curiosity will never be content. Even today, when we know so much, curiosity has not unravelled the riddle of the birth and sex-life of the eel. Perhaps these are things, like many others, destined never to be learned before the world comes to its end. Or perhaps—but here I speculate, here my own curiosity leads me by the nose—the world is so arranged that when all things are learned, when curiosity is exhausted (so, long live curiosity), that is when the world shall have come to its end.

But even if we learn how and what and where and when, will we ever know why? Why? Why?

A question which never baulked an eel. Any more than the distance between Europe and 50° longitude. Any more than the appearance upon the scene of man with his unique possession of precisely that unremitting question Why, and with his capacity to find in the domain of the eel—water—not only a means of transport and power and a source of food (including eels), but a looking-glass for his curious and reflective nature.

For whether or not the silver-coated *Anguilla anguilla* ever reaches the Sargasso, whether it performs its nuptial rites there or before, nonetheless it is true that, just as the young eel is driven not only by marine currents but by an instinctual mechanism more mysterious, more impenetrable perhaps than the composition of the atom to make for some particular watery dwelling thousands of miles from its place of birth, so the adult eel, moved by a force which outweighs vast distances and the crushing pressure of the ocean, is compelled to take again to the sea and, before it leaves the world to its spawn, to return to where it came from.

How long have eels been doing this? They were doing it, repeating this old, epic story, long before Aristotle put it all down to mud. They were doing it when Pliny posited his rock-rubbing theory. And Linnaeus his viviparity theory. They were doing it when they stormed the Bastille and when Napoleon and Hitler contemplated the invasion of England. And they were still doing it, still accomplishing these vast atavistic circles when on a July day in 1940, when the southern skies were full of sinuous vapour-trails, Freddie Parr picked up out of a trap one of their number (which later escaped and lived perhaps to obey the call of the far Sargasso) and placed it deftly down Mary's navy-blue knickers.

GRANTA

ROSE TREMAIN
MY WIFE IS A
WHITE RUSSIAN

Rose Tremain was born in London in 1943, and was educated at the Sorbonne and the University of East Anglia. Her first book was a history of the Women's Suffrage Movement entitled *Freedom for Women* published in 1971. She has also published a biography of Stalin. She has written three novels, the last of which is the *Cupboard,* and has begun work on a fourth. She has also written extensively for radio and stage. She lives in Norwich.

298

I'm a financier. I have financial assets, world-wide. I'm in nickel and pig-iron and gold and diamonds. I like the sound of all these words. They have an edge, I think. The glitter of saying them sometimes gives me an erection.

I'm saying them now, in this French restaurant, where the table-cloths and the table-napkins are blue linen, where they serve sea-food on platters of seaweed and crushed ice. It's noisy at lunch-time. It's May and the sun shines in London, through the open restaurant windows. Opposite me, the two young Australians blink as they wait (so damned courteous, and she has freckles like a child) for me to stutter out my hard-word list, to manipulate tongue and memory so that the sound inside me forms just behind my lips and explodes with extraordinary force above my oysters: '*Diamonds!*'

But then I feel a soft, perfumed dabbing at my face. I turn away from the Australians and there she is. My wife. She is smiling as she wipes me. Her gold bracelets rattle. She is smiling at me. Her lips are astonishing, the colour of claret. I've been wanting to ask her for some time, 'Why are your lips this terrible dark colour these days? Is it a lipstick you put on?'

Still smiling at me, she's talking to the Australians with her odd accent: 'He's able to enjoy the pleasures of life once more, thank God. For a long time afterwards I couldn't take him out. Terrible. We couldn't do one single thing, you know. But now—he enjoys his wine again.'

The dabbing stops. To the nurse I tried to say when I felt a movement begin: 'Teach me how to wipe my arse. I cannot let my wife do this because she doesn't love me. If she loved me, she probably wouldn't mind wiping my arse, and I wouldn't mind her wiping my arse. But she doesn't love me.'

The Australian man is talking now. I let my hand go up and take hold of my big-bowled wine glass into which the waiter has poured the expensive Chablis my wife likes to drink when she eats fish. Slowly, I guide the glass across the deadweight distance between the table and my mouth. I say 'deadweight' because the spaces between all my limbs and the surfaces of tangible things have become mighty. To walk is to wade in waist-high water. And to lift this wine glass...'Help me,' I want to say to her, 'just this once.' Just this once.

'Heck,' says the Australian man, 'we honestly thought he'd

made a pretty positive recovery.' His wife, with blue eyes the colour of the napkins, is watching my struggles with the glass. She licks her fine line of a mouth, sensing I suppose, my longing to taste the wine. The nurse used to stand behind me, guiding the feeding-cup in my hand. I never explained to her that the weight of gravity had mysteriously increased. Yet often, as I drank from the feeding-cup, I used to imagine myself prancing on the moon.

'Oh, this is a very positive recovery,' says my wife. 'There's very little he can't do now. He enjoys the ballet, you know, and the opera. People at Covent Garden and the better kind of place are very considerate. We don't go to the cinema because there you have a very inconsiderate type of person. Don't you agree? So riff-raffy. Don't you agree?'

The Australian wife hasn't listened to a word. The Australian wife puts out a lean freckled arm and I watch it come towards me, astounded as usual these days by the speed with which other people can move parts of their bodies. But the arm, six inches from my hand holding the glass, suddenly stops. 'Don't help him!' snaps my wife. The napkin-blue eyes are lowered. The arm is folded away.

Heads turn in the restaurant. I suppose her voice has carried its inevitable echo round the room where we sit: 'Don't help him! Don't help him!' But now that I have an audience, the glass begins to jolt, the wine splashing up and down the sides of the bowl. I smile. My smile widens as I watch the Chablis begin to slop onto the starched blue cloth. WASTE. She of all people understands the exquisite luxury of waste. Yet she snatches the glass out of my hand and sets it down by her own. She snaps her fingers and a young bean pole of a waiter arrives. He spreads out a fresh blue napkin where I have spilled my wine. My wife smiles her claret smile. She sucks an oyster into her dark mouth.

The Australian man is, I was told, the manager of the Toomin Valley Nickel Consortium. The wife is, as far as I know, just a wife. I own four-fifths of the Toomin Valley Nickel Consortium. The Australian man is here to discuss expansion, supposedly with me, unaware until he met me this lunch-time that despite the pleasing cadences of the words I'm unable to say Toomin Valley Nickel Consortium. I can say 'nickel'. My tongue lashes around in my throat to form the click that comes in the middle of the word. Then out it spills: *Nickel!* In my mind, oddly enough, the word 'nickel' is the exact greyish-white colour of an oyster. But 'consortium' is too difficult for me. I know my limitations.

My wife is talking again: 'I've always loved the ballet, you see. This is my only happy memory of Russia—the wonderful classical ballet. A little magic. Don't you think? I would never want to be without this kind of magic, would you? Do you have the first-rate ballet companies in Australia? You do? Well, that's good. *Giselle*, of course. That's the best one. Don't you think? The dead girl. Don't you think? Wonderful.'

We met on a pavement. I believe it was in the Avenue Matignon, but it could have been the Avenue Montaigne. I often get these muddled. It was in Paris, anyway. Early summer, as it is now. Chestnut candle blooms blown along the gutters. I waited to get into the taxi she was leaving. But I didn't get into it. I followed her. In a bar, she told me she was very poor; her father drove the taxi I had almost hired. She spoke no English then, only French with a heavy Russian accent. I was just starting to be a financier at that time, but already I was quite rich, rich by her standards—she who had been used to life in post-war Russia. My hotel room was rather grand. She said in her odd French: 'I'll fuck for money.'

I gave her fifty francs. I suppose it wasn't much, not as much as she'd hoped for, a poor rate of exchange for the white, white body that rode astride me, head thrown back, breasts bouncing. She sat at the dressing-table in the hotel room. She smoked my American cigarettes. More than anything, I wanted to brush her gold hair, brush it smooth and hold it against my face. But I didn't ask her if I could do this. I believe I was afraid she would say, 'You can do it for money.'

The thin waiter is clearing away our oyster platters. I've eaten only three of my oysters, yet I let my plate go. She lets it go. She pretends not to notice how slow I've been with the oysters. And my glass of wine still stands by hers, untasted. Yet she's drinking quite fast. I hear her order a second bottle.

The Australian man says: 'First rate choice, if I may say so. We like Chably.'

I raise my left arm and touch her elbow, nodding at the wine. Without looking at me, she puts my glass down in front of me. The Australian wife stares at it. Neither she nor I dare to touch it.

My wife is explaining to the Australians what they are about to eat, as if they were children: 'I think you will like the turbot very much. *Turbot poché hollandaise.* They cook it very well. And the hollandaise sauce—you know this, of course? Very difficult to achieve, the lightness of this sauce. But here they do it very well. And the scallops in saffron. Again, a very light sauce. Excellent texture. Just a little cream added. And fresh scallops, naturally. We never go to any restaurant where the products are frozen. So I think you will like these dishes very much....'

We have separate rooms. Long before my illness, when I began to look (yet hardly to feel) old, she demanded her privacy. This was how she put it: she wanted to be private. The bedroom we used to share and which is now hers is very large. The walls are silk.

She said: 'There's no sense in being rich and being cooped up together in one room.'

Obediently, I moved out. She wouldn't let me have the guest room, which is also big. I have what we call 'the little room', which I always used to think of as a child's room.

I expect in her 'privacy' that she is smiling: 'The child's room is completely right for him. He's a helpless baby.' Yet she's not a private person. She likes to go out four or five nights a week, returning at two or three in the morning, sometimes with friends, and they sit and drink brandy. Sometimes, they play music. Elton John. She has a lover (I don't know his name) who sends her lilies.

I'm trying to remember the Toomin Valley. I believe it's an immense desert of a place, inhabited by no one and nothing except the mining machinery and the Nickel Consortium employees, whose clusters of houses I ordered to be whitewashed to hide the cheap grey building blocks. The windows of the houses are small, to keep out the sun. In the back yards are spindly eucalyptus trees, blown by the scorching winds. I want to ask the Australian wife, did you have freckles before you went to live in the Toomin Valley, and does some wandering prima ballerina dance *Giselle* on the gritty escarpment above the mine?

My scallops arrive, saffron yellow and orange in the blue and white dish—the colours of a childhood summer. The flesh of a scallop is firm yet soft, the texture of a woman's thigh (when she is young, of course, before the skin hardens and the flesh bags out). A forkful of scallop is immeasurably easier to lift than the glass of wine, and the Australian wife (why don't I know either of their names?) smiles at me approvingly as I lift the succulent parcel of food to my mouth and chew it without dribbling. My wife, too, is watching, ready with the little scented handkerchief, yet talking as she eats, talking of Australia as the second bottle of Chablis arrives and she tastes it hurriedly with a curt nod to the thin waiter. I exist only in the corner of her eye, at its inmost edge, where the vulnerable triangle of red flesh is startling.

'Of course, I've often said to Hubert' (she pronounces my name 'Eieu-bert', trying and failing with what she recognizes as the upper class *h*), 'that it's very unfair to expect people like you to live in some out-of-the-way place. I was brought up in a village, you see, and I know that an out-of-the-way village is so dead. No culture. The same in Toomin, no? Absolutely no culture at all. Everybody dead.'

The Australian wife looks—seemingly for the first time—straight at my wife. 'We're outdoor people.'

I remember now. A river used to flow through the Toomin Valley. Torrential in the rainy season, they said. It dried up in the early 'forties. One or two sparse willows remain, grey testimony to the long-ago existence of water-rich soil. I imagine the young Australian couple, brown as chestnuts, swimming in the Toomin River, resting on its gentle banks with their fingers touching, a little loving nest of bone. There is no river. Yet when they look at each other—almost furtively under my vacant gaze—I recognize the look. The look says: 'These moments with strangers are nothing. Into our private moments together—only there—is crammed all that we ask of life.'

'Yes, we're outdoor folk.' The Australian man is smiling. 'You can play tennis most of the year round at Toomin. I'm president of the tennis club. And we have our own pool now.'

I don't remember these things: tennis-courts and swimming-pools.

'Well, of course, you have the climate for these things.' My wife is signalling our waiter to bring her Perrier water. 'And it's something to do, isn't it? Perhaps when the new expansions of the company are made, a concert hall could be built for you, or a theatre.'

'A theatre!' The Australian wife's mouth opens to reveal perfect, freshly-peeled teeth and a laugh escapes. She blushes.

My wife's dark lips are puckered into a sneer.

But the Australian man is laughing too—a rich laugh you might easily remember on the other side of the world—and slapping his thigh. 'A theatre! What about that, ay?'

She wanted, she said, as she smoked my American cigarettes, to see *Don Giovanni*. Since leaving Russia with her French mother and her Russian father, no one had ever taken her to the opera. She had seen the posters advertising *Don Giovanni* and had asked her father to buy her a ticket.

He had shouted at her: 'Remember whose child you are! Do you imagine taxi drivers can afford seats at the Opéra?'

'Take me to see *Don Giovanni*,' she said to me, 'and I will fuck for nothing.'

I've never really appreciated the opera. The Don was fat. It was difficult to imagine so many women wanting to lie with this fat man. Yet afterwards, she leant over to me and put her head on my shoulder and wept. Nothing, she told me, had ever moved her so much—nothing in her life had ever touched the core of her being—as this had done, this production of *Don Giovanni*.

'If only,' she said, 'I had money as you have money, then I would go to hear music all the time and see the classical ballet and learn from these what is life.'

The scallops are good. She never learned what is life. I feel emboldened by the food. I put my hand to my glass, heavier than ever now because the waiter has filled it up. The sun shines on my wine and on my hand, blotched (splattered, it seems) with the oddly repulsive stains of old age. For a second, I see my hand and the wine glass as a still-life. But then I lift the glass. The Australian wife lowers her eyes. My wife, for a moment, is silent. I drink. I smile at the Australian wife because I know she wants to applaud.

I'm talking. The words are like stones weighing down my lower jaw. *Nickel.* I'm trying to tell the Australian man that I dream about the nickel mine. In my dreams, the Australian miners drag wooden carts loaded with threepenny bits. I run my hands through the coins as though through a sack of wheat, and the touch of them is pleasurable and perfect. I also want to say to the Australian man: 'I hope you're happy in your work. When I was in control, I visited all my mines and all my subsidiaries at least once a year. Even in South Africa, I made sure a living wage was paid. I said to the men underground, "I hope you're happy in your work."'

But now I have a manager, a head-manager to manage all the other managers, including this one from the Toomin Valley. I am trundled out in my chair to meet them when they come here to discuss redundancy or expansion. My wife and I give them lunch in a restaurant. They remind me that I still have an empire to rule, if I were capable, if indeed my life had been different since the night of *Don Giovanni.*

When I stopped paying her to sleep with me, her father came to see me. He held his cap in his hands. 'We're hoping for a marriage,' he said. And what more could I have given—what less—to the body I had begun to need? The white and the gold of her, I thought, will ornament my life.

Yet now I never touch her. The white and the gold of her lies only in the lilies they send, the unknown lovers she finds in the night, while I lie in the child's room and dream of the nickel mines. My heart is scorched dry, like the dry hills of the Toomin Valley. I am punished for my need of her while her life stalks my silence; the white of her, the gold of her, the white of Dior, the gold of Cartier. Why did she never love me? In my dreams, too, the answer comes from deep underground: it's the hardness of my words.

A.N.WILSON
SCANDAL

A. N. Wilson was born in 1950 and grew up in Wales. He was educated at Rugby and New College, Oxford. He has published five novels, plus a study of Sir Walter Scott, and a biography of Milton. He is currently working on a life of Hilaire Belloc. A. N. Wilson writes reviews for newspapers and journals, and is now the Literary Editor of the Spectator. He writes: 'Some "biographical notes" state that I am an academic or a don or a teacher. This is not the case. Just a hack.' 'Scandal' is selected from a recently completed novel that will be published later this year.

For Julian Blore, there was no worse agony than the day he had to return to school. And the beginning of an autumn term was always worse than the others. The longer summer holidays had allowed him to re-establish the roots of home affection; the worse was the wrench when they ended. And instead of the merciful ten or twelve weeks of other terms, he had fourteen weeks of exile stretching ahead of him.

The agony began about a week before the day. On this occasion, it was the very day they got back from France that his mother began to prepare the packing of his trunk. He dreaded it being brought down from the attic. He loathed the last-minute visits to Harrods—which followed the perusal of the clothes list—the purchase of dull grey socks, grey shirts, sleeved vests, serge football shorts.

And this year, the family was in turmoil about Daddy. The newspapers said that he had done something very wrong. Julian had read the articles avidly as they appeared. His father had visited a prostitute and had been a spy. It was quite obvious to Julian that this was true. He was almost pleased to read it, for it justified his sense, never admitted to himself before, that Daddy Spoilt Everything.

Julian was convinced that if it were not for his father, and his father's career, he would not have to go away to school. Mummy, he was sure, would have allowed him to go to the Hall, and then on to Westminster like everyone else. It was Daddy who had found this hateful prep-school in Malvern, and Daddy who had ambitions later on to send him to Repton, where none of his friends were going.

While the trunk was being packed, items on the clothes list ticked off ('One Teddy bear: first term only'), Mummy was brisk, trying to avoid the pathos of it all, and Kate (home for a week or two) was positively exultant. His elder sister smoked Gauloises now, as she strutted about the house in her scarlet boiler-suit and her espadrilles.

'Honestly, Julian, I think you're *really* wet, never *known* anyone make such a fuss about going back to school.'

'You didn't have to go to Hillbury.'

'Mine was just as bad. All schools are foul,' she puffed and belched.

He hated her for it. This term was Rugger. One would get back and see with dread the H-shaped goals established on what had been the comparatively civilized cricket pitch. Fourteen weeks of it stretched ahead, each colder than the next; games every afternoon; runs on the Malvern hills; cheesy milk drunk out of third-pint bottles; the grazing of knees on coconut matting as one jumped from ropes in the gym; the drab melancholy which hung over *everything*.

In normal circumstances, his mother took account of his misery, and treats were devised to lighten the burden of the last week (the trunk was dispatched to Paddington days in advance). Tickets for shows would be purchased, knickerbocker glories consumed at Fortnum's, tense little games of Monopoly. Always, there was the feeling that his mother had the power to save him from his impending fate; always, it was a sense which he did not dare to put to the test. If he made her fight for him, his father would be foul. The household had to revolve around Daddy's needs. Julian, certainly in this particular week, was the last to be considered. Poor Daddy must have breakfast in bed; Daddy must see his solicitor; be quiet do, Daddy is trying to work on his papers. This tending on the lecher and the spy superseded any claims Julian might have had on his mother's time. She asked Kate to take him to the cinema: they went a couple of times. The first, it was stupid, because she took him to a French film at an Academy cinema and you had to follow what was going on by reading the subtitles. She laughed a lot, too, which was annoying, because there was nothing funny in the film at all. In fact very little happened in it. There were a lot of close-ups of dust-bins and dew-drops. When he had registered disapproval, she had taken him off to a really childish Walt Disney film, which he had seen most of anyway in excerpts on *Screen Test*. So they were miserable, miserable days....

On the last evening, which Mummy would normally have spent with him, they went out together to a State Banquet. She had held his hand before they left and looked intently into his eyes.

'Daddy needs me to help him, now that these horrible men have said such wicked things about him,' she said. 'We've got to go out to show them that we know they aren't true. If I didn't go out tonight, everyone would say it was because I thought Daddy had done all these *terrible* things.'

'Are you sure he hasn't?' Julian asked.

Her great blue-grey eyes had not flinched as they stared back at him. There was reproach in their steely strength.

'Julian, don't ever ask that again.'

'But are you, Mummy?'

'Of course I'm sure,' she had said; but she had looked away again almost at once.

'It would be very bad if they caught him, wouldn't it, Mummy? I mean, if they proved he really *had* done those things—been spying for the Russians and everything?'

'Julian, they are not going to catch him because he is *innocent.* You really mustn't talk in that way. When you go back to school tomorrow, you must be terribly careful what you say to people. You will, won't you? You promise me?'

'I never talk about Daddy at school, anyway.'

'Look, *darling.* We've spoken to the headmaster, and he is going to make sure that no newspaper men talk to you or anything like that. But if any of the other *boys* ask you about it, you won't say anything, will you? You see, there are some really *awful* people in the world. They would even use *boys* to get information about your father. You know, they might ask quite casually where you spent your holidays, or something like that.'

'Can't I even tell them *that?*'

'Of course you can. It was a silly example. I just mean, be careful. If they start talking about your father....'

'*Mum*-my. No one talks about their dads. I keep telling you.'

'Let's hope that's true,' she said, and kissed his forehead. He hated, in these latter days of home, to be kissed. The time stretched ahead in which there would be no hugs, no kisses; in which her lovely face, and the smell of her, would be miles away, and he would be imprisoned in a vile dormitory full of children discussing masturbation.

'Mummy.'

'Yes, Julian?'

'I was just thinking.'

'Yes, darling?'

'I mean, if it's so dangerous for me to go back to Hillbury; I mean, if you think I might be tricked into saying something about Daddy....'

'Oh, *darling.*'

She hugged him so closely now that he started to cry. She had seen through the ruse at once.

'I really thought that was a good idea, too,' she said, over his shoulder, stroking his hair. 'But Daddy thinks we've all got to be brave, and behave *exactly* as normal. Think how awful it is for him at the moment.'

'But, Mummy, it's his fault.'

'If someone told lies about you, would you say it was your fault?'

'No, but it wouldn't be. I don't believe you think he's telling the truth. I think you're just covering up for him.'

'Oh, Julian, you *mustn't*, not even as a joke.'

'I'm not joking.'

'Well, well, well, you're keeping your mother from a State Banquet, young man,' said Derek, entering Julian's bedroom without permission. To the boy's eyes his father looked frightening in his evening dress. The colours of his countenance were set off by the high white winged collar and white tie. The cheeks were the colour of bricks; the whole head was an even reddish-brown, except for his scarlet ears, which stood out like tea-pot handles, and his very pink, moist lips.

'We must go,' said Derek, crossly.

Julian reached up to be kissed by his mother one last time. Derek leaned forward and implanted a kiss on his son's brow.

'Good night, old sausage. Sleep well.'

It was a ridiculous injunction. Julian couldn't settle the night before term. He found himself hatching escape plots. Supposing he were to ask his mother to drop him at Paddington, rather than actually seeing him on to the train. Could he not then catch *another* train, go into hiding in Bristol or Wales or somewhere; send them a telegram saying he was all right, but that he would only come back if they let him leave Hillbury? Or he could try a last attempt to *implore* them, to beg them to let him leave....

He was still awake when they returned from the banquet. Daddy looked rather drunk, even redder than when he had gone out. Mummy was in a long swooping gown with a tiara on her head.

'What on earth d'you think you're doing?' she said, really crossly when she encountered him, pyjama-clad, on the landing.

'Mummy, do I have to go back to school, do I *have* to?'

'Of *course* you do, now *go* back to bed!' She had really snapped.

He had mustered so many good arguments while he had been lying there. He had thought of pointing out that it was much cheaper to go to day schools. Daddy was such a 'nana, he probably didn't realize all the money he'd save. But this very reasonable tactic could not be advanced. It was horrible that Mummy was so cross. It made him wish that he had stayed in bed; because now the whole of his last night at home was wrecked. He was just standing there in tears.

'I know someone who's varry over-tired,' said Derek.

'We're all tired,' said Priscilla. She was really angry.

Surprisingly, Julian went to sleep quite soon after this.

I n the morning, she was being nice again. She did not apologize for losing her temper with him the night before, and he half wondered whether she was going to punish him by getting Kate (an abominable driver) to convey him to his train. But she was not as cruel as that. They expected him to eat breakfast, but the boiled egg made his gorge rise, and it was as much as he could do to stop himself openly blubbing over the toast and marmalade.

'I think you're a real baby,' Kate mercilessly observed. 'I only cried my first term at Cheltenham. You don't cry in your seventh term, for heaven's sake.'

'I'm not crying!' he paradoxically howled.

'Well, goodbye old chap,' said Derek. Absurdly, a handshake was thought appropriate as a mode of paternal valediction. That suited Julian. Mummy helped him carry his case to the car. It felt horrible to be in the prison uniform again; stupid shorts, rough grey flannel against chapped legs, a blazer braided with hideous yellow, black, and white edging, and a tie of the same design around the collar of his grey shirt. On his head, the ignominious yellow cap, with a black H.

'We'll come and see you in a few weeks,' said his mother, trying to talk through his grief. He wanted to behave well for her, but now they were alone together, he could not help weeping openly. 'It'll be alright when you've settled in. You say so yourself.'

'It's *not* all right.'

'Darling, we all have to do things we don't like.'

'But why do *I* have to...' he gulped with the sobs, 'go away...other children...don't go...away.'

'I went away. Kate went away. Daddy went away.'

There was no answer to that.

'I'll tell you a secret,' she said. 'Daddy hated it; he used to cry, too. But he learned how to be brave. Don't you *see* how brave he's being now? One day you will. He could be Prime Minister, you know. And that's why these *horrid* newspaper men are spreading lies about him. It's because they want to stop him being Prime Minister.'

If so, it seemed such an eminently reasonable line of conduct that Julian could not see what was wrong with it.

'Will you come next week-end?' he asked.

'There's no *exeat* the first week-end,' she said. 'You know we're not supposed to come until you've had time to settle in. As it is, the headmaster said I come too often.'

'*Please*, Mummy.'

'And we'll *write* to each other.'

'Sorry,' he sniffed.

As the car approached Paddington, he became dimly aware that too much sobbing would embarrass his mother, and he tried to stem its flow. He more or less had it under control when she opened the flood gates by saying 'Now, be brave.'

They parked in Praed Street, on double yellow lines. This time, he was to carry his own over-night bag. As they made their way into the great glazed terminal, his eye unwillingly absorbed the sight of a gaggle of Hillbury boys, waiting by the barrier with the master who was responsible for their safe conduct to Worcestershire—Sir Caradoc Pass, an obesely ugly man with whiskers and a tattered sports coat with pins sticking out of the lapels.

'Lady Priscilla,' the master's tone with parents was always obsequious. 'Hallo Blore,' he said, 'have a good holiday?'

Julian mumbled something inaudible.

'No need to cry, Blore,' said Sir Caradoc, sadistically.

'I think I'll go, darling.' She crouched over him in the warmth of her embrace.

'Oh no, Mummy, there's ten minutes before the train goes.'

'You've got all your friends, now.'

'Oh, please don't go.'

He did not want to be making a scene. He knew that he was eleven, and that when you were eleven it was no longer quite natural to cry. But he was clinging to her neck and sobbing, and would not let her go.

She struggled free callously, and ran, not looking behind her, into the Great Western Hotel. Crumpled with shame, his eyes and cheeks stinging with grief, Julian allowed himself to be loaded into the train on platform four. When, as a grown-up, he watched old films of the Jews or Cossacks being bundled into trains, his disgust was of a peculiarly personal character. When it was airily said, 'Why did they let themselves be butchered? Why did a thousand men and women allow themselves to be put on a train by a handful of bullying sergeants and corporals?', he could not answer the mystery, but felt again the completely crushing power that captivity had over the soul.

Crushed then, too miserable to read or speak, he swayed and rattled towards Malvern. Sir Caradoc sat opposite, playing with the pins in his lapels, occasionally withdrawing one to prick his cheek bones and make them bleed.

The baronet, come down in the world, made no effort to speak to the boys until they got to the station, when he arrogantly said, 'Your family has been in the news a lot lately, Blore.'

It was not the thing to talk about your family at school. Sir Caradoc was hitting below the belt. Julian was sure that the other boys would recognize this, but to his horror, they didn't. There was a general tittering.

To his shame at being the only one blubbing was added a wounded family pride and a fury with his father for having landed him in this intolerable position. Once back in the hateful confines of the school, there was enough activity to enable him to escape this intrusive line of questioning. There was finding where one's bed was. Julian found that he was in the largest, coldest dormitory in the school, in a house with the least beautiful matron, between two boys he had never liked. Peterson, the only real friend, was in another dorm. There was always a hideous poignancy about unpacking, and seeing the things which had been spread out on the bed at home, piled on the locker beside the cruel little iron bedstead which was to be his resting-place for the next three and a half months. Then there was a diving around the school, unnecessarily seeing what had altered since the previous term. Which corridors had been repainted, which tables revarnished? The notice-board had been re-felted in green baize and

315

the notices were pinned with an unnatural symmetry. There was a list of the names of new boys, and a new master, Major Stokes, was to teach Geography and PT, replacing Mr Shotover.

High tea was presided over by the headmaster's wife, a well-bosomed sadist, whose summer holidays had been devoted, at least partly, to the purchase of new mohair cardigans and auburn hair-dye. The sausages on toast which the boys were required to consume were half cooked, but she would not hear of any protest. Every scrap must be consumed. Afterwards, they were to be addressed by her husband.

The prissy-voiced, snowy-haired Scot who enjoyed the distinction of being Mrs Fraser's husband was produced, as if out of a hat, at the end of tea. The image was not wholly absurd, since the white locks and faintly protuberant teeth suggested the rabbit, as did the watch-chain suspended from a dandified fob. He hoped that they would all enjoy their term, and that they would work hard. He would like them especially to welcome Major Stokes. Major Stokes was a stooping, yellowing man who looked like the semi-successful product of an experiment to re-animate the dead. He was to teach, nevertheless, physical training. It was hoped that under his tuition, they would all become *fit little bodies.* How primly Mr Fraser said the words, and how knowingly Mrs Fraser smiled as they were spoken. There was an old Latin saying, and he hoped they would all be able to understand it: *mens sana in corpore sano.* And then they had to be asked to bow their heads in prayer and he had thanked—a sure sign in Julian's mind that he was round the twist—God for the beginning of a new term. And then he had said they could go, but that he would like to see Blore.

In the study afterwards—that room of dread, where one normally went only to be caned, upbraided, or told bad news from home—Mr Fraser asked Blore to be seated on the sofa. When Julian found himself sinking down into the back of this commodious article, Mr Fraser had joined him, and the tweed of his trousers had pressed most unwelcomely against the embarrassingly bare knees of Blore.

For, he was Blore now. Julian was a label discarded for another few months. It would be seen in his mother's handwriting at the top of a weekly letter. Apart from that, it had no connection with him.

'Blore,' said Mr Fraser, punctiliously, politely, 'we have all watched with very great concern the terrible ordeal that your father has undergone in recent weeks.'

'Yes, sir.'

'I have promised your parents, Blore, that we shall take very especial care that you are not bothered, Blore. You know what I mean.'

'Yes, sir.'

'Don't talk to people about it—there's a good chap.'

'No, sir.'

'Gossip is a very terrible thing, Blore.'

'Yes.'

'I'm sure the other boys will be kind to you. It must be worrying to you, Blore.'

There! He had got what he wanted. The mention of kindness was enough to make Blore blub again.

'But you must look on Mrs Fraser and myself as your friends, Blore. And if you are in trouble, or worried, you must come to us.'

He was crying helplessly now, and wishing he could stop, for the more he cried, the more likely it was that the old man would do what he did, in fact, next. An arm had reached round him, and Blore was being squeezed. 'You're growing up into a nice boy,' he said. 'You'll always regard me as your friend, won't you, Blore?'

Blore mendaciously averred that he would, and escaped. An hour had to be killed before the bell summoned him to the dormitory. He perambulated bushes, tennis courts, lawns, round the back of the scout hut, and down to the opposite border of his confines, the drive leading to that happy world outside. In the same way, animals pace around their cage when first entrapped. His hour of solitude was, in the event, too short. In the dormitory, he knew the drill. Clothes were folded neatly on the chair at the end of the iron bedstead. Then, clad only in underpants, Julian made progress to a line of basins in the middle of the room where teeth were brushed and faces swilled with cold water. It was a relief to bathe his tear-hot face, but he knew that hours of crying lay ahead. These ablutions were performed in obligatory silence, presided over by a fat matron with a warty face. Silent prayer, again of obligation, was offered, kneeling beside one's bed. There was then a quarter of an hour for recreational talk or the reading of approved books.

Blore could not understand how nearly all the other boys were able to be so cheerful. Did they not have homes? Did they not love their mothers? They japed and quipped; they hooted and ragged; they cheeked the matron and made faces behind her back; they boasted of their summer holidays.

After lights out, when the noise of matron's footsteps had died away and they knew her to be absorbed in the evening's television programs, they talked again. Blore lay silent, quivering with grief.

'My dad took us to Spain.'

'My dad took us on a Boeing 707.'

'That's nothing. We went on *Concorde.*'

'Has Blore ever been on a plane?'

From Blore's bed, silence. From all the other beds in that darkened room, there were giggles.

''Spect Blore went on a plane to Moscow.'

More laughter. From Blore, more silence.

'Did you, Blore? Did you?'

The chorus grew louder.

'Did you go on a plane to Russia, Blore?'

He covered his face with the coarse linen sheet, but someone was coming over to his bed.

'Did you, Blore? Did you go on a plane to Russia?'

There were several of them now standing round his bed.

'Can't you answer, Blore? Don't you know English?'

'Comrade Blore!'

'I bet he's wanking.'

'My dad says Blore's dad ought to be hanged.'

'Traitor!'

They had got hold of him and were dragging him out of the bed.

He kicked and wriggled, but lashing out only seemed to increase their blood-lust.

'Get a leg, Chester-Jones.'

'I'm trying to.'

They bumped him on the floor, up and down, but it was too benign, too jolly a torture for their tastes. Chester-Jones, the leader of the pack, had forced him face down on the floor and was kneeling astride him now. One of Blore's arms was being pulled up in an agonizing half-Nelson. Someone else was holding his hair and banging his head up and down on the splintery boards. When they were bored with that, they filled one of the basins with water and ducked him. In the struggles which ensued, his pyjamas were not the only ones to get soaked. His punishment was to be made to eat a bar of soap, and it was only when he had retched up his sausages on toast that they left him to drag his throbbing, aching body back into a bed which someone had, in the duration of the fight, amusingly made into an apple pie.

ICA IN CONVERSATION AT THE INSTITUTE OF CONTEMPORARY ARTS

The ICA runs a unique programme of lunchtime events —
In Conversation — in which the readers can meet the writers
and talk to them about their work .
Other ICA events include debates on cultural issues , poetry
and polemic and the liveliest conferences in town on topics
as diverse as architecture and cable TV .

Coming soon ....

Tuesday **Jorge Ibarguengoita,** one of Mexico's most remarkable writers
1 March talks about The Dead Girls (the first translation of his work in
English) with **Bill Buford,** editor of Granta.

Tuesday **Emily Prager,** New York writer, wit and ex-contributing editor
8 March of National Lampoon, talks about her new collection of stories
A Visit to the Footbinders.

Thursday **D.M.Thomas,** author of the extraordinary The White Hotel,
24 March talks with one of the Best of Young British Writers **Maggie Gee** about his new book Ararat.

Also **Russell Hoban,** author of Riddley Walker, talks to writer and
in March broadcaster **Edward Blishen** about his new book Pilgermann.
Rosalind Coward talks about her new book Patriarchal
Precedents with anthropologist **Annie Whitehead**.
Barbara Taylor, talks about her book Eve and the New
Jerusalem, in which she reforges some of the early links
between feminism and socialism.

April **Poets Pourri**
An eclectic festival featuring the most exciting voices in
poetry today — from performance poets to literary gurus.

May **Living Culture**
A series of discussions which examines the way in which
popular culture, from James Bond to the music business,
influences our thinking and effects socio-economic and
political processes.

June **Arts and Television**
A two day conference which examines the nature of television
coverage of the arts.

As an ICA member you receive advance mailing of all events,
priority bookings and discount on ICA publications as well
as free entrance for you and a guest to all ICA exhibitions ,
special offers on ICA Theatre tickets and other benefits . . . .
. . . all for £10 . 00 a year .
Write or telephone now for details
Membership Secretary , ICA , The Mall , London SW1 .
01 930 0493 ICA Box Office: 01-930 3647.